Mason's Link

A Novel by

Bill Andrews

Copyright © 2007 by Bill Andrews

Mason's Link
by Bill Andrews

Printed in the United States of America

ISBN 978-1-60266-830-0

All rights reserved solely by the author. The author guarantees all contents are original and do not infringe upon the legal rights of any other person or work. No part of this book may be reproduced in any form without the permission of the author. The views expressed in this book are not necessarily those of the publisher.

Unless otherwise indicated, Bible quotations are taken from the King James Version of The Bible.

www.xulonpress.com

Acknowledgements

To my wife, Marilynn, thank you for being my strength. To my sister, Janet, and to my daughter, Wendy, thank you for reading the bad drafts and your helpful responses. To Dr. John King, Jr., thank you for your encouragement and your courage in life. To Dr. Martha Mims and Dr. Millie Moore, thanks to each of you for your ideas and comments to help make this project readable and your encouragement not to give up.

Chapter 1

Stewart rolled over on the floor as he turned from the television program he was watching and asked, "Grandad, are you gonna get old and die?"

Startled, George Mason put down the sports section in his lap and peered over the rim of his reading glasses into the boy's wide blue-as-the-sky eyes. They were more serious than he had ever seen. "Why do you ask?" he replied.

"Well," Stewart said as he slid around facing his Grandad, "I was watching this story about this boy and his grandfather who was really sick. The little boy told him he would miss him if he didn't get well. What'll happen if you get sick, Grandad?"

"Goodness, Stewart, you're onto a pretty deep subject here. Yeah, I guess you could say that I'm getting old. I'd hope if I get sick I'll get well. Otherwise, I'd miss you too," Mason carefully said, hoping his grandson wouldn't wade into this subject any deeper yet thinking about his angina problems.

Stewart was not to be denied. "What if you get sick and die," he said more seriously than before with furrowed brows beneath his blond buzzcut. "I'd really miss you and being able to talk to you and being able to do things with you," he added with a voice beginning to tremble.

George looked closely at his six year old Grandson, the oldest of his seven grandchildren. Stewart was not only the wisest of that group but sometimes he seemed to show signs of maturity matching most young adults. "Yeah," he replied, now on the edge of his recliner, "I'd miss you too, and I'd really miss getting to see you get bigger and older."

"Grandad, have you ever missed anyone like that?" he asked. He was standing now looking straight into George's eyes from a distance of twelve inches away with his small hands propped on his Grandfather's old knees.

George's thoughts quickly traveled back thirty-five years to a darkened hospital room where he watched and held the hand of Katherine as she struggled and drew her last breath after a long battle with leukemia. He was there sitting on her bed beside her, surrounded by her family and his family as they all bade her a last farewell. She had fought desperately and bravely but, at the end, she was mercifully unconscious as the pains subsided and as she slipped silently away from their world and into her new world wherever and whatever that was. As tears streamed down his own cheeks, George kissed her good by on her yet warm cheeks knowing they would forever be cold from that moment on. These thoughts had never strayed far from his stream of consciousness over all these years.

"Yes, Stewart, I've missed someone like that," George tenderly replied as his throat tightened and as he reached up to grab the boy's shoulders

"Are you talking about my first Grannie?" he asked, still face-to-face.

George looked at the boy for a long moment before he drew him in for a tight hug and said, "Yes, yes, I am. She'd have been very proud of you." What else could Mason say; that he never misses her? As good as he believed his life had been all these years with Dana, he still missed Katherine.

"How do you know?" the boy asked unrelentingly as he backed away from his Grandad's embrace.

This boy was just full of questions. "How do I know?" he repeated as he removed his glasses, wiped back his few remaining hairs and touched his eyes as he sensed a small welling of tears. "I can just sense her sometimes, it's hard to explain," he said with a slight quiver in his voice.

"Do you ever talk to her?" he asked, drawing George even further into this deepening and strange conversation.

It was an eerie feeling having this conversation with Stewart. It made him wonder later if his grandson was delivering the words from his own exceptionally bright mind or if perhaps he was being fed tidbits of thoughts that resulted in the innocent torrent of questions now being delivered. "No, not really but I'd like to sometimes," George said.

"Then why don't you?" Stewart asked with his head cocked and hands on his hips.

"Well," he said as he prepared to give a long and eloquent answer, "I guess memories are a good source of thinking about your first Grannie, but they don't give me the opportunity to talk with her. Dreams may be the best way. Occasionally, she'll appear in a dream, and we seem to be talking together."

"Wouldn't it be great to be able to talk with her sometimes?" Stewart ventured but only halfheartedly, as he turned his attention back to the TV and slouched back to the floor without really expecting an answer.

"Well, what in God's name did I just experience?" George asked himself as he stared at his grandson. He sat there, not paying attention to the movie or the newspaper, and began to go back over the conversation. What was the boy doing? Was he leading him with a line of questions with answers already known just as some smart lawyer might do in leading a witness on the stand? What if, in some form or fashion, a conversation could be had with her, Katherine, the high school sweetheart with whom Mason faithfully shared the first ten years of his adult life? No, no, all reasoning says otherwise. Such thinking was just fantasy.

Katherine and George had dated since he was in the eleventh grade. She was a tall slender dark haired sophomore, shy beyond reason. She thought she was too skinny but she didn't see what he saw. True, she was slender, but she moved with the grace of a gazelle and a lioness all rolled into one. Every move she made was calculated by her to draw attention away from herself as if she was trying to blend into her surroundings. Her problem was the more she tried, the more he liked it. To him she was beautiful although amply sprinkled with freckles. Her smile produced just the slightest hint of dimples. Her laughter, once she was provoked out of her shyness, was hearty.

George guessed he unfairly used his influence as an upper classman to have her be his date at the spring dance. From then on, they were almost always together. Their summers on the Chesapeake Bay were spent crabbing, fishing or skiing behind his dad's boat.

After graduation, George entered school at Georgia Tech while she stayed for her senior year in Baltimore. After her graduation, she almost followed him to Atlanta, enrolling instead just up the road in Athens at the University of Georgia. This enabled them to spend a lot of their undergraduate years together. They saw each other as much as possible. Her dad transferred to Atlanta as an investment banker. This meant she didn't have to return to the Baltimore for weekends or holidays. So George went back home as little as possible himself.

As soon as he graduated and settled into an engineering job in Atlanta, they were married. She had another year before she graduated but decided to stay for her master's. She wanted to teach. They started their family rather late. She was in her late twenties before Jackie came along. Two years later Jason joined them. Within a year, she was diagnosed with leukemia; the bad kind. Nothing they tried seemed to work. Nine months later, everyone was huddled around her in a hospital room at Emory Hospital watching her draw her last breaths. George's world as he knew it ended at that moment.

Everyone was sure Katherine was now in Heaven. George missed her then and spent many nights fighting tears as he tried to find some peaceful sleep, knowing all the while that just down the hall tucked into beds were the two beautiful children she left with him as her legacy in this world. She knew she was dying and after awhile, she seemed to accept her fate. He thought she'd made peace with God. Between her battle and her final acceptance of what was to come, she once told him in a tearful conversation, "What I hate most about all this is knowing I'll not be able to watch our children grow up."

Stewart was the six year old son of Jason. Stewart, a first grader, was bright and as curious as a monkey. Everything seemed to be fair game for him to look at, take apart and ask about. He reminded George a lot of Jason. He was also sensitive about feelings and relationships way beyond his few years. George hated to admit it, but the boy was probably his favorite of the group.

Jason and Jackie were really too young to understand the loss of their mother. Unlike George, they had few memories to recall. Time passed slowly at first. Their lives seemed to stand still. Then all of a sudden, they found their lives going on. Jackie was about to enter kindergarten, and Jason was beginning to form words.

Then, along came Dana. Like a breath of fresh air off the ocean, she entered their lives. A woman of extraordinary character and beauty with blond hair and ocean blue eyes coming out of a bad relationship and worse family conditions, she was looking for love and security. These things George could offer her as well as a ready made family. They met through a church outreach program. She was trying to pull herself out of the hole she was in from her divorce. He was trying to make sense of his life after Katherine. God smiled on them as Dana became a key part of their family and their lives. Dana brought order out of chaos. She was a budding artist, and she had a heart overflowing with compassion.

She generously spread her compassion on Jason, Jackie and George. They absorbed it like a sponge. They adopted her; she adopted them. Her family was from somewhere around Montgomery. She attended Auburn where she earned an art degree and was the number one player on the Auburn tennis team. She might have been full of compassion, but put a tennis racket in her hand and she became an aggressive competitor.

Having Dana with them, they were happy again. Painful memories receded to make an appearance only when something jolted them loose. Something like the questions Stewart brought to bear in this conversation.

Several days passed. Stewart had returned home to his parents, his spring break now over. By now he was back in school and had likely forgotten the conversation he and George had over the weekend which caused a mild earthquake in George's mind. He, unlike Stewart, has been unable to get this out of his thoughts for any period of time longer than an hour.

What prompted the child's outburst of questions? Was it the show he watched about the grandfather and grandson? Was it triggered by some other external source designed to cause Mason to explore these very questions? Could that external source have been something supernatural? Did someone somewhere trigger those questions inside his young mind? Were those questions designed to make George explore the possibility that somehow a way to communicate existed between him and someone in another place? Could that place be Heaven?

"Communicate?" George wondered, "Whatever am I pondering? Why am I even thinking about such a possibility? Who would I talk to? My mom? My dad? Katherine? Who? Crazy, all these thoughts are so crazy."

"Wow! The thoughts and questions were mind-boggling," George thought, always the worrier about things he couldn't conveniently get his arms around. Certainly, prayer had been around for eons. Many people prayed everyday as a regular routine. Many prayed only in special situations usually in time of great need. Many, he supposed, rarely prayed or not at all. He wondered, though, of those falling into the latter category, how many secretly prayed but wouldn't admit it. A lot, he bet. Prayers were usually directed to God, or Jesus, or Allah, or whoever occupied the Deity they worshiped.

What if, just what if, there existed another avenue of communication that could be used to talk to someone other than the Deity one holds in esteem as the extreme being. If so, and what a BIG IF, how could it be done?

Would it have to be done in a dream? One heard stories all the time about people who told of being visited in dreams. This seemed like a rather disorganized way to have a meaningful exchange due to the randomness of dreams. Maybe there was another way.

Accounts existed of people having out-of-body experiences at times when they were near death. Though, it seemed those stories rarely related the presence of other, non-worldly beings.

Stories also circulated of people seeing ghosts or apparitions. However, those stories rarely involved reports of conversations with them. Certainly, these seemed to be limited to specific locations and rarely when people themselves wanted them to happen.

Then, there were stories of people in near death situations who claimed to be traveling through a tunnel toward a bright light. Standing in the bright light would be someone or several people who had passed on and who they were particularly close with such as a spouse or parents. They would be smiling. There would be a few words offered to the new arrival along the lines that they were glad to see them again but they must go back. Their time hadn't yet come. This scenario seemed pretty real to George; however, the communication link and dialog seemed short and perhaps mostly one sided.

George wondered again who he might talk to. His dad was a distinct possibility. After all, when his dad passed away, George had no chance to say goodbye. They had a great relationship up to the time of his heart attack. Katherine, for sure, was one person he wanted to speak with. Unlike the situation with his dad, George certainly had a chance to say goodbye over the long time he spent with her during her illness. After her final acceptance of her situation, they sometimes spoke of the impending separation, although he was unprepared for the loneliness that followed in the weeks and months after she was gone. He missed her, for sure, sometimes unbearably whenever he was alone with their two small children or at night when he would reach his arm out to the other side of the bed they had shared together to see if, by chance, all of it had been just a bad dream.

If he could talk to her one more time, what would he say? His mind explored this question as much as he did the seemingly absurd possibility that such a conversation could even be had. For sure their life together was interrupted. They each thought they would have many, many years together. Would she want to know how his life was going, how the kids were doing? He certainly wanted to know about her life whatever it was.

What about Dana? She had been such a key part of George's life for over 30 years, his most important partner and the glue that held him together. What would she say if she knew he was harboring all these thoughts? He shuddered to think about facing her. He loved her with all his soul and wanted to avoid anything that might hurt her or lead her to think that he was thinking of another woman.

Hold on, what if Katherine was not in Heaven? What if there really was no Heaven or afterlife? What if she simply passed into nothingness? He couldn't even fathom thinking she may have gone to ..... Hell. Even though he'd never been a devout Christian or even considered Katherine to have been extremely devout, George could not accept a scenario where she was not there somewhere maybe watching and listening and waiting. Waiting? What if she's not waiting? What if she has found another life and another person to share it with? After all, that's what he did. Was something like that even possible wherever she is?

Nope! George believed in God and that He has provided a place as He promised in the Book of John, Chapter 14, Verse 2 where He told Peter, "In My Father's house are many mansions: if it were not so, I would have told you. I go to prepare a place for you." She was there; in his heart and Soul, George knows she's there. Some day, he hopes to be there. Some day, he hopes Dana will be there. Some day, he hopes all his children and their children will be there. His hope and dream was they would all be there together. "Wait," George thought, "What about Katherine and Dana? What if we aren't together because they aren't with me? What if one or both of them decides we can't be together because they don't want to be a part of my family anymore? Is there such a thing as jealousy in Heaven? Also, what if I don't make it? Heaven forbid such a thought. What if I've done something in my life to pile up the points against me? Nothing comes quickly to mind but I can never be too sure. I should be more careful about all I do and say. After all, my dream won't work if I'm not a part of it."

"Back to my original question," he thought, "is someone suggesting it's possible to do it another way? What parameters would enable and enhance such a communication link? Seems to me an ideal environment might be a quiet setting, with no one around, where you could put yourself into a near state of sleep not enhanced by drugs or drink; one where you're not asleep but where you could block out as much of the present world as possible yet remain conscious and aware of your surroundings. Does this make any sense? Sounds absolutely preposterous doesn't it?"

The more George thought about this, the more skeptical he became. The great science fiction writers Jules Verne and Isaac Asimov came to mind by even contemplating such a task. Another week went by as he tried to sort out how crazy an idea like this sounded versus how simple the logic seemed. No matter how hard he tried, he couldn't dismiss it from his mind, so he decided to give it a try.

An ideal time presented itself on a Saturday afternoon. Dana was out of the house with some friends on a shopping trip to Perimeter Mall. That was a scary thought unto itself. Dana was a shopper's shopper. She loved to hit the malls. She planned her forays. On her shopping days, she spent the morning and night before pouring over the sale brochures which arrived over the past week with the Atlanta Constitution. There were always a lot of them. Her friends did the same. She hated to shop with George because he was so one sided about such adventures. His idea of shopping was to think of something he needed, look on the internet to see who had it, go to their store, buy it and return home. To her line of thinking, this was absolutely no fun at all.

On this day with her out of the house, he decided to put his theory to practice to see how crazy he really was. Outside was a beautiful spring day. The sky was dotted with lazy slow moving clouds. The temperatures had yet to climb into the hot days the upcoming summer would bring.

George was sitting in his favorite recliner in their family room, which to some people would seem cluttered, surrounded by nearly fifty years of memories. His back was to the window looking at a space in the far upper corner of the room. After going through the mental checklist of clearing his mind and thoughts, he closed his eyes and quietly to himself, he asked, "Katherine, are you here?" His next thought was, "Boy, I hope no one finds out what I'm doing or I'll surely be planted in the funny farm along with all the other nuts."

A few moments went by then, "Hello, George. How are you?" was the answer that rang out in his head.

With that, he shot straight out of the chair, looked around the room and asked, "Who said that?" His first thought was someone had come into the house and found him nearly asleep. He got up to look around sure that someone was there. No one was around.

What was it he heard, 'Hello George, how are you?' Who said it and how did he hear it if no one was around? Then he remembered his theory-to-practice scheme. Thinking further, it occurred to him the comment and question appeared in his head and didn't come through his ears.

George nervously settled back into his chair once again and re-focused on the corner of the room. He had trouble clearing his mind but closed his eyes once again and asked, "Katherine, are you here?" Was it really this simple as he waited for a second response?

"Yes, I am, and don't be jumping up like that again. You startled me," the Voice said.

"Are you Katherine?" he asked timidly almost cringing as he posed the question.

"Yes. It's been awhile since we've talked, hasn't it?" She said.

"Are you real? Is this real?" he asked, amazed.

"That's for you to decide. If I said yes and you asked me to prove it, how would I do that?" she ventured.

"So I may be having a conversation with myself after all?" George added as a question.

"Could be, but you invited me in, so here I am," she said.

He sat quietly for some time thinking about the situation, "How's this possible? She was right in her comment on proving this. I'd love to be able to have some proof but what would I say about this to other people? They'd quickly assume I'd lost all sanity and would probably want to put me away somewhere and throw away the key." So, for the time being, he decided to see where this led. "Sorry for being so quiet, are you still here?" he meekly asked as he squinted with his eyes closed, halfway expecting to be hit with a wall of silence. His body was rigidly tense as if he were sitting in a dentist's chair even though he tried to force calmness on his mind.

"Yes, I am and you're right to be having questions about this," she replied.

"You can tell what I'm thinking?" he shot back.

"Not exactly," was the answer. "I took your hesitation to mean you were thinking about what just happened," she said.

"Well, what exactly does 'not exactly' mean?"

"Your inner thoughts are your own. If you ask me a question though, either verbally or non-verbally, I can hear and sense it. Don't ask me how, because I don't know," Katherine added.

Then he became concerned. "Is this a one time shot at talking to you or will we be able to do this at other times?" George asked. George was so engrossed at the fact that a conversation was going on that he completely forgot the other questions he wanted to know about her life.

"As far as I know, we can do this as often as you like," she said, "However, our conversations can only be initiated by you. In other words, you have to invite me," she added.

He pondered this for a minute and then added, "This is so unreal. A miracle, even. Am I unique in having this ability?"

"No," came her answer. "I'm told everyone has the ability but few ever discover it. Apparently, even fewer realize what they've done," she said. "Just remember even though we've opened this means to talk, you're still living your life among your family and friends and you have a responsibility to honor those obligations. We can talk as often as you like, but your important time should be devoted to those you care about there," she added.

"I can't believe it, the first time we talk in thirty-five years and I get a lecture?" he thought.

Still feeling as though he'd discovered a pot of gold, George asked, "So we can talk, I can ask questions and you'll answer them? Are you in, in ... Heaven?"

"Yes, I'm in Heaven and yes, if I know the answer and if I'm permitted to, I'll answer your questions. However, there're things I've learned here I may not be able to tell you. That's because knowledge about certain matters about the world and the universe haven't yet been discovered by humans. We aren't allowed to pass anything like that back to you until the discoveries are made on Earth in their normal course of events. Is that okay?" Katherine asked as she settled into a comfortable chair beside him even though he couldn't see her.

Katherine thought, "He would really freak out if he knew I was here in his family room watching him. Better not tell him that yet."

"Yes," he replied still in a quiet state of awe at what he had discovered.

"If you like, I can give you a few items of terminology so we'll be clear about how I express myself. Okay?" she asked as she looked at him stretched out in his recliner. He looked old to her. She knew he was only sixty-seven but there was something about him that belied his age. "I wonder if he's feeling as well as he should," she thought. He was a little overweight but not excessively so. She'd watched him enough over the years to be accustomed to his absence of hair and all his little idiosyncrasies. She realized she still loved him but could have no claim on him in their current situation, so she would simply be the teacher as was her profession.

"By all means," he said completely oblivious to anything about her watching him except her voice being there.

She began, "First, you call this place Heaven. We simply call it Home. We know most people call houses on earth their homes. But after you've been here awhile, you come to realize here is the real Home. The earthly spaces we occupied were simply way stations before we arrived here."

"So," he thought, "my house here is but a way station. Some day it'll be left to others to fill with their memories and stuff. Will I have to abandon all this when I take the next trip to ....wherever?"

"Second, we didn't 'die' or 'pass away' to get here. We 'Passed Through.' Think of the process as you would a butterfly metamorphosing from its cocoon into the beautiful creature you see flitting around you," Katherine continued.

"Didn't die! My goodness!" George thought, "So the Good Book is really right about all that."

"Third, when we passed through, our 'Souls' are the part that make the journey. This is the part of the human makeup God deposits into us after conception. This is the center of our being. The rest is just flesh and blood and stays behind. The Soul comprises our memories and feelings and travels with us as we pass through."

"Oh," he said, "so we get to keep our memories. They don't get left behind in our way stations."

"That's right. Since this is also a first for me, let me ask you this," she ventured as she looked closely at his facial expression as he lay there, "Do you see me or just hear me?"

All of a sudden, Katherine looked up to see another figure enter the room. This figure was of her world and not George's.

George replied, "I hear you inside my mind. The only vision is one from some years ago when we were young. You're wearing some sort of pants outfit and you're smiling, but I don't see your lips moving as you speak to me. Why, are you hideously ugly or something?"

"That's because the vision you see is from your memory. I can't see what you see but it's enough that you can. I can see you as you lie in your family room stretched out in your recliner, but you can't see the image of me as I am now. By the way, did you think I was ugly when we were married? And also, you're not exactly the slim and trim George you were on our wedding day either." she said as she peered at the other individual, a man, but she could tell he wasn't a resident like her.

"No! No! Please let me take my foot out of my mouth. I'm sorry for asking such a question. Yeah, I've put on some extra weight. I need to do something about that. But you were always beautiful to me," George said as he felt himself sweat just a little. "What do you look like now anyway?"

"You can't see me as I am now because I guess it's not permitted. I don't fully understand why and frankly, it's not important to me. 'What do I look like now?' Well, I sure hope I wouldn't seem ugly to you. I can't believe you asked that question. One of the beauties of being Home is I can take on any of my former appearances I choose. I can look as I did as a child if I want. That's not my preferred choice. I can look like a teenager. Sometimes I do that. Most often I take on the appearance as I was at about age 30, in earth years." The man who had quietly entered the room was smiling and held his finger to his lips as if to tell her not to betray his presence.

Wow! "I remember you were really good looking at that age. Do you have to take on an appearance at all? Do you wear clothes? Do you have wings? Can you fly?" George asked.

"Slow down a little, George. I find it helpful to have an appearance as I travel among others here who I want to visit. Usually, though, if I'm with my parents, I'm a teenager again. That's how they want to see me. Sure I wear clothes; after all, we're not heathens. I don't have wings; none of us do. How would you ever fit clothes around them? And no, I can't fly like a bird," she said.

George felt his head beginning to swell from hearing all of this. He hoped this conversation was real because some of this seemed to be important stuff. He wondered if she was standing with her arms folded as she used to whenever she lectured him. She used to furrow her brow when she was in this mode too. Was she doing this as well?

"You mean to tell me you can see and talk to your parents? How about other relatives and friends? How about others you never even met before?" George fired back. Even he was surprised at the questions coming out. These weren't even the questions he wanted to ask.

"Hold on, George. You're asking a lot of questions. Slow down. You don't have to ask all of 'em at once. I'll answer as many as I can," Katherine answered as she continued to look at the man now standing beside her.

The visitor finally said to her outside of George's hearing, "My name is Eli. I'm an Elder and I'm here to observe. Are you okay with that? If so, please just nod."

Katherine nodded as she watched first him, then George.

"All right, I'll try to control myself," George said overflowing with anticipation.

"As to my parents and other relatives, yes, I can see them as often and as long as I like. Even relatives I've never met. It seems many of my ancestors are interested in meeting me as well as other descendants. You have no idea how many I've met so far. They all want to know how I lived and about my other family members who haven't yet passed through. Depending on where they are in my family lineage, they can often tell me stories about my parents and grandparents when they were little kids. We've had some great visits and a lot of fun. It seems they have a never ending curiosity about their descendants and if their family lines are going to continue. All of this should be of interest to you since you have a deep interest in genealogy. Even if they don't seek me out, I can visit them and do so sometimes if they're here." She hoped Eli was not going to stop the conversation.

"That is fascinating stuff," George added, now grinning, "I'd like to do that some day. I'd be asking them all sorts of questions about how they lived and their uptake on historical events of their day and age."

"Yeah, I thought you'd like that. As to friends, yes, there've been some who've passed through. You have to remember, George, I passed through at such an early age, not many of my friends and not even my parents were here then. It seems I've been filling the role of greeter on an increasingly frequent basis as they've started arriving in greater numbers in their older age.

"As to new friends, yes, one of the great benefits in being Home is you have an endless supply of new people to meet. People who were famous on earth, smart people, funny people, and children, lots and lots of children," she added.

"As to new friends, have you, have you ...you know, met anyone you like?"

"You mean like a guy?" She asked.

"Yeah, I guess I do, not that I have any right to ask or know."

"There have been several over the years; nothing permanent, however. Right now and for a long while now, I've been what you might call unattached. I've always been too close to you and the family to consider anyone else too seriously," she replied.

George thought to himself, "I had no right to ask that. Why did I ask that? Stupid me! Here, I've been living with another woman, Dana, for over 30 years in a wonderful relationship. Do I still harbor some ancient feelings for Katherine? I guess if truth be known, even as much as I love Dana, I never finished my life with Katherine, so yeah, there must be feelings of some kind inside me somewhere." Then, he remembered something else she said.

"Hold on a minute," he said. "You mentioned you can visit them and do so sometimes 'IF they're here'. What does that mean?"

"We've learned not everyone passes through to become residents here. While we don't know exactly where they go, some people don't always make it Home," she answered as she walked around the room looking at his and Dana's things while keeping an eye on the Elder.

Wondering about this last statement which seemed significant, he asked, "Why do you think they don't make it Home? What kinds of people fall into this category and how many are there?"

"As best we can figure, even though we can't confirm it, these are the people who, when they were on Earth, fell into some category of evil doings or those who perhaps mistreated others without remorse. They seemingly had no conscience when dealing with their fellow human beings. There must be another place for them. Hell, perhaps, or maybe they simply died and ceased to exist in any form. We've no idea how many there are," she replied. The Elder continued his vigil. He seemed to watch George more than her. Maybe that's a good sign.

"Hey, I bet there are a slug of them trying to get in who were involved in sending spam on the internet before they passed through," he ventured jokingly. Well, maybe not jokingly! Just then, a car door slammed. Dana was back from the mall and gathering her parcels as she made her way into the house. "Katherine," he said, "Can we continue this later?"

"Sure, George! Go see Dana and see if you can help her. I'll be standing by," Katherine said, her voice ringing in his mind.

After George signed off Katherine asked, "Elder Eli, can you tell me why you're here? I don't think I've ever had a conversation with an Elder before."

Eli said, "You need not fear my presence. I was asked to come watch the opening of this communication between you and George. I know you were told some time ago this was possible, but believe me, this is the first instance of this happening in a long time. We can sense when these occur, and we're very much interested in them. It sounds like George will try to contact you again."

Katherine said, "I believe he will. So you are not upset about this?"

"On the contrary, we hope he does. What we don't know is what he will do with this knowledge."

"Do you want him to tell Dana and others?"

"Could be, we'll see how this goes. What he does with this will be entirely up to him," Eli said, "I may see you again if he makes contact with you later." With that, he was gone.

Katherine began to worry about Eli and his comments even though he seemed straight forward. "Was this going to come back to haunt George or me, for that matter?" she thought. She always had a tendency to look for things that sometimes weren't there.

Chapter 2

Dana entered the kitchen, loaded down with packages, just as he rushed in from the family room. "Hi," he said sheepishly, "Need any help?"

"Yeah, there's another load in the trunk," she replied as she sat them on the counter. "What've you been up to while I was gone? I thought you were going to play golf."

With his best smile, George replied, "Well, Marvin has a sprain in his lower back, and Bill had a honey-do list about a yard long, so we canceled. I just stayed home and straightened up in the garage," George lied, not wanting at all to tell her he'd been talking to Katherine; at least he thought he had. "How could I?" he thought as he rushed into the garage for her other packages, "I'm not near ready to explain a heavenly conversation with my ex-wife to my current wife and best friend on earth." Looking around, he realized he really did need to straighten up out there.

"By the way," She added as she pulled a diet drink from their refrigerator, "Jason called and said they had a really great time while they were here during spring break."

"Did he mention anything about Stewart?" he asked nervously as he re-entered the kitchen.

"No, why?" came her response as she turned to look at him. "But, I think he had a good time as well."

"I'm glad," he added, gingerly laying the packages on the counter alongside the others careful not to break anything. "He's such a great kid, Nicole too; both of them smart as whips."

"That's all I'm going to say about him," he thought, "No reason to run up a red flag by mentioning the grilling I took from him, if indeed, the questions were his."

Dana continued as she began to pull out salad materials for dinner, "Monica asked if I wanted to play tennis tomorrow after church. Do you mind?"

"Okay by me. There's a golf match on TV I want to watch anyway," he replied, not wanting her to know he would again test the strange connection he had discovered.

George sat down at the breakfast table and watched as she puttered about the kitchen in her dinner preparations. His mind wandered back to the strange events of the afternoon. What would he ask Katherine next? Heck, was he sure he even had the conversation or was all of it just a figment of a dream he had? Did he go to sleep or did he actually make a heavenly contact?

Dana busied herself while keeping watch over her husband of almost thirty four years. What was he doing? He looked like he had the weight of the world on his shoulders. "You okay, George?" she finally asked.

He jumped slightly at her question, and turned his head slowly to look her in the eyes, "Yeah, I'm fine," he said as he nervously smiled not wanting to take this any further. At that he jumped up and returned to their family room where he turned on an NBA game. The Hawks were getting hammered by the Celtics. So what else was new?

Dana's eyes narrowed as she watched him go. "What is he up to?" she asked herself. Sometimes he could be elusive whenever she stumbled upon something he didn't want to discuss. She resolved to watch him a little closer from now on.

George hardly slept that night. Sleep came late and when it did, he dreamed fitfully of his earlier conversation with Katherine. He wondered again if he really had the talk or if it was the result of an afternoon nap that included the visit from her.

All of this didn't go unnoticed by Dana but she never mentioned his preoccupation with whatever was going on inside that balding head. She would bide her time and see what she could learn through observation and what he might tell her. She had learned over the years that this was the way she had to conduct herself to get him to open up. She loved him but sometimes he drove her a little batty.

The next day, their visit to Church was relatively uneventful. George admitted to himself, however, he was more attuned to Rev. Richard Casey's comments looking for anything that would offer comfort and confirmation about the strange experience of yesterday. Nothing was forthcoming. He made a mental note to find some way to probe Richard about what he'd experienced to see if he'd ever heard about similar episodes. George thought, "He'll probably label me as some sort of heretic if I am too straightforward about all this."

He wondered if he looked like a heretic. If he looked in the mirror, all he would see is a non-descript sixty-seven year old individual, within a tiny fraction of an inch being five feet eleven, balding, slightly pudgy but not truly obese. His hair used to be brown, now it's mostly gray, what little he had displayed over his ears and around the back of his head. No doubt, he could stand to lose some weight. He'd have more wrinkles if he weren't carrying the extra weight. He realized he needed to exercise more, however. So far, there was no problem with his cholesterol or blood pressure. He had the type of outward appearance that went mostly unnoticed by anyone passing him on the street. That's good! He didn't particularly like to stand out. He'd rather just be in the background watching everyone else; which was probably why he became an engineer, that plus his natural ability with numbers and mechanical aptitude. He got all that from his dad. But even his dad was more outgoing. In the final analysis, he guessed he could be labeled a heretic, even if he didn't look like one.

Sunday afternoon turned out to be a carbon copy of Saturday. It was another great spring day with puffy clouds overhead, birds chirping softly and temperatures in the mid 70's. The azaleas were at their peak with a variety of colors and the dogwoods were in full bloom. Dana had left to pick up her friend, Monica, for their tennis match.

George wandered around the house trying to decide where to undertake his next session with Katherine. His home in Atlanta was over twenty five years old. Dana and he bought it new as their family began to expand beyond Jackie and Jason. At the time, the neighborhood was just being developed from a series of lots nestled among tall pine trees alongside steep winding streets. At the time, Atlanta was in the midst of explosive growth; so much so that existing main roads received very little attention as to width and the subsequent traffic they would be forced to bear. Looking from the street, their yard in front of the red brick house slopes slightly downward left to right with a two car garage underneath the two main floors. The back yard slopes likewise and backs up to an undeveloped stand of long leaf pines giving a lot of privacy.

This was the only home his children remember. His heart was here; most of his significant memories were here; Christmas' past when they would be awakened on Christmas morning as the younger ones would race through the house with exciting news of visits by the guy in the red suit; first days of school; first teeth falling out; first news about boy friends and girl friends; first news as those friends began to plan marriages; first news about grandchildren. He thought,

"My goodness, so much has gone on under this roof; it had been my and Dana's whole world seemingly. I guess she felt that way; I hope she felt that way."

George settled into a lounge chair in a shaded corner of their patio. Dana had found a good patio set on sale as a result of several shopping forays at the end of last summer. One of them happened to be a comfortable lounge with nice soft cushions. He focused on an overhanging branch of a large oak tree sitting in their back yard with its small new growth leaves. He slowly closed his eyes and cleared his mind.

"Katherine, are you here?" he asked in a more straightforward manner than yesterday as if he now expected her to be here.

A few moments later, came the reply, "Yes, I'm here. Looks like you're having another beautiful day."

George felt relieved to know this still seemed to be working and not a figment of a simple daydream. "The day's just great. I hope I didn't take you away from something important, but I wanted to know if we can continue. I have a lot more questions," he ventured.

"Sure, but can I ask you something first?" she asked as she settled into an adjoining chair and out of his sight. After all, he could only hear her voice in his mind.

"Yes, go ahead."

"Did you tell Dana anything about our talk yesterday?" She asked even though she already knew the answer. She'd been hanging around after they had talked watching him and Dana to see what he'd do.

"I haven't said anything to her about our conversation," he answered.

"Why not?"

"I don't think I understand enough about what's going on to say anything yet. Afterwards, I wasn't even sure it happened. Until just now, I wondered if I wasn't just dreaming," George answered, "Also, I guess I was a little nervous about telling her I talked to you. I didn't want her to get the wrong idea."

"And what idea is that?" Katherine asked as she watched his facial expressions carefully. She wanted to see if he started fidgeting as he talked.

"Well, you know, about us, I guess. I'm not sure how she'd feel about us talking."

"Do you think she might be jealous or something?"

"Well, I'm not sure. I guess that could be possible," he said as he was a little uncomfortable at this line of questioning. He, indeed, was fidgeting.

"Do you think you'll ever tell her?" as she smiled enjoying the moment in making him so nervous once again after all these years.

"Yeah, later maybe after I've had a chance to think more about all this," he said unsure at all about what needs to be done with this information.

"I can live with that. You said you have more questions?" she replied satisfied with his answers and his expressions.

George began with his questions although this dialogue made him more than a little fidgety, "I noticed today and remember from yesterday, it seemed to take a few moments for your response. Is there a reason for the hesitation?"

"Yes, yesterday, I wasn't at all anticipating your beckoning call. I was off watching Jackie and her kids playing at a park in their neighborhood. When your request came through, I had to make my way to you," Katherine replied, "Today, I was with some other friends at our local arrival station waiting for one of our old high school friends to pass through. Again, I had to make my way to you," she added.

"Who was the high school friend?" he asked.

"That's one of those things I'm not permitted to tell you. You'll probably hear about it from your own sources and then we can discuss it," she said rather sternly as she frowned knowing he couldn't see her.

"Okay, sorry 'bout that. Was it someone I might know? If it takes some moments for you to make your way to me, can you tell me how that works?" he ventured curiously.

Her carefully worded reply followed, "Yeah, I think you'd probably remember the person. When people on Earth form close bonds such as between a husband and wife or parents and children, their Souls create a permanent link which acts much like a direct phone link. When you asked for me, your Soul sent out the message I received. At Home, travel from one place to another is usually very quick. All I have to do is will myself to be where you are. Today, I had to explain why I was leaving to the other friends who were waiting with me. Does any of this make sense to you?"

"It only makes sense because you're telling me. I accept what you're saying as the way it is," he said. "Are you able to answer calls from anyone or does it have to be someone close to you?"

"No, apparently there're no links established with anyone other than someone you're very close to," came her answer as she turned to look out over their yard at a small rabbit that just emerged from the woods. She had no trouble keeping the conversation going as she looked around.

"You said you were watching Jackie at play in a park with her children, did I hear that right?" George asked.

"That's right. The beauty about Home is that you can go anywhere you want including any place on Earth. I often visit her and Jason to see what's going on in their lives. Do you remember a comment I made toward the end of my time on Earth when I regretted not being able to watch them grow up?" Katherine asked gingerly as if she knew how he would reply. She turned from the yard to watch his expression at his answer.

"Yes, I do. It was a statement I've often thought about over the years, usually everyday. It's haunted me all these years that I was unable to respond to you when you said it," he replied as he moved his hands up to his face. He could feel his face start to redden and his eyes tear up at that long ago statement and his inability to respond to her then. He wasn't doing much better now.

"Well, I need to put your mind at rest. Almost from the start, I've watched them everyday, often for days at a time. I've also watched you with them and Dana with all of you. I cannot begin to tell you how happy I am they've turned out so well and for the way you and Dana have raised them. Even when Stacie and Mike were born, Jackie and Jason never had a moment's concern about their relationship with both of you. I'm so proud of all of you. You're a good man and Dana seems to be an exceptional woman," she added with emphasis.

By now, his eyes were tearing freely as he smiled at her comments about the way he'd tried to lead his life. After losing her all those years ago, he made a vow to himself to never waste any time when it came to his family. They were the most important part of his life. "Thanks," was all he could manage with a trembling voice. "I've loved every minute of it," he finally managed to get out, as he was now outwardly moved.

She smiled to herself as she bent over to plant an invisible kiss on his cheek, one he couldn't feel and would never know about. He was a tender, caring soul. That much was obvious to her even when she was in the tenth grade looking up to him as an upperclassman. He never took her for granted and always did his best to see to her happiness and well being all the years they were together. Occasionally though, she would have to remind him about doing his share of the chores around the house. "Yes, George, I know you have. I've watched you too much to feel otherwise."

"Can you see me now?" he asked.

"Yes, as we are talking, I'm standing beside you, watching."

"Well, you've made me look like a mess."

Back to his questions, "How is it that I can talk to you and sense you now and I can't sense you at other times?" he asked.

"When you invited me in today, and yesterday, it's as if your Soul opened a door for me to enter. I'm inside your Soul now as we talk but I'm on the patio with you watching you and all the other things going on around here. At other times, when I'm just visiting, my Soul is only present watching as a spectator," Katherine explained as she walked around him. "As we're talking, my Soul's inside yours but we can't tell what each is thinking. We can only respond to questions and comments we make to each other. I don't understand all this myself but this is the way it seems to works. This is probably as clear as mud to you, right?" she added.

"You're right about that," George added, as his head seemed to swim while he gripped the arms of the lounge. "I feel as though I fallen into quicksand as I struggle to understand all this marvelous stuff you've told me. Are there others watching us now?"

"I'm reluctant to tell you this, but yes, there are quite a few others here right now," she said looking around at all the others from Home who had arrived while they had been talking. "After our talk yesterday, word spread, not sure how, but right now, we have quite an audience. A conversation like we're having is quite rare and has attracted a lot of interest among Home residents. Your parents are here among others you'd know as well as a lot of people you've never met. There're even a couple of Elders watching us. The patio, the family room and the yard all seem to be full of people," she added as she looked around acknowledging those she made eye contact with.

George's head was swimming worse as he struggled to keep his head above the quicksand. He felt as though he was about to fall off the lounge. "Let me digest some of what you just said," he shot back to her. "You said my parents are here, people I don't know and a couple of Elders, right? Can they just come and go as they please?"

"Yes!"

"Can I say hello to my parents?" he asked resisting a temptation to rise up and look around.

"You can and they'll be able to hear you but they can't respond because there's only one of us allowed into your Soul at one time to talk with you. You can talk to them later or I can leave to allow one of them in," Katherine said.

"No, no, let's continue for now. Maybe I'll try to contact them later," he added.

"Talk about learning more than you can digest, I'm there," he thought as he wondered how he'd ever keep all this straight. "What am I going to do with all this?"

"The Elders, who are the Elders?" he asked.

"You might think of them as Angels in earthly terms. You should feel honored. They rarely attend meetings of residents, and it's even rarer when more than one of them is present," she replied.

"Angels, huh! Well, I guess I'm honored and a lot confused I might add. Welcome to my home, all of you, if you can hear me," he blurted out as he hoped he was presentable and not making a complete fool of himself as he made a mental note to dress better in the future, at least to make sure his pants were zipped up.

Katherine looked at the group attending again and continued, "They all heard you and they're all smiling. It seems you're a hit after all."

One more Elder question, maybe two, "Do the Elders work for ....God? Why are they here?" he queried.

"Yes, although I'm not sure if they report directly to Him or indirectly somehow," was her reply. "Probably indirectly since this is such a large place. I can explain this later. I'm not quite sure why they're here. Wait," she hesitated, "One of them says he's to report about this directly to Him."

"Him, do you mean God?"

"That's exactly what I mean."

George thought to himself as his mind was now racing like the wind, "What in the world will this Elder say to God about Katherine and me just talking? Are they afraid she'll say something that's not allowed? Are they going to zap my mind after all this to erase any memory of what I'm doing? Have I inadvertently opened a forbidden door with whatever I've done here? Hell, I don't even know what I've done. What if I've just assigned my Soul to Hell?" His head started spinning again as he tried to fathom what was going on. "Its no use, I can't make any sense of this. I guess I'll just roll with the punches."

"Can I ask what you've been doing all these years aside from watching us and meeting other ….people?" he asked as he decided to stay away from the word 'guys'. "There I go again, am I jealous?" he wondered to himself.

"First of all, the concept of years is less meaningful here. Were it not for tracking activities with you and other family members on Earth, time really means little," she started. "During my orientation period, it became obvious to me and others that my teaching skills would be useful in bringing along the children who pass through and who hadn't achieved adulthood yet," she added as she paced back and forth. The other visitors gave her plenty of space.

"I know I seem to be rambling here but can you back up one step and tell me what you mean by your 'orientation period'?" George asked. "Maybe, it'd be better if you can start at the beginning …when you arrived there which, to me, was so long ago," he added.

Chapter 3

A long moment passed before Katherine said anything. She looked at the Elder who nodded his approval. At long last she started, "First, George, you have to understand when a Soul passes through, all past memories and feelings, good and bad, come along. The days leading up to my passing through were filled with memories of you and my other family gathered around me in the hospital. I heard and felt your sorrow as you watched me. Also, I was in a lot of pain and was heavily sedated, if you remember. Let me add though, as soon as I passed through, all the pain disappeared. One day, you'll understand better. All physical pains stay behind. No one here is burdened with any afflictions; however, all the memories of the pains remain and follow us through."

"I'm really glad your pains ceased. I remember the suffering you went through as if it were yesterday," he stated.

"The moment I passed through, I remember seeing new faces in the room. I remember getting out of bed and seeing you and the rest of the family so distraught. I wanted to tell you I was all right. Just then, I saw one of the new faces looking directly at me and smiling," Katherine said.

"The face introduced herself as Helen and said she was there with John and they were going to guide me Home. She was pleasant looking about five feet four with soft blond hair, hazel eyes, dressed in a white pleated skirt, and looked to be about forty.

"Not fully comprehending what was happening; I looked back and saw myself, or my physical body, lying in bed. I glanced back at Helen," Katherine said.

All Helen said was, "Shall we go?"

"I remember she took me by the hand and we began to move; I guess we were walking. Only, we seemed to go straight through the window into the outside air. As we did that, I turned my head and glimpsed you for the last time before the wall filled my vision. It was about two months, Earth time, before I saw you again. Once we were outside, it seemed as though we were still walking but from the perspective of being suspended in mid air. I remember marveling at what was going on. After a while, I sensed that we were walking on a long winding path through a beautiful meadow filled with flowers leading up to this huge building," Katherine told George.

Katherine continued her story as she related her next thoughts and conversations with her guide, "Helen, I hope it's OK for me to call you Helen, did I just pass away?"

"Yes, from the perspective of describing the event in earthly terms. Here, you may say that you 'Passed Through', as in passing through the veil. Your Soul that God gave you before you were born has been freed of your earthly body and we're bringing you Home where you'll live from now on," she responded.

"Is this Heaven?" Katherine asked Helen.

"Yes, but we prefer to call it Home for reasons you'll come to understand later," Helen replied.

"Is this building we are approaching Heaven or Home?"

"No," John answered this time, "This is the arrival station where you'll stay for awhile and where you'll learn about your new Home. You'll find you've undergone a remarkable transition which will allow you to do many new things and meet many people including perhaps some old friends and family members who have passed through before you," he added. John was slender, maybe six feet tall, with dark hair, almost black, brown eyes, and a light complexion. He was wearing a light blue suit with matching shirt and solid red tie.

Katherine asked, "What about the family I just left? Will I ever see them again? How're they doing? Will I ever talk to them again?"

Helen picked up the conversation, "Please don't worry. They'll all be fine and you'll be able to see them again in a short while. I'm not sure about talking to them," she added as she looked at John, "You'll undergo an orientation program here and, as part of the program, you'll learn how to visit them and to observe them wherever they are. After a while, and as they complete their time in the physical world, we expect them to join you here where they'll also see you again."

Katherine added, a little worried, "An orientation program, does that mean I'll be brainwashed or something like that?" as they continued walking along the path through a meadow full of flowers alongside a small brook.

John answered this time, "No, it simply means we'll teach you the capabilities you now have and how to use the new skills you now possess. We'll teach you a lot about Home, how large it is and how to travel around. We'll teach you how to enjoy your hobbies and how you can adopt new ones. We'll help you decide how to use your old skills or learn new skills to help other residents or new arrivals. We'll help you decide about a new place to live where you can spend your free time. We'll teach you how to stay abreast of what's going both here and on Earth."

Helen continued, "Katherine, you may sense that your orientation has already begun. You'll soon realize all of the senses you enjoyed on earth are part of you here. You can see, you can talk, you can smell the flowers around us, you can hear and you still have your sense of touch and taste. Your Soul doesn't need to breathe, you don't have to partake of food to sustain your strength, nor do you have to sleep, if you prefer not to."

Katherine brought the conversation back to the present by saying, "You can see, George, from the first moment, Helen and John were bringing me into my wonderful new world and leaving me little time to contemplate the events just past."

"So you moved from one world into another with no chance to go back. How would you ever want to go back to what you went through?" George added.

"The hardest part of passing through was leaving you and Jackie and Jason. The easiest part was getting away from all the suffering. There was no way I would go back if I had to put up with that," Katherine said.

"Sure can't fault you for that. What happened next?"

"As John, Helen and I approached the huge building; I noticed something familiar about the entry way ahead of us. Strangely, it resembled our front porch and front door on our home in Atlanta. At that point, Helen said it often helps new arrivals if they can see something familiar. I stopped at that point. Both Helen and John turned to look at me. I asked them if they were Angels."

"No," John said, "We're residents just like you who've chosen the role of guides for new arrivals. We're at your front door and we'll leave you now as you begin your new life here. Please go on in."

"Both of them waited as I nervously approached the door and turned the handle," Katherine said.

"George, I was really nervous and apprehensive as I pushed the door open."

"I guess so, I would be nervous too, though it sounds like everything was prepared in such a way as to put your mind at ease," he added.

"Yes! The interior was just like our home from the size of the rooms to all the furniture and pictures. Even all my clothes were there. It was just like I'd gone home. Turns out our whole house had been duplicated inside this huge arrival station simply to enable me to begin to feel at Home," she added.

"What happened next?" George quickly asked, mesmerized at what he was hearing.

George lost all track of time as they continued to talk. In fact, Katherine brought him back to reality when she said, "George, I believe it's time for you to re-enter your world."

"What," the next thing he remembered was hearing Dana as she walked out onto the patio, tennis racket still in hand.

"There you are, you sleepyhead. I believe you'd sleep your life away if given the chance. What happened to the golf match on TV, and what exactly have you been doing?" She asked as she quizzed him in a tone only an overly curious wife can use.

"The golf match wasn't that interesting," was the partial answer he gave as he arose from the lounge. Then he took a chance by adding, "To tell you the truth I've been thinking about Katherine and my parents and what they're doing now."

"Now that's a strange thing to say about such a strange subject. I know you realize they passed away a long time ago. So what do you think they're doing now?" she said as she walked to stand directly in front of him as she repeatedly tapped her left hand with the tennis racket. The hairs on her neck began to prickle at the mention of the name, Katherine. Why was he saying this?

"My guess is they're in Heaven," he replied, careful to use a term Dana was familiar with. He wanted to break and run but he stood his ground.

Katherine was still present watching this scene unfold as were most of the other visitors.

"Well, that would be my guess also," she added with her neck hairs still tingling and still tapping her left hand, "So what brought all this on?"

"It came about as a result of a strange conversation and a lot of questions I had from Stewart when they were here last week," George ventured, hoping she would not carry this much further.

She wouldn't let this go quite that easily, "And what was the general direction of his questions?" Dana added now with a little more emphasis as the tapping seemed to grow with intensity.

Realizing that he had trapped himself, George added, "He wanted to know if I was getting old and what might happen if I got sick and didn't get well. Then he wanted to know if I had ever known anyone who had gotten sick and didn't get well. You might guess the situation with Katherine came to mind and we talked about that a little. I hope that doesn't upset you," he was starting to sweat just a little; actually more than just a little with the swinging tennis racket directly in his eyesight.

She sat down on the lounge and pulled him down beside her. She took his hand as she was now feeling better about all this, looked him square in the eyes and said, "Listen, I love you very much. I also know that my chance at a life with you only happened because of the terrible ordeal Katherine went through. I know you loved her very much and she's the natural mother to two of our children and five of our grandchildren. As far as I'm concerned, she's a welcome member of this family now and forevermore. I never met her when she was alive but from all indications from our family, she was a class act."

Katherine smiled as did George's mom and dad as they continued their vigil.

"Thank you for saying all that. Indeed, she was a class act, as are you. But you have to know even as much as I cared for her then, I love you now and have built over thirty great years of memories with you and our family. Those will never be traded for anything. Please remember that," George managed to say over and around the lumps in his throat realizing he hadn't told her any of the significant stuff.

Katherine and the Elder realized that as well.

"So how was the tennis match? Can you still beat Monica?" he asked as he managed to change the subject. Dana was a good tennis player and a fair golfer. They played golf together but not too much tennis. She was far too good for him. Her tennis skills earned her a partial scholarship at Auburn a long time ago. He was older than her by a good five years and taller by a good five inches. She could have easily passed for his daughter. Sometimes he was reminded of that by strangers they meet. Indeed, she had managed to age very slowly. She was still slim and had a full head of naturally blond hair. Her smile, the blue eyes and dimpled cheeks always caused his heart to skip a beat.

She laughed. He loved to hear her laugh too, "Oh yes, we played a couple of sets and I managed to lose only four games. Monica asked if we wanted to come over next weekend for a cookout. What do you think?" Dana asked.

"That'd be great," George answered. Monica was married to Marvin, one of his golfing buddies. Being retired, he expected to play at least one round with him between now and the weekend.

In addition to being a good tennis player, Dana was also an accomplished artist with a paint brush. Her works adorned homes all over the city and had been sold at several galleries in the area. At least one painting had made its way onto Ebay as an item for sale. Every time someone had a silent auction, she was always asked to contribute one of her works for whatever charitable cause the auction was supporting. She was a soft touch for such things.

Then she said, "I've a confession to make. I got another speeding ticket this afternoon on the way to the club."

"My goodness, Dana," he replied. "You'd better slow that BMW down. Your heavy foot's already making its impact on our insurance rates. Not only that but you may find yourself going through some remedial driver training." This was about the third or fourth time in the past two years. Her intent on fast speeds made her scary to ride with. George almost always insisted on driving whenever they went anywhere.

He decided it was not yet time to tell Dana anything about the communication link he had discovered. After all, as Katherine made clear, how was he to prove the existence of such a portal? He supposed he could instruct her on using it with a loved one from her past. The only thing was, with her family history, who would she able to make the link with, since it required a connection with someone you were once really close to? Perhaps her mother, Rose; they seemed to have been pretty close. Her parents divorced before she finished high school. Anyway, George felt as though he first needed to learn more. Also, how would she react to him just talking to Katherine? Was she secure enough in their relationship for this not to be a problem?

Chapter 4

The next chance to speak with Katherine came the following Wednesday. Dana was at a church auxiliary meeting with other ladies and wouldn't be back until after lunch.

In thinking about the other two sessions with Katherine, George was still in awe at what had transpired. To communicate with someone so close yet so far away in another dimension decried all rationale and reasoning. He believed his talks with her were real. Yet the concept seemed so unreal, like something right out of a Steven Spielberg movie. He knew of nothing else on the planet even close to this.

There was so much to ask, so much to learn, if she would be willing and permitted to tell. The list of questions and topics he wanted to know seemed endless. Still, after all was said and done, what would he do with this information? Forgetting about potential issues with Dana, should he try to tell others?

He thought to himself, "If this indeed is real, why's this not already common knowledge among those who still live on this Earth? Why isn't this mentioned somewhere in the Bible? How will the Church react to such a phenomena? Will they want to keep this quiet? Will they believe they have too much at stake to risk in losing status among their congregations? No, I think the time hasn't yet come to reveal much if anything about this. There's too much I feel I need to know yet. Soon, maybe, maybe never."

"Besides, who'd ever listen to someone like me? I've always considered myself smart but I never thought my career was that distinguished. Sure, I put in my 40 years as a career engineer and had over 40 patents to my credit, some of which are producing a nice stream of retirement income. I've raised a great family who are, in turn, doing pretty well in getting their own careers off the ground and their young ones out of the cradles; some day, but not yet. Maybe I'll pass this information along only to them and let them sort out how to tell the world. My guess is the world is a long way from being ready to have this information."

Wednesday was overcast and windy with the temperature hovering around 60 degrees. Not a day to be out on the patio. Instead, he was sprawled out on the couch in their living room studying the clock on the mantel as its pendulum slowly swayed back and forth.

"Katherine, are you here?" he gently asked from within his mind with the expectation now of a reply after a few moments. Its funny how quickly one learned to take things for granted.

Sure enough, after a short hesitation, "Yes, George, I'm here," was her equally gentle response. "Looks like all's well with you. How are you absorbing all of this information? Have you mentioned it to Dana yet?"

"No, I haven't told her anything yet. I'm still trying to make some sense about all this. I can assure you it's quite overwhelming. Yet for all that you've told me so far, I find myself sleeping quite well at night. It's as though the news has a rather unique ability to calm the Soul, so to speak. Quite reassuring actually but not so satisfying that it's squelched my thirst to learn more," he replied as he stretched out on the sofa. "Okay if we continue with questions? I sure don't want to offend anyone there. That wouldn't seem to be a wise course of action given the audience at last Sunday's discussion. Do we still have an audience? First though, tell me how you're dressed so I can visualize you."

"Let's see, I am wearing a pair of bib overalls with hiking boots and no shirt."

"You're what!" he exclaimed as he almost came off the couch.

By now she was laughing as were others from Home in attendance, "Made you think twice didn't I? Actually, I'm wearing a two piece black pants and top outfit with a white blouse under the top. I have a pair of open toed dress sandals on as well. Is that enough detail?"

"Well, you're still a crazy woman, I see that. Yes, thank you very much, I now have the picture firmly in my mind. But I'm also trying to picture you in overalls too," he said laughingly.

"Yeah, that'll keep you awake at night for sure. As to your other questions, there're a few others in attendance with more arriving as we speak, including one Elder, but not nearly as many as the other day. Yes, we can continue to talk. I'll tell you what I can," she added.

It's weird he ccouldn't see or sense anyone else here as he forced his eyes open to look around. Had to be careful though, didn't want to lose his concentration. "I remember you telling me about entering a door into a room that looked exactly like home, can we pick up there?" he asked.

"Yes, as I walked in, I remember seeing my grandparents, both sets of them. There was one other person who introduced herself to me as Margaret. She told me she was a resident whose task it was to answer any questions I might have and to tell me about what would happen next. I remember hugging my grandparents. They all told me how excited they were to see me. Grandma Tess hugged the tightest. If you remember, she was the last one to pass through only a couple of years before me. They all looked so young; about 50ish I guess," Katherine said.

"Considering what you'd just gone through, seeing them must've really been uplifting. I guess just being there must've been uplifting as well," he added.

She continued as she walked around the living room, "Probably more so than what you were going through. Was it pretty tough for you? As soon as I saw them, I knew deep down everything was going to be all right for me, but I was still very worried about you. We visited for a long while. They told me how they'd been keeping watch over me and you and all the rest of the family during my final days. At the time, I didn't understand how that was possible but I accepted their comments as fact anyway."

"You have no idea the pains I felt after you passed. I felt alone even with Jackie and Jason. The world collapsed around me. Your life went in one direction and ours in another. But what about the other person there...Margaret you said, right?" George asked.

"After I settled down a bit and caught up with my grandparents, I took a short time to look around the rooms we were in. They looked just like I was home; even the outside view. Margaret said she could start to fill me in when I was ready. She was a petite lady, probably no more than five feet tall. Margaret looked relatively young, but I learned that looks here can actually belie your age. She later told me she had been at Home for about 150 years. I looked at her and thought she was vaguely familiar. She assured me we hadn't met and she was simply a resident whose task it was to be a part of the welcoming group, answer questions and to begin the Orientation process," Katherine added as she paused to study the pictures on the mantel.

"What was the Orientation process like?" he asked, hardly knowing how to ask these kinds of questions. "How long did it take?" he added.

Katherine hesitated for a moment as if deciding how to proceed, then she began as she restarted her pacing, "Orientation has two main purposes. One purpose includes all the instructions about how to live in this new place. I hadn't learned yet to call it Home. The other main purpose is the Reconciliation."

"The Reconciliation...what's that?" he asked immediately sensing this might be important.

After looking at the Elder sitting across the room, she continued, "There's a lot about Reconciliation I can't tell you because I'm not permitted to. It's an important step we go through before becoming full fledged and free roaming residents. If you remember me saying that once a Soul passes through, the Soul retains all memories, both good and bad. About the only thing I can say is during the Reconciliation, most bad memories and experiences are addressed and reconciled. You have to figure the rest out for the time being and simply wait your turn at the process."

"Well, Okay," he said feeling a little short changed. How quickly he became spoiled with just hearing all the new information she was relating. "What about the other instructions; what did that entail?" he asked.

"Envision your first day at school where you arrive in a bus or car and are ushered into a classroom with a bunch of other little strangers. You realize you're in a totally unfamiliar place full of unfamiliar people who look just as dazed and lost as you. Your best friend at that moment is the teacher who begins to bring order out of the chaos with kind words and a smiling face.

"My first time was basically like that. I was still at the place that looked like my home. I had already finished the Reconciliation process. Margaret asked if I was ready to take the next step. I said yes. She took me by the hand and by the time I blinked my eyes, I was in a room full of other people; must've been a couple of hundred of us. Margaret said she'd be back later to pick me up, then she was gone, disappeared before my very eyes, which were, by the way about as wide as they could get. I felt lost, as if my security blanket was missing. I looked around and saw others disappearing as well. When all was finished, I guess there must have been a hundred or so of us left. I had no idea where we were in relation to the rooms which looked like my house."

"First day at school, huh? Hope you made some friends," he ventured.

"Yeah, I did, many of them as a matter of fact. One in particular became my training partner. All of us there were adults. I learned later that children, who pass through, go through a different process. Shortly, a middle aged gentleman spoke up. He said his name was Henry. He said he was a resident like us and was there to begin a period of instruction that would enable us to function as useful and happy residents. Again, someone asked where we were. He said that if you look at the big picture, we were at Home; 'a place you may have called Heaven only a short time ago,' he added.

"Someone else asked how we got to this room. 'Aha,' he added, 'A very good and important question.' He went on to say he would explain how we arrived and where we were in relation to where we had been," Katherine said.

"Sounds like Heaven 101." George commented.

"Precisely," as Katherine continued, "We were taught as new residents, our Souls now contain several new functioning tools. One's a tool for navigating. Home's a big place, infinitely big it seemed. The new tool is one that enables us to go from place to place merely by visualizing the destination and adding the words 'go there.' If it's a place you haven't been to yet, just say the name for the destination such as 'library' plus 'go there' and you're there; turns out to be really simple and very effective. This instruction works for traveling to Earth as well."

"You mean there are no cars or planes there; how about taxis and rickshaws?" he asked.

"Rickshaws, huh! Well, you can travel by any means you want. If, for example, you wanted to travel by car, you could do so. Most people who do this do it like a vacation trip just to get the feel for being in a car again and to see the scenery of the countryside. Maybe they want to go up into the mountains," she replied as she sat down on one of their wingback chairs.

Seemed as if each question of his and an answer from her led to even more questions deeper yet into a subject. "Okay, how does one buy a car?" he asked.

"That," she said, "was another subject of instruction during our orientation. How do you get stuff? Turns out this is almost as simple as going places. If, for example, you wanted a car, all you have to do is visualize it, or say its name and say 'bring here.' It's as simple as that. No money or credit cards are used here. It's not needed or permitted."

"No money or plastic? How in the world is that possible?" he said wondering aloud.

"George, remember we're not in your world of physical limitations anymore. Other than saying that, I'm just as amazed and confounded about how things work here as you'd be. God, when he made this place for his children, was really ingenious. There're many things which go on here that boggles all of our minds. We're just thankful we're here and He cared enough for us to give us this place.

"We were able to practice our new abilities by getting out and going places and going shopping. Shopping's a little different here. We visit places where things are displayed. When we see something we want, we get it by the means I just told you," Katherine said.

"Shopping sounds like fun. How about a place to live or did you simply stay at the place which looked like our house?" he asked.

"Shopping is fun, particularly with all the new gadgets available. I did stay there for a while. Part of the orientation was how to find other housing. I had a choice of continuing to use the quarters they first gave me or I could redesign a new place located wherever I wanted. I could live in a city or I could have a place outside the city. They have other residents who help in new designs; sort of like architects. I have a small house located by a lake and a large park. Once I'd decided on the design and the location, I acquired it by the same process as the car," Katherine explained as she began wandering through the kitchen. She was keeping an ear out for Dana in the process.

"Sounds like nice digs. Do I remember hearing you say that you work a teaching job there? How did that come about? Since that was your old job, did they make you take the same job?" George asked.

She explained, "No, they don't make you take a job you might not like. During orientation, they explored various options with me. I considered a number of roles. When I learned about all the children who're here, I thought working with them would be easy and uplifting at the same time."

This provoked yet another series of question on another tangent, "What children? Is their training different than the programs set up for adults?"

"Yes! Most adults, when they arrive here, already have skills from their jobs and schooling on Earth. Children who pass through can arrive at any age and in almost any stage of schooling and social level. As tragic as their passing may seem on Earth, all children arrive here with the greatest of fanfare and often with a great need for social skills as well as a need for completing their educations. All of them had their lifeline disrupted with their passing, and we find there can be huge gaps in what they know and what they need to know to be successful and happy residents at Home.

"Each child is put under the care of two resident adults who provide not only education but also love and support particularly if their parents haven't passed through yet. Many of their closest relatives who've passed through such as grandparents are often involved in their care and support while we finish their schooling. Some arrive here never having experienced love from anyone on Earth, or perhaps they were abused in some way. They get the most attention. Believe it or not, but we have to teach them to accept love and teach them to trust. Some of them come from shattered homes or are so young they never felt the loving touch of their mothers."

"Those must really pull at your heart strings," George interjected as he began to feel some of the pain he sensed in Katherine's voice.

"That's the reason for all the attention we lavish on them. The orientation program for children generally lasts a lot longer than for adults because of their educational needs. They not only need the education but they also need to develop their adult appearances. All of this is accelerated when compared to Earth time but can still take up to ten times longer than the adult programs.

"The biggest challenge for us occurs with children who're extremely young in Earth time. This includes children who are unborn," she said as she began to pace around the room at a faster rate because of this subject being so near and dear to her heart.

"Unborn huh! Exactly how young can they be when they arrive there?" he asked.

"Some of what you're asking we're not sure about," she began as she glanced again at the Elder, "Shortly after a child is conceived on earth, God, with the help of his network of Elders, puts a living Soul inside this new child sometime during the period of development in it's mother's womb. We believe the Elders fit the new Soul to the situation, so to speak, and to match it to the makeup of the parents so we're pretty sure it doesn't happen immediately after conception. We're just not sure when.

"At any rate, if something happens to the mother or the child before it's born, such as an accident or abortion, the Soul of the child arrives here for us to care for and nurture to near adulthood. We deeply feel it's our responsibility to provide for the care and education of each child even though the process might be accelerated," she passionately added as she sat down again.

Hearing tiredness in her voice prompted George to ask, "Can I assume from your tone and words this may be the area you're involved in?"

"Yes!"

"Would this, by chance, have anything to do with when Jackie and Jason being so young when you passed through?" he gently asked.

After a long pause and with a detectable quiver in her voice, she added, "Yes, I guess it did. I want so badly to see these small children brought along as normally as possible, the same as I wanted for my own children. I'm with these children as much as possible. I often have them in my residence while they're going through their schooling. It's so fulfilling but you probably know all that. Since I've been here, I've had the great opportunity to help many of them along and have created lasting friendships with a lot of them. Someday, I'd like to introduce you to some of them."

"I look forward to that. I do know how fulfilling it can be to watch and help children grow and develop but tell me this; do they sometimes just want to be children and have to be corrected?" he added.

"Yeah, at times they can be little imps. I've never disciplined any except by putting them in timeout or denying them privileges. I'm not sure I could spank them anyway, the way things work here. They receive limited freedoms to start with and gradually earn more as they demonstrate the understanding needed for higher levels of responsibilities.

"Also, it's okay to look forward to meeting some of them but just remember your responsibility there. Even though your children are grown, they still look to you for guidance and they respect your opinion more than you might imagine. You also have a bevy of grandchildren who look up to you. Even though they don't know me, I watch them as much as I can. I've envied you and Dana over the years even though I'm in this great place. Then, there is Dana. You've yet to enjoy all the time with her both of you have available," she ventured.

There goes that lecture again, "Just how much time do you suppose that is?" he asked in a manner that surprised even him.

"George, I can't tell you that," was her short answer.

"Can't or won't?" he shot back sensing that they might be having some kind of argumentative discussion.

"First, if I knew, I wouldn't tell you. Second, we don't know the future here in spite of what many might believe on Earth. The future for us unfolds just like it does on Earth, day by day. There may be some here who know the future such as God or Jesus, or perhaps some of the Elders, but none of the residents know, I assure you. We live here in the present time; which means we can't travel back in time either," she replied as she glanced at the Elder again. He was just sitting listening and watching and offered no comment or hint of his own feelings.

Jesus, now there was a name that hadn't been mentioned yet. But, George wasn't going to get the opportunity to ask about Him yet; Dana was home from her auxiliary meeting. George's anxiety over her learning of these conversations just shot up again.

Chapter 5

George heard Dana arriving when the garage door started to open. He jumped off the couch and rushed to meet her at the back door.

"Enjoy the auxiliary meeting?" he innocently asked.

"Yes, I did, and George, you've never asked me about these meetings before. What've you been up to? Did you get the hall closet cleaned out like I asked?" she fired back as she came into the kitchen with eyes searching for answers.

"What?" he muttered, knowing full well he never touched the closet. "I guess I forgot."

Then she stopped, turned and looked at him as she sat her church materials on the counter, "Okay, have you been asleep again? Where this time?" she asked in a definitely unfriendly voice.

Sheepishly, he replied, "On the living room couch."

"George Mason, what's going on? This is the third time I've come home only to find you asleep or coming out of a sleep," Dana was almost shouting now, "Something's going on and I want you to tell me what it is. Are you all right? Are you passing out or something? Please tell me. I'm starting to worry."

"Okay, okay, I believe you deserve to know, and it's probably time for me to try to explain," he said as he finally gave in. Now he had to figure out the best way to bring her into this crazy loop without her calling for someone with a straight jacket or flying off the deep end when she learned who he'd been talking to. "Please sit down." They settled uneasily into the two wingback chairs in the living room facing each other. All was quiet in the rest of the house. Neither knew that Katherine was still present as were some of the other visitors including the one Elder. They started to crowd into the living room all wanting to hear and witness what was about to happen.

George began, "First, I hadn't really decided yet on exactly the best way or with the best words to tell you what I've discovered. Second, I want you to promise to hear me out completely without getting angry or jumping to a bunch of crazy conclusions when I tell you what I've been doing lately. Third, I promise you I'm not crazy and what I've discovered seems real to me. It could be very important." He paused, then quickly blurted out, "What I've discovered is a communication link which allows me to talk to someone who has died and is in Heaven!"

Dana looked incredulous; eyes wide, no smile, not much of any kind of expression, lips tightly closed. This scared him.

"Say something," he pleaded as most of the visitors crowded around to see her reactions.

After another pause, she said, "I don't rightly know what to say or how to respond. I'm glad you told me not to think you're crazy. That's the only thing keeping me from either laughing out loud or calling your doctor. Why would I be angry anyway? You're serious, aren't you?" Dana asked as her eyes narrowed and pierced him, like arrows.

"I'm deadly serious. You're my wife and my best friend, and I love you very much. I wanted to tell you....eventually. Actually, I wanted to tell you earlier, but I had so little information about what I had found and I was so overwhelmed,

I knew I'd sound like I'd jumped off a bridge somewhere. I probably still sound that way. But, I've had three sessions now, and what I'm learning will blow your socks off," George added trying to sound confident about what he knew. He still had no idea how she'd react when she learned about Katherine. He had no idea such a crowd was on hand seeing him struggle.

"All right, what've you learned?" she asked with a most unbelievably harsh tone as she sat perched on the edge of her chair.

"In summary, I'm learning how Heaven works and, by the way, they don't call it Heaven there; they call it Home. I have to be honest with you. There's no way I can prove this. I was warned about that. I can explain how it happened and you can try it but there's a catch," he explained as he was likewise perched on the edge of his chair except he was wondering if he wasn't ready to bolt out of the house.

"Yeah and what's that?" she asked in the same tone.

"As best I can understand it, the communication link occurs between two Souls. Mine would be one. The other would be with someone who's already passed on. For the link to work, it had to be established while both people lived on earth and the two people had to love each other very much. Much like the feelings between parents and children or……perhaps between two people married or otherwise," George carefully said.

"You mean between married couples, say?" Dana asked with her eyes narrowing even more and boring into his. The crowd of invisible visitors continued to grow, filling in other rooms of the house.

"Yes," was his measured reply.

"You mean between you and Katherine?" she asked almost making a statement out of it in capital letters. Her frown deepened. He'd seen these before. She is definitely on the verge of being very unhappy.

"Yes. Remember me telling you about the questions Stewart asked when he was here?" George added trying desperately to keep a level voice and not make a run for the door.

"Yes, but I thought he was asking about your health and what'd happen if you died," she added still in a very excited state, standing now by the fireplace and extremely close to the fire poker. George noticed, as did a couple of the visitors.

"He did, but his questions and the way he asked them put me to thinking about whether it was possible for a person to figure out a way to talk and communicate with someone who has Passed Through, which, by the way, is the term they use to describe death. I wondered if the questions he was asking weren't being fed from someone somewhere else and were being used to guide my own thought process. If so, I wondered if it weren't possible to talk back to such a person. It took a while to come up with a way I thought might work. I was lucky and did this on the first attempt," he said still sitting perched, ready to run and trying to make himself as small a target as possible as he watched her by the fire place not that she'd ever threaten violence. No, not Dana. Actually he loved her very much and wanted desperately to help her thought process get through this.

"George, I have to tell you that none of this makes the least bit of sense and I don't believe it. If you've been having conversations with Katherine, I think it's something going on strictly in your head. I'm very skeptical about this and more than a little upset," she added sternly with arms crossed and clearly on the edge as she thankfully moved over by the window. None of the visitors had left.

Questions flooded Dana's mind. "Why Katherine? Is there something going on here with George that he feels some special need to talk to her, either real or imagined? Is something going on in my marriage I don't know about?

Is George unhappy with me for some reason? Is he having some kind of affair in his head? I went through this when my first husband cheated on me. I don't think I can handle this again." All of these questions were draining her energy, and she sat down again.

"I can't say I blame you for being so skeptical or upset. Nobody would believe this, and it can't be proved except by doing. If you want to think about this and if you want to try it, let me know and I'll tell you how it worked for me," was all George could think to say in an effort to soothe her feelings. He wasn't aware of her other concerns...yet.

"Yes, indeed, I'll think about this. I'm not at all sure how I feel about you having all these long talks with Katherine after all these years even if it is only within your head. Are you unhappy with me for some reason? Have you been unfaithful to me? I'm not sure I could stand it if you have been," Dana exclaimed, now almost in tears.

"No, no, no; that's not how it is at all," George exclaimed as he rushed over to embrace her. She pushed him away, "I was afraid you might have some fears but nothing like this. I never want you to think I've been unfaithful. I love you with all my heart and Soul. You and I are linked tightly and will be forever. All I'm trying to do is explain something else that is wonderful. I believe it's real. All I ask is for you to try."

After a long while, "Tell me how this works," she finally said as if she was giving in to some inevitability.

George wiped the sweat from his brow and began, "Using their terms, first, you have to think of someone who has passed through who you were really close to. I thought perhaps your mother, Rose, would be that person. Second, you have to find some quiet time and place when nothing else is going on; no TV or radio or any other distractions. You have to concentrate. You have to put yourself into a kind of controlled trance. By controlled, I mean you have to remain conscious but totally concentrated on the person you are trying to connect with. You have to clear your mind of extraneous thoughts and distractions. Once you feel you've achieved this state, simply ask the question 'Mom, are you here?' If it works, you should hear an answer inside your mind within a moment or so. You won't be able to see her but you should be able to hear her speaking in your mind."

"Goodness!" is all she could say for a moment. "So that's all I have to do to make this work?" she added still with a healthy amount of disbelief and with an unhealthy amount of suspicion as she continued to glare at him from across the room.

"Let me ask you about Rose. Were you really close to her?" he asked trying to get a sense about their relationship and trying to move her thoughts away from his relationship with Katherine. He realized if she wasn't close enough to Rose; then there may have been no one before him with whom she'd made this vital Soul-to-Soul connection.

Reluctantly, she replied, "Well, after her and Dad divorced, times for us were pretty tough. She had her hands full trying to keep our family together. I was old enough to help with my younger brother and sister, but I was mostly rebellious as they were. However, by the time I went off to college, I began to see the strain and extra effort and sacrifices she made to hold our family together. I became really close to her after that; particularly so, once we learned that Dad got into all that trouble with the law. Toward the end of her life, I made an effort to be with her every chance I got, as you should remember," she explained as she sat back down wringing her hands.

"Yes, I remember. She was a courageous, heroic woman in my humble opinion. I thought you had reconciled with her. Okay, so think about what I've told you. If you get a chance, please try this. If not, then there's no other way to convince you. I believe what I'm doing is real and I really don't want it to stop. There is so much more to learn, and that's all I'm doing in my conversations with Katherine. There's no hidden agenda here. I'd like to have similar conversations with my parents," George said now kneeling beside her chair hoping this was going to calm things down a bit. He sure didn't want it to create a rift in their otherwise special relationship. "I'm not crazy. It's hard to explain, but I have much better peace of mind from all of this happening. It's like I can sense how all this is going to end for all of us. It feels great," he added trying to sound enthused, "and reassuring."

"Someday, you'll have to tell me about your vision. Okay, I'll think about it," she said, but only half heartedly with a voice tired from the emotions of the past half hour.

The matter wasn't mentioned again as if both of them wanted to avoid any more involvement with such a strange and volatile subject. He'd finally come clean with her. To be honest, the discussion about the connection went better than he'd envisioned. The part involving Katherine could have gone better, but at least she didn't dismiss all this out of hand....he didn't think.

By this time the visitors started to disperse. The Elder had left. Katherine was ready to leave. She spoke for awhile with George's parents and Dana's mom who had also been present from the beginning. All of them felt the situation was stable and everything would work out. They all hoped Dana would have the courage to try the connection.

Chapter 6

The following day, Thursday, George had a tee off time at nine with Marvin and Bill. They picked up a fourth at the clubhouse as they were prone to do. The three of them hadn't yet found the right person for the open slot in their foursome. The day was cloudy with a promise of isolated thunderstorms in the afternoon. By that time, they should be finished with their round and be firmly ensconced in the clubhouse.

At home, Dana started her morning chores which, today, consisted of washing a couple loads of clothes, making the bed, doing some light house cleaning and making herself presentable, which never took a lot of time. She didn't have a good night's sleep for obvious reasons. She wasn't sure if she was more upset at discovering George was having imaginary conversations with Katherine or at the possibility that they were, indeed, real. Actually, the latter possibility seemed way less probable than the first. Still, she wondered....and wondered. More importantly to her psyche, what were they talking about? She went to sleep with a gnawing pain in her stomach which returned the minute she thought about them again when she awoke.

By midmorning, she finished her initial to-do list for the day and found herself sitting in the family room looking out over the patio and the woods in the distance. Somewhere out there, she heard the familiar warble of mockingbirds with their strange varied melodies as if they were talking to each other. Somewhere else in the background, there was a radio playing soft music. "I probably left the radio on in the kitchen," she said to no one in particular.

She found herself thinking about the process George described the night before. What was it he said; relax, clear the mind, concentrate and don't go to sleep? And be ready for a response.

"Well why not?" she thought.

When she thought she was at the right stage, she asked, "Mom, are you here?" She waited a few moments. Nothing happened. "Yep," she thought, "He was crazy after all."

Thinking through what she did, she realized the radio was on. She got up and turned it off. The mockingbirds were singing in the woods and were flooding the family room with their conversations through the open patio door. She closed the door. "There," she thought, "Quiet at last."

She settled back into the chair, relaxed and began to breathe deeply again. Then, she tried a second time, "Mom, are you here?"

A few moments went by. She was about to abandon the process when a reply came back, "Yes, Dana, I'm here."

Unlike George, she didn't spring up and search the house for the source of the reply. George had conditioned her to be ready for a response. "Is it really you, Mom?" she asked, leaning forward.

"Yes, it is. I see that you're trying the process George told you about. I'm present in your mind and we can talk," Rose said, not mentioning the other conversation she'd witnessed between the two of them yesterday. Rose had passed through some fifteen years before. She died at the early age of fifty five, the result of a hard life raising three kids alone. At the end, she carried herself in a stooped over frame weighing no more than one hundred pounds and like someone twenty years older. She never had the help of any of her family members. She was an only child and both of her parents died when she was a young adult. Rose never felt sorry for herself, though. She knew her responsibilities and pushed herself one day at a time tackling the ever incessant problems at hand, hoping to make it through to the next day. She loved her kids, and she loved her Church. She wished tearfully many times she could've provided better for them. Today, she was standing straight and without pain in Dana's family room looking at the sweet face of her oldest; a face she believed really cared about her in the latter years before she passed through. Dana had called her and she was proud to answer.

Dana's heart quickened and her breathing became shallow. She had a feeling she was losing the connection so she forced herself to be calm. "Mom, please excuse me for reacting this way. Are you still here?" she asked in a steadier voice.

"Yes, I'm still here. Please try to remain calm. We have some catching up to do, and I imagine you might have some questions," Rose replied.

"Forgive me, Mom, but George said he's been having some conversations with Katherine," Dana said.

"That's right. I was present during the last two," Rose replied.

"You were where?" Dana asked, not believing her good luck. She was about to find out what they were talking about.

"Well, actually, the last two of his sessions were at your house where we are now. I think the first one was here as well," Rose said. "I'm here now, watching you as we speak. While he and Katherine were talking, there were others of us observing what was going on. Basically, we were just nosey and listening in. Nothing really went on but their conversation. It was interesting. He's asking all kinds of questions. Let him tell you what he's learned so far."

"How...how's all this possible? He's just asking questions? What's he said about me? Does he still love her?" Dana asked, her head beginning to swim with the enormity of what was taking place and with all the questions she was unloading from her cluttered mind.

"Dana, let me try to put your mind at ease," Rose began. "Later I'll explain how I know this but I listened to your conversation with George yesterday when you become so upset upon learning they were talking. It's hard to explain exactly what he's thinking but I have to assume there has to be some residual feeling toward Katherine since they were married so long and since their relationship was severed by reasons which were no fault of either of them. But that doesn't mean that he loves you any less. From all I see between you and George, he's deeply in love with you and has been all these years. I saw nothing yesterday that would contradict my opinion on that. He's simply asking questions about the way we live here in Heaven or at Home, as we prefer to say. I strongly suggest you not apply the hard issues you faced with your first marriage. I saw how that impacted you before I passed through. None of those issues are present in George."

Dana began to weep. She was trying hard to control her emotions so she could continue talking to her Mother.

Rose went on to explain as she continued to watch and worry about her daughter, "As to your other question, we really don't understand how this is happening any more than you do. We do know that God left this process or channel open for anyone on earth to use if they sought it. George found it, somehow. It's very rare. I guess no one on earth has used this channel for over 50 years. It's created quite a sensation here at Home or Heaven as you know it."

"George said you called your place Home. He hasn't explained much else yet. I guess when we talked about this yesterday, I wasn't very receptive. I had considerable disbelief and other issues to get over as you seem to know. My talking with you pretty much clears that up and settles my mind although this is still quite unbelievable," Dana responded now under a semblance of control.

"Yes, this is Home now for me. It has been all these years since I passed through and will be for… for who knows how long," Rose explained much relieved that Dana seemed to be settling down.

"Do you get to see Dad much?" Dana asked.

"Dana," Rose said, "I haven't seen your dad since he passed through. I've looked for him, asked about him, but it seems he's not here. I've concluded that he ran into some trouble during his Reconciliation and was turned out or something to that effect."

"What do you mean 'during his Reconciliation'? What's that?" Dana queried.

"The Reconciliation is part of the Orientation process. George can explain it to you because he and Katherine talked at length about it. I can't reveal much about it except to say that it's the process where prospective residents are forced to look at the way they lived while on Earth. All I can figure is that something must have gone terribly wrong for him during his Reconciliation," Rose answered. "I knew when he passed through, but I don't believe he made it out of Reconciliation. That's one of the first processes we have to go through when we arrive. You'll see when you get here," Rose added.

Dana responded, "That is a little disconcerting, but I'll think about what you said. By the way, how're you doing and what're you doing?"

"I'm doing great. You'll learn this is a pretty marvelous place. You can do just about anything you want. I've met loads of new people and made a lot of new friends. We can work as much or almost as little as we want. I'm pursuing the hobbies I never had time for on Earth and have added new ones. They only want us to work about five or ten percent of the time."

"Mom, I am so glad you've found time for yourself. I may never have told you before, but you have earned a world of respect over the years by all you went through. I'm not sure I could have done that. Even George said as much. I thank God every day that George was not like my dad. I'm so sorry for all you had to face."

"Dana, thank you for saying all that," she said as she continued, now smiling as Dana's words warmed her heart, "I have a job in the communications group here helping catalog and classify the news coming out of Earth for our residents to call up and review from our system here," Rose explained.

Dana absorbed all this and immediately came up with another list of questions. "I wonder if this wasn't the way it was for George in his conversations," she thought to herself. Seems like the more you hear, the more you want to know. "Mom," she finally said, "What do you mean cataloging the news? Do the residents have the ability to see it for themselves? Do you get to watch us yourself?" Dana fired in rapid succession.

Rose responded, "I do get to see you a lot. I visit quite often and see you, George, my grandchildren and your grandchildren. My visits to see you are quite wonderful. I've watched them grow and develop. I've done this for years. I was there yesterday watching you and George.

"As for the news, yes, the residents can watch what's happening on Earth. Many try to be eyewitnesses to events and some even report their observations in programs much like network news programs. There's so much going on at one time, no one here can possibly be everywhere at once. You can only be in one place at a time.

"So, a job our group has is to accumulate much of what's going on, catalog it, and classify it so residents can recall it when they want to or when they have time. I would say it's like 'movies-on-demand' on Earth; except they can recall pretty much any earthly event to watch at their convenience. I don't know how it works but it does. Everyone seems to like the system. It's pretty amazing to me," Rose finally concluded as she was now standing looking out over the patio.

"This is overwhelming," Dana said.

"Yes, it was for me when I was introduced to all this during Orientation," Rose added.

Rose continued, "I've a place up in the mountains. You'd love it with your talents as an artist. Such scenery is difficult to find even on Earth. I have a roommate, my best friend from my high school days, Tricia. Do you remember her?" Rose asked.

"Yes, I do. I think that's great, and you sound so happy," Dana responded. "Are there a lot of people there?" she added.

"There are millions, maybe billions; so many that we don't really know. From all generations, seemingly, that ever existed on earth," Rose said.

"So you can meet people who died, uh, passed through, a long time ago, like the Middle Ages for example?" Dana asked.

"Oh yes, lots of people from lots of ages and from lots of places," Rose replied.

"If they're from a lot of places and times, how do you communicate with them? How can you tell the time period they're from?" Dana inquired.

"Our ability to communicate is another one of those unexplainable things. During Orientation, we learned if someone is speaking to us in a language we don't know, a translation is somehow provided for us from within our Souls. We respond in our own language and the other person has the same ability to translate our words into their language. It's like magic. That's the best way I can explain it.

"As to the time period they're from, it's difficult to tell unless you attend one of the events they stage from time to time. That's where a group of them meet in period garb and period environments. I'd say it's sort of like a Civil War enactment on Earth when all participants dress in old uniforms and pretend to be at war again. The only difference is, here the reenactments are much more real; except there's no violence. Everything is re-created even down to the smells and food. I understand some participants even elect to live in these environments for long periods of time. It's just another of those things you can do here," Rose explained.

"Mom, what about the Church?" Dana asked. "Here on earth, many believe that you have to be a member of the Church, accept Christ or perhaps follow some other religious rites in order to be assured of a place in Heaven.... Home, I mean."

"Dana, the Church is very important there and here. When I lived on Earth, I tried to go to Church every Sunday, dragging you and your brother and sister along when I could. At Home, I still go to Church every Sunday. Anyone who passes through and who followed one denomination or the other on Earth will find that same denomination here. We're free to continue practicing our religion here. Obviously, some aspects of worship are modified to recognize the fact that we're indeed Home. There's so much to be thankful for. It is always a good thing to thank God for all He's provided," Rose said.

"There are a lot of Christians here. There are a lot of Jewish people here. Even people who have very limited exposure to teachings of the Church are here in abundant numbers," she continued. "If a person leads a decent life, stays out of trouble, respects others and is tolerant of other people's rights, then it's likely that person will pass through regardless of their ethnic or religious background."

"So there are non-Christians at Home....and in abundant numbers. I wonder how that knowledge will sit with some of the Church groups on Earth. Sounds like Heaven though," Dana quipped.

"Yes it does, doesn't it?" Rose replied.

Just then the doorbell rang. Dana said, "I have to go. Can I talk to you later? Thank you so much for answering my call. I love you very much," she told her Mother.

"Thank you, dear Dana, for calling me. Yes, please call when you can," Rose answered as the voice in Dana's head faded. Rose stood there with her tears now streaming down her own cheeks as she continued to watch Dana. How blessed she felt to have this chance.

Dana looked at the clock on the desk. Some two hours had passed while she was talking with her mother. "I guess I owe George an apology....a rather big apology," she said to herself as she stood. The doorbell rang again.

Dana opened the inner door and discovered a small girl with a bright smile dressed in a Girl Scout uniform. She recognized her as Amy from about three doors down and across the street. Amy was with a friend also dressed in uniform. Dana noticed Amy's mother standing on the sidewalk in front of the house looking on and waved to her.

"Why hello, Amy. You look all spiffy in your scout uniform. What're you doing out with your friend on such a great day?" Dana smiled.

"Mrs. Mason, this is Melanie and we're here to see if you'd like to sign our cookie sheet for some of our world famous Girl Scout cookies. See, here's the list," Amy beamed back as she handed the list to Dana.

No wonder Girl Scouts sell so many cookies, Dana thought, as she looked onto these two beautiful young faces. "Sure, let me take a look," Dana said.

The transaction proceeded to a quick conclusion as Amy told her it would take about a month before she would deliver the cookies.

Dana closed the door and leaned back against it as she contemplated the events of the day so far. What would she say to George?

Chapter 7

Dana didn't have long to wonder. George came in from the golf course smiling as usual. He always enjoyed his days on the course even if he broke his own record for high score. He played for the pure enjoyment of the sport. It may have something to do with the fact that he and his buddies never gambled except for who will buy the beer at the 19th hole.

Dana was waiting and smiling in return. "Good day on the course?" she asked.

"Yeah! I didn't lose but I didn't win either. Bill is kicking our butts with his new clubs," he said. "And your day?" he asked, hoping she had recovered from some of the stuff she was espousing yesterday about his fidelity.

"Strange, yet exhilarating," she said.

"How so?" he wondered aloud. This was a good comment from her. He suspected, but he had to hear her say it. This may be better than he expected.

"I didn't get a good night's sleep. You unloaded a lot on me yesterday. You need to find a way to give me that kind of information in more bite sized chunks. I may have overreacted. I kept thinking about what you said. Then, I thought some more. After I finished cleaning, I settled into a comfortable chair and began to clear my mind. Lo and behold, after a couple of false starts, Mom answered my call. You were right. You have to concentrate without distractions for the process to work. What a rush! What a strange experience! What you did was really rare according to Mom. Although I was really taken aback with your conversations with Katherine, I guess you are forgiven," she said.

George smiled, walked over and hugged her tightly. "Thank you! You had me worried. I thought I'd really stepped in it this time. You never ever know how glad I am to hear about Rose. Tell me all about it, and I'll tell you what I've learned," he said with great relief and anticipation.

They settled onto the couch facing each other. She began. He listened. Then he talked and she listened. They traded observations and opinions. They laughed and giggled at their newfound wealth of information like a couple of school children who suddenly found the teacher's answer sheets.

At the end, Dana casually mentioned that Rose had been around the last two times he talked to Katherine and only alluded to the special questions she posed about him. George had more sense than to press that issue. His only concern at this point was whether or not she was beyond the Katherine thing; guess that one would have to play itself out.

"What're we going to do about all this?" she asked.

George said, "I've thought about that a lot. Seems to me that there is a lot of risk in trying to spread the word about this. No one's likely to believe us. Also, I'm more than a little concerned about how the Church will react; I mean the mainstream denominations. We could literally be labeled as Heretics. As to reactions from others, we could get run or laughed out of town. Or more simply, ignored and labeled as crazy."

"Yes, I think there is considerable risk. Still, if we could figure out a relatively safe way to get this out, do you think it would be beneficial?" Dana asked.

"Maybe; maybe not. I need to noodle on this some more. For this to work, there should be a clear benefit and not just be labeled a novelty. I just have to think some more. This isn't something to try to profit from, either," he added. "For this channel not to have been used for fifty years or longer and for it not to be common knowledge, others may have had the same thoughts. I'm just suspicious the Church may have played a role in this not being more commonly known. I'd like to find a way to talk to Richard about this; see what I can learn from him but not yet. We need to know more."

"Okay, then, why don't we sit on this for now. We both want to learn more. Could be sometime down the road before we decide to reveal anything about this," Dana said.

"Sounds okay to me."

Then they rehashed what they had talked about already from all the conversations with Katherine and Rose. This kind of news deserves rehashing to see if either of them overlooked something. This went on for the rest of the day and well into the night with a short break only for dinner; only today, dinner was composed of fresh-from-the-freezer pizza.

The next morning, George planned to mow the lawn. The yard was fairly small, and the task should take no longer than an hour including edge trimming. Dana had a hair appointment and then planned to go to the market to pick up some items to prepare for the cookout at Monica and Marvin's.

"While you're gone, I may try to contact my dad," George said.. "Katherine told me he'd been hanging around while we were talking."

"My gosh," he thought, "How casually I said this, as if we'd been doing this for years."

Her answer was just as matter-of-fact, "Sure, and you can fill me in later."

George added, "Dana, you know that Katherine said, in addition to Rose, my parents were also present when she and I were talking. You know what that means? It means even though you or I aren't talking to Katherine or Rose now, all of them could likely be here right now observing and listening. Is that scary or what?" George's dad nodded his head affirmatively as he stood close by listening.

Dana paused from her dinner preparation activities, "Indeed, that's very scary….. and unnerving too. All these years, we may have been under constant observation. I guess I may have to be a little more conscientious about what I do. You too!" What she didn't say is now she's wondering if Katherine was around when she was talking to Rose. If she was, then Katherine heard her questions about George. "Am I creating problems for myself?" She thought.

"Well, it seems I learn something new every day. The more I think about this, the more of a bombshell it seems to be," he added. "I'll have to ask one of them about that."

With that, George made his way to the garage to get out the lawnmower while Dana readied herself for her outing. Dana left while he was mid way through mowing. When he finished, he cleaned up a bit and prepared to start a new session; except this time, he planned to try to contact his dad.

Chapter 8

Jefferson Allen Mason was a self made man in every respect. His roots were from a middle Tennessee farming background. He was the youngest of five children. His dad was a farmer and his grandfather was a farmer.

In the early thirties, George's dad wanted to break the mold. He scrimped, saved and worked every odd job he could find around the farm and in their nearby town to save enough to go to college. He was good with his hands and machinery. His ability to figure out what made things work set him apart from almost everyone.

Jefferson entered the University of Tennessee as a freshman in 1933 in the school of engineering with just enough money to pay his first year's tuition and books. He took jobs off campus to earn his room and board. After six years of working, scrimping and attending classes, he emerged with a brand new degree, the first in his family, and was ready to conquer the world.

Unfortunately, there were other events at play in the world which seemed intent on self destruction as the Axis powers were on their way to bringing much of the rest of the world under their control by whatever means necessary.

Jefferson realized, as did the rest of the United States, it was only a matter of time before this country was pulled into the fray. He, along with a friend, enlisted in the Army in early 1939 and was posted at Ft. McClellan near Anniston, Alabama. Part of his initial activities included testing for placement in a military occupation. His math and mechanical aptitude scores were among the highest ever recorded. Recognizing this raw talent, the Army wisely offered him a commission as a first lieutenant to be assigned to weapons development which he promptly accepted. He was assigned to the Aberdeen Proving Grounds in Maryland where he spent the rest of the war effort in weapons development for all branches of the service.

It was in Maryland that he met his bride and George's mother, Annie. They were married in the spring of 1939 and promptly began a family. He was born late that year.

After the war, Jefferson left the service and founded a tool and die business where he could use his native talents and the contacts and skills learned during service. The business flourished as he took on defense contracts for both the Army and Navy.

Jefferson and Annie had three boys, and Jefferson managed to generously give of his time to each of his sons. They enjoyed fishing, hunting and sports of all sorts, particularly golf.

Jefferson died of a heart attack in his late 60's, and George now hoped he had passed through safely. He intended to see if he could use his new communication tool to reach his dad.

George settled into his favorite recliner in the family room, cleared his mind and asked the question, "Dad, are you here?" By now he was expecting to get an answer.

Shortly the reply came, "Yes, Son, I'm here." Jefferson's familiar voice rang out in his head and George felt himself smile. Jefferson stood looking at his son stretched out in his recliner. Always the slacker, he chuckled to himself. Before Jefferson answered George's call he took the time to let

Annie and Katherine know. He expected them to join him shortly. Several other residents were already there.

"It's been so long since I've had a chance to talk to you. When you had your attack, I wasn't able to reach you before you passed through. Thank goodness you're at Home," George replied, proud of himself for using all the correct terminology.

"Well, where else do you think I'd be?" Jefferson asked, chuckling as he did. His father's sense of humor was still intact.

"Yes, I guess I've always known you'd be there. I'm glad. I'm still amazed at how I'm able to talk to you and Katherine. She told me you were around when we were talking. How're you and Mom doing?" George asked.

"We're doing great. She'll be here shortly to watch us. We check in to see you and the kids a lot. You've done a great job and we're proud of you. I see, though, that you could be doing better with your golf game. You need to get the same sticks that Bill has," Jefferson said.

"Thanks, Dad, for the advice and compliments. I can't believe you even watch me on the golf course. You must really be hard up for something constructive to do. Tell me what you're doing and where you're living," George requested.

"Your mom and I have a place across the lake from where Katherine lives nestled up next to the mountains. I get to fish and do a lot of golfing. You wouldn't believe the golfing that's available here," he added as he walked around looking at pictures.

"Well please tell me. I sure hope you've managed to improve your game," George said.

"Well, there's a course right near our home that's plenty challenging. I play at about the same level as when you and I used to play. But the best thing is almost any course you can imagine on Earth is available here at Home. The course layouts are almost identical to the courses there. Pebble Beach, Augusta, St. Andrews, you name it and you can play it. There're always guys ready and willing to play with me," Jefferson said.

George chuckled to himself, "Well if you're still playing at the level when we played, there must be plenty of guys beating you. Is that all you do there…play golf?" he asked laughing, "Don't you have a job or something?"

"I bet I could beat you. And yes, I do have a job. I get to use my skills from earthly times. I'm in the Technology Section here. We're responsible for all the gadgets that residents here ask for. We provide whatever they want," he answered as he silently welcomed Annie and Katherine to George's family room. The Elder also arrived.

"You mean you design and make them like you did in your business here?" George was now curious.

"Not exactly," Jefferson said as he acknowledged the Elder, "There's a lot of gadgetry that's unique to us at Home. These are the type of things not yet invented on Earth and I can't tell you much about them. Also, as new things are invented on Earth, we can duplicate them here and make them available to residents. Ipods, for example, are a hot item now just like they are there."

"How can you duplicate something that's made here? Some of the things that come out of stores these days seem pretty complicated," George said.

"That's one of the great things about Home," his father said, "I can't tell you exactly how the process works because I have to confess the process is beyond me. The laws of physics don't exactly apply here, if you know what I mean.

"This happens to be one of the areas I work in," Jefferson continued, "For example, say some resident here asks for something following the acquisition process the way Katherine explained it to you. My job is to see if we've produced it here before. If so, the process is that we simply…

'configure' the item. That's the best way I can describe the process we use. People like me with good mechanical minds can do it easier than others and that's the reason I work in this section.

"If someone asks for something that's new on earth, one of us goes back to earth, usually to the place where the items are produced. We study the designs and characteristics of the item. I've even studied a couple of your designs. We then return Home where we use our new skills to 'configure' a copy of the earthly item. Once we have one here that works, we simply duplicate it for anyone else who may request it. All of this is pretty interesting," Jefferson said.

"So you studied my designs, huh. Am I getting any royalties from that? You know if someone on Earth did that, they'd be accused of patent thievery or something like that," George ventured, "You don't call it stealing there?"

"Hey, be careful how you use that word. There's no stealing here. We can't very well pay the guy on Earth who made it, now can we, even in your case? We give him all the credit and put in a good word for him with his pastor and all that. If he makes it this far, we'll thank him when he arrives. So consider yourself thanked; besides, we improved on your designs," his dad said.

"Well, you're welcome, I guess! All of what you do does sound interesting. Sounds like a section I'd like to work in one day," the son said.

"My guess is with your skills, you'd fit right in here. I'd love to have you work in my section. But, like Katherine said, you have a lot of living yet to do there. Don't forget your responsibilities," Jefferson replied in his best fatherly advice voice as Annie and Katherine grinned and nodded their approval. The Elder just listened and watched. George didn't have a clue.

"No, I won't. At least your lecture is shorter than Katherine's. All this is so astounding," George said as

Katherine laughed. "I'm learning so much. Not only am I getting to talk to you again but the information you and Katherine have told me has created a huge desire to continue to learn. Maybe I've already learned too much. When Katherine made the comment that this is for me to believe or not believe; I choose to believe all this is real. The certainty of there being a Heaven or Home is such a profound revelation to Dana and me. Maybe my faith in God before was weak but no more. And yes, I have responsibilities here with not only my children and grandchildren but with others. I have to decide what to do now with what I know. Maybe others will like this as well, who wouldn't. I'm really in over my head with this."

Jefferson said as he looked at the Elder, "I hate to say this but there's nothing I can do to help you in your dilemma. You've discovered us. I can answer your questions, at least some of them. It's your prerogative about what to do with this. After all, free will is the rule."

"Well, now, that's an interesting term, free will. What does it mean?"

"This is a pretty deep subject. In its simplest meaning, you are free to do what your conscience and laws allow. When humans evolved to a point, God gave them Souls. As part of His overall plan, He gave them the ability to do things on their own; without His intervention. Humans are free to act as they see fit toward others and toward their surrounding environment usually only restricted by the rules that humans impose on each other through laws. Human nature takes hold. Love toward self and fellow man eventually triumphs over the evil that some people do. Love is stronger than evil. We believe God knew this when He set everything in motion all those millenniums ago. We also believe that's why so many pass through and, conversely, why so few never arrive here," Jefferson explained, this time with the Elder nodding his approval.

"Whatever you decide to do, nothing basically will change here. Things might go differently on Earth but people will continue to pass through as their lives spend out on Earth," he added.

"I have much to think about," George said and left it at that for the time being. "If God gave humans free will, what does that say about the world itself?"

"What do you mean, Son?" Jefferson asked as he glanced at his son.

"Well, if humans are free to act on their own, how much does God do in directing the way the world operates?" he asked in order to clarify what he wanted to know. The Elder was paying close attention.

"We aren't totally sure, but we believe he does very little. When God created this world and this sun, He put the natural law of physics into play. Everything has evolved over millions of years, including humans. God is very patient. We believe he intended the world to evolve to the point to where it would primarily sustain humans. It's up to humans to manage the world as best they can in order to sustain themselves as long as possible, maybe forever or at least until Christ comes to earth again. We assume that'll be the case. If so, then humans will continue to procreate and God will continue to install Souls in them. Eventually, the Souls will pass through, at least most of them anyway, and God's plan is carried out. That's how we see it here at Home. From all we can determine, Home will continue to expand to absorb all the Souls who'll pass through," his dad explained.

"My gosh, this is indeed profound information. You guys have all this figured out," George said. "You know, the universe is a pretty big place. Do you know what's going on elsewhere outside our little solar system?"

"I hate to say this," Jefferson exclaimed as the Elder continued his vigil, "but we really don't know. The Elders don't discuss this with us even though we ask. We believe, however, other solar systems are evolving much the same as our world, and there are likely other worlds like ours which are in some state of evolution. Many may be ahead of ours, and many may be behind ours. With the universe being as large as it is, there could be countless others. We believe God's an extremely busy fellow in attending to all of this. I bet this makes your head swim too." The Elder neither confirmed nor denied the statements.

"You got that right," George replied. "All this makes me feel so insignificant yet glad to be one of His. Okay, so here's the $64,000 question. I know you with your engineering and scientific mind, and others like you there, must know how all of this is done? What's the essence of Home relative to Earth?"

"You're lucky in one respect," his dad said as the Elder watched, "If we knew, if we'd figured this out, I wouldn't be able to tell you anything about how things work here. We don't know but there are theories. Yes, we're curious. Yes, we discuss this among ourselves often and vigorously and for long periods. The most popular theory is that God has put us in something akin to a fourth dimension. Rod Serling is at Home and he thinks he's arrived in the twilight zone. It seems we exist somewhat parallel to the physical world. Here, however, conventional laws of physics and the physical universe don't work. You should see Newton re-trying his apple experiment, it's hilarious."

"You've met Rod Serling and Sir Isaac Newton?"

"Yep! I've met Mr. Serling just in passing, but I've had a couple of conversations with Sir Isaac. He's quite interesting, you know. Anyway, once here, a person possesses unique abilities including the ability to travel between Home and Earth. Although once on earth, we only have a sensory presence and not a physical presence. We can see and hear and travel but can't affect anything. We're only witnesses to what you and everyone else does."

"And now, I'm something of a witness to what you've told me. What am I to do with this?" George said more to himself than to his dad. "Without others calling their loved ones there and doing what I'm doing, I'll be one of the great kooks or, perhaps, a great science fiction writer. The more I learn, the more I want to keep this close to myself and Dana. I'm afraid someone else may have to figure out how, when and if to bring the rest of humanity this knowledge."

"Yeah, I might feel the same way," his dad said as he looked at the Elder who seemed just a little disappointed.

"So I guess what you said about the other worlds are just theories as well," George stated more in the form of a question.

"Yes, just theories, but you have to admit, the recent discoveries on Earth about the existence of other planets circling other suns lends some credence to our theories," he stated.

"I guess it does. Do you have any sense that anyone from Home has ever traveled to other 'Heavens' which God may have set up to serve humanity from other worlds?"

"No, nothing of the sort has ever come to light here; after all, the other worlds' existence is still just theoretical," Jefferson said. "With the extreme distances between stars, it also seems the likelihood of anyone on earth ever traveling to another world capable of supporting humans seems remote as well, wouldn't you say?"

"It does seem so. Still, God must get around somehow," George added. Jefferson noticed the Elder cracked a little smile. "Dad, you've said you and others there have discussed these theories at length. What others?"

"Well, I have friends with similar backgrounds to mine. We like to talk about these things. There're also gatherings, like symposiums, which are attended by some fairly high powered scientists, physicists and theoreticians where I can mingle, listen and occasionally ask questions. Some of these people you'd have heard of from the contributions they made on Earth before they passed through," Jefferson explained.

"Gatherings? What type of gatherings?"

"Here at Home, we have a lot of free time on our hands. There's an infinite variety of activities available outside of the work. Some of these activities involve bringing together people with backgrounds where exchanges of ideas, information and conjecture occur. These are excellent for keeping our minds active. Most of the time, they're highly organized and publicized for anyone who has an interest to attend. No one's excluded even if they have no inkling of the subject matter. Otherwise, they probably wouldn't let me attend," his dad said as Annie and Katherine chuckled.

"Don't start being modest. That coat doesn't fit you," George said as he laughed.

"Me modest, never!" Jefferson snorted as Annie, Katherine and the Elder laughed, "Often, these gatherings are organized around someone of note who's just passed through so they can meet cohorts and maybe add new insights from their recent work on Earth. They're quite exciting. It's interesting to bring new people in and watch them as they meet others whose work they're familiar with from when they were alive on Earth; people they knew only from published works or inventions; people like Einstein or Bell or Edison," his dad added, "Most of the old guys are only too happy to accommodate new arrivals."

"That is really amazing. You've met them too?"

"Yes I have, would you like me to recount everyone I've met?"

"No, not now. Free time, huh? I guess that means lots of leisure time. I know you play golf. Have you developed other hobbies? What else goes on there that's popular with the residents?" George asked.

His father replied, "I discovered I love woodworking. I've built a lot of the furniture we use, and yeah, most of it's still standing. As far as what's popular, just about anything you can imagine goes on here; racing, mountain climbing, skiing, football, baseball, basketball, and tennis….just to name a few. In baseball for example, there're teams comprised of former major leaguers. You'd call them professional leagues on Earth. Not here, since there's no money in circulation. Teams are formed and play against each other simply for the love of the game. Games are scheduled, players show up and fans are in the stands. It's great! Same thing goes for football and basketball. Golf! You can actually schedule rounds you can play against some professionals and others like Bobby Jones."

George's head was swimming again, "You've played golf with Bobby Jones?"

"Yep! Racing's big here too. You can find races involving anything that runs from cars to horses to sailboats. In horse racing, for example, people maintain stables of their favorite animals. Car racing's another big sport. Residents who have the knack can design, build and maintain their own cars. If they have decent driving skills, they can drive'em as well.

"About the only thing that doesn't go over big here is gambling as you might envision. There is gambling but without money and usually the participants are friends and the stakes are where the loser has to host the next big party or something like that."

"Parties! Tell me about the parties. Don't tell me you and Mom have become party animals,"

"Nope, we're just about as conservative as you remember. Aside from us, though, there're some spectacular parties here. Anyone can give a party. Big or small; it doesn't matter. Big parties usually involve bands or other entertainment. It's a real coup whenever someone can entice a former big band leader like Glenn Miller to provide the music. Lavish food and beverages are plentiful. However, since alcoholic drinks have no impact on our metabolism, most beverages are non alcoholic. Instead, they go in for flavors rather than alcoholic content," Jefferson responded.

"So, do you and Mom still practice your ballroom dancing? Hey, what about work? Is there a wide range of occupations?" George asked. "I've heard you and Katherine allude to the fact that so little of your time is required in doing assigned tasks."

"Practice ballroom dancing? I have you know, we are considered experts. That's another thing we like to do. We've won trophies. Work? There're a lot of occupations here; almost as many as on earth. However, there's a lot missing from here. If you think about it, you could probably name several career fields absent here which require a lot of people on earth," his dad said.

"For example, there's no crime here. Therefore, there's no need for police officers. There are no fires here that require the use of fire fighters. Since there's no crime, there's also no need for jails or other places of incarceration. There're no geographic divisions of land that require the use of standing armies or navies to maintain. There's no sickness or disease; therefore, there's no need for the medical professions or hospitals.

"Interestingly enough, there're a lot of statesmen here from the ranks of political leaders on Earth but no dictators. I don't think I can name a single dictator that has passed through and become a resident here. There may be a few classified as benevolent dictators but I don't know of any. My guess is the dictators faced a relatively short Reconciliation process before someone quickly decided their fate. There're a number of kings and queens, however.

"Financial occupations such as bankers and legal occupations requiring lawyers and judges are not present here. But don't be misled by what I just said. There are former bankers and lawyers here; lots of them, but they really have no professions to practice," he said. "Accountants and CPAs, on the other hand, have jobs to do here. Yeah, we keep score like we did on earth; only most of the numbers are statistics and not sales and profits.

"So what do the displaced professionals do then; I mean, look at all the lawyer jokes; are they just wasted?"

"People like police officers, fire fighters, doctors, bankers and lawyers all had interests of one kind or another aside from their professional leanings. Usually, these form the basis of most of their job activities and certainly their leisure activities. I've never heard anyone express a desire not to be here simply because they couldn't practice their former profession," Jefferson added.

"Now, I've heard you and Katherine talk about visiting or observing us on earth. I'm glad that you're able to watch and keep track of us but some aspects of your visits are a little unnerving to me," George said.

"How so?" Jefferson asked as Katherine listened a little closer.

"Well, I mean there could be instances where we might wish to have moments of privacy like when we're in the bathroom or perhaps when there are moments of intimacy between two people. You know...examples like that," the son added as he started to sweat just a little. Katherine grinned as did the Elder.

"Ha, ha, ha," his dad laughed as he walked over and slapped at George.

"Those laughs I remember well." George thought.

Jefferson added, "I bet this is your real $64,000 question." And he laughed some more as he slapped George again. Of course George couldn't feel it, "Don't worry! There're some rules here, mostly unwritten, which say we are not to impose on moments of privacy involving Earth residents. The general rule is if you guys are involved in something that we ourselves would've wanted privacy given the same situation, then, we extend that courtesy to you. The rules are pretty much adhered to."

"I'm glad you got a kick out of that. I guess I'd have laughed as well. That's good news but I'll have to tell you I haven't dwelled on the issue. Frankly, I just now thought about it," George said a little sheepishly.

"Sure you did. Since we've sort of skirted the subject, let me add another tidbit of information that you may or may not have thought of," his dad added. "Ordinarily, I wouldn't say this except to answer a direct question of yours but sooner or later you'll want to know," Dad said, "Residents here do not have sex."

George sounded stunned as he ventured a reply, "Well, I guess I was curious and was wondering how to get around to this subject. After all, when you were here on Earth and I was a young lad, we didn't exactly have very good conversations about this subject. Also, I hesitated to ask Katherine and certainly wouldn't have asked my mom. But why is it that way since you brought it up and since it seems to be such a driving force on Earth?" Katherine and his mom were rolling by this time and the Elder was grinning.

"Well, I am not a hundred percent sure of this answer but the best as I can figure it, sex acts, per se, are physical in nature and such physical acts don't carry through here at Home," he replied.

"So people who're friends there are really friends and not lovers, so to speak,"

"Yep, that's the way it is. Seems to work okay for us. After all, there's no need for us to procreate which is another, more basic reason, for that particular activity to occur only on Earth," he added as he laughed.

"Well, let me be so bold as to sum all this up. Let's see, there's no sex there, no money, no violence and no wars. If I announced this to the world, there could well be a lot of people who might decide it's not worth it to go Home,"

George added as the others continued their silent laughing, "Also, I bet your television and movie producer residents, if there are any, have a hard time coming up with subject matter when it comes to programming decisions with no violence or sex to write into their scripts," George added.

"You know, that's an interesting observation," Jefferson interjected as he settled down, "When it comes to us sitting down and requesting some entertainment, most of us simply tune into the broadcasts from earth which we can get here. You'll be amazed at the clarity and quality of broadcasts we pick up here. For movies, we can ask for DVD's or we can simply visit a movie theater on earth. Problem with that is we can't enjoy the popcorn in a theater even though we can smell it. I hate that. Your mom and I go to the movies quite often, particularly new releases. We often go with you and Dana or one of our grandchildren when they go; particularly if they're taking their children to see something funny. We love to be a part of all of your activities."

"I can't tell you, Dad, how happy all of this makes me. I'll sleep even better now," George said. Just then, he thought he heard a car turn into the driveway. "I'll relay all this to Dana. I think she just arrived. Can I call on you later? This has been a good father and son chat, has it not?"

"Yes indeed, call me anytime. This has been a lot of fun. It's meant a lot to me. Remember to work on that golf game," Jefferson said as they signed off. Katherine and the Elder looked very pleased. Annie gave Jefferson a nice hug.

Always the dutiful husband, George rushed out to the garage to help Dana bring in the bags from the market.

"Hi, beautiful!" he said remembering that she also had a hair appointment. "How was your morning? Mine was great," he added with a grin before she could answer.

She looked at him and gave him a knowing grin. "You've had another session, haven't you?" she asked.

"Yeah and I can't wait to tell you about it. I was talking with my dad, and we had an unbelievable conversation," George added. He started in with the debriefing even as they moved indoors with the sacks of food and ended with the comment about no sex.

"No sex?" she stated in a most incredulous way. She tucked that little detail away for further thought.

"What a day! And it's only half over," he thought.

Chapter 9

Saturday dawned to crisp blue skies. Late afternoon thundershowers from the day before and a cold front moving in from northwest promised to sweep the hot muggy air out of Atlanta for at least a couple of days. Highs for the day were forecasted to be in the upper 70's with temperatures dropping to the lower 60's by Sunday morning.

The stage was set for a great afternoon at Monica and Marvin's with their manicured back yard surrounding a swimming pool and a barbecue grill setup that most people would love to have even in their kitchens. Built in fridge, double grills, outdoor oven, and even a kitchen sink complete with disposal. All of this was built between their house and the pool. Sitting to the left of the pool was a pool house complete with bedroom, bath and sitting room/kitchen. Their only son recently occupied this outdoor bungalow for the past two years until he graduated from the University of Georgia and relocated to Charlotte as a budding investment banker.

Marvin was a retired executive who had been a Senior Vice President for Delta Airlines. Monica, at one time, had been a flight attendant. George guessed they had found their own version of the friendly skies. He met Marvin when they were both students at Georgia Tech. Monica and Marvin were dating at the time. After he lost Katherine, Monica was the person who introduced him to Dana through a church outreach group. Dana and Monica had gone to Auburn together and apparently knew each other from high school.

The other players in this scene were Laverne and Bill. Laverne was one of those stay-at-home moms who, for some reason, continued to stay at home even after her children left to go out on their own. She dabbled at writing and had several short stories to her credit which had been published by the local Sunday magazine. She also liked to audit courses at one of the local community colleges.

Bill, a semi-retired attorney, had a light case load and could be found at his downtown office three to four days a week for about half a day each. He had handled George's estate planning and tax return work for years. George thought, "I need to remember to talk to him about scheduling an appointment maybe next week to discuss an idea I have concerning my and Dana's wills." Bill attended LSU and was from somewhere in the Louisiana bayou country. When encouraged, he could give a good rendering of any story in the old Cajun dialect. George met Bill shortly after he graduated from GT when he discovered that doing his own tax returns could be inherently dangerous. Bill saved him some significant tax dollars from a rather stupid error which was caught by the IRS.

They were all gathered at Monica and Marvin's house by 4 o'clock to start the festivities. For some reason, none of them ever availed themselves of the beautiful swimming pool. "Now, I remember the reason," George thought, "Us guys are all carrying a little extra weight packed into spare tires around our waists giving the appearance of waddling walruses when sporting swimwear. That's not necessarily the case with the girls. They've all tried to remain fit and trim through the years. The most successful has been Dana. The other two are losing the battle in a couple of spots but this is never discussed. Their unwritten rule is they, like their spouses, will not display themselves in front of their friend's spouses. So no one ever uses the pool at these gatherings."

Marvin was in his element as he rushed back and forth in his outdoor kitchen. His compact five foot nine frame belied the fact he was such a handy man around the grill. He still had all his hair, although mostly gray rather than brown as was the case in his GT days. He had ribs going on one grill and was preparing to steam some crab legs on another along with some veggies. The beer was flowing freely. The guys were talking up the last golf outing where Bill, once again, waxed their cans. Bill, on the other hand had jet black hair with dark eyes and olive skin, a gift from his parents through the gene pool known as the southern Louisiana Cajun.

The girls were chatting about…..well whatever girls chat about on Saturday afternoons. Their two favorite subjects were the latest fashions and stories about their husbands, particularly stories of the more outrageous nature.

Monica laughed easily. She came wrapped in a less than slim and trim five foot six frame but blessed with naturally blond hair and emerald green eyes. She was always dieting but the visible evidence indicated the futility of her efforts. Her face was dimpled but with excess sun spots. She was, nevertheless, a perfect match for Marvin.

Laverne was close to five foot ten, skinny though she was. She was from New Orleans and had met Bill at LSU. She could have used a little extra weight, but who would have the courage to suggest such an idea to her? However, she carried a beautiful face which was starting to wrinkle in the usual places beneath dark brown hair with a light tan complexion with piercing dark brown eyes. Her serious demeanor was often broken with a beautiful smile showing two rows of almost perfect teeth.

By 5:30, all was prepared and the friends sat down to enjoy a great meal. Crab legs as an appetizer, and ribs with corn on the cob, slaw and new potatoes as the main meal.

The crab legs could have been the main meal as far as George was concerned. He loved 'em. "Maybe there are crab legs in Heaven too," he thought.

After an hour, most of the dishes had been consumed. What followed was some banana cream pie that Laverne had brought. George was stuffed and a little bit looped with the beer he'd consumed. After dinner, the conversations cranked up slowly. Someone casually threw out a question about what everyone had been doing all week.

Bill related the story about dealing with a cantankerous little old lady and her estate planning. Seems she wanted to leave the bulk of her estate to her cat, Heathrow, to the exclusion of her two children who were pretty old themselves. Bill finally talked her into the idea of approaching one of her children and extracting a binding promise to take care of Heathrow until his final days.

Marvin piped up and said, "George, what have you guys been doing all week?"

Without a thought and still half looped, he replied, "Well, Dana and I've been talking to dead people." He realized when the last words were out what he had said. He didn't look up. For about five seconds, the silence was deafening.

Then, everyone started to laugh; slowly at first and then building to a crescendo. George grinned sheepishly. Dana was giggling but was looking at him with a definite glare. When he finally looked at the others, they were all pretty much rolling... except for Bill who was laughing as well but he also had a puzzled look directed at George. Thankfully, Dana changed the subject.

As Dana and George were leaving, he casually mentioned to Bill that he wanted to call for an appointment this week about a question concerning their wills. Bill said, "Okay, and I want to talk to you about your comment earlier."

Whoa! They stood for a moment, looking at each other and George finally replied, "Yes, we can do that." He suddenly realized that Bill took some part, not sure which, of his comment seriously. "This could be an interesting conversation. I have to think about what and how much I'll say," George thought.

Dana and he talked later about the incident. "Why in the world did you say something like that?" she asked.

"Good question. I'm not sure why. I guess me being a little out of it and with all of this on my mind and just under the surface of my consciousness, it just slipped out," he answered.

"By the way," he said, "I want to talk to Bill about an idea I have. I need to run it by you first. I've been struggling about what to do with all we've learned. Maybe you have too. I'll have this conversation with Bill, but I really don't want to tell him too much. I've been thinking of talking to Richard to get his reaction. I'm still most concerned about the Church." Richard was Rev Richard Casey, their pastor at Pinecrest Methodist Church, "My thought, at least for now, is to compose four letters, one for each of the kids, which summarizes what we've discovered and have Bill deliver them after we have passed on to coincide with the reading of our wills. This would be done after the last one of us passes. The letter would explain everything and convey a simple set of instructions about how they could contact us. What do you think?"

"Well, how would you keep Bill from learning the contents of the letters?" she asked.

"I'll compose them myself, seal them in individual envelopes and just let him pass them out at the reading of the will," George said.

"That sound's okay," she added. "I'm like you. This is all too radical for me to want to announce to the world just yet. Just think, if we told the kids now, all they can do is listen to us. If the part about needing someone close to you to contact is correct, then they likely won't have anyone they can call yet. Katherine passed through when Jackie and Jason were so young, they likely haven't formed the link needed to call to her. Besides, if something happens, we can always change our minds."

George worked on drafts of the letter all Sunday afternoon. At the end of the day, a version existed that both Dana and he were satisfied with. Regardless of the wording, their kids would probably think they were both a little nuts as they read these sometime in the future. One of them would just have to have the courage to give it a try.

Monday morning, George made the call to Bill's office to set up an appointment for Tuesday at 9 o'clock.

Tuesday came, and George was ready and on time. Bill met him in the law lobby on the 30th floor in one of the high rises just off of Peachtree. The office appointments looked expensive and George concluded that this law firm was one of quality. "Good morning, George. It's not often that I get you down here," Bill said.

"It's not often that I make my way down town. I like to stay in the burbs. The pace of life there more closely matches mine. Here, I have to step just a little too fast or else one of those taxi maniacs will get me," George replied.

Bill closed the door and they both sat down; Bill behind his lightly populated desk and George across from him in a leather wingback. "I remember in earlier days when his desk would be brimming over with client files. You could tell that he is indeed cutting back," George thought.

"Well, what brings you all the way down here today?" Bill began. "You mentioned that you wanted to talk about your wills but my review of your files says that we did an overview last year and besides Dana isn't with you."

"You're right, this visit is not so much about rehashing our wills but a special procedure I'd like you to do for us at our passing. This'll be something to attend to after the last one of us passes," George explained. He really just wanted to give him the instructions without saying why or what was in the letters now tucked in his coat pocket.

"I can do that. Is there anything I need to work up for this?" he asked reaching for his notepad.

"No, this entails simply passing along to each of my children at the reading of the will a letter that Dana and I've composed and placed in sealed envelopes. Do you think this will be a problem?" George asked.

"No problem. Just one question, though," Bill said. George inwardly cringed as he thought he was going to have to go into the details about why they were doing this, but he asked, "There's nothing in them illegal or constituting a confession to some crime or anything like that, is there?"

"No," George said as he laughed, "It's just a last set of instructions that'll only make sense to them after we're gone."

"Good." With that, George passed over the letters; four of them with a child's name on each, along with a letter of instruction to Bill or whoever would be handling this at his firm. Bill reviewed the letter of instruction. "Looks pretty simple to me. I'll place these with the original copies of your wills in our files. Your children do know we have your wills, don't they?" he asked.

"Yes, they do," George replied.

"Good, now is there anything else I can do for you today?" he asked.

"No, that was it. We really appreciate you doing this," he said feeling lucky that he was getting out of here with no more of an in-depth conversation than this.

"We are glad to do it. Now," Bill said and the hairs on George's neck became aroused, "I've something to ask you."

Yep, now they were standing straight out. George hoped he didn't notice. Bill began, "You remember the funny comment you made at the cookout Saturday?"

George's radar was running full speed. "I barely remember it. As I recall, I was feeling quite good at that point after all we'd eaten and all the beer I'd consumed."

"You said, jokingly I might add, that you and Dana had been talking to dead people during the week," Bill said in a definite questioning manner as if he were leading his witness.

"Yes," was his reply in the best witness answering manner he could conjure up.

"My guess is you were joking but I wasn't a hundred percent sure. I'd like to tell you a story if you have time," Bill offered.

"Sure," now George's interest was piqued. What was he about to say?

"A long time ago when I was a young boy in Louisiana, I had a great grandmother that I barely remember. She was Cajun through and through. You've said you like me to tell tales in my Cajun dialect? Well, she spoke that way all the time. She was born sometime in the late 1800's. Her name was Annette, and she was married to my great grandfather whose name was Boudreaux. They raised a family of eight children. Families were pretty large in our parish in those days. They were close-knit. All of the kids survived and had large families of their own. My grandmother was the oldest girl in the family.

"My great grandfather, with a sense of compassion for France and a great sense of patriotism, went off to Europe in World War I and never returned. I guess it was months later that our family learned that he perished in some battle there. By then, my grandmother had established a family of her own near the old home place. Annette went to pieces. She moved in with my grandmother and basically went into total denial about what had happened to Boudreaux.

"Every day and week that passed seemed to take her further and further from reality. My grandmother could not bear the thought of putting her away some where, so she cared for her until she died in the mid 1950's.

"Here is the really weird part. The story goes that nearly every week, Annette would awaken from the stupor she seemed to live in and relate story after story about having talked to Boudreaux. None of the stories made sense but it was as if he was talking to her from across the grave. No one paid much attention to any of this. It's so strange that you made the comment like you did," Bill finally concluded.

George sat there listening to the whole story picking up the pieces that seemed to him now to be so familiar with what Dana and he had been through. It seemed pretty certain Annette had discovered the link they were using but had no inkling about its significance. He had to be careful how he responded to Bill when he said, "Bill, it seems to me your great grandmother must have loved Boudreaux very much and probably missed him greatly. The loss was just too much for her to handle. The dreams she had seemed real to her. She probably couldn't tell the difference."

"That's kind of what we all thought. But your comments brought all those memories back to life," Bill added.

"Well, I am sorry for that."

"Don't be, most of those memories are good ones to be relived and savored," Bill added as a final note, "Take care of yourself. Maybe we can get back on the golf course later this week."

"Let's do that. Someone recently advised me to get some of those new clubs like you have and maybe I'd have a chance to beat you for once," George said as they were leaving Bill's office and making their way to the elevator.

"Hey, buddy, news for you. There are no clubs anywhere that'll let you do that," as he laughed with the elevator doors closing.

"Whew, seems like I dodged a bullet there," George thought to himself as the elevator descended to the lobby. He made a mental note to mention this to his dad or Katherine the next time he connected with them. He also remembered the information Dana learned from her mom about the last earthly contact being over 50 years ago. Was there a connection here?

Chapter 10

Dana was already home by the time George arrived at about 11:30. He had taken her BMW to Bill's office and had stopped to fill it up. She hated to do this chore herself and she hated even worse to get into the car only to find out it needed fuel. He loved to drive her car and was always looking for excuses to get behind the wheel. It was some spirited vehicle; too much for him but it suited her to a tee.

As soon as he walked through the door, the aroma of grilled steak hit his nostrils. By past experience, he knew that lunch today would consist of steak fajitas with refried beans accompanied by chips and cheese dip. She did this about once a month. It was a heavy lunch but was always good.

Dana turned from the stove and threw a big smile at him. He loved her smiles. He melted a little whenever one of those came his way. They always made him feel like he was floating on air. "Hi, Baby, I'm glad you're home," she said.

"Glad to be home!" George managed to say as he recovered from her initial smile and shed his jacket.

"Guess who's coming by later this afternoon," she commanded.

"Well, I'm certain I have no idea, who?" he asked.

"Michelle's dropping by with Stewart and Nicole," she answered. Michelle was Jason's wife. Nicole was their last born who was now five years old. Stewart, the six year old grandson, was the one who had started all this with his incessant questions.

"After lunch," she continued, "and before they get here, I need to run over to the mall. I ordered something from Talbots and they called to say it's in."

"Nothing too expensive," he said in jest as they sat down to eat.

"Yep," she jokingly replied, "you're going to have to go back to work to pay for this one. Don't worry; I plan to be back before Michelle gets here. By the way, how'd the meeting with Bill go this morning?" she asked.

"It went well. I gave him the envelopes. He'll distribute them sometime in the future…way in the future, I hope," George added, "But he told me the strangest story."

"How so?" Dana asked.

"He told me about his great grandmother who passed away over 50 years ago. She was one of the old time Cajuns, I guess. Spoke all her life with a heavy accent. Anyway, her husband was killed during World War I and, according to Bill, she never quite recovered from the loss. Apparently, she would be out of it, from reality that is, for a week or more at a time. Each time she awakened, she would be filled with tales of detailed conversations she had with her long-dead husband."

"Why would Bill bring something like that up?" she asked.

"Remember on Saturday when I made that stupid comment about you and me talking with 'dead people?" he responded.

"Yeah, you almost gave me a heart attack," she said, "Before everyone started laughing, I thought we were in deep doodoo."

"Well, Bill was listening a little too closely. I guess that was the lawyer in him. Anyway, he wanted to relay the story of Annette, his great grandmother. Seems that she died sometime in the 50's. Now, do you remember what Rose said to you in your session with her?" George asked.

Dana thought a minute and finally said, "Hey, hold on, do you think there's a connection between Rose's story of the history of the linked sessions and the one Bill was talking about?"

"Maybe, I guess it could just be coincidental. But it did come to mind. Who knows how factual Bill had the story. Annette could have been completely bonkers with her experiences. But think about it, how would we sound to the world if we came up with similar stories? I may mention this the next time I'm linked in," he said.

"Linked In; hmnn, maybe I've coined a term to describe our little sessions," he added.

"Maybe so, I like the sound of it too. Okay, I'm off to the mall; one of my favorite things to do," Dana said as she turned to look at him.

George turned at the same time. Their eyes met across the room. "You know I love you very much," he said as he looked at her standing there looking great in her chic outfit, still beautiful after all these years, at least in his eyes. Sure, there were the crow feet wrinkles surrounding her eyes and a few other wrinkles that had appeared on her neckline, but to him, she was still the perfect beauty he remembered from that church social all those years ago when she first floated into his eyesight.

"I know. You've been my friend and my husband and my lover for as long as I want to remember. Wouldn't it be great if this could last forever?" she said with a smile he would never forget and a request that matched his desires to a tee; except.....can there be a place for Katherine too?

He moved toward her, took her in his arms and kissed her. "That's for sticking with me all these years," George said as he released her.

"Wow! We'll have to follow up on this later," she said as she grinned impishly. She turned and was gone.

As she pulled away, he thought now would be a good time to have a quick session with Katherine to see how things are going with her and to ask about Bill's Annette.

George turned off all noise makers around the house, closed the doors and windows and settled into his favorite recliner. After allowing a few moments to calm down, he asked, "Katherine, are you here?"

A few more moments passed. Then, "Yes, George, I'm here; and a good afternoon to you," she answered.

It was still amazing to him; this Link he had discovered. Yet now, he found himself taking it more for granted. He guessed this was just human nature. "I hope I didn't take you away from something important," he stated.

"No, I was about to go to the arrival station to see if any new children had come in, but I was still at my house," she said.

"I have a question for you," George started and then led her into the story about Annette and Boudreaux. "Can you find out if perhaps she was talking to him as we are now?"

"I can tell you for a fact that she was, George. Another fact, Annette was one of the visitors here during our second session. I got a kick out of her. Her Cajun accent is still heavy; enough so that I had to use my translation routine to understand her. She and Boudreaux are living happily here. Here's another fact, her conversations those fifty years ago were the last which occurred in this fashion until you came along," she explained.

"By the way, among residents here, you're something of a celebrity for having uncovered this Link again after all this time. What do you think about that?" she asked.

"It's incredible, all of this," George added.

David Lane was really proud of himself. He'd just turned sixteen and was seated behind the wheel of an almost new Trailblazer his dad brought home yesterday to celebrate his birthday and his new driver's license. "I gotta go somewhere," he told his mom as he ran into the kitchen to grab the keys and head out the door. He was starting his campaign to take it to school tomorrow where he was a sophomore.

"Wait, where're you going?" she asked intending not to let his casual driving get out of hand.

"I'm going down to the car wash. I saw some dust on the hood awhile ago," he stated grinning sheepishly.

Dana was cruising down Wyndcliff Road at her usual speed which was about fifteen miles over the posted limit. She knew she was pushing it but she wanted to get to the mall and back before Michelle showed up. Wyndcliff Road was like other roads across northern Dekalb County; two lanes, hilly with huge light poles, pine and oak trees and mailboxes set close to the driving lanes. It was something of a main road in that it led to the mall and its outlying retail stores.

Dover Street was a feeder off Wyndcliff which intersected below the crest of a hill. Even though there were warning signs posted on Wyndcliff about the dangerous intersection ahead, most drivers, Dana included, who traveled this road frequently more often as not chose to ignore the warnings and not slow down as they crested the hill.

David, himself, was driving way over the speed limit and had his radio blaring to the world. The world was listening because he had all of his windows down. He was really proud of his Trailblazer and loved playing with all the gadgets that GM had so thoughtfully placed about the vehicle and across the dash.

Being a young new driver in a city populated with narrow winding roads, he was not paying attention as he should have to the task at hand of guiding the Trailblazer safely along Dover Street. The thought never crossed his mind that he might not be invincible. As he rounded a curve and was approaching the intersection of Wyndcliff where he was supposed to stop, he was fiddling with a cup holder that pops out of the dash.

Unfortunately for both David and Dana, he arrived in the intersection at the same time that Dana arrived. The Trailblazer plowed full speed into the driver's door of the BMW. Dana had too little time to react. David was not aware of his predicament until the collision occurred.

His air bag deployed throwing him full force into the bag as it came out of his steering column. He suffered a concussion and broken legs. He survived.

Dana's side air bags and her steering column air bag deployed and should have been enough to safely cushion her impact, but not today. As the force of the Trailblazer hit the left front side of the BMW, it was not enough to stop its forward momentum. It continued for another fifty feet down Wyndcliff but at a thirty degree angle heading off the road directly into a twenty inch pine tree. The force of the BMW's impact with the pine tree was enough to drive the engine block back into the passenger section pinning Dana into a fatal position. There were no additional air bags to blunt the force of this second impact. The pine tree survived. Dana died instantly.

Katherine was smiling as she replied to George's last comment, "Yes, this is all too incredible. I know it is for me and for you….," She paused mid sentence for a long moment. The smile faded quickly and turned to controlled panic.

"Katherine, have I lost you?" he asked, sensing that something had interrupted their session.

"George, listen to me carefully. I have to go. You have to go. Our current session has to end….now. After our session is over, I want you to stand by the phone and wait for a call that'll come to you shortly," she explained quickly but with an even tone though she was close to tears.

"What's happened? What's going on? What can you tell me?" he implored.

"I'm sorry, George. The rules prevent me from telling you what I just learned. You'll know soon enough. You'll understand one day. I'll talk to you later. Take care of yourself, meanwhile," and she was gone, literally. She was already at Rose's place watching as Rose learned the news about Dana, her firstborn.

George sat there stunned. A few moments passed before he could get his thought processes working again. "Katherine,…. Katherine,…..are you still here?" he pleaded. Something had happened he needed to know and she could not tell him because of the rules of not revealing information before the mechanics of Earth's communications systems played their role.

His thoughts began to come in panic sized bursts. "Something must have happened to Dana. No, something has happened to Michelle on her way here; and she has Stewart and Nicole. No, something must have happened to Jackie or Jason or Mike or Stacie," George thought quickly as he paced the floor in a panic.

"Oh dear God, please take care of them all," he prayed aloud.

He was beginning to choke up when a car pulled into the driveway. It was Michelle with Stewart and Nicole. He ran outside just as they were getting out of her van. Michelle knew something was amiss when she looked up into his eyes.

"What's wrong, Dad?" she asked quickly. She always called him Dad. Her small petite frame housed green eyes beneath sandy colored hair but did little to reveal her high level of intelligence except through her piercing looks.

"I don't know. I can't say. I'm waiting for a phone call," George answered realizing he probably wasn't making any sense. He was sure she sensed his distress. Just then, he remembered Stewart and Nicole. He mustered all his courage and with a big smile, he gave them each a bear sized hug. Even in the direst of circumstances, he could never envision a reason for not giving them a hug. Seeing them warmed his heart and created the grin he displayed across his face. "How're you guys doing?"

"Fine, Grandad," they said almost in unison. "Can we play?" Nicole added.

"Yes, sure," George automatically responded. "Let's go back into the house. I think a call may be coming through shortly."

"Okay kids, let's go inside like Grandad suggested," Michelle added as she continued to watch him, certain that something was wrong here.

Once inside, George turned to Michelle and hugged her saying, "Sorry for forgetting this outside but I wanted to get back in as soon as possible. I'm really, really glad you and the kids are all right. How's Jason?"

"Jason's fine. I just talked to him and he was going into a meeting at the office," she answered "But you don't look so good. What's happening?"

"I wish I knew," he responded. Another piece of good news, apparently whatever set Katherine in motion did not involve Jason, so George put him into the okay column.

"I've a feeling that a call is coming through shortly with some not-so-good news," he said to her hoping this wouldn't go further than that.

"How's that? How do you know that you're going to get a bad-news call?" she asked with a really strange look on her face.

"It's hard to explain," he added, "This may not be the best time to explain this. But, hey, tell me what's been happening with you, Jason and the kids," George implored.

As she was about to answer, the phone rang. They both stared at it. It rang again before he walked over to pick it up. "Hello!" was all he could say.

The voice on the other end asked, "Is this the Mason residence?"

"Yes, this is George Mason" he said, "Who's this?"

"This is Deputy Johnson with the Dekalb County Sheriff's Department. There's been a vehicle accident involving your wife, Dana. She's been seriously injured. She's in the process of being transported to Emory Hospital. Can you meet us there in the Emergency Room area?" he asked as George's face began to contort into sheer panic. This was not lost on Michelle.

"Yes, yes I can. The Emory emergency room? I can be there in about ten minutes," George said as he looked at Michelle. She was already pulling out her cell phone to call Jason. George hung up the phone, "Michelle, Dana has been involved in an auto accident and is on her way to Emory," he said in his best strong voice with a quivering chin.

"I'll call Jason and ask him to call the others. I'll follow you shortly as soon as I collect the kids. You go ahead," she said and then asked, "Are you okay to drive yourself there?" The others she referred to would be Jackie, Mike and Stacie. Michelle was near panic herself but with her children at hand, she maintained the strong control over her nerves as mothers often do.

"Yes, I can make my way there," he responded. Already, a daze was starting to settle over him but he was functioning. He grabbed his keys and headed for the door.

"Please drive carefully," she implored, "We'll be there shortly."

He had no idea he was going to be met by Deputy Johnson and a doctor from the emergency room staff with news of incredible horror. "Dana has to be all right," he reasoned. "I wish I could talk to Katherine right now," he thought as tears were starting to flood his eyes. He had to wipe them off to maintain a good view of the street. The loneliness was already starting to envelop him.

Chapter 11

Dana's first thought was, "What was that?" The impact happened so quickly she didn't have enough time to realize what was going on or to react. All she remembered was a blur of black metal coming at her from the side. She remembered the air bags going off but it blocked her view of the tree coming at her. She didn't remember losing consciousness.

She did remember pushing away from the airbags and crawling out the right side of the car past what looked like a motor. "Why is the motor sitting beside me?" she asked herself. She stood up and looked around. "My goodness," she thought, "I got hit by that black SUV. I hope the other driver's okay."

She turned back around and looked inside the BMW. "My beautiful BMW," she thought. "I hope they'll be able to fix it. I need to get my purse out." Then she looked at the driver's side. "What's that?" she asked herself. Something was caught up in the air bags. Then she saw the hair, the right arm. "On no," she thought, "There's blood on her arm. Her arm…that's my arm….that's me?"

Just then, she felt a tap on her shoulder. She turned to see a lady standing there. Over her shoulder, she saw a gentleman. Both of them were smiling at her.

"Hello, Dana! My name is Helen and this is John. We're here to escort you Home," the lady said.

"Well, thank you! I'll need a lift. Look at how my BMW looks. George will be furious. He's said repeatedly our insurance rates are going through the roof because of my driving....Wait, what's going on here? Isn't that me in the car there?" Dana asked as she turned back to her car.

"Yes, that's you," Helen answered gently, "And we aren't going to the home you shared with George. We're going to your new Home."

Dana turned to look at Helen, then she looked back inside the car, and finally the realization set in. "That's me there and I'm dead, aren't I?" she asked Helen as she turned again to her.

"Yes, I'm afraid so. Your life has changed. By the way, you're not dead; you've just 'passed through' as we say.

Dana remembered her conversations with Rose and George. "So this is how it begins. Will George be all right?" she asked.

This time John responded, "Yes, he'll be fine. He'll be lonely but he has the children and grandchildren. He also has the memories of you which will sustain him until you and he can talk."

"We'll be able to talk like Rose and I?" Dana anxiously asked.

"Yes, you will," he responded. "It'll be awhile until your orientation is complete but he'll definitely be calling you. Also after orientation, you'll be able to go back and visit him and your other family members on your own. We just need to show you how that's done."

Dana then realized that Helen and John were holding her hands, and they were walking down a path surrounded by beautiful flowers and trees. Birds were all around chirping and singing, and there were butterflies, lots of butterflies. She looked behind her but could not see anything that reminded her of the accident. She didn't remember getting to this point. "All of this is so new and confusing. Will it ever make sense to me?" she asked.

"Definitely!" Helen reassured her. "You face a wonderful life here. You'll see people, such as your Mother, who you haven't seen in a long time. You'll make new friends. You'll learn a lot of neat things about how your new world works, a world we call Home."

"Will I meet Katherine?" Dana asked, "I've heard a lot about her over the years and recently, with the Link George discovered, she's come back into our lives." She wasn't sure how she was going to react to their first meeting. Already, her fears were increasing. Did she really have anything to fear? She wondered how she would react to their first meeting. They have a lot in common but what about their individual desires and wishes? How closely are they aligned? Are they really different? Let's face it, the question will come down to George. Does she want him all to herself? Does Katherine? Is there common ground for both of them to be with George? What about George's wishes now that she won't be a part of his everyday life? Whenever he passes through some time in the future, how will he see the two of them? Will he have another partner by then? He will certainly have that choice. That's what happened after Katherine died. All these questions flashed through her mind as they walked along this beautiful path.

"My guess is you'll meet her soon," John said smiling.

"Why would he smile?" she wondered. He must not know what was coursing through her mind like a raging river.

As the three rounded a curve in their pathway, a huge building came into view, causing Dana to pause for a moment. "Is this the arrival station I've heard about?" she asked.

"Yes!" John said, "And if you look closer, you should be able to see something familiar."

Dana peered ahead and, indeed, jutting out from the massive wall of the station was what appeared to be the front of a house. Not just any house, but the front of her house complete with porch, swing and flowers. The flowers looked just like the ones she planted two weeks ago. "My goodness!" was all she could say.

Helen added, "We do this to make new residents feel at home in familiar surroundings after they arrive. This will be your home for the next couple of months unless you decide to relocate sooner. You'll spend your time here when you're not in the Orientation programs and until you learn to navigate around your new Home. It would be unfair to do anything different since you are new and don't know your way around or even how to get around yet. We wouldn't want you to get lost."

"We'll leave you at your front door," John said. "You'll meet some more people on the other side. We're sure you'll enjoy your life here. No need to knock, just go right in. After all, this is your home."

Dana said, "Thank you for bringing me this far. Will I see you again?"

"Maybe, there're lots of opportunities to interact with our residents. You'll be able to visit us if you want just by calling our names. You will learn how to do this," Helen said.

"How long have you been doing this?" Dana asked.

John responded, "I've been at this about 350 earth years. Helen's the rookie. She's only been doing this 250 years." John remembered well his first day at Home. He had been in the New World only four years, having landed in Connecticut in 1650 with his family of four. They had made the arduous trip from England seeking some peaceful setting where they could worship God without the influence of the Church of England. They had moved by foot and horseback across the Hudson toward the upper regions of the area called New York when they were set upon by a small band of Indians who wanted all they had. That day, all members of his family arrived Home.

Helen, on the other hand had been a member of high society in New York City in 1750. She was a daughter of the newly elected mayor. On the day of her arrival at Home, she had been horseback riding with her friend, Emily, when the horse took a turn she wasn't expecting throwing her into a tree trunk head first. Her young life on earth was cut short at the age of fourteen.

"It's amazing to me you've been here that long," was all Dana could add.

"We've guided most of your family members to the arrival station over the years and most of George's family as well," Helen added as they were now standing in what would have been the front yard.

"That's interesting," Dana commented, "Can I ask you another question before I go in? When I was talking to my Mother, I asked her about my Father whose name was Jack Taylor. Did you guide him here?"

Helen and John paused to look at each other and then back at Dana. "Yes, we did but we also had some assistance."

"How's that?" Dana asked, "Was that because of my father's background? My mom told me she hasn't heard from him or seen him since he passed through."

"Have you heard of the Reconciliation process?" John asked her.

"A little, from George and Rose," Dana replied.

"I wasn't aware of your Father's situation until you just mentioned it," John began. "When prospective residents arrive here who had known issues back on Earth, we often have special assistance to guide them to the arrival station. My guess is he was examined pretty closely in Reconciliation and may have been found unsuitable for residency here. That's just a guess but it could've happened that way."

"That sort of confirms what my Mother suspected," Dana replied.

At that point, they were at the front door. "If you've no other questions, we'll say goodbye here. We wish you the best as you sort out your new life. Call us if you need us," Helen said in conclusion.

"Thank you," Dana replied. She shook both their hands, turned and opened her front door; or at least one which looked exactly like hers even down to the decoration she hung on it a month ago. Helen and John had already turned to leave.

As Dana entered her foyer, she couldn't help but notice that things appeared exactly like she had left them this morning with the exception there was no George and there was an absence of normal clutter. "Oh well," she thought to herself, "I'll take care of that if I'm here a while."

As she entered the living room, Dana saw her mother. Beyond her mother stood her grandparents, both sets of them, all smiling and holding their hands. Rose rushed forward to give her a huge hug. "Welcome Home," was all she could say through a big smile.

"My, it's so good to see you all," Dana said also with a huge smile as she hugged her grandparents.

Rose said, "Let me introduce you to the others here."

Dana hadn't noticed but two other ladies were present. Immediately, she recognized the face of Katherine.

Seeing Dana's look of recognition and before Rose could say anything, Katherine stepped forward and said, "Yes, I'm Katherine. I'm so glad to meet you at last. We have a lot to talk about and maybe sort out. There's a lot of catching up I'd like to do when you are up to it." With that, Katherine also gave Dana a hug and said, "Welcome to your new Home. Also, this is Margaret. I believe she'll be your guide through the orientation process."

Dana returned Katherine's hug, turned toward Margaret and extended her hand, "I'm pleased to meet you, Margaret,"

"Yes, me too! Katherine is correct. I'll be your guide through Orientation. Right now, I'm going to leave and return later. I know you have some catching up to do with your family," Margaret said.

Katherine added, "I could leave and return later as well, if you like."

"Please, Katherine, if you don't have anywhere else to be, I have questions perhaps you can help me with if you can you stay for a while?" Dana stated as she turned to Katherine.

Katherine nodded sensing some of Dana's concerns, "I'll be glad to stay around. I've been around the children along with you and George so much through the years, I feel like one of my family has arrived. I've visited you and George so many times in this very home I feel like I'm home here as well. I want to do whatever I can to make your arrival as seamless as possible.

"Let me also say I'm really sorry your arrival here was under the circumstances which occurred earlier. George contacted me shortly after you left the house this morning. We were talking about Annette and Boudreaux, of all things, when I learned about the accident. I had to break off the conversation without giving George a good reason why. He's just learned about your fate. He's in a lot of pain now, but please trust me, he'll be all right. Michelle's there with him and Jason's on his way. Jackie, Mike and Stacie have all been called," Katherine explained before she stopped.

Dana asked, "I appreciate the update. Do you suppose it's possible for me to visit George sometime later?"

"Yes," Katherine replied, "I believe I can take you. We can check on our entire family." My goodness, Katherine thought, it sounds so strange to be talking with Dana in this fashion after all this time, and someone she had watched all these years now in her presence and in need of her help. She wondered if there was any chance they could be friends or perhaps grow to be good friends. Was there a chance they might be roommates?

Dana was so confused by the events of the last hour; from driving to the mall to sitting in a look-a-like home in Heaven. She wasn't yet able to say Home, but that would probably come later. She was surprised to feel relieved that Katherine was here. She had questions that only she and Katherine could resolve. How would this work out? Could they come to some amicable understanding? Was there a chance at something better than an amicable understanding? Was there a chance for them to be friends; just friends or perhaps good friends? When would they be able to talk about this? Soon she hoped.

She turned to Rose, "Mom, it's so good to see you and all of you as well," as she looked at her grandfathers and grandmothers.

Chapter 12

George sat stunned in the small conference room off the emergency suite. Deputy Johnson and Dr. Anderson had just left. Both had been extremely compassionate and understanding as they used carefully chosen words to describe the sequence of events surrounding Dana's accident and her demise. Jason had arrived and was learning the details from Michelle. Stewart and Nicole were surprisingly quiet as they listened to the subdued conversations going on around them as if they knew it was a time for their best behavior. "He would have to make this up to them later," George thought.

For the time being, however, reality was slowly settling in on George's psyche. It had just occurred to him that twice in one lifetime, he was experiencing what no one should have to endure even once. Once again, his life had been shattered. "I have to pick up the pieces and move ahead. I'll probably have days when it'll seem like I'm in hell and I've been there before. What do they call it, de-ja vu?" George thought.

Jason was distraught. George could tell even if it was not visible on his face. He was trying to maintain a countenance for Stewart and Nicole but he was wringing his hands incesantly. Jason carried himself on a six foot frame. He was blessed with rugged good looks. He had blond hair and blue eyes, slim but with the beginnings of a bicycle sized mid waist spare tire. He kept himself in shape even with a full time work load and two demanding but loveable children.

"Jason," George said, "Why don't you call Jackie and tell her we're going back to the house. She may be trying to make her way here but there's nothing she can do. We may as well go home."

Jason looked at him and tried to say something, but his voice failed. Michelle said, "Sure Dad, that's a good idea. I'll call her. Jason, let's gather up our things and take Stewart and Nicole to Dad's."

This time Jason nodded. Michelle saved him from having to say anything.

As a group, they moved into the parking garage to three separate vehicles. Stewart was going with Jason and Nicole would ride with her mother. Jason now with his recovered voice asked, "Dad, will you be all right getting home by yourself?"

"I'll be okay," he answered even though he was still in a daze.

"Well, just in case, I'll wait out on the street and follow you home," Jason said.

As George drove, he thought of Jason, the second born of his four children. Jason graduated from Georgia Tech and had fallen in line with his grandfather and George. He was a good engineer with a level head on his shoulders and gold in his heart. George knew that he, himself, would be all right, but he worried about Jason. Jackie, Mike and Stacie were emotionally stronger than Jason who, George believed, was closer to his mother than the other three.

Jason's mother, adopted in this case, was Dana. His memories of Katherine were very limited. He could only recall bits and pieces of her so Dana was the only mother he knew. After Katherine left, Jason had a big void that George alone was unable to fill. Dana fit that role perfectly.

Jackie had a few more memories of Katherine than Jason. When Dana came along, Jackie clung to those old memories. She and Dana grew close, however, because of Dana's willingness to provide comfort and care when Jackie slipped into periods of regression over Katherine.

Naturally, Mike and Stacie grew up in a house where they only knew the family which, until a couple of hours ago, had been around all their lives. "I'll need to talk to them and watch them," George thought, "All of them may feel that I'll need care and attention. I will, but not in the way they might imagine. I'll be lonely, as I already am, when I think about our home and all the memories which lurk around every bend and in every corner. However, I'm certain after a while, I'll establish links to Dana and will be able to call upon her and Katherine to carry me through the days ahead. This is a luxury I didn't know about after Katherine was gone. I'll survive and I'll go on. I'll enjoy the moments I can have with my children and I'll strengthen my ties with their children. Those ties will serve me well long into the future after all of us have departed this Earth."

The trip home from the hospital took about fifteen minutes. Jason followed George, and Michelle followed him. Jackie had just arrived and was standing in the front yard with her children. Jackie, with tears streaming down her face, was almost the spitting image of Katherine, tall at five ten and slender, dark hair with hazel eyes, fair complexion.

Monica was there with Laverne. None were in good shape emotionally. They stood in the drive way crying and comforting each other.

Within the next thirty minutes, Marvin and Bill arrived with Rev. Casey. How did word about this spread so quickly? Within the next thirty minutes, George talked with Mike and Stacie who were preparing to fly into Atlanta tonight. "We'll have to send someone to the airport to meet them," he mentally told himself. He also talked with Dana's brother and sister who were coming in from Montgomery.

Thank goodness Dana always kept an immaculate house. Very little straightening up needed to be done. Monica and Laverne took charge in that department anyway. They were already receiving neighbors and church members, most of whom were bearing gifts of food. George hoped they were keeping lists as he would need to send acknowledgments and thanks later.

He wanted desperately to contact Katherine. It was probably too early to call for Dana. With all the activities going on here at the house, there was no way a quiet place could be found, maybe not for days. He would just have to wait and see.

It was amazing how the direction of life can change on a moment's notice. Dana had passed through, no longer available to walk and talk with her family. "My life took a 90 degree turn today. I am now heading in another direction, alone. The life Dana and I planned together has ended. New plans now have to be laid. No matter how hard the children will try to care for me and to include me in their plans, I'll be alone once again," George lamented to himself.

Dana and George knew that some day, only one of them would be left. That much they had discussed and planned for. It's just this was not supposed to be that day. Nevertheless, it had arrived, unannounced, with all the force of a sledgehammer. Dana was not here. She's there, beyond the veil. She has passed through. She had begun the next segment of her existence. Her soul was alive and she would flourish. She might miss us, but yet, she could watch us. Soon, they would talk again. Meanwhile, here he went….on with his life here with all his 'inherent' responsibilities about which Katherine and his dad had recently reminded him. Rev. Casey came through the house with a cup of coffee in each hand. He found George on the patio talking with Bill who was still unsettled by the day's events. "George, here, take this cup of coffee. I know its warm out here but the coffee may shake loose some of the cobwebs which have formed up there," pointing to George's head.

"Thanks, Richard. This will be helpful," he said.

George had known Richard for a long time. Richard's father and grandfather had both been Methodist ministers, and his grandfather had even been a Bishop in South Carolina for a period of time. Both of them had passed on along with his mother. Richard was about five years younger than George.

"Bill," Richard said, "Are you going to be all right?"

"Yeah, I'll be okay. I need to get myself together. Whoever would have thought we'd be doing this today after we just spent the time together this morning," he stated to George. "I'm here for you, George, to do whatever you need," he added.

"I know. Thank you for your friendship. You've meant a lot to Dana and me over the years; Laverne too. Please let her know," he said. "And Richard, can we spend a little time talking about the service and the days ahead."

Richard said, "Yes, that's why I came out here to the patio. We may have some quiet time away from the household."

Their discussions went on for at least an hour. Jackie and Jason came out to listen and to add their views at various times. All input was welcome. None of the plans could be finalized, however, until they visited with the funeral director tomorrow morning. Jackie went off to call for an appointment.

For a short time, Richard and George found themselves alone. They'd walked out into the far corner of the yard. "Richard, can I ask you a question about your trade?" George asked. He wanted to put out a feeler for what Richard knew or what the Church knew about his discovery even though this was probably not the best time.

"If you mean about the Church, go ahead?" he added to clarify George's comment for himself.

"I know you're a pretty good historian on what has gone on in the Church over the years, not only with the Methodists but also in other branches. Do you ever recall anything written about people who claim to be able to talk to the dead?" George asked as he laid it out for Richard to chew on.

"My goodness, George, are you thinking about some way you can contact Dana?" he came back in a surprised tone.

"Yeah, I guess I am," George said. "If this sounds too crazy, just chalk it up to the stresses of the moment."

"Well," Richard began, "You've every right to be stressed out but let me think a minute. I think there've been quite a few reported instances, but when looked at by those in the Church who were assigned to investigate, almost all were explained away. I can only think of a couple of reports over the centuries which have survived the scrutiny of investigation and have gone down without plausible explanations. I believe one was out of the Presbyterian Church in Scotland in the sixteenth century and another one was reported by the Roman Catholic Church in the 1950's from somewhere in Louisiana. There may be others I can't bring to mind. They're so rare that no one even took those two seriously. Remember, in the absence of a good explanation, it doesn't mean one didn't exist. It just wasn't discovered."

"By chance, do you recall the general demeanor from Church leaders when those were written up in the historical accounts?" George asked wanting to see what kind of slant was put on the stories.

"Seems to me, the Church was bent on explaining away the incidents more so than trying to look at them as something new, if that's what you mean," Richard replied.

"Like there was no way the incidents could have really happened? Like they may have been trying to protect their interests?" George asked trying to understand what he heard.

"Well, I don't know about the 'protecting their interests' part but certainly looking at the incidents in a disbelieving manner," Richard added.

George thought for a minute and said, "Well, I guess I'll have to give up on that idea." At this point, he didn't need to have Richard distraught over his mental state by insisting that not only was it possible but that it was being done. Richard did confirm one thing. Indeed, the occasions were rare and far between. Also, George had no doubt about whom the Louisiana report was centered around and he certainly wasn't going to raise any red flags with Richard by mentioning names. George also didn't want Bill to hear any part of this conversation. In a way, he felt he was hiding something which all needed to know. "Maybe later, or maybe I'll just let my children deal with this," he thought.

Jackie came out just as their conversation was wrapping up to report on a 9 o'clock appointment tomorrow with the funeral director.

Afternoon shadows were lengthening. The house was still full of people and would likely be so until late in the evening. It was always good to be surrounded by friends and neighbors at times like these. A lot of people felt close to Dana, and George as well. They had made friends easily through the years in this neighborhood and at church. The fact that someone died suddenly and had not been ill can cause a lot of abrupt unhappiness in people's lives. One moment, you think of a person and when you would next talk to them or see them. The next moment, you were forced by circumstances to think of them in the past tense knowing that you would never come face to face with them again on this Earth. These two moments were gigantic and were on opposite ends of the spectrum; yet, they were the moments which occur whenever someone you're close to passes on.

Everyone faced death at some time or another and under some circumstance or another. The certainty of that event never lessened the impact on those who were left and who must adjust their lives to continue forward toward their own final earthly event.

The evening quieted down around 9 o'clock. Most guests had gone home. Many they would see again over the next couple of days as they began to move through the formal rituals most Americans observe in laying loved ones to rest. There would be a visitation period, a funeral service and a graveside service. It happened everywhere all the time. Dana's would be no different.

After nine, the only people left were Jackie and Tom, her husband, and their children, Michael, Justin and Traci. Jason and Michelle were there with Stewart and Nicole. Mike and Elizabeth and their two year old, Todd, had just arrived from the airport. Likewise, Stacie and Robert, her husband, with their two year old daughter, Lisa, in tow had also arrived from the airport about thirty minutes earlier. In other words, George's Family was home once again but without Dana and Katherine, who should be included in this category even though she'd been absent for thirty-five years. After all, she had been visiting on a regular basis all these years unseen and, until recently, unheard.

Chapter 13

At the arrival station, Katherine was discussing with Margaret the possibility of escorting Dana back to her Atlanta home where her family was gathered. Margaret said traveling so early after arrival was risky because Dana hadn't been trained yet to travel around by herself.

Katherine said, "If I hold onto her hand and if Rose also accompanies us, do you think it'll be safe enough to try?" as she put the request to Margaret. Rose nodded in approval. "We'll only be gone a short while. I know this is probably a rare request but you have to understand how much Dana already knows about us and Home. We'll be sure to call you as soon as we get back."

Margaret thought a minute. "Taking a little extra time before we start her orientation isn't a big deal," she said to herself and then out loud. "Okay!"

Then she turned to Dana who'd been listening to all this. "Dana, please understand this is a rarely granted request. It's rare because you haven't had the training to do this on your own. Our fear is that you might somehow become separated from Katherine or Rose and not be able to find your way back. If you want to do this, you have to stay with Katherine or Rose. Do you understand?"

Dana looked first at Rose and Katherine then turned to Margaret and said, "Yes, I understand. I really appreciate this."

Katherine and Rose approached Dana and each took one of her hands. Katherine uttered the words "George Mason home – go there." In half a blink, they were gone.

In the other half of the blink, Katherine, Rose and Dana arrived in the family room of George's house. Dana jumped as she said, "My gracious, that was fast." She found herself standing with Katherine and Rose watching George hug Stacie as they came in from the airport. Jackie and Jason were both there along with Michelle and Tom. They all seemed to be crying. Dana said to them, "Hey guys, what're you crying about, I'm right here." No one paid her any attention. No one turned to look at her.

Katherine said softly, "Dana, they can't hear you. You're now an observer just as we've been over the years. They can't see us. They don't know we're here."

Dana looked first at Katherine then at Rose and asked, "Mom, is this what you've done all these years?"

Rose said, "Yes Dana, this is the process we go through when we go back to see the family."

Dana looked at her family. Then she looked beyond them. Standing on the far side of the room were George's mom and dad. The full realization slowly dawned on her about what was happening.

When Jefferson and Annie saw Dana looking at them, they came across the room and gave her a hug. "I didn't expect to see you here this soon," Jefferson said to her.

Katherine said, "We got special permission to make this visit. We've been allowed to bring her because of her foreknowledge about Home. Rose and I agreed to accompany her."

"Well," Jefferson said as he gave her another welcome hug, "It's good to see you. You can see that they're all pretty torn up by the day's events. With George's knowledge, he'll guide them through all this. I think everything will be all right."

Dana was riveted by the scene in front of her. There was her family, her earthly family, trying to cope with losing her. Here was her heavenly family being where they need to be, that is, with the grieving family. She, herself, was very disturbed in seeing what they were going through.

Thinking back now, she realized everything going on now would not have happened if she had just stayed home today. She would be enjoying a boisterous evening with George, Jason, Michelle, Stewart and Nicole. She muttered to herself, "Why in the world did I have to go to the mall?"

Katherine, not quite hearing what she said asked, "What did you say?"

Dana, upset with herself said, "Mall!.... Go there!" as she half heartedly attempted to clarify herself to Katherine.

Katherine and Jefferson both said at the same time, "Nooo!!!"

Too late! Dana faded from their eyes. Unknowingly, repeating those last words happened to be the necessary travel statement to go from one place to another. Dana was gone.

Jefferson said to Katherine in a panic, "What was it she said?"

Katherine, also in a panic, replied, "She mentioned something about going to the mall."

"Why'd she want to go to the mall now?" Jefferson asked incredulously.

"My guess is she didn't want to go to the mall. My guess is she was trying to accept some blame for what happened today by lamenting the fact she didn't really need to go to the mall this morning at all," Katherine explained after a moment but still in a panic.

"Well, maybe she'll be right back," Jefferson added.

"I don't know about that," Katherine added. "She hasn't yet had any training about traveling around. She may not realize what happened or how to undo it. She may not even know where she is. We don't know where she is."

Katherine looked at Rose. "If you don't mind, Rose, why don't you hang around here and I'll check in with Margaret," Katherine said to her.

Jefferson said, "I could go to the mall to see if she's there. Come to think of it though, which mall would she be in? There are a lot of malls around Atlanta and she's been to them all. Which one was she going to this morning? For that fact, she may have landed in a mall at Home. What a mess!"

All the while, the other scene in the room was being played out between the earthly residents. The tearful greetings for Stacie and her family were over and things were starting to settle down oblivious to the other emergency happening out of their sight and hearing in this very room.

Katherine looked at them and said to her group, "One day we'll probably all laugh at this. I bet there aren't many days at Home or on Earth, when one person can cause such an uproar in both places." Unknown to Katherine, the day wasn't over yet.

At that, all the Home folks grinned or chuckled, as did Jefferson.

Katherine uttered the words, "Margaret – go there!" and she was gone.

Dana jumped as the scene changed in front of her eyes. One moment, she was standing in her family room watching her family grieve; the next, she was in one of the strangest places she had ever seen. "What just happened?" she asked herself. "How did I get here and where is here?"

The sun was shining bright but not so much that she needed sunshades which she normally carried. No clouds were to be seen. She found herself standing in the middle of a huge square; must've been at least a half mile on each side. Wide multiple avenues were leading off of all four sides. Between the avenues were buildings of various sizes, mostly huge and multi story. Small kiosks were set up around the square. People were walking through looking at the displays. Every once in awhile someone would stop and chat with the person at one of the kiosks. All sorts of things were on display; clothes, hats, shoes, books, food, drinks and many kinds of art work.

Being the artist she was, Dana naturally gravitated toward one which displayed paintings. There was quite a gathering around this particular display. The crowd was really diverse. Clothing reflected all sorts of cultures. She heard as many as seven languages; yet, strangely she was able to understand everyone. "How's that possible?" Then she vaguely recalled something Katherine told George.

These particular paintings were unusually vivid with colors. The style looked somehow familiar. Then she remembered, "These look like Monet's" she said out loud to herself. Then she looked up at the top of the kiosk and saw the simple sign, 'Monet'. She stared at it for a moment, and then looked down at more of the paintings. As she turned the corner, she bumped into a gentleman who was talking to a small group.

"Oh, pardon me," she said.

"That's okay," the gentleman said as he turned to face Dana; only he spoke in French, but she understood the words in English.

She looked into his eyes and blurted, "My gosh, you're the spittin' image of Claude Monet." She knew his face well from the art history courses she'd taken over the years.

He smiled. Then he bowed to his waist. "Thank you for saying that. I try so hard to look like him since I am him," he exclaimed.

Claude Monet was one of the most famous and prolific of the Impressionists. He lived on Earth from 1840 to 1926 and happened to be one of Dana's idols among the artists of years gone by

"What? You are?" Dana stammered. "I am so sorry. Please forgive me."

"There's nothing to forgive. Do you like these paintings?" he asked as he stepped back and motioned to the multitude of works hanging on the kiosk.

"I have loved your work all my life," Dana managed to say.

"What's your name? Have you been here long?" he asked.

"Uh, my name is Dana, Dana Mason. Have I been here long; I don't think so. Actually, I'm not sure at all where I am," she said as she glanced around again.

"Not sure where you are, huh? Well, where did you come from?" he asked.

"I guess I sound stupid or something. One minute I'm standing in my home watching my grieving family and the next thing I know I'm standing in this huge square."

Monet looked at her more closely and with a puzzled expression asked, "Did you say your grieving family? You mean on Earth? Who was it that passed away?"

"I think it was me," she replied. "Yes, I was at my home on Earth. My mom and another friend took me out of the arrival station to check on my husband and children."

"Dana, have you been through Orientation?" he asked with a puzzled look.

"No, I was about to start it when all this happened," she said.

"Well, I hate to tell you this, but I don't believe you are supposed to be here, or anywhere, except in Orientation," he ventured.

"You're probably right but, to be honest, I have no idea how to get back there from wherever I am right now," she replied.

"Well, first of all, you're at the Gateway Center. This is a place you can come to see what is available for just about anything you'd want, like a shopping mall. See all the buildings surrounding this square?" he asked as he gestured with his arms at the structures around them.

"Yes, but I've no idea what they are," she said, glancing around. Her interest piqued at the words 'shopping mall'.

"They're stores where you can view anything from Earth and anything made at Home here all for your taking if you want," he said.

"Interesting," she thought.

"Would you like to have some assistance finding your way back to your area in the arrival station?" he asked.

"Oh, Mr. Monet, I'd appreciate anything you can do in that regard," she said as she smiled.

"Well then," he said as he pointed, "Do you see that building over there with the large glass windows?"

Dana replied, "I do see it."

"Go over to that building! When you enter the lobby, look to the right and you'll see a large set of doors labeled 'Information and Assistance'. There'll be someone available to help you find someone who can get you back," Monet said smiling at her.

"Thank you! Thank you! I want to say again how much I enjoy your paintings. Are these some that you've done here?" she asked in an unsure manner. After all, she was talking to one of the greatest painters on earth....probably here as well.

"Yes, I've done these over the last couple of months. I'll occasionally bring a group of them down here to see how the crowds react to them. I usually wind up giving them away," he said.

"You give them away? You don't sell them?" Dana asked incredulously.

"Don't need money here. I just do it for pleasure it gives me," he said grinning. "Would you like one?"

Dana gasped as she took a step back and drew a hand to her chest, "Are you kidding? I've wanted one of your paintings all my life. I do paintings myself, and I've always admired your work."

"Ah hah! So you paint too. Maybe that'll be your calling here. Let's look around and you tell me if you see one you particularly like," he said.

"My goodness," she said as she could not believe her good fortune, "I like this one here," she said looking at a small painting of a seashore and seascape.

He picked it up and handed it to her. "Take it with my compliments, and welcome Home," he said.

She was beaming, "No one will believe what's happened to me here," she said. "If there's ever anything I can do for you or to help you, will you let me know?" as she reached out to hug him.

"I will! Good luck," he said, returning her hug.

Dana turned and began walking toward the building with all the glass as he suggested. "Now this is what I call a shopping trip to the mall," she said to herself as she walked tightly clutching her Monet painting. Walking, heck, she realized she was almost skipping as she carried her precious cargo. Katherine, Mom and George won't believe this. "Goodness," she thought suddenly, "I hope I see them again." She realized she had no idea how to get in touch with them. Maybe someone here could help.

Everyone had gone home for the night except the family. George thought, "Thank goodness we hadn't downsized our house yet." The kids moved back into their old bedrooms for the night and the grandkids,...well, they were sleeping in various nooks and corners, on pallets and couches and a couple, Michael and Stewart managed to root their way into Grandad's king size bed. Michael was about six months younger than Stewart, and they were always the best of buddies whenever they were together. George realized the last time they were all together was last Thanksgiving. Two of them had Christmas commitments at their in-laws.

He lay there with Stewart and Michael for a little while. Usually, they'd have asked for the TV to be turned on but the request had yet to come. They were not as boisterous as usual as if something else might be on their minds. Stewart, in particular, was unusually quiet. During a lull in conversation, Stewart turned and looked at George for a long moment before saying, "Grandad, do you remember that talk we had awhile back when I asked you if you were getting old?"

The hairs on the back of his neck began to rise. "Yes, I do Stewart. Why do you ask?" George ventured.

"Well, Grannie's not going to get any older, is she?" he asked.

The question tugged at his heart as George answered, "No, Stewart, she's as old as she's going to be here on this Earth. But you know what, she's now in a place where she will live forever and never get any older. Does that make sense?"

"Nope! That doesn't make any sense at all. You're joking, right?" he answered.

"Yeah, Grandad, you're joking," Michael piped in.

"No, no, listen and I'll tell you a little story," he began, "Today, Grannie left us to go to another place; a place the Bible calls Heaven. She's there now. One day, you and Michael will see her again just as I will, but we all have to wait our turn. Also, one day you might be able to talk to her. Did you two love her; I mean really, really love her?"

"Yeah!" replied Stewart closely echoed by Michael.

"Well, I'm going to tell you a secret. Can you keep a secret? You have to promise you won't tell anyone." George charged them.

Both boys were quiet for a moment as they looked at each other and back to George. "Yes, yes, we can keep a secret." Now, he had their attention.

"Okay, there's a way for you to talk to her. If you ever want to, here's what you do. Find yourself a quiet place; turn off the TV and anything else that's making a racket. Then, you ask this question, 'Grannie, are you here?' You have to listen for a moment and if she's there, she'll say hello. Then you can talk to her," George explained.

Stewart asked, "Is that all there is to it? Can we do it now?"

George replied, "I think it best if you wait a while; maybe sometime after you get back home. Also, remember this, if she doesn't answer right away, don't give up. Wait a couple of days and try again."

Stewart said, "Boy, I can't wait to try. Thanks, Grandad."

"Can we watch TV?" Michael asked.

"Sure!" he said as he clicked on the TV. He was sure all this was already forgotten; although he wasn't so sure about Stewart who was turning out to be more attentive and more serious than most six year olds. "Finally, maybe I'll quit nagging myself about what to do with the information which I, alone, now possess. I finally told someone," George thought.

He'd turned on the bedroom TV for the boys with the expectation they would soon fall sound asleep. It worked. He was still wide awake as he turned off the TV a short time later. The rest of the house was pretty quiet by now. One could never tell, however, how long that would last. Small children are prone to their loudest behavior when they awake in unfamiliar surroundings in the middle of the night.

He thought, "Now may be a good time to see if Katherine's around. I can chat with her without verbalizing our conversation if I can focus properly."

George lay down in the bed and found a corner of the mirror on the dresser he could just barely make out from the dim glow of street lights seeping in around the curtains and shades. He decided to focus on that spot as he went through the now familiar routine of clearing his unusually cluttered mind. That process took a little longer today given all the activities, but he thought he had it conquered as he murmured, "Katherine, are you here?"

After what seemed to be a few moments longer than normal, the now familiar answer came, "Yes, George, I'm here. Are you doing okay? Everything seems to have settled down around the house. Is everyone else okay?" Katherine answered trying to maintain an even voice for his benefit.

"Thank goodness you're here," George began, "First off, we're fine for now. Have you been monitoring us?"

"I've been in and out. I was just at the arrival station talking to Dana's resident coordinator," answered Katherine, not wanting to say much more than that.

"Is anyone else here with you? Dana? Have you seen Dana?" he asked with a little more urgency.

"Your dad and mom are here as well as Rose, Dana's mom. Dana's fine. I've seen her and finally met her face to face," Katherine added but not wanting to say anything else about Dana's whereabouts. Again, she hoped her voice didn't give away her own concerns. While Katherine was pacing around the bedroom, the others maintained their distance as they tried to stay out of her way. She didn't want to tell George that Dana had been here observing all the grief earlier; nor that Dana had suddenly and inexplicably disappeared.

"That's great. I hope you two can grow to respect each other. How's she doing? Better question, how does any resident hold up when they pass through with the suddenness that occurred to her today? Is it just as devastating to new arrivals as it is to those of us who are left to put our own lives back together?" George asked.

"I guess it can be," Katherine said, "In Dana's case, it happened so fast and with such finality that she didn't suffer. She passed through instantaneously and is now in perfect health, so to speak. She was perplexed about what happened as most residents would be. However, with her foreknowledge of the way things are, she recovered quickly."

"I'm glad. Any idea when I might be able to talk with her?" he asked.

"It won't be until after she completes her Orientation. Sometime during that process, she'll be taught how to do all this."

"Okay! Do you think you'll see her again anytime soon?" George asked.

Katherine hesitated a little before answering his rather loaded question, "Yes, I certainly hope so. Matter of fact, I may ask her if she wants to stay with me while her orientation is going on. If she does, one of the first things she'll learn is how to get from the arrival station to my house and return."

"Super!" George said, "Katherine, do you mind if I say good night. I'm really tired and who knows when we'll be up again around here," referring to the current state of affairs with the house full of small children.

"George, we hope you get some rest. You need it. You've done really well with all this so far, good night," she ended, but not before she walked over to give George a kiss on his cheek, a kiss he couldn't feel.

"Good night, and good night to everyone there," he added. He was addressing his mom and dad as well as Rosa. His mom walked over to gently caress his cheek. She had no intention of leaving, however.

Katherine stood there along with Jefferson, Annie and Rose looking at George and the two boys as he moved into his night of sleep. Even though it was dark in the room, the four of them had no problem seeing in the dim light; just another benefit of being Home. Katherine thought about the other problem at hand and glanced at the others. She said, "I was at the arrival station talking to Margaret when George called. They haven't heard from her yet. I got a well deserved lecture on why we shouldn't have brought her here. I guess none of this would have happened if she'd stayed there. But Margaret admitted she's partially to blame. It seems there's a process where she's supposed to be registered as a new arrival and Margaret hadn't done that yet. If she'd been registered, then she could be located very quickly wherever she is."

Jefferson spoke up, "Is this something unusual for this sort of thing to happen….to lose someone?"

"I'm not sure," Katherine responded, "Margaret didn't seem that upset. I guess there's something they can do… maybe like issuing an all points bulletin to Elders and residents who're working in their Information and Assistance locations. Home is a big place; yet, it's pretty organized when they need to get something done. That's been my experience anyway."

"Mine too," all three of the others chimed in.

Jefferson added, "I can't help but speculate. Does this make her a Lost Soul?" he threw out with a big laugh.

At that, they all laughed. Better to keep your sense of humor than give in to panic was his motto. He added, "Katherine, were you serious when you mentioned to George about asking Dana to stay with you during her orientation?"

"Yes, I was," she said, "I believe she and I'll get along fine. I hope she feels the same. Seems like I've known her for a long time with the many visits I've made here. Besides, if George calls and she's there, I can always bring her along to hear our conversations even if she can't participate yet."

Jefferson replied, "Excellent idea! I bet George will get some comfort knowing that as well." The rest nodded in agreement.

Katherine said, "Well, I think I'll go back to the arrival station and wait for word about Dana. If anything comes up, I'll let you know." All said okay to that and with their acknowledgment, Katherine was gone.

Dana was understandably nervous as she walked into the Information and Assistance office. This was a huge area like all the other things she had observed thus far. There were many people inside. Everything was orderly and neat, however. Everyone was talking with someone who seemed to be rendering assistance or dispensing information. There was no line of people waiting for help.

As she paused and looked around, a petite middle aged woman of Asian extraction approached her and asked in what sounded like Chinese, "Hi, my name is Mei Ling, may I help you?"

Chinese was being spoken to her. She knew because she could hear the sounds of the language. At the same time, she heard Mei Ling's question in English. "This is amazing," Dana thought to herself.

Mei Ling was newly assigned to the Information and Assistance office. In fact, she was a relatively new arrival at Home. A year ago, she was the Assistant Shipping Manager for Asian Exports out of Taiwan. Shortly, she would discover she had breast cancer, and shortly after that, she learned she had about six months to live. At age 52, she felt cheated at life. This meant she would leave her husband of thirty years and three wonderful children. The doctors misestimated the diagnosis. She passed through within three months instead of six. After her Orientation program, she was assigned to the Information and Assistance Group. She had only been in this location for four weeks. The training she was given was excellent and felt she could handle any request.

"Yes, maybe, I don't know. Can I just tell you my predicament?" Dana inquired.

"Please do!"

"I don't know where I am or how I got here."

"You feel you're lost?" Mei Ling said in the form of a question.

"Yes!"

"Well now that's a bit unusual, being lost. But, it seems as though you may have met Mr. Monet," Mei Ling said after looking at the object Dana was carrying. By this time Mei Ling was smiling. "Tell me your name and where you were before you arrived here."

"Yes, Mr. Monet was wonderful. He gave me this. I was at my home with my mom and some friends watching my family. My name is Dana Mason," Dana added.

Mei Ling was beginning to guide Dana towards the back to another office. She sensed something was amiss here. "Dana, let me ask you this, where were you this morning when you got up?"

"At my home in Atlanta with my husband, George. About mid day, I left home and was driving to the mall when I was involved in an automobile accident. Then, I met Helen and John who escorted me to a huge building to my front door; only it was not my front door in Atlanta. Then I met Margaret. My mom, grandparents and Katherine were there. Katherine was my husband's first wife. Is any of this making any sense to you?" Dana asked as she obviously had told Mei Ling more than she asked for.

"Sort of!" Mei Ling replied. With that, Mei Ling opened the door to the office and asked, "Ralph, did you hear all that?"

Dana entered the office to see a short gentleman standing there. This must be Ralph.

Ralph was an old timer, relatively speaking. He had been here a little over 140 years. His home had been in Philadelphia, but that wasn't where he was when he passed through. He was at a little church named Shiloh in early spring. He remembered the peach orchard blooms but didn't remember the mini ball that struck his left ear. He does remember a number of other arrivals here at Home, including him, that April day in 1862. He wasn't a tall guy by today's standards, probably five feet six, a moderately good looking guy in his prime at the age of 27. His only family in Pennsylvania was just his mom, dad and five brothers and sisters. Two of his brothers would join him at Home within the next two years.

Ralph said to Mei Ling, "Yes, I heard." To Dana he said, "Hi, my name's Ralph. Mei Ling and I both work here at the Information and Assistance office. Sometimes, she'll ask me for help whenever an unusual situation comes up. Your situation seems to fit that bill. Is it okay if we ask a few more questions?"

"Yes! Sure! I apologize for being such a problem," Dana replied. Dana wondered how it was that Ralph had heard when they were in the other room. Oh well, she could ask about that later.

Ralph assured her, "You're no problem. It sounds like you passed through today and were brought to your temporary home at the arrival station. Does that sound about right?"

"I think so," she replied.

"Okay, give me just a minute," Ralph requested. With that he stood there looking as if he was in deep thought. Then he said, "I've looked in our data base and you're not registered in any of the arrival stations. I do see an entry where Dana Mason passed through today from Atlanta, Georgia. I assume that may be you?" he asked.

"Yes, that's me unless there were two of us from Atlanta," Dana said.

"Well, there was only one Dana Mason today and you were in an automobile accident on Wyndcliff Road," Ralph said.

Dana was much impressed with what was unfolding here. Already, she felt much better about her situation. How did he know all this? More questions to ask later. "That was me," she said.

"The question is 'how is it that you're not registered at the arrival station and how did you get here?' Do you remember exactly what you were doing the instant before you arrived here?" he asked.

"I was standing in my home in Atlanta watching my family. Katherine and my mom had received permission from Margaret at the arrival station to take me back to see them. I remember I was lamenting about the fact that I should not have gone to the mall," she said in reply.

"Aha, I believe I understand how you got here. You must have uttered the phrase for Home travel in talking about the mall. In doing so, you arrived at this mall. Is Margaret your coordinator at the arrival station?" he asked.

"I believe she is," Dana said.

"Margaret must have granted permission for you to travel before she put you into the arrival station's system. That's probably the reason you aren't registered there. Now why did she allow you to travel so soon after arrival?" he asked aloud more to himself than to Dana.

"There was some discussion between Margaret and Katherine about the fact that I already knew some about Home because of the conversations my husband and I have been having with Katherine and Mom," Dana answered.

Ralph looked up at Dana for a long moment. Then he looked at Mei Ling who was standing by, listening. Ralph was a former policeman and was good at performing in a role where you had to get to the bottom of something. A look of recognition slowly came over him.

"What?" Mei Ling asked as she recognized the look.

Ralph looked back at Dana. "Your name is Dana Mason. Your husband's name wouldn't be George Mason would it?" he asked.

"Yes, it is. Do you know him?" Dana asked with a puzzled look. This is getting deeper and deeper she thought to herself.

Mei Ling was now smiling. Ralph was also smiling as he said to Dana, "I've never met your husband, George. But I've certainly heard of him. Heck, most of us here at Home have heard of him, right Mei Ling?" She nodded in agreement. "He made the news here by uncovering the communication channel between earth residents and residents here at Home. That hasn't been done in over fifty years. He's famous. Katherine is now famous. You are almost as famous because he told you, and you also opened the channel to your mom.,"

"My goodness! Katherine said what George did had made a stir here, but I had no idea," Dana replied. "Can I tell you something else that we found interesting?"

"Please do!"

"George learned that the incident you mentioned which happened over fifty years ago occurred to the great grandmother of George's best friend. I think her name was Annette," Dana added.

"Yes, I believe that was her name. She was also mentioned on the newscast. This is amazing. Dana! You have made my day. We're going to get you back to your home at the arrival station right ricky-tick. Is there anything else we can do for you today?" Ralph asked.

"What you've done plus all that I've seen has just been amazing to me. Thank you, and Mei Ling, very much," Dana said.

"Well, trust me, as a new arrival, you ain't seen nothing yet," Ralph added. Then he looked up and said, "Margaret – come here please."

After a few moments, Margaret materialized seemingly out of thin air. "There you are," she said as she smiled at Dana. "You gave your friends and me quite a scare. Have you enjoyed your time here?" she asked as she saw the painting Dana was carrying.

"I sure have. Everyone that I've met here has been great, including Mr. Monet," she said as she waved her painting.

Ralph said, "It's been a pleasure meeting you, Dana Mason. I expect to hear great things about you. If we can ever be of service to you again, please let us know. Drop by any time."

Mei Ling added, "The same goes for me. Next time you go shopping, drop in."

Dana grinned. Margaret said, "All right Dana, take my hand and we'll get you safely back home. Don't forget your package." Then they were off.

As they appeared in the temporary Dana Mason home, they arrived to see Katherine waiting on them. "I truly apologize for the mess I've made," Dana said.

"Well, the important thing is, did you have a good time?" Katherine countered.

"You bet! Look what I have," Dana held up the painting, "I met Claude Monet, and he gave me this. He had a kiosk at the mall I dropped into."

Katherine gasped, "No way! He didn't."

"Yes way! He did. Also, I met some great people who work in the Information and Assistance office there. And the mall, the Gateway Center I believe Mr. Monet called it, was fantastic. I'd like to go back there sometime soon. I love malls. I've no idea how I got there and, right now, couldn't get back," Dana explained.

Katherine looked at the painting and commented, "You know, I've got a great spot to put this painting. I currently don't have a roommate and was thinking of adding some extra rooms at my place. How would you feel about staying with me while you are going through Orientation? I know this place looks like your home and can provide some comfort from all its familiar surroundings but if you want to visit my place and look around, maybe you'd like to make it your temporary home until you decide about a permanent place to live. Besides, it can give us plenty of time to talk unencumbered without other people around."

"Hmmn," Dana thought, "This could be a way to talk to Katherine alone and get to know her better."

"I think that would be a good idea and will give us time together. I mean, after all, we have so much in common," Dana told her as she immediately began to warm to this person from the past; from George's past. Could there is a way to be good friends with her?

"Okay! Thinking out loud and without being too presumptous, keep this in the back of your mind. If you like what you see and if you believe we might become friends, I can see adding an extra living complex along with an art studio. I think you'll like the backdrop of the lake and mountains. I can envision you there painting and creating to your heart's content. I can see you having a kiosk at the mall alongside Mr. Monet. Tell me if this is worthwhile considering."

Dana grinned and said, "My goodness, you aren't nearly as shy as George told me. I actually like the sound of that plan. It could be an ideal arrangement. When can we go?"

"We can go as soon as you master the art of traveling. Margaret says that'll be very soon," Katherine added.

Margaret broke in, "Okay girls, if it's all right with both of you, I believe it's time for Dana to begin her Orientation program."

Chapter 14

George woke up slowly. The rest of the house still seemed quiet. "That's good," he thought. "Maybe they all got a better night's sleep than I did." he looked over at the clock; 6:15. Even he wasn't supposed to be awake yet. Then he looked back the other way and understood why.

Stewart was lying perpendicular to him with his head nestled up close to his chest. Michael was also lying perpendicular to him but in the opposite direction. His feet were nestled up next to George's left leg and his head was almost off the bed on what used to be Dana's side. On top of this, they were both lying on top of the covers. It's a good thing the house was a little warm last night.

How in the world did they manage to do this little dance in his bed during the night with neither of them or him aware of it? Undoubtedly, this would go down as one of the great mysteries of life.

As George continued to lie there, it occurred to him, "This is the first day of the rest of my life, the first day I'll face alone without my life's partner with me." It wasn't supposed to be this way. Although he was past 65, he felt there were plenty more years yet to run on this little playhouse Dana and he built here with her and him acting out their roles as a loving and happily married couple. Now, it appears this would be a one-man act for the foreseeable future.

Thinking further though, "There'll be some pluses to this. Some that no one else in the world may know about, it seems. I'll have the good fortune to talk to them as often as I like. And, you know what, my conversations with them will be on my terms when I choose. That's a definite plus. The down side, however, is they may well be watching every move I make. Do you suppose nagging from Heaven is allowed?"

Today, they would have some difficult decisions to make. Not that the things they must decide would be particularly difficult but their states of mind would force them to bring to bear things none of them wanted to think about. Oh, the funeral director would be very helpful as he guided them through his mental checklist of things needed attending to. When they leave, he would see to it that they had very little left to do except to show up at the appointed times at the various activities.

First thing George had to do though was to get out of bed. There would be no one from now on to provide direction to do this or that. By the time he finished in the bath room, he heard other activity coming from other parts of the house. He walked into the kitchen to see Michelle working at the coffee maker and Jackie peering through the refrigerator for something that looked like breakfast food.

She mentioned as she saw him, "It could be worse. Could be that we have to eat a spinach casserole for breakfast if the eggs and bacon don't stretch far enough. How does that sound to you, Dad?"

"Sounds okay to me! Just feed me first," George said as he laughed. He laughed! Then they all laughed. Mike, Tom and Jason were sitting around the table. Seemed as they looked at each other, they realized they still had a family here.

This is life. Families grow and wane. As the thinning process occurs when loved ones pass, the remaining members pick up the slack and carry on. There could be less harmony or more harmony depending on who the remaining leaders were but the family survived nevertheless. George's stated desire was to keep the family together and communicating with each other for as long as possible. His ultimate desire was for all of them to be together on the other side of the veil. He knows now that was possible without question, and they should be able to build on this as they grew and as other family members came onto the scene. One thought, this depended to a great degree on how Dana and Katherine saw each other. Would they develop a bond strong enough to allow each of them to be a part of the long term extended family or would one of them be on the outside looking in? He hoped for the former.

The meeting with the funeral director went smoothly. Jackie, Jason, Mike, Stacie and George were in attendance. Visitation would be tonight at six; the Service at ten tomorrow at Pinecrest Methodist Church, with burial at Pleasant Hills Cemetery. Dana would be buried next to Katherine.

Funerals were occasions which brought remote members of family together. Cousins, surviving aunts and uncles, nieces and nephews were usually in attendance. Seeing them is good because as time goes by, there were fewer and fewer of them. Gone were the times when family reunions occurred. Once the grandparents passed on, the reasons for family reunions passed on as well it seemed. So, the occasions for visiting with them were funerals.

Sometimes, weddings were another place when family members gathered but usually not all of them. Of course, lots of family members received invitations; same as for graduations. The expectation usually was that not all family members would attend. Funerals, weddings and graduations created family gatherings, but the main one was funerals.

Once George passed on, his children would find fewer and fewer occasions to be together at one time. That was too bad, because they all got along so well and were close. Maybe one of them would take the lead to host parties for the whole group on occasion. When do they cease calling them parties and start calling them reunions?

George knew when they would start them up again. When they passed through, they would begin having their gatherings as they assembled at Home. At any rate, Dana's funeral went well. Maybe she was watching. He wondered, "What is the rule about someone watching his or her own funeral. I think she would have been proud of the turnout with the messages delivered and all the flowers and gifts made on her behalf. I'll spend the better part of a week acknowledging all our friends and relatives for attending and for their support."

Unknown to George, the attendance at Dana's funeral also brought out a near record attendance from Home. Every relative from Dana's and George's respective families who had passed through were seemingly in attendance. Even a large contingent of relatives from Katherine's family was there. This spoke well of her reputation. Like on Earth, many of the attendees had not seen each other for a long time. And like on Earth, these occasions proved to be the catalyst for family reunions of sorts. Everyone visited and everyone was caught up in a festive like atmosphere. All seemed to have a good time.

To tell the truth, there were usually more family residents from Home at funerals than family members on Earth. At Home, the probability of relatives coming from further up the ancestry line, such as great grandparents or great-great grandparents, attending were pretty good. After all, this was the best chance for them to see family members who were

Home residents as well as descendents who were still on Earth.

Yes, Dana was escorted to her funeral. In this case, her mom and grandparents were the escorts. She had a first chance to visit with a lot of relatives she hadn't seen in many years. She enjoyed the occasion, if you can call a funeral an enjoyable occasion. What bothered her the most, of course was seeing George and her children as they went through the agonies of saying farewell for one last time. Of this group, she knew, however, that George and she would be talking before long. She thought he held up well for that very reason.

It'd only been two days since the accident. Katherine and Dana had a chance to catch up at the funeral as well. Dana had just completed the reconciliation part of orientation and was ready to finish up the rest of the orientation program.

"I talked to Margaret yesterday to see if you have any time on your schedule to let me take you out to my house," Katherine mentioned. "If you want to go, we can take the trip sometime tomorrow."

"I'd like that," Dana said. "Come around anytime and we'll go out. From your description and the one I got from George's dad, it sounds like a beautiful area full of scenery waiting to be put on canvas. If it works out, Margaret says I could move my temporary residency there soon."

"I've been working on some ideas for adding a complex for you if you like what you see," Katherine said not forgetting that they still need to talk about other issues. "When you're there and if you're ready, we can go over the suggestions. If they're close enough, we can visit the group who design living quarters."

"How long will that take?" Dana asked.

Katherine replied, "The Design Section, as they are called, will take a couple of days. We can look at their plans one more time. At that time, if you're satisfied, all I have to do is go through the routine of requesting the addition. At that point, have your bags packed because the addition will be ready for you. Stuff like this happens fast here at Home. You'll be pleasantly surprised."

"Sounds good! There are still some things we should probably discuss. Maybe we can do that tomorrow," Dana replied. "I've had some travel training so I shouldn't be a burden on anyone to get around; at least on a limited basis. I want to thank you for the invitation to stay close to you and George's folks. I mentioned this to Mom and, if we decide to be roommates, she may try to put a place nearby so I can see her on a more regular basis. Do you think that'll be all right?" Dana asked.

"That'll be fine. I hope we can make this work," Katherine said.

After the funeral, almost everyone went back to George's home for a final get together before the family started to break up and return to their respective homes. Mike and Stacie decided to stay on through the weekend. They talked to Jackie and Jason and decided that George needed someone close by for a couple of days. Since Jackie and Jason both lived in the Atlanta area, they went back home but expected to return for the weekend as well.

George was glad they were staying and glad that the two oldest would be back for the weekend. It seemed to him there were plenty leftovers from all the food that came in, so no major cooking projects loomed for anyone. He was glad for the extra time to spend with Mike and Stacie's children, Todd and Lisa. Being as they all live outside Atlanta, he sees them the least. They're into everything. They can navigate well but haven't quite learned the meaning of the word 'No' yet.

For him the worst time of the whole affair occurred Sunday afternoon as Mike and Stacie departed for the airport. Jason transported them in his big Chevy Suburban. Jackie was already home with her family. Jason's family was home as well.

George found himself home alone for the first time. It was more devastating than he thought it would be. Fresh memories of Dana, his children and grandchildren were everywhere. This was going to be a bad night. It would be good if he could contact Katherine to check on her and Dana. He hoped he was emotionally stable enough and could get himself calmed down so that the link could be made.

After turning off the TV and making sure the outside doors were closed, he sat in his favorite recliner and began to force a level of calmness on himself. When he thought he was ready, he said, "Katherine, are you here?" Nothing happened. He waited a good five minutes and began the routine once again; only this time he tried to concentrate harder.

Once again, "Katherine, are you here?"

Katherine was nervous as she made her way to Dana's temporary home in the arrival station. She knew this was the time for her and Dana to have their chat. She hoped it went well. Deep down, she had the feeling that a lot was riding on what would transpire today.

Dana was ready. She knew some of the things she wanted to talk to Katherine about. She knew those things would likely branch off into other areas. Deep down, she wasn't at all sure how this would come out. She only had the vaguest of ideas of the outcome she wanted. Katherine had presented her with a really good outcome. Secretly, she hoped this could be achieved.

When Katherine arrived, she found Dana looking through some old family albums; some pictures that George maintained were taken during the time she was leukemia free with Jackie and Jason as toddlers. He always wanted all four children to remember how the family was originally formed.

Dana looked up from the pictures and smiled as Katherine made her way in from the foyer, "Good morning! Well, it seems like morning to me for some reason," Dana said.

"Good morning to you, too. From a time standpoint, morning is as good a descriptor as any," Katherine said as she gave Dana a warm smile in return, "I see you're looking through some old albums. I hadn't realized you and George had hung onto those old pictures of me and the kids," she added as she glanced over Dana's shoulder.

"Yes, George felt it was important for the kids to realize how we all came to be together. You were an important part of the initial equation. Thinking back on it, I agree with his thinking. Do you want to sit down or do you want to go on back to your place?" Dana asked.

"We could go back and give you a chance to look around. Not that we need it but I've put together a tray of food along with some coffee and juices. You can bring the album with you if you like," Katherine said in return.

Dana stood and took Katherine's hand. With the other hand, she held onto the album. "Might as well let Katherine keep this if she wants," Dana thought.

Katherine issued the travel instruction and they were off. They arrived into a great room filled with light and flowers and plants. Though the outside door, Dana could see a swimming pool with the lake and mountains beyond. What a beautiful place. Her immediate thoughts were, "This is a great place. Who wouldn't want to live here? But first things first, there are some discussions to get through."

Katherine gave her a thorough tour and explained how they might change things around if Dana thought she might like to live here. She showed her a couple of extra rooms that could be used as temporary quarters until Dana decided. They returned to the great room and walked out to the patio to a table with food and coffee Katherine had set up.

Dana helped herself followed by Katherine. They both took comfortable chairs facing the pool and the expanse beyond. "This is a beautiful place," Dana said to Katherine.

"Thank you!" Katherine responded, "It wasn't always like this. It has evolved over the years as I thought of other things to add."

"I love it," Dana added, then, on a more serious note, "Katherine, can I say a few things which have been on my mind since before I passed through?"

"Yes, I've felt for some time now there may be some things we need to say to each other," Katherine said.

"Okay, first, let me give you some things from my background. I was raised in a home with a brother and sister by my mom who provided the bulk of the care and support we received. My dad was in and out, mostly out, for extended periods of time and rarely helped her either financially or physically. Mom finally became fed up and forced him out altogether. My brother, sister and I were very bitter, sometimes blaming Dad and sometimes Mom. I didn't realize how tough it was on Mom until I was in college. To a degree, however, I was lucky. I was able to land a tennis scholarship to Auburn. However, before I started my first semester, I stupidly ran off with a high school sweetheart and was secretly married. This almost derailed my chances at the scholarship. Worse though, the guy turned out to be a first class jerk. He didn't attend college and only took menial jobs. Soon, he was running around on me. After my third year, I was so messed up mentally, I almost flunked out of school. He and I parted ways and I vowed never to let that happen again. Then after about six months, I was visiting Monica, and she insisted we go to this meeting at her church. That's where I met George. Monica introduced us. I guess it'd been some months after you passed through. He was pitiful looking. I felt sorry for him, but for some reason, I was attracted to him. We started dating. That's when I learned about Jackie and Jason. I fell in love with them and George at the same time. We were married as soon as I graduated and my life changed forever. I was so happy; George seemed so happy. I hoped my bad memories were behind me forever.

"Then came the day, actually the third day, I found George coming out of what I thought was a mid day nap. This was unusual for it to happen one time let alone three. I panicked, I guess, and forced him to tell me what was going on. I thought he was having some sort of health problems what with his elevated weight. Instead, the news of the Link hit me like a wall of water. The second wave was, unfortunately, when he told me he was talking to you. I didn't believe the story about the Link and I couldn't believe he was thinking or talking to you. All the past issues I had with my first husband flooded my mind and I reacted badly. I'm so sorry." Dana said as she sat looking alternatively at Katherine and into her lap with her hands folded.

Katherine sat listening closely to Dana's story as she watched her face and felt a wave of compassion overtake her as she responded, "Dana, dear Dana, there is absolutely nothing for you to apologize to me for. You had some tough times until George came along. I know how wonderful he is and how he can build you up to where you feel like you're on top of the world. Almost from the start, I watched as you entered their lives and how you so beautifully gave of yourself and gave them the hope and love they needed to pull themselves out of the terrible doldrums they were in from my passing. I was so happy for all of you. Never, ever did I experience the first pang of jealousy for what you had and what I had given up. Even now, I want so badly for you to be okay with all that's happened. Together, I believe we can help each other. Together, I believe we can help George as he struggles to bring his life back into order. Having said that, I don't want you to think I am trying to come between you and George or to make any decisions for you. My purpose is to support both of you and help however I can. I've been here too long and have too much else going on for me to try to force myself back on George to the exclusion of you. He loves you; you are the one he grieves for now. He needs your support and will want to know that you are okay with your present situation. I want to help you, not only because of my past feelings for George but out of the great respect I've developed for you over the years."

Dana found herself weeping, no sobbing, as Katherine delivered those last words. She had no idea you could sob in Heaven. She was watching Katherine with the tears streaming down her face. She stood and walked the few steps toward Katherine. Katherine stood to face her. They embraced for the longest time as they both were now crying. Slowly, peace and calmness fell across them as they pulled back and looked at each other. Both were smiling and started to laugh as if they had found long lost friends.

Dana backed away from Katherine and looked around. Her critically artistic eye began to take in the landscape seemingly now for the first time. She realized again how beautiful this place was. "Katherine," she asked, "Is the offer for me to move here permanently still open?"

"Yep!" Katherine replied with a big smile she couldn't seem to wipe off her face.

"Katherine," Dana began again, "Sometime in the future, maybe the way off future, George will be passing through. If he hasn't found anyone else to be his partner by then, do you think he might like to live here with us? After all, I've heard there is no sex in Heaven that might hinder our relationships."

Katherine laughed for the second time, "He might! Let's hope he will." She couldn't believe her ears. Dana has already taken this way beyond anything she could possibly have hoped for. They hugged again as they made their way over to the table to refresh their coffee and grab more snacks.

Katherine was relaxing at the lake home when she thought she heard the call. Dana happened to be with her. "Dana, I believe George may be trying to contact me. If this is him, please be ready and we'll go together. Be ready to take my hand when I signal you," she said.

"I'm ready," Dana said. She hadn't been around George since the day of the funeral and wanted desperately to see him. The added bonus would be to talk to him through Katherine.

A few minutes went by. No call came through. Then, Katherine heard the call again, stronger and more distinct this time. She gave Dana the signal and took her hand and issued the travel instruction. Next she said, "Yes George, I'm here."

George was much relieved and almost lost the link with her but he held on. "Thank goodness you've come. I'm alone for the first time and it's killing me. I was hoping against hope you'd come," he said.

"If you like the news that I'm here, then I'll double your happiness. Dana's with me. She's watching you and listening as we speak," Katherine said as she stood on one side of the recliner watching George's face while Dana stood on the other side. Neither wanted to be too far away from him.

He almost lost the link again. He thought it a good idea to warn them, "If the link breaks, please hang around and I'll try to re-establish it. I've learned my emotions are getting in the way today. I'm having to force myself to remain as calm as possible. I can tell you though, the thought of both of you here with me at one time is just about more than I can take. Needless to say, I'm pretty happy about all this," he explained.

George thought, "At least, I'm happy they're together. If they can't be with me then they need to be with each other." He, of course, had no idea about the emotional exchange they just had. These two people have been the most important people in his life. He could almost characterize his life as two lifetimes, one with each of them. Now he expects them to be there until he can join them, whenever that is.

Katherine said, "George, dear George, we both want to know how you're holding up."

"Well, I'm doing pretty well, I think. I had a burst of emotions when you both showed up now. I believe it's under control. No doubt, it'd be much worse if this link didn't exist. I wish she were here with us. How's she adjusting to things there?" he asked.

"She's fine. She is here with us. The only problem is you can't hear or see her. Whenever she completes her orientation and you two can begin to talk, I'm sure she'll fill you in on her first impressions," Katherine said not wanting to bring up the fact that Dana got lost her first day and had a grand adventure. "She's with me now because she was at my place by the lake when you called."

"Is she through orientation? I don't understand how she can be with you."

"She was taking a break. I'd invited her out to go over plans to add some rooms for her to live with me. How do you like that?" Katherine asked as both of them smiled.

"Live with you! I think that's great; actually it makes me very happy," he added quickly.

"During her orientation, she'll be at my place in her off time rather than staying at the arrival station," Katherine added.

"How long will it take to have the rooms added? Do you have space for her meanwhile?" he asked.

"It'll take about three or four days before it's all done and yes, I have the space for her until that's done," Katherine added.

"Three or four days? My word, how can it get done in that short a time?" he asked in an astounding tone.

Katherine said, "That's the way things get done here. Most things I get take a lot less time than that. Don't forget, we're not on Earth anymore."

"By the way, I forgot to tell you last time we talked when the boys were sleeping with me I got into a question and answer session again with Stewart. Did you know he was so curious about all this stuff?" he asked Katherine.

"Yes, I've noticed. He has some special qualities for a boy his age," she said.

"I know he's a small boy but the way he probes, tells me he has a really sensitive mind. You, by chance, didn't put him up to the questions he asked me that got all this started, did you?" he asked her.

"No, that wasn't me," Katherine said, "I can't say I know of anyone who did that. I'm not aware of any way one of us who could have prompted him."

"I told the boys a secret that night," George said. "I told them how to contact Dana. First, though, I asked if they loved her enough to form the Link needed for all this. I doubt anything comes of it but now someone else besides me knows about the link. Tell Dana not to be surprised if Stewart makes contact someday if he doesn't forget what I told him. Is there anyway to determine if a Link like this is possible?"

"She heard you. I don't know," Katherine replied. "Dana is nodding. She'll ask about this during orientation."

"Well, I don't know about you guys but I'm dead tired. Unlike you, I do need my beauty sleep. Tomorrow, I have to start getting my life and this house in order and establish new routines. I remember all this from my first time through this. At least this time, I don't have two small children looking at me through those big eyes they had then. Is it okay if I call it a day? Can I contact you tomorrow? Can I contact you every day? I think this will be part of my new daily regimen, if you don't mind," he stated.

"George, get a good night's sleep. You deserve it. Dana sends her love as do I. Call me every day if you like," Katherine said as they both, in turn, kissed him on each cheek unbeknownst to him. They had both started crying as they listened to his last few sentences.

"Good night, I love you both," George said as a last comment. He broke the link as he pulled himself out of the recliner. All of a sudden, he was starving. "Wonder what's left in the fridge after all this company. Gotta clean it out this week anyway," he said to no one in particular, except Dana and Katherine heard him, "I guess talking to two women at once will work on your appetite." They laughed at this last comment.

Dana and Katherine watched as George pulled himself off the recliner and made his way to the fridge. Katherine had to make a comment, "Dana, did George's comment about his love for both of us upset you?"

Dana looked at her as she thought about the question, "No, not anymore. My mind is at peace and my desire is to help George. He had feelings for you well before I came alone, feelings that were disrupted by your passing through. He's entitled to those now as he sorts out all that's ahead of him." They both watched as George quietly ate his snack and made his way to bed. They left after he turned out the light, both still close to tears knowing how lonely he must be feeling.

The next couple of months went by slowly. Routines were newly established for a single older gentleman of whom George was now one. Much of the house remained unchanged except for the clothing and other personal items Dana left with him that day. He invited all the girls, that is, Jackie, Michelle, Elizabeth and Stacie, in to see if there was anything they might want. After they finished, he made a trip to Goodwill which was very appreciative of the quality and quantity of items they received.

George learned that being retired was now more of a burden than before, primarily because he had no one in particular with whom to share the large blocks of time retirees often have. He thought about going back to work full time. His old boss let him know that he could use him if that's what George wanted. He thought, "I think maybe I'll look at more part time activities either as a volunteer or in a paying job. Maybe I'll do some consulting."

Besides, if he had some part time activities, he could continue his twice weekly outings with Marvin and Bill. They re-started their golf outings the very first week after the funeral. George wanted it and his friends were glad to accommodate. Interestingly, he found himself being the first one at the club and the last to leave. After all, they had responsibilities at home he no longer had.

In addition to golf, Bill and Laverne along with Marvin and Monica always included him in their plans. Whether they went to a movie, to dinner or both, he was always invited and almost always attended. He went to all the cookouts. He even hosted some on occasion. They were fun. He, for sure, was always the odd man out but he didn't mind. They seemed not to mind either. It was too early for them to consider any sort of matchmaking activities. He had absolutely no desire to do anything like that anyway and awaited the first opportunity to make them aware of his choice to stay single. He figured one of them would bring it up one day and he was ready with his answer.

George had spent a lot of time with Jackie and Jason's families. Whenever he was at Jason's, it never failed but that Stewart gave him a run down on his attempts to call Dana. Obviously, the boy had not forgotten and, just as obvious, he was persistent. It was too bad Dana was still in Orientation; or else, she would likely be having conversations with him. It would be interesting to see if a genuine link exists between the two that'll enable their talks. Apparently he and Michael have kept their secrets.

George had also traveled to visit Mike and Stacie's families and spent about a week with each one. Their little ones were growing and beginning to form words. Stacie seemed to be agreeable to expanding their family.

George had daily conversations with Katherine; usually, about the same time every day. It was a hit or miss as to whether Dana was available. Apparently, their schedule of hours for orientation activities was significantly different than work schedules here on Earth. Here, work consisted of eight hour shifts as a regular regimen. There, in the orientation programs, the sessions appeared to go for hours longer. After all, residents apparently required no sleep so they go for much longer periods of time.

George also stayed in touch with his dad and mom. She worried about him. He had added a little more weight. He didn't have Dana to watch his diet as before. His annual physical was coming up shortly and the bet was his lecture this year would be about the dangers of carrying this extra weight, same lecture as last year. He was not much overweight, however, maybe only ten pounds.

George had been unable to find out what Dana was going through in orientation except information about the new skills she was mastering. It seemed she had mastered the art of travel and of shopping and acquiring things. She said she had been to a huge mall to acquire who knows what. He got the impression there was some kind of story about the mall that he didn't know yet. That would come, he supposed. No information at all had been forthcoming about her reconciliation process except she seemed to have passed with flying colors.

Maybe there would be some news tonight when he contacted Katherine. At 8 o'clock, he sat down in his recliner. This was about the time he called every night. It helped

Katherine and her scheduling. So far, he hadn't sensed her tiring of these nightly chats. He began to concentrate and clear his mind, "Katherine, are you here?"

Very quickly, she answered, "Yes George, I'm here. Dana's with me tonight with some news. Why don't you try calling her?" They'd been anxiously waiting.

"You mean she's graduated and I can talk to her directly?" George quickly asked as he felt his pulse rate jump.

"Yes, you have my permission to sign off. I'll just listen if that's okay," Katherine stated.

"Okay, good night, Katherine, and thanks," he said quickly.

Now, he had to redo the routine of beginning his concentration stage followed by the clearing of the mind stage. He was very excited. They were probably watching. Yes, they were watching.

Dana had, indeed, been watching George as he began his conversation with Katherine. Since the calls had been nightly and at about the same time every day, Katherine had taken the advance step of arriving at George's house just ahead of his call. This eliminated the hesitation George experienced in his early calls.

Dana watched as George signed off with Katherine and as he began the process of initiating the call to her. She was excited. Just then, she heard the message, "Grannie, are you here?"

This was confusing. Why would George call her Grannie? Then it dawned on her. This wasn't George calling. Her senses told her it was Stewart. She could ignore the call but decided against it. "Katherine, I have a call coming in from Stewart. I'll be back here as soon as I talk to him. Will you please wait in case George gets confused?"

"My goodness," Katherine said, "Yes, I'll wait," as they exchanged glances.

In an instant, Dana departed from her old home and was now in Stewart's bedroom, "Yes Stewart, I'm here. This is Grannie." Dana said gently.

The shout came loudly and almost broke the link that Stewart all of a sudden found himself tied to. "Grannie, is it really you?" Stewart said very loudly.

"Yes, it's me, how're you doing?" Dana asked. She couldn't believe it. Seems George was right after all. There was no telling how long Stewart had been trying this; let's find out. "Stewart, how long have you been trying to call me?"

"Grannie," she could still hear the excitement in his voice, "I've been trying everyday for a month. I'd just about given up. I miss you. Why can't I see you? I can hear you but I can't see you," he said.

"I don't think that's allowed," she said.

"Are you in Heaven, Grannie," he asked.

"Yes I am," she decided to keep the sentences short. No need to overload this six year old with technical details such as correct names. Go with what he's familiar with.

Suddenly, from the hallway, Dana heard Michelle say, "Stewart, who're you talking to so loudly?" as she opened the door to Stewart's bedroom. Michelle looked at him in bed; she looked around the room and saw no one else. "Are you on the phone with one of your friends or were you asleep and talking in your dreams?" She went over and felt his forehead to see if, by chance, he had a fever.

As soon as the door opened, the link between Stewart and Dana was broken because he had to direct his attention to his mom. "Mom, I'm sorry I was talking so loudly. I was talking to Grannie," he said in his best proud voice as he sat up and thrust out his chest. Indeed, he felt as if he deserved a medal.

Dana continued to watch the drama unfolding. No doubt, Stewart was going to have a hard time convincing his mom he hadn't been dreaming.

Michelle said, "So you were dreaming. That's okay; Grannie would love to know that."

"She does know. She said she was in Heaven. If you don't believe me, ask her yourself. Go ahead!" Stewart implored. "Grannie, please tell her."

Michelle and Dana could do nothing more than just stand there watching his sweet face. Dana couldn't answer either of them. The link was with Stewart and without knowing it, the link broke when he turned his attention to his mom.

Michelle, however, could talk to him. She reached down with her hand and gently caressed his cheek as she leaned over and kissed his forehead. "I'm sorry, Stewart, I can't hear her. Perhaps it was a dream after all. Why don't you go back to sleep and see if you can reach her again?"

"Mom, it was real. I heard her. Grandad told me how to do it and this was the first time it worked. Can I call him?" Stewart implored. He was now thoroughly confused. After all this time following what Grandad had told him about the link, he found himself talking to Grannie; only now she won't say anything. Was he dreaming?

"Grandad, huh," she made a mental note to talk to him tomorrow or the next time she saw him, "Okay, I'll talk to him. Meanwhile, you need to get to sleep. You have a lot of playing to do tomorrow and you'll need all the strength you can muster," she said smiling at her very bright son.

"Yes," Dana thought as she watched the drama unfold and Stewart's frustration, "I'll talk to him myself."

George tried for the third time to reach Dana, "Dana, are you here?" If this didn't work this time, he told himself, he would call Katherine back to see if he had missed something in the routine.

This time Dana heard the call. She left Stewart's bedroom and returned to their old family room. Katherine was still there and she smiled as Dana re-entered the room. "Yes, George, I'm here," she replied.

"Is it really you? It sounds like you. You sound so good. Are you okay? This was my third try to reach you. Did I mess something up?" he kept saying.

"George, relax. I'm here. You didn't mess up. What you got was a busy signal," she explained.

"A busy signal; you mean you were on another call," he said.

Dana laughed, "Yes, that's what I mean. Apparently, just as you were getting ready to call, Stewart dialed in ahead of you. Do you remember that secret you told him some months back? Well, according to him, he's been trying every day since then. This was the first day I'm allowed to receive calls and he beat you to it. Don't you think that's a hoot?" she laughed some more. Katherine was also laughing.

George thought a minute and laughed as well. Oops, he had to be careful not to break the link, he told himself. "You're telling me he's tried to call every day? He told me several times that he was trying. I thought by now perhaps he'd given up. I give him one thing, he's persistent."

"You know George," she said, "I noticed something about what Stewart was doing. I've watched you several times as you readied yourself to call Katherine. I remember myself having to concentrate and clear my mind as much as possible. Stewart was lying in bed, eyes open and looking around when I got there. Not like you and me when we had to be still and focus. He only broke the link when Michelle asked him why he was talking so loud."

"That is indeed interesting," George replied. "So Michelle heard him talking to you."

"Yes, and he confessed everything to her. He seemed pretty upset when I wouldn't talk to her. Of course by that time, he'd broken the link to me when he started talking to her and I couldn't talk to him either. I guess he was pretty frustrated. Michelle did a good job calming him down. She believes he was dreaming. She told him she'd talk to you later. Just a heads up," she explained.

"Thanks," he said, "You know, I never thought our first conversation would be this complicated. You sound great. I miss you terribly but things are getting better around here."

"I've watched you often over the past several months," she said, "I'm proud of the way you've held up and the way you've dealt with friends and children. I still love you. You are a good man, George Mason. I realize now how lucky I was all the years we were together. We can talk at your leisure from now on."

"Thanks, I'm still in love with you, too. Now I know I won't have to stop loving you because some day, I'll get to pick up where we left off. I guess this means you made it all the way through orientation and reconciliation. Was it tough? What kind of work will you be doing?" George asked.

"Everything went very smoothly; even the reconciliation process. I can't tell you anything about it but there were no hiccups. With my background, I'm going to work in the Art Institute. I expect to be teaching and I'll get to do my favorite thing, paint. This reminds me, I have a story to tell you about my first day here. Katherine held off saying anything until I could give you all the details," Dana stated.

"Well, I hope it was a positive experience for you. I certainly remember that day as well," George replied.

She winced a little at his statement even though there was no sadness in his voice now. He must've been absolutely devastated that day. "Yes, you'll like this," she started and hoped she sounded upbeat as she began the story from getting lost to meeting Monet and back home again.

George listened and thought to himself, "She's adjusted quite well." It was indeed a great story not to mention being unusual. "So, some people there think I'm a celebrity," he said picking up on the comments from the guy in the Information and Assistance Office. "Do you have the Monet hanging in a conspicuous place? By the way, how is it living by the lake with Katherine and Dad hanging around all the time?"

"You are a celebrity of sorts. I get a lot of comments and questions about you from other residents. More than a few are asking what you're going to do with your discovery. I have the Monet hanging over the mantel in our great room. The addition we put onto Katherine's place included a complete set of living quarters for me as well as a renovated great room where we spend most of our time together and talk about you. Quite often, your mom and dad visit us as well as my mom. She moved out to a new place close to us. Living there is great. If I can't be with you, I wouldn't want to be anywhere else," she stated.

George heard her comment about the questions on his intentions. Maybe it was time he did something. He was beginning to feel a little like the kid whose parents went home and left him at the mall. At the mall, there were plenty of things for the kid to do but after a bit, the ones who loved and provided comfort were not around. That's how George felt about now. The mall was great but he wanted to be among those who loved him. Only they could make the pain go away; the pain which was weighing his heart down.

"If I said I miss you all, would you understand?" he asked her.

"Yes, I believe we all would understand," she replied carefully.

"If I said I want to be with you all, would you understand?" he asked. He wanted their reaction to this seemingly innocent question but one that was loaded with dangerous undertones.

A few moments went by. He guessed they were talking among themselves; at least the ones who were here with

Dana. That was exactly what was happening. Katherine and Dana were trying to decide what he meant. At last came her reply, "No, this question has more than one connotation. Your real meaning is not understood very clearly. We understand you'd like to be with us. But, this is not your time yet. There'll be a day when you'll see us. We're pretty sure that day isn't today. No one knows when it'll come. We do know you're not the one who decides what day it'll be. Do you understand this statement?" she declared as a person speaking for many.

"Yeah, I think I understand. I have a role to play in this life on this stage. That role has more lines to deliver. I have people here who I care about very much and who care about me as well. I want to fulfill this role and take the final bows to my audience at the end of the final performance. I'm not about to abandon them by doing something to cut this run short. Nature will take its course and the good Lord will have his way. Please rest assured on that," George was careful to explain.

"Now, we understand you, and you understand us. We'll talk whenever you like. We'll visit whenever we like. You have things to do there. We have things to do here. One day sometime ahead of us, you'll be among us. Until that day, you're among your earthly family. Enjoy them as they grow and multiply," Dana said in summation as she stood with arms crossed looking at him. Katherine was similarly posed.

"You sound like the Dana of old. You always had a knack for keeping me on the straight and narrow," he added with a wide grin.

"Well, don't forget, I now have a lot of help with all the collective knowledge from your family here. There's only Katherine here with me now but perhaps I should bring the whole family if our conversations are going to lead us into these areas. I felt like I could've used their help for a moment back there," she added.

He was yawning and felt it was about his bedtime. "You guys may have all the energy in the world but I have to get my beauty rest. After all, I'm not as young as I used to be." He also felt some pains in his left arm and wondered what that was.

"Maybe a little exercise or smaller portions at the table is what you need," Dana volunteered.

"Don't start, woman. You're not supposed to be lecturing me, correct? Isn't there something about free will in play here?" he asked jokingly.

"Yeah, Mr. Smarty Pants, you go do what you will. You're the one who'll have to pay the price," she shot back as she glared down at him.

"This has been fun but I am a little tired. I'm really glad we can talk once again. It's too bad we can't bring all the family there into the conversation at one time," he said.

"In time! In time!" she exclaimed. "Good night, George," more than a little exasperated at their first conversation in months but extremely happy they were once again talking.

"Good night, Dana; good night, Katherine. My love to you both," George said as he broke the link. He thought, "I'm tired and going straight to bed. Maybe I'll watch Jay Leno first. Maybe tomorrow, I'll give Jason a call and invite all of them over for hamburgers and hot dogs this weekend. I want to see how they are treating Stewart after his little discovery. On second thought, maybe I'll wait until July 4th. All the family will be together then and it's only two weeks away. Maybe, it's time to bring this discovery out of the closet as some residents at Home seem to want."

Chapter 15

Sleep that night came quickly. George dreamed of Stewart and Dana. He dreamed of Katherine and Dad. He dreamed of Home. Would it really be like it has been described? He thinks so. The conversations he had no longer left him in doubt about either its existence or what it's like. Indeed, both of these characteristics seem worthy of advertisement.

He was awake at morning's first light. He has a new purpose. It seemed as though he had made the decision to go public. Yes, he has made the decision. Other questions now came to mind. How to go about this? Who would he tell first? Why should he do this?

The latter question is the one that deserved his immediate attention. Why do this? After all, there was a high degree of likelihood he would be ridiculed, labeled a nut case and a heretic and generally dismissed by most people. Why subject himself to all this at his advanced age? After all, sixty-seven seemed to be an advanced age, at least to him.

First off, if knowledge of this Link could become generally accepted by mankind, it stood to reason it may have a positive influence over behavior in general, at least over behavior between people. True, the existence of Heaven or an afterlife had been at the forefront of mankind's beliefs for millenniums. Except for the atheists or those possessing truly evil minds, almost everyone else strived to learn more and behave in such a way that they would become accepted in the version of afterlife they believed in.

Most people, Christians included, hoped there was a Heaven and hoped that one day they would pass through its pearly gates. There was that phrase, 'pass through'. If knowledge of its existence could become more or less fact, then the expectation of entering some day would heighten. With this knowledge in hand, people would begin to pay attention to the process which would enable them to increase the likelihood they would be among those who enter and not among those who don't.

The key to confirming Heaven's existence using this discovery, aside from the traditional route of developing faith from the teachings of the Bible, was to believe you could contact someone who had passed through already. This could only be done between two people who had developed a Link through the abiding love one gave another and receive abiding love in return.

The next important element in the process was actually making the first contact. Without making the contact and learning about Home through the Link, there could be no way this discovery would be meaningful. Those who made contact could help spread the knowledge. This knowledge and the spreading of it would begin to have positive influences over behaviors between people simply because the existence of Heaven would be more certain.

So then, what would be the best way to spread the news? It seemed to George that either going on TV or calling a press conference or writing a letter to the editor would not be effective in getting the news out. Certainly, more people would hear of it quicker. Just as certain, however, too many might dismiss the news out of hand. The subtleties about how to achieve a Link and who to achieve it with could likely be lost in the message.

No, it seemed to him the best way is to relay this message would either by one-on-one or in small groups. Such methods would give those who hear the message a chance to express their disbelief, question the messenger's sanity, waylay concerns and pinpoint the best way for them to achieve success. Members of the target group would probably need to be prescreened to make sure a person might be on the other side with whom a viable Link could likely be established. Once the subject was introduced, a follow up phone call or session would be helpful to allow time to establish a Link and provide feedback.

George believed he could effectively use Stewart's example as a way to get his children's attention. They were his first target. First, though, he must call this in. It's only 9 o'clock in the morning. He hadn't made a call this early yet. It would be interesting to see if anyone is awake at Home this time of day.

George assumed the now familiar position in his favorite recliner. He might have to get a new recliner if these calls continued at this pace. His cleared his mind as he asked, "Katherine, are you here?"

More than a few moments passed without an answer. "I'll give this a few moments more," he thought, "After all, there's no telling what goes on at Home this time of day."

Finally, "Yes, George, I'm here and how're you doing this fine morning?"

"I feel great. I appreciate you being available. Did I take you away from something important?"

"Well, I was beginning a new session with a new student. I had to bring in another teacher so I could answer your call," she said.

"I'm sorry about that. I apologize to you and your student. I know this is early but I've made a decision and wanted to tell you about it. To me, this seems important enough to let you know and to have you let anyone else know that might be interested. Is there anyone else with you?" he asked her.

Katherine hesitated as she thought about what type of decision George had made that would cause him to call this early, "No," she finally replied, "I'm alone. Do you think anyone else needs to hear this?"

"Could be! I'll let you decide after I tell you. Here goes! I've decided to go public with the discovery."

"You mean the discovery about the Link and what you've learned about Home?" she asked to confirm her understanding.

"Yes, but only about the discovery part. I'm not sure it would be wise to relay all that I've learned about Home. Could be if anyone believes me and tries the Link, they can learn about Home on their own," George responded.

"George, has anyone told you about the Elder who's been assigned to monitor these Links, as you call them?"

"No, I wasn't aware this had created such a stir," he responded.

"Okay, well give me a moment or two to see if he's currently monitoring us or if I can reach him otherwise. Don't break this Link, please. I'll just be a moment," she implored.

"All right, I'll standby."

She was gone many moments. How long is a moment anyway? After about a minute or so, she came back, "George, are you still here?"

"Yes, I'm here."

"George, an Elder by the name of Eli is here with me. If it's okay with you, he would like to join our conversation and speak to you. I will listen in," she added.

All of a sudden, he was confused. How could the Elder speak to him if he's already on a call with Katherine?

The answer came in a smooth rich baritone voice, "Hello, George. My name is Eli. As Katherine has told you, I'm an Elder here at Home. I have been assigned to watch over you since you discovered how to communicate with Katherine for which you have adopted the term 'Link' as a descriptor. I like it. Is it all right if I talk to you for a moment?" Eli asked in a more formal tone.

Eli has been an Elder for about 1500 years. Prior to that, he had been a resident like everyone else for another 300 years. Not many residents here even know that most Elders were once been residents themselves. Most residents believe all Elders were part of the Home scene from the beginning of the world. Not so! The need for Elders was greater now because more residents were at Home than there were in the beginning. There were so few of them then. Also, recruitment of Elders from among residents was fairly secretive. It involved many factors and involved changes in physical appearances to shield their true identities. Eli had been here so long, he rarely thought of his prior status and even less about the time when he walked the Earth.

"Certainly!" George responded with more than a mild curiosity about Eli.

"By the way," Eli explained, "Katherine told you only one can talk to you at a time. That's true only between residents. Elders, as we are called, have a few more capabilities and can enter conversations if needed. I picked this concern up from your thought processes just now. Maybe one day, we can explain more about these abilities to you. This Link gives you the ability to carry on a three way conversation with both of us."

"I'd love to learn more about that one day," George said as this seemed like an important offer.

"Fine! Katherine tells me you have made a decision to tell other people about the Link," Eli stated.

Wow! It seemed that he had readily adopted his term for this process. "Yes, I wanted to let Katherine and anyone else know before I began the unveiling process to see if this was all right," he added.

"First, yes, I do like your term 'Link'. I believe we'll adopt it to describe these conversations. Remember, I can hear your thoughts even though Katherine cannot. Secondly, at this point, I can't tell you to go ahead or not. What I'm interested to know is the thought process you went through in making the decision. At first, I was aware of your hesitation to tell anyone about this, including Dana. Now you have changed your position. Can you tell me why?" Eli asked.

"Well, it seemed to me that if the information about the Link could be properly communicated here on Earth that it could act as a positive influence on people's behavior. They'd have a higher certainty of the existence of Heaven, and this might motivate them to behaviors that would aid them in gaining entrance. It might also help prevent behaviors that would act against their entrance. If this makes sense, I'm willing to put myself through the potential trouble and problems with trying to spread information of this magnitude. I hope no one labels me a heretic. I believe this information is pretty important. One reason I've hesitated this long is that I couldn't figure out a way to approach the issue," George explained.

"George, remember, we cannot tell you what to do," Eli explained, "I believe you are familiar with the concept of 'freewill'. With freewill, you can do as you see fit. I can tell you, however, that your reasoning is well thought out and well founded. Your concept of doing what you feel is best for the people will always be well received here by all of us ... and the Powers that be. If you decide to carry forward with this idea, we wish you the best of luck even if there's not much that we can do to aid and assist you."

"Thank you for your comments. I didn't hear anything negative about the idea in your statement. My plan, therefore, is to proceed but in a cautious manner. I want to be effective, and I want to build a force of believers who'll help spread the word. I'm not trying to negate any efforts by the Christian faiths as they go about their work. I hope all of this will eventually be embraced by the various Faiths as their members begin trying the process," George added as further explanation.

"Again, your reasoning is sound. Good luck to you, George," Eli added, "We will be watching. It could be that we'll have to add another department here just to monitor these Links if they begin to multiply and spread."

"Can I ask why this has not happened before?" he asked.

"All I can tell you is that it's not because of something here. In my opinion, the world was not ready to accept this concept in the few instances when someone on Earth uncovered the Link. In fact, I believe the word Heretic was used in at least a couple of cases. With your ideas however, I doubt this will happen to you. I say stick to your plan and you should be okay," he explained. "We believe you are a good man, George. A lot of people here will be watching, residents and Elders alike. One day, perhaps we can have more conversations about all this. If you have no other questions or comments now, I will bow out of this Link and let you and Katherine continue. Good luck!"

"Thank you for your comments. I would, indeed, like to have more conversations with you. Good day, sir," George answered with more than a little bit of awe. Some of his original suspicions about the Church seemed well founded. Church leaders of olden days were very suspicious of anything off the beaten path. Anyone bringing forward progressive or new ideas were, for the most part, dismissed or perhaps drummed out of the church as in ex-communicated.

With that Eli was gone, out of the Link. He had no idea if Eli was still around or not. "Katherine, are you still here?" he asked.

"Yes, yes, I am," she said, "I must say, that was most impressive."

"What're you talking about?"

"The fact that an Elder came; the fact that he spoke to you and the fact that he spoke so long and in such a complimentary fashion," she added.

"So this is unusual?" he asked.

"I really believe so," she said, "Several people, maybe twenty or so, have joined us. No one can ever recall this happening. We're kind of speechless. This has to mean your undertaking will be considered a significant event and will be watched by many. I would venture the opinion that you'll have lots of visitors from now on particularly as you begin the process of rolling this out, not that you'll ever know."

"Well," George thought, "Freewill or not, looks like I've committed myself to this in a much bigger way than I anticipated. I've put a target on my back and probably on my chest as well. I don't know if this will mean anything in history, but it'll sure have an impact on me and my life ahead. It doesn't change my basic plan to go at this slow, however. Right now, I've got some planning to do and a July 4th party to get ready for. My guests are going to play a more important role this year than ever before."

The 4th of July fell on Monday this year. George expected his children and grandkids to be here most of the weekend. Mike and Stacie would be here with their families. They were driving in from Cincinnati and St. Louis, respectively. He understood they would be hanging around during the week following his gathering to visit with their in-laws.

Of course, Jason and Jackie, with their families, would be here. He expected them all to arrive Saturday and be at his house until late Monday. He had an outing planned for

Six Flags on Sunday. "It'll probably be really crowded but we'll have fun; we always do, of course, unless it rains," he thought.

Dana would not be here this year to manage the affairs in the kitchen. Jackie would take charge of that. He would be cooking pork shoulders from early Monday until about mid afternoon when they would begin the feasting. "Makes me hungry just thinking about it," he thought.

George had a lot of preparations to do, house cleaning, yard work, buying up supplies, laying things out, even pre-buying some Six Flags tickets, the kind where you don't have to stand in line.

He also had to plan his session with the kids about the Link. He would like to do this late Saturday before bedtime. Hopefully, he can spend a little time with Stewart beforehand to find out how he was doing and if he had any further conversations with Dana. He had to 'arrange' for all his children and their wives to be in one place at one time and to guide the conversation around to Stewart's experience. The boy didn't know it, nor would he understand, but he would be the catalyst. George had not quite figured out how yet, but Stewart would be a main player.

George intended to retrieve the letters he gave Bill and give them out at the end of their discussion. That's so they would have something in writing that described the process. Hopefully, he would give them something to think about before they got to sleep the first night. Having made his decision, he'd rather tell them face to face than have them read something Bill would give them after he was gone. He thought, "If they're going to think I'm crazy, I'd rather have the chance to defend myself. Besides, I want to encourage them to try the Link, preferably the weekend before they go home. Knowing them, some will try it. Maybe one or two will succeed."

For all of his kids, their Link would probably be with Dana. He should alert her. Maybe Katherine would tell her. For their spouses, he was not sure who they would Link with. He needed to probe this in their session. "Oh boy, they're all gonna think I'm nuts," he thought.

The two weeks flew by very quickly. George stayed busy and even managed to get in a couple of rounds of golf with Bill and Marvin. However, he did forget to retrieve the letters he gave Bill. That was all right, he could reprint them from his computer. The holiday weekend was slated to be hot and muggy. Thunderstorms could be expected to visit any afternoon. Maybe they would stay away for the Sunday outing.

Luckily, all the kids arrived within about an hour of each other, Jackie with her family first; followed by Mike, Stacie and lastly, Jason. This was the first gathering of his group since Dana's accident. All of them, grandchildren included, seemed somber when they first arrived. However, after they saw what he'd done with the place and all the effort he put into planning the weekend, they brightened up and, pretty soon, all were back to normal. It probably helped them to see he was feeling okay about the new state of affairs and was smiling and laughing.

George's moment with Stewart came right after they arrived. Jason, Stewart and he were unloading their van. Jason had walked into the house from the garage leaving Stewart and him struggling with the next load. Of course with Stewart only being about seven now, he was doing this mainly for show. George admired his courage in wanting to help.

"Stewart, my man, how have you been?" he asked.

"Fine!"

"Have you been staying out of trouble?" he probed a little further.

"Yep, huh, I mean yes sir," the boy corrected himself.

"You know, I've been meaning to ask you something," George said as he looked at him and then looked around to see if anyone else was within earshot. "Do you remember the last time we were together when you, Michael and I were about to go to sleep in my big bed?"

"Yes, I remember."

"Do you remember the secret I told you and Michael about talking to Grannie?" he asked as he watched Stewart closely.

Stewart stopped struggling with the bag he was trying to dislodge, turned and looked at George a few moments before replying, "Yes, I remember."

"Did you try what I suggested?"

"Yes, I did. I tried a lot of times. One time she answered me and you know what?" he asked as he peered into my eyes.

By now, George was kneeling beside the boy and they were eyeball to eyeball. "What?" George asked.

"My mom heard me. I guess I was talking too loud. When I told her I was talking to Grannie, she said I was dreaming. Was I dreaming, Grandad?" he asked in a pleading sort of way.

George smiled at him, hugged him tight and said, "No, you were not dreaming. Have you talked to her since then?"

"Yes… some… a couple of times, maybe more. I haven't told Mom. Why? You aren't going to tell Mom are you?" he implored. "She doesn't know. I might get into trouble, you think?"

"First, I'll tell you that I've talked to Grannie too. I haven't told your mom…or your dad either as a matter of fact. I'm glad to hear that you've talked to her again. I think that's important for you to do that. You know what else I think?" George asked smiling at him.

"No, what?"

"I think I need to tell your mom that I've talked to Grannie too," he said.

"Aren't you afraid that she'll fuss at you like she did me?" Stewart asked.

"Well, I'll bet she was more concerned about you getting your sleep than her meaning to fuss at you for doing something wrong. When I tell her that I've talked to Grannie, she might be concerned about me like she was you. In fact, your dad might be concerned and Aunt Jackie, Aunt Stacie and Uncle Mike. But, I'd really like to tell her... and all of them. Would you like to help me?" George asked him.

"Help you do what?"

"Help me tell them. You wouldn't be afraid to do that would you?"

"Wow, I don't know," he said drawing back a little.

"You see, Stewart, when I tell them, I want to tell them what I told you. I want to tell them how they can talk to Grannie, too. I bet they miss Grannie like you and I do. I bet that if they could talk to her, they would feel better. What do you think?" George asked gently as he held onto Stewart's little hands.

Stewart looked at George for a moment and began to smile, "Yeah, they might feel better. Yes, I'll help. What do you want me to do?" He was now on board.

"Maybe tonight, I'll get'em all together and start telling them. When I do, I may come get you so you can hear. I may ask you some questions about how you did it and all you have to do is answer some questions. Does this sound okay? You can sit by me or on my lap if you want to," George added.

"Okay, I'll do it," he smiled.

Just then Jason came back outside and said, "Well what have you guys been up to? Am I going to have to unload this van all by myself? Boy, where can you get some good help around here?" he said as he walked by and tussled Stewart's hair.

"We were having a little chat, if you don't mind," George said to Jason, "Grandson to grandfather talk, no fathers allowed," he added.

Jason grinned, "Well, okay then. Can I get some help now?" They all laughed.

George winked at Stewart who had a wide grin. "I'm not sure if he knows how to wink yet," George thought.

Everyone finally settled in for the afternoon and evening. Grandchildren were running around, George's children were catching up with each other. Everyone had an enjoyable afternoon. The evening meal was particularly difficult to prepare. It consisted of calling in a pizza order to Domino's. Lots of cheese pizza for the young ones and various combinations for the older group.

George helped the others clear the tables after the meal. Toward the end and before any of the adults scattered, he casually mentioned, "Hey guys, before you start giving baths and taking care of the kids, I have something I want to tell all of you."

Everybody stopped in their tracks and looked at him. "Don't worry, I'm not dating anyone nor have I squandered all your inheritance."

At that, there were a couple of chuckles but mainly stares as if to say "What are you up to, old man."

The rest of the meal clearing went at something like record speed. Everyone wanted to know what was behind the sudden and unexpected announced meeting. Soon, everyone was settled into the family room. George had casually found Stewart and was leading the boy to his favorite recliner. The other grandkids were in and out and were being monitored by their parents with the third eye and third ear that all parents seemed to have. The other two eyes and ears were focused on George. He knew they must be wondering why Stewart was among them.

"Michelle, I know you are wondering why Stewart is sitting with me," as he began.

She only nodded affirmatively.

Continuing with his comments directed to her, "I remember you were raised by your maternal grandparents, right?" George asked simply because he wanted to focus on them for a moment. He already knew the answers, they all did, but he wanted to use it as an example for the four members present who were married to his children. Everyone also knew why her grandparents raised her. Her father and mother divorced when Michelle was young, and as it turned out, neither were the best of parents. This, George would not get into.

"That's right."

"My guess is you loved your grandparents very much," George added.

"I was very close to them," Michelle added hoping he wouldn't dwell on this for long and wondered why he was even asking about it.

"You know we were all very sorry when they passed away," George continued.

"Yes, thank you very much for all your kindnesses."

"I know you felt bad about it as we all felt when we lost Dana. Tom, I know you also lost your father awhile back. Were you very close to him?" he asked Tom, Jackie's husband of ten years.

Michelle was visibly relieved that George's attention was focused away from her.

Tom replied, "Yes, I was. I know how Jackie felt at losing her mother." Tom, a computer technician, was a strapping guy about six feet two with muscles everywhere. He was balding prematurely with sandy hair, blue eyes, clean shaven, and seemed devoted to his family.

To Elizabeth and Robert, Mike and Stacie's spouses respectively, George said as he looked at them, "You two are very lucky to have both of your parents still with you. I wanted you to hear this even though some of this may not apply to you yet."

They both nodded but did not speak.

"Stewart misses his Grannie in many ways similar to the way we miss our parents and grandparents who have gone on, don't you, Stewart?" he asked him as the others were watching me.

He only nodded. He was doing fine so far.

George looked up at Michelle who seemed to understand why he was saying this to her son.

"Some, if not all of what I'm about to say to you will sound absolutely preposterous," he began. "You may even think I've gone off the deep end. The problem is what you'll hear from me cannot be proved in any rational way. It can only be experienced. I'll tell you how to undertake the experience. Then it'll be up to you to try it or not. If you decide to try it, it may not work for you. I can only suggest you keep trying or decide to forget about it. I can almost guarantee it'll work for some of you if you follow the steps carefully.

"And no, this doesn't involve strong drink or any other artificial stimulants, if you get my drift. You have to be stone sober, in a quiet environment, fully awake and in control of your senses. You have to concentrate on the process at hand. Any extraneous thoughts may likely hinder you from fulfilling the experience. All of what I've just said and the other important information will be given you in a letter at the end of my little speech."

"The last time we were all together, I told Stewart and Michael this little secret, didn't I Stewart?" he said as he looked down at him. Stewart was looking up at George intently.

He nodded affirmatively again but didn't speak.

"Michelle, I understand you found him one day talking loudly in his room to no one in particular," he said as he looked back at her.

"Yes!"

"What did he tell you he was doing, if you don't mind me asking?"

"He told me he was talking to Grannie," she replied as she looked at me, then at him. The rest also looked at him.

"And what did you make of that?" George asked her.

"I told him he'd been dreaming," came her reply still looking at Stewart.

To Stewart he then asked, "Stewart, my man, when your mom heard you, were you talking to Grannie and were you doing what I asked you when I told you the secret?"

"Yes, Grandad; you aren't mad are you?" he asked me as he looked up at me with big eyes and wondering now if he had made a mistake in agreeing to help his Grandad.

George smiled warmly at him, "No Stewart, I'm not mad at you. It sounds to me as if you did exactly what I said." To the others, "Stewart was talking to Grannie, I have talked to her also....many times since her accident and neither of us is crazy. Stewart told me this afternoon he has talked to her several more times." George hesitated a moment before adding, "It's now time for your disbelief to show and be heard."

He looked around the room. No one made a sound. All mouths and eyes were wide open. So he carried on, "A link is formed permanently between two people's Souls on earth when they love each other unconditionally. Such can be the case between spouses or between parents and children or, apparently, between grandchildren and grandparents. When one of those Souls dies, the link survives and can be used much like a phone by the person left behind; in this case to allow Stewart to contact Grannie and me to contact Dana. I told you this is unbelievable. Before you collectively decide to have me committed, I ask that you simply try it. I feel sure you children have links established with your mom. Michelle, you probably have links formed with your grandparents. Tom, yours may be with your father. Elizabeth and Robert, I'm not sure about.

"The method is surprisingly simple. Follow what I said about finding a quiet place to concentrate and simply say, "Mom, are you here?" George said as he looked at Jackie, Jason, Stacie and Mike. "Keep trying if you don't succeed the first time. If you succeed, she'll answer. Ask her questions, something only you and she would know. Ask her other questions about where she is or anything. She can answer most questions. Be ready for a lot of surprises."

By now, the crowd before him started to come alive. They looked uncomfortable. They had started to squirm. They looked at each other. They looked at George. They looked back at each other. They looked at Stewart. "Does anyone have any comments or questions? Someone say something." George said. He couldn't believe no one had said anything yet. He reached into the side table by his chair. "Here are copies of letters your mom and I signed and had intended for you to have later. They may be useful now as you sort this out."

Jason was the first to speak, "Dad, I don't know what to say. This is all so far fetched, so far beyond anything I would have guessed you were going to say. How can you be sure you were talking to Mom and not dreaming or hallucinating? Have you talked to any others like Mom?"

"Yes, I've found that I have links with four people: your mom, Katherine and my mom and dad. Your mom was also involved in this before her accident. I've learned much information about where they are. They are in a great place. Ask her, she'll tell you. I'm absolutely convinced what Stewart and I have done is real. I know you won't believe until you have made contact yourselves. Short of you making contact, there's nothing I can do to prove this. Just don't write this off as ramblings of an old fool," George felt like he was starting to babble just like an old fool. That was not his intention. In fact, he wanted to tell them as little as possible about Home so they could learn on their own. Once they made contact and were comfortable with the process, he wouldn't mind sharing more information with them.

Jackie was next to speak, "Let's assume for a moment you're right about this. Why haven't you said something about this before now?"

"Good question, I've debated with myself for months now about what to do with this. I had the hardest time even telling your mom. It took me three sessions with Katherine before I had enough confidence in what I'd discovered just to let your mom know. Even then, she had to try it before she believed. She linked up with her Mother. After that, we thought the idea of telling anyone about this would sound so absurd that we would both be labeled as kooks or heretics. It may yet happen but I've concluded that this discovery is too important not to let others know.

"After you link up a couple of times, you'll understand why I'm doing this. I want your feedback after you've tried this. If you succeed, you're free to decide about what to do with what you learn. My only request is for you agree not to sell this to anyone. I believe God put this process in place for someone to discover and use. Don't ask me why but I believe he wants this to be known. To me, it seems to be further proof he wanted people to love and trust and respect each other and then to enjoy their lives after death in the Heaven he created especially for them.

"By the way, I can tell you this link has been discovered in the past. There is Church history about a couple of instances where its discovery went unexplained. Unfortunately, they didn't understand what had really happened or the information was deliberately suppressed."

Mike said, "Dad, I'm willing to give this a try but you'll understand my skepticism until it succeeds." Mike, the baby of the family, was a district sales manager. He inherited his dad's looks and physique and would likely be bald by his mid fifties. At five eleven, he currently had a full head of hair dark brown in color with blue eyes. The hair would likely disappear over time.

Stacie agreed. Stacie, Dana's first born, has her mother's good looks but not her athletic skills. They more closely match her dad's. She is five four, blond with blue eyes with deep dimples when she smiles. She was a little overweight and has struggled to shed the pounds gathered from her last pregnancy.

Michelle spoke up, "All this sounds so weird. I'm also like Mike; I'm going to have to experience this to believe it. Do you think I could link up with my grandparents?"

"I don't see any reason why not. If you were as close to them as you've said, the link should work. Try it with the one you felt closest with first," George stated. "There's something of a lesson here for all of you. I can see you have reacted much like I and Mom did the first time. When it first happened to me, I heard the voice in my head and was convinced someone had come into the house without me knowing it. The lesson is if you tell someone, you should know ahead of time if they've lost someone they have loved dearly; enough so to have formed a strong link with them. Okay, any more questions?"

Once again everyone was speechless. Apparently there weren't going to be any more questions. He looked down at Stewart. His head was bobbing as if he were about to go to sleep. He'd been a good trooper about this.

Michelle had one other question, "Dad, how did you know Stewart had been talking to Dana. Did he tell you when I wasn't around?"

"No, as a matter of fact, Dana told me. I simply confirmed with Stewart this afternoon that it had happened. I did ask him to help me explain this to you all. He did his job perfectly. I'll let you in on another secret. Stewart was the one who set me on course to discover this process. He asked me some very pointed questions one day about Katherine that put my mind in motion. The questions were so good I often wonder how he came up with them. Maybe one day I'll find out," George explained.

Michelle and Jason just shook their heads, "He is always coming up with 'pointed questions' as you put it," Jason said. "He seems to be pretty smart. Here, Dad, if you are through with him, I think I need to put him to bed," he said as he got up to take Stewart from his dad's arms.

At that, they all began to move around. Apparently the going-to-bed process had begun. The other kids seemed to have slowed a bit like Stewart. "I bet a couple of them are already asleep somewhere around here. I know for a fact I'm tired after having just gone through this session. I was dreading it but now it's done. We'll see how successful I was and who'll be the first to make contact. Maybe we'll know tomorrow." George thought.

Now that he has told them, he wondered how many residents from Home were here observing. Maybe I'll contact Dana, Katherine or Dad later.

Dana, Katherine and Jefferson were, indeed, watching as were about a hundred other residents including one certain Elder named Eli. Eli was shaking his head in apparent amazement at how George pulled this off. Katherine and Jefferson were whispering among themselves with Dana listening, wondering if anything would happen tonight. Dana suspected she might get a call from one of them but didn't know which one. Little did she know. None of them had any intentions of going anywhere, not this night anyway as they milled around talking among themselves, waiting for someone to call.

This night could be historic as the word of the Link has now been explained in earnest to a small but interested group. George had harbored the information for months and finally had the courage to let it out. He did it with good reasoning and forethought. There were hundreds of residents praying for his success, praying that perhaps a loved one of theirs somewhere on Earth would hear of this night and this Link to make the call to them.

Jason and Michelle finally had Stewart and Nicole down for the night. Trying not to wake them, they were talking in whispered tones. Jason was waving the letter his dad had given him. "Look at this, Michelle. This can't be real. It's too simple. It's too far fetched. Are you going to try this?"

"I think of Stewart and what I saw him doing that day a couple of weeks ago. Then tonight, he was perfectly serious when he was answering your dad's questions. And your dad seemed perfectly lucid and serious himself. I love and respect your dad. He asks nothing of us but to try. I think I have to try. If it fails, then we can tell him. But my gosh, what if it works? Think about it, a way to talk to someone who's passed on; someone you miss and loved when they were here. Yes, I'm going to try but I'm gonna try to keep my expectations down," Michelle exclaimed as she put the finishing touches on her nighttime attire.

"When are you gonna do this?" Jason asked as he walked around trying not to step on Stewart or Nicole sprawled out on the floor.

"Well, if you can be quiet, I'll try after we lie down. I guess I'll try to call my Grandpa. Then maybe you can try if you like. We have to be quiet so I can concentrate. Your dad says that's a key ingredient to the process."

Jason and Michelle laid down and turned down the lights. Jason was quiet and still with the covers up around his neck as was his sleeping habit. He didn't want to jeopardize what Michelle was trying to do. A few moments went by. He wondered what she was doing so he turned his face ever so slightly so he could see her in the dim light coming from around the windows. Her face was serene, no smile, no frown with eyebrows slightly furrowed. Her arms were out of the covers as was her sleeping habit. Then, he heard her whisper, "Grandpa, are you here?"

A few more moments passed and she whispered, "My gosh, is it really you?" Jason, with his pulse racing, wondered what was going on. Was she really talking to him or was she pulling one of her tricks which she sometimes did just to aggravate him. He continued to watch her wanting desperately to ask. Now she was smiling with her eyes closed, even chuckling under her voice. She mouthed more words that he couldn't hear. Jason sure didn't hear anyone else talking but she seemed to be listening as if she was hearing something or someone. He watched for what seemed to be the longest time. It must have been an hour. He was absolutely mesmerized. Then he heard her say, "Can I call for you again?" a moment went by and she said, "Good night to you, Grandpa. Please give Mamaw a hug for me."

Michelle laid there for a moment before she opened her eyes. She turned to see Jason anxiously watching her. A big grin crossed her face, and she touched his face. He returned her smile as he touched her hand. "It worked. It worked unbelievably well. What a rush. You have to try this," she said in a tone that said she had forgotten there were sleeping children in the room. She hugged him really, really tight.

Jason was surprised, "Well what did he tell you?" now caught up in the moment as well and also forgetting to whisper.

Michelle suddenly remembered, "Shhh! Let's whisper. I still can't believe this. He said he and Mamaw were living together in a beautiful house by a lake. I asked him if they were in Heaven. He said 'yes, but we call it Home instead of Heaven'. He said they and a bunch of others have been watching us all evening. Can you believe this? I guess they were all expecting your dad to make the announcement. Your mom was among those watching. But I bet you couldn't reach her right now."

"Why not?"

"Apparently, she's talking to your sister, Stacie. I still can't believe this. Should we go tell your dad? He'll want to know. Do you want to try your mom first? Grandpa said I can call him whenever I want to." Michelle said as she couldn't seem to get the words out fast enough.

"Yeah, let's do it."

They eased out of bed, tiptoed across the floor, careful not to step on Stewart and Nicole. Michelle remembered that Stewart and Michael were not sleeping with their Grandad tonight probably because he expected some of us to visit him sometime like we were about to do.

Down the hall they almost ran. As they approached Dad's bedroom door, they heard voices on the other side. After tapping lightly on the door, they heard an invitation to enter.

George was sitting up in bed, sidelights on and chatting with Jackie, no, almost laughing together as Jason and Michelle rushed in. He looked up grinning, "Well, do you guys have something to report?"

Jason and Michelle were standing there looking first at Jackie and then at his dad. "Yes," Jason said, "Michelle has something to report." He then became slightly embarrassed as he realized that he almost repeated his dad's words.

"I talked to my Grandpa," Michelle blurted out laughing to George. "It was unbelievable. You were right. It was unbelievable. I said that already didn't I?"

"That's great!" George said laughing, then turning to Jackie, "You want to tell them your news?"

Jackie looked up sheepishly, "I talked to Mom. You're right," as she looked at Michelle, "It was great, unbelievable. We all seem to be using the same words."

At that point, Tom walked in grinning, "After Jackie talked to her mom, I was able to get my dad. It took me a couple of tries because it was hard concentrating after what I had just witnessed with Jackie. This is good stuff."

Michelle added, "Well that's not all, my Grandpa said that Dana was talking with Stacie right now."

Jackie spoke up, "Dad, Mom told me there were a lot of other people here watching all this. She said to tell you someone named Eli was here. Can you tell us who that is? And what about all the other people? I don't see anyone except us."

George looked first at Jackie then at the rest as he replied, "First, let me tell you that residents of the other world, a world they call Home, can come and go as they please. Apparently, their souls have strange and wonderful abilities to do things they couldn't do when they had a physical presence here on Earth. As you talk further with them, they will tell you these things. I understand from talking with Katherine that what we're doing here tonight is unique. Apparently, we are the first to use the Link in an organized fashion. I imagine we may have quite an audience of interested people, even as we speak, watching and listening to us. How does that make you feel?"

They all looked at each other, then at George, then around the room and back at him. They couldn't see the smiling faces of the residents crowded into the room.

Katherine, Jefferson, Eli and a whole host of others were watching and would be laughing out loud were it not for the fact that they wanted to hear the conversations going on between George and his children. Dana was not present because she was in Stacie's bedroom talking with Stacie. Eli contentedly told himself and other Elders upstream using his telepathic pathway that the Link was now public and to get ready for the consequences. In this case, he knew they had been waiting 2000 years for this event.

"I can't tell you much more than that. I don't understand their capabilities much more than what I've told you," George explained further, "Eli, on the other hand, is a very special person. He is an Elder; a person we might call an Angel," They all gasped, "From what I gather, he's been assigned to me, to us, with instructions from someone higher up to watch and observe what's going on with the Link process. You may find this as strange as I did but during a conversation I had a couple of days ago with Katherine, he actually entered our conversation. I actually talked with him."

"Strange! Strange?" Jason said, "All of this is strange, weird, crazy, zany, unbelievable, you name it. I think we'd believe about anything you told us at this point. Where does all this go? What do we do with all this? I guess I better call Mom pretty soon; else, she'll think I've forgotten her."

"The beauty of all this ...and you," George said as he sat in the middle of his king sized bed surrounded by his offspring, "is that you can do pretty much what you want with all this. You can use it. You can explore it with questions to whoever you're talking to. You can keep this to yourselves. You can tell whoever you want; although I caution you to think about how you do that. From my standpoint, I believe I'll slowly bring other people into the loop, people who I know to have lost love ones they were particularly close to just like I did with you guys tonight."

Stacie came running into the room waving her arms, "You guys won't believe what I just experienced," she blabbered out at breakneck speed.

"Oh yeah, we would. All of us, except Jason here, have just done the same thing. You've talked to Mom haven't you?" Jackie said as she and the others began to laugh.

"Yeah, it was exhilarating, wasn't it? Dad you were right," Stacie added as she rushed over to give him a tight hug.

Just then, Mike slowly walked into the room. "I've been hearing a commotion going on in here," he said. "Anything I should know?"

Jackie told him, "Most of us have tried the Link process Dad told us about. It worked for us. I take it that you haven't tried it yet."

"Yeah, I tried it. I guess something was wrong. I had trouble concentrating. I asked but received no answer. Then I started hearing all the commotion in the hall so I thought I'd see what was happening," he explained with a disappointed tone in his voice.

"I bet one reason you didn't get through to Mom was that she may have been busy talking with Jackie and Stacie," George added while Jackie and Stacie nodded. "Concentration can be a problem. We have a house full of people who can provide a lot of distractions. Don't give up on it, Son."

"Okay! I'll keep trying."

By now, it was in the wee hours of the morning. The excitement was contagious but fatigue slowly quieted the group. Yawns were becoming more prevalent. Slowly, they all drifted off to bed. George was left with a feeling of euphoria and great satisfaction. He had not let his children down, and they had discovered that life continues and, indeed, thrives at a place called Home.

"Before I call it a night," he thought, "I would make one attempt."

"Dana, are you here?" he asked after forcing himself to settle down.

Almost immediately came her reply, "I sure am. George, as I heard it on my side here tonight, you're the man. I've been waiting around hoping you felt up to calling. Katherine, your folks and a whole host of others have been in and out. We're all quite proud of what you did for the children tonight and, I will admit, a bit in awe as well. I don't know of anyone who could have handled it better. Stewart was a perfect gentleman through it all."

"Well, that's a bit overwhelming, I must say. Thanks! I was really worried about how it would go. I'm glad they listened. I'm glad they tried. I'm glad they got through. I hope Jason and Mike make it sooner than later. I'm glad it's over," George finally added and probably sounded pretty tired in the process. His arm was hurting a little and there was tightness in his chest.

"My guess is it's a far cry from being over. My guess is its just beginning, at least the important part," Dana replied. "By the way, I believe Mr. Eli would like to speak with you, if that's okay."

"Oh, yes, that's okay," as he lay on his bed.

"George," Eli began, "I just wanted to let you know I've been here all evening. I echo what Dana has said. You did a superb job. You planned it well. It went exactly as you would have liked, I imagine. We are all very pleased with the way this is getting started. I will be reporting on this as soon as we finish our conversation. It'll be well received, I can guarantee you."

"Thank you! I really appreciate that. Can I ask to whom you will be giving this report, if I'm allowed?" George asked hesitantly.

"Yes, you certainly can. There is a large group of Elders assembled awaiting this information. I have an associate here who will help me. This will go all the way up the ladder, trust me. Let me say, since you have started the knowledge expansion process tonight, all of us here deem your efforts to be of the highest importance. This is a landmark step. Since I've seen how you approached telling your children, I have every confidence that you'll continue to do this in an outstanding fashion. By the way, if you find yourself in a situation where you feel a need to talk to me, just call me. You'll find it easier to reach me than you do your loved ones. I'm available to you on a '24/7' basis as you would say in your world. Unless you have other questions or comments, I'll bow out of this conversation and wish you good rest and good night," Eli concluded.

"Good night, Sir," George managed to get out.

Dana spoke up, "He's gone, George. All of us here tonight listening to all this, are just astounded. As your grandfather would say, you are plowing new ground, fellow."

"I'm a little overwhelmed," he said. "Take that back, I'm a lot overwhelmed. I have no intention of turning back, but now, man, I'm plowing forward with renewed vigor. I'm still going to take this cautiously. I don't want this to become sensationalized. I want to introduce it to people who can use it and will also carry it forward responsibly. To me, that makes the most sense unless someone can advise me otherwise. Yeah, I know, you guys can't advise me."

"Sorry! To be honest, George, I'm not sure anyone here could've improved on the approach you took," she said as she sat beside him on the huge bed she used to be a co-tenant on.

"I'm indeed tired. I guess I should say good night and see if I can get to sleep. I expect we'll be talking about this all weekend. Besides, we have a full day at Six Flags tomorrow. I'm looking forward to watching all the children," he said.

"So am I, good night George, sweet dreams," Dana replied as she smiled; a smile that George couldn't see. She looked up to see Katherine, Jefferson and Annie all smiling and nodding their approvals. She bent over and kissed him on the forehead and cheek. She looked at Jefferson again. He gave her thumbs up.

Chapter 16

George broke the Link, turned over and turned out the two bed lamps. "I hope sleep will come quickly," he thought as he began to lose consciousness.

Seemingly, the morning light came quickly. He didn't remember dreaming at all. He guessed the activities and stress from last night overtook him. The bedside clock said it was 7 o'clock. He could already hear noises from the rest of the house. Their big day was on, not that yesterday was not just as big, the way it ended. Come to think of it, yesterday actually ended today, some five hours ago.

It took him fifteen or so minutes to get the cobwebs out of his head and his few remaining strands of hair in some semblance of order. He walked into the kitchen and you would have thought he was at a Chinese fire drill. Chaos seemed to rein. Everyone was talking, laughing and seemingly having a good time all at once. Bacon was frying, eggs were scrambling, biscuits were cooking, the aroma was great.

Everyone stopped when they sensed him being there. Three or four of them rushed to give him good morning hugs. Even the grandchildren seemed to be involved in this fire drill.

"Good morning, all," George started, "Did everyone manage to get some sleep."

"Not much," several of them replied almost in chorus.

Jason said as he held his head in his hands at the table, "I don't think I got any."

Mike added as he looked similar to Jason, "Dad, Jason and I finally managed to contact Mom. It was so great and exhilarating. I bet she didn't get any sleep either."

George laughed, "News to all of you, neither she nor anyone else at Home require any sleep."

Michelle laughed as she piped up, "Well, nothing you say will ever surprise me again. We have so much to learn."

First lesson of the day as he began, "Okay, I need to give you the standard lecture they've all given me in case you haven't heard this yet. This discovery will be great for your lives and your outlook as it will be for anyone you pass this along to. Remember though, you're still earthly residents subject to all the perils of living physical lives. Your children are in the same boat with you. You have responsibilities to yourselves, your spouses and to your children. You have responsibilities to your Church, to your country, to your communities, to your neighbors and you have a responsibility to live your lives to the fullest including enjoying, loving, and caring for each other. Your day will eventually come for own your trips Home. Until that day, and no one knows when that'll be, make your presence felt here with your hearts and minds. Does everyone understand this?"

As he looked around, he had everyone's attention. It was hard to tell but everyone seemed to be standing a little straighter.

Jason responded now with a clear look on his face, "Yes, you're exactly right, Dad. This discovery should in no way be used as an excuse not to live our lives and be a part of our children's lives and be good neighbors, Christians, and citizens. This I promise to do."

"Here, here," the rest said almost in unison.

Jason added, "I can also see we have a new responsibility. I agree this seems to be an important discovery. We have to help you spread the word. I give you my pledge to do just that. When you figure out how I can help, please let me know. Meanwhile, if opportunities present themselves to do this on my on, I intend to try."

George responded, "Thanks for your pledge of assistance. As soon as I figure out how to move this ahead, we'll talk more."

Michelle also added, "I'd like to help, too."

To a person, the rest agreed.

"Well, I think we all make a pretty good team. This'll be fun and it'll be significantly important. On this day, July 3, we begin. Let's wish ourselves luck," George told the group. Everyone raised their orange juice or coffee mug to toast the moment and seal the pact.

The outing at Six Flags went well except when it rained. A thunderstorm came up late in the day and cut their time by about an hour. Stewart and Michael were on a roller coaster ride when the thunder came. They were scared by the time the cars stopped at the end point and just barely got wet. Aside from that, the kids had a good time. By the time they got home, it was late afternoon. Everyone crashed. George cooked hamburgers.

The next day began early as George ramped up the barbecue pit to cook the pork shoulders. He had them on the pit by 6 o'clock. He started out alone but within the hour, everyone was stirring around. There were more reports of Links with Dana and from Michelle. Everyone started talking about friends they wanted to pass the information to. The day went well. They feasted about mid afternoon. By the end of the day, the crowd started to disperse. Jason and Jackie went home with their broods. Mike and Stacie migrated to their in-laws with theirs.

Another gathering successfully concluded, the first without Dana's presence. She was here, however as we spoke to her off and on over the weekend. She was probably getting tired of answering calls. George knew she was watching them as well. He was alone again, lonely as usual after such a crowd, but fulfilled at the accomplishments of the weekend. Seemed that the rollout was off to a good start.

Dana wasn't the only resident from Home present. A majority of the recent ancestral family members from all ranks were around as well. Eli was in and out and was pleased at the progress made.

Monica and Marvin were hosting one of their cookouts next Saturday. George thought the time was ripe to open the doors to them and introduce them to the Link. He would need to prepare special versions of the letter he just passed to the kids. This version might serve as one of his tools wherever he introduced this to others.

If memory served him, George believed Monica, Marvin, Laverne and Bill had all lost at least one parent. He would need to probe each of them about how close they were to gage whether or not Links had formed. He was counting on at least one viable Link in each of their families. If he was going to tell them in a group, which was currently his plan, he needed for at least one person from each family to try the Link.

Saturday arrived and he was ready. He had his usual supply of beer and wine along with chips and dips to take. This seemed to be the standard complement of items his friends had relegated him to bring to their get-togethers. Apparently, no one trusted or liked the things he cooked. That was okay with him. Truth was he was a lousy cook. He tried once to make a black bean casserole. No one actually got sick, at least no one said as much, but even he, when he tried it, turned up his nose. That was unusual because he usually ate most everything set before him. "There's no reason to subject my friends to the lower-than-acceptable quality of my prepared foods. I also have my letters ready," he thought.

The letters were about a page and a half in length. The specific instructions didn't take but a paragraph located near the end. The bulk of the first part of the letter comprised a lot of explanation along with some examples. After all, it would be unfair to simply blurt out the instructions without some sort of lead-in. The lead-in was important in preparing them to accept the seemingly absurd instructions, simple though they were. The last part of the letter just suggested they try the process before passing any final judgment on the letter or George, as far as that was concerned.

George arrived mid afternoon and moved his stash of goods to the backyard. Marvin was puttering around his outdoor kitchen as usual daring anyone to bother him with un-solicited suggestions. Monica was inside working on other dishes. Laverne and Bill hadn't arrived yet. They came in about a half hour later. The fellowship was great as usual. Always, a few golf stories appeared; most of them at George or Marvin's expense since they were substandard players to Bill. There was always an unspoken element about Dana's absence. It was never mentioned but it hovered over them like a thin wispy cloud, not entirely clouding out the good times, but not quite allowing the full rays of sunshine through either. That would be George's entry into the discovery discussion.

They sat around the outdoor table under the awning by the pool after dinner. Marvin cooked great prime rib. The side dishes were compliments of Monica and Laverne. George was not quite sure what Bill brought to the gathering except for his usual brand of Cajun humor and jokes. There was a lull in the conversation and George took his entry shots.

"Boy, it would be great to have Dana here to enjoy all this again," he said with his head half way down but just high enough for him to see the other reactions around the table.

After a moment, Monica spoke, "You know George, you're right. We enjoyed our times together so much over the years."

There! The door opened. This was the first mention of Dana in months. It was appropriate for Monica to have responded since she was the closest to Dana outside him.

"I miss her, yet I don't miss her. Even though she doesn't live with me anymore, I feel like she's there in spirit all the time. I'm sure she's happy wherever she is and is likely smiling at us now. She could even be among us now watching and listening," George continued.

Indeed, she was watching along with a hoard of other visitors including Katherine, Jefferson, Annie and Eli, the omnipresent Elder. Eli had a particularly critical interest in how this session would go between George and his friends. The hopes and expectations upstream were high and all riding on George's shoulders to make this successful.

There was some shifting around the table but no one had any response to these strange sentences they just heard from him. They probably wanted to see where he was going with this.

"Monica," George continued, "I know you were close to Dana."

"Yes, I was. She was probably my best friend. I loved her like a sister," Monica added. Now, there was a possibility that might be worth exploring, he thought to himself.

"I know you lost your father some time ago. How many years has it been now?" he continued with his comments to her.

"It's been ten years now. I miss him every day."

"Do you feel like you were close to him?" George asked her.

"Yeah," she hesitated a moment before continuing, "I was devastated when he had his heart attack. None of us saw it coming so none of us were prepared for the sudden loss."

"Was he a good man?" George had to ask because he didn't know him that well and he had to be reasonably sure that he'd be there when she called him later.

"He was a model citizen in our small town. He was always volunteering for almost anything that came along. And even though we weren't that well off, he saw to it that his children were always number one on his concern list," she added not at all sure where this was going and getting a little irritated at the single direction toward her.

"I'm sorry to drag all those memories out but I wanted to let you know that we all have someone really close to us who has passed on. Marvin, I believe your mother has passed. Yours too, Bill. Laverne, my memory tells me that both of your parents have passed on, isn't that correct?"

"Yes, George! That's right. We've all had losses from good people that we've loved very much. Out of the four of us, one day two of us will know the loss that you have," Laverne responded as she listened carefully trying to figure out where George was headed with this.

"I want to tell you something that has helped me cope with my loss," George said. "This is gonna sound crazy; maybe a lot crazy but hear me out. Bill, do you remember the story you told me about your great grandmother, Annette?"

Bill was surprised at the question. He jumped like George just woke him up, "Yes, yes I do."

George stepped in to keep him from having to tell the story. "Would you mind if I describe a little of your story?"

"Yeah, that'll be okay, I guess," he said as he shifted from one hip to the other in his chair wondering also where all this was going. George seemed to have a purpose, though. The other visitors were listening intently, particularly Eli.

George started in, "Seems that Bill's great grandmother was married to Boudreaux back around the first part of the last century. He was a patriot and volunteered to serve in the American forces when we entered the First World War. Boudreaux never returned from Europe. He perished over there on some battlefield. Annette never quite recovered from the loss. Seems that she was just as close to him as I was to Dana, or perhaps you were to your parents who've passed on.

"The story goes that Annette seemed to go off the deep end. She spent a lot of time withdrawn from others around her only to come out of it occasionally when she began telling stories of talking to Boudreaux; detailed stories of long conversations. Did I represent the story pretty closely, Bill?"

Eli looked at another couple standing, listening from the corner of the patio. They were nodding and smiling.

Bill was visibly uncomfortable by now as were a couple of others as he said, "I think you got most of it, George."

"Bill, that's okay. I didn't mean to embarrass you or reveal a deep dark family secret. The truth is Annette was indeed having conversations with Boudreaux. The only problem with Annette is that no one believed her or understood what was going on including her. The Church even investigated it. I bet you didn't know that, Bill."

"What, huh? How do you know that, George? What're you leading up to?" Bill responded now with a slight edge in his voice. George didn't blame him. He'd probably feel the same way.

"That's a good and fair question, Bill. The other truth is I've been talking to Dana. I have discovered a way for us to talk. The process is probably the same as Annette used. I asked Rev. Casey about the history of such occurrences. He told me there was an unexplained case out of Louisiana in the 1950's and another one some centuries before."

Marvin couldn't contain himself any longer, "George, do you hear what you're saying. You're saying you talk to dead people. Wait, you've said this before haven't you, I remember now. But that was before Dana had her accident. What's going on, for Pete's sake, George?"

"I realize this sounds preposterous. Just hear me out a little longer before you call the guys in the white coats. I discovered this process a couple of weeks before Dana's accident. I even told her about it and she used the process to talk to her mom before the accident. I told my grandson some weeks ago. He's talked to Dana. I told my children this last weekend. All of them have talked to Dana. Michelle talked to her grandfather and Tom talked to his Father. You're free to call and talk to any of them about their experiences. As crazy as this sounds, it's the real thing," George and all the others, including the extra visitors, were all now on the edge of their seats, "The process is really simple. I want to share this with you. All I ask is that you try it and let me know the results. I have a letter here for each of you to read. Bill, it's similar to the letters you're holding for my children. Not only have I talked to Dana, I've also talked to Katherine and my mom and Dad," George implored as he passed out the letters. Katherine and Dana were standing on either side of George as if to give him whatever support they could muster.

Bill was looking at me rather intensely. George wasn't sure if he was just angry or really angry. "George, something struck me odd about that statement you made at the party those months ago. It also struck a familiar chord as I recalled some of the events surrounding my great grandmother. The reaction of our family was divided over all Annette went through and all she said. I was too young to understand any of it. I remember some people from Church coming around and asking a bunch of questions. For the moment, I'm gonna give you the benefit of the doubt," he said as he began to read the letter.

All of them were now reading their letters. George let the silence carry on. There was no use saying much else until one of them responded. The other visitors were shifting around trying to look over the shoulder of one of the readers to glimpse the wording for themselves.

Monica was first, "So, it seems this Link you describe is the key to this?"

At least she didn't wad it up and chunk it into the trash can, "Yes, I think so. If you are not close enough with someone to form the irreversible Link, then the process won't work. I figure it has to be between people like spouses or parents and children or grandparents and grandchildren. I haven't tested it with relationships between good friends like you and Dana."

By now, all had finished reading the letters. "The other key is to put yourself into a state of deep concentration with a clear mind and away from external distractions. Once you're there, you ask the short but key question like 'Dana, are you here?' If any of you decide to give this a try, I really would like to know how it comes out," George repeated.

"George, let me ask you this," Marvin said, "I'm pretty skeptical about all this in spite of Bill's comments about Annette. There're four of us here besides you. If we all try this and if none of us are able to Link up, will you agree to see a psychiatrist? I'm more than a little concerned about all this. You certainly have found a way to make a regular outing something spectacular. What do you say?"

"I'm not crazy. But I'll see the shrink if you all agree to give this an honest try. Don't forget, you can call any of my children to get their uptake on this. All of you know them and I put their phone numbers in a separate note with the letter. Laverne, you haven't said anything. Care to put anything on the table?"

Laverne looked up from the letter at George then at Bill, "I've listened to some of the stories from Bill's family gatherings over the years. Indeed, there was a wide division of opinion. Those who wanted to believe Annette could never get enough information from her to figure out how it happened, however. They couldn't tell from just watching her. You'll get your honest try from me."

At that, Marvin, Monica and Bill all nodded in agreement. The conversation drifted after that. George thought a conversation like this gets to a point when people want it to end, him as well. Anyway, he had gotten the message out. It didn't go as smoothly as he would have liked but the story was out and commitments were made. He was afraid to ask when he might hear back. He figured if someone succeeded, the word will get around quickly. If no one succeeded, then Bill or Marvin would tell him. The afternoon wound up shortly after. George returned to his empty house.

For the time being, this was the last time he planned to do this in a group environment. He felt he could have a better conversation one-on-one than in a group session. The drift of the conversation seemed easier to control that way. His next target was Rev. Richard Casey. But first, he wanted to wait awhile to see how his friends managed this. It was funny, he felt like he had just tried to sell them his used lawnmower. "I hope none of this jeopardizes our great relationship. I feel confident at least one will succeed," he thought.

The call came about three PM on Sunday. Bill was on the other end, "George, this is Bill. Laverne and I wonder if you're free to come over to our house this afternoon." That was it? No hint about what happened. Could be that when he arrived, he would be greeted by the big men in white coats. Why not?

"Sure, Bill, give me fifteen minutes to change and another fifteen to make my way over these busy streets," George replied.

"Good! See you in thirty." Short call! His voice was level and gave nothing away. Made George wonder.

Bill and Laverne lived about ten minutes closer to George's house than Monica and Marvin. They had lived there probably twenty years. The home was a two story cracker box style home. The shrubbery and trees were mature as were those of almost all their neighbors. The over hanging limbs from the trees blocked most of the sunshine from their yard. As a substitute, they had a lot of ivy growing around. It always made George think they must have a lot of snakes. Don't know why he felt that way because he'd never seen the first snake.

He drove up and noticed Marvin's car in the driveway. Well whatever the message, they'd decided to tell him together. George was trying to be upbeat about this. After all, he deemed their support critical in his quest to expand the knowledge base.

The door opened just as George stepped on the front stoop. Apparently, they were looking out for him. He walked into a scene that just about floored him. Banners were hanging everywhere. Champagne was open and glasses were being poured. Someone thrust a glass into his hand.

"George," Bill shouted, "I don't know how you did it but you've discovered the secret of the millennium. This'll make you rich and famous. You have to tell us how all this happened. We've all contacted our closest loved ones. Monica has additional news for you."

He winced a little at Bill's second sentence. Monica was bubbling, "My gosh, George, it was great. At first I didn't believe my Father's voice in my ears. I can't wait to tell my Mother in Montgomery. George, do you think she can call him?"

"Depends," George said, "On whether or not they had a close and loving relationship. If they loved each other, she should be able to. If they weren't that close, maybe so, maybe not."

"Well, let me tell you what else," she continued, "I called Dana and she answered."

That caused him to stop and look at her for a moment. He'd not talked to anyone last night. Exhaustion set in and he went to bed early. "You what?" George was now almost shouting. "That's unbelievable. I had wondered if Links could form between really close friends. That's really great news."

"Yep, she said you hadn't called and you'd gone to bed early. She said she was watching you along with a lot of other people. You'll have to explain that. She said she was here yesterday during the afternoon...along with a lot of other people. You need to explain that as well," Monica responded.

Outside of their view, a host of Home visitors were smiling and clapping their hands on their own. Eli was nodding his approval.

"Well, she was right. I was tired when I got home. I guess I'd used a lot of emotional capital in rolling this out to you guys yesterday. Bill, let me say first, that I do want the word to get out about this. However, I have absolutely no desire to be famous nor will I accept any money as a result of this discovery. I figure the Link has been waiting for all this time for someone to uncover it. God put it in place and I want you guys to spread the word but please promise me that you'll not accept any money for this either. If you do, find yourself a favorite charity to give it to.

"As far as the other people Dana mentioned, they are interested in this process. Anyone in heaven can join any gathering, as I understand it, which they find interesting. This discovery is starting to be known and they want to observe the occasion. Maybe they want someone to call them. Maybe they're just hopeful. That's the best explanation I can give you."

Eli's facial expression was almost unreadable except Dana thought she sensed a certain amount of respect hidden behind his steady gazing eyes.

Bill started up, "I've got news for you. My guess is you'll be famous as news about this spreads whether you like it or not. When I was talking to my mom, she said you were already famous there, at Home as she described Heaven to me. She was here all afternoon and up until I called her. Not only that, but my great grandmother and great grandfather were here watching as well. Man, you know how to draw a crowd. We must have talked for an hour or more. She told me some amazing things about Home."

Marvin spoke then, "George, I owe you an apology for ever doubting you."

"You know what, Marvin, that's exactly why I encouraged you to simply try it. Few people are going to accept this just on my word or your word or anyone's. It'll be years before people are comfortable with this. Does anyone see that this may hold the power to affect people's behavior?" George asked the whole group.

Laverne answered as she paused to look at him, "Sure, I can see that. Once people understand this, it'll give them great hope. It'll encourage them to act with more love and respect toward others. It may even curb some acts of violence once it's known that not everyone gets to stay in Heaven." The others looked at her. "Sure, I had a long conversation with my dad who told me that not everyone gets to stay there. If they have a history of violence against people, they are held accountable. If their earthly behavior is bad enough, they go somewhere else."

"Where do they go?" Marvin asked.

"I don't know. My dad didn't know. He said that certain people don't pass through. Did you guys learn about that term as well?" she answered.

Two of them nodded affirmatively. "They don't use the term 'die' there. They say that people pass through from this world to their world," Laverne continued.

"I'm proud of all of you. I guess my instructions worked. You're starting to learn about Home. There is so much to learn and all of it is breathtaking. Here's a key question. Will you be willing to help spread the word about this to others?" George challenged them. Eli was listening closely. "I'm not talking about going on TV or anything like that. I'm talking about looking for opportunities either in a one-on-one or in small groups. I'm talking about possibly putting yourself in a position to be ridiculed or laughed at or labeled something unkind"

They all looked at each other then at him. Bill spoke up, "Absolutely! Count me in." The others said the same. Eli smiled.

Marvin said, "Is this a miracle? Will this make us your disciples, George? Will I have to kneel and kiss your hand or feet or anything else?"

"Marvin, I tell you what, you can kiss my butt for starters and if I like it, we'll go from there," George said.

The room erupted from laughter on both sides of the veil. "I'll tell you this, to me this is not a miracle. I think this Link has existed from the beginning and mankind has not understood it or perhaps it's been suppressed. God made this possible. It may be a discovery of sorts but certainly not a miracle even as marvelous as it is," George exclaimed. Eli nodded once again.

Monica chimed in with her thoughts, "George, I'm glad you took the approach you did. You told us just enough to get us to try the process. You spent time to understand that there were people we might be able to Link with. You didn't oversell the unbelievably marvelous characteristics of Home that could have been a turnoff before we tried the process for ourselves. You let us use our own imagination in coming up with questions for our folks there. Guys, there's a valuable lesson here about how to spread the word."

"I agree," Bill said.

"Why don't we have a little more champagne? I feel that a great weight's been lifted off my shoulders. You can't imagine how important it was for my best friends to embrace this," George felt he had to add.

"Are you kidding?" Bill said, "As far as I'm concerned this may be one of the three most important events that's happened to me in my life alongside my marriage," as he looked at Laverne, "and the births of my children. Let me pour." As he hoisted another bottle, Dom Perignon, George noticed.

Their impromptu gathering went on for perhaps another two hours before the old people decided it was time to retire to their respective homes and prepare to face another week. George labeled it a great success. The past two weekends had been great from his standpoint.

Chapter 17

George's challenge for the week ahead was Rev. Richard Casey. First though, he needed to call his backup support group. As soon as he got home, he made a beeline for his favorite recliner and promptly called Dana even though he had to force himself to discard some of the euphoria he was carrying from the afternoon gathering in order to create a semblance of calmness in his mind.

"Dana, are you here?" he asked.

Almost immediately, "Yes George, I'm here. I bet you're feeling pretty good the way things are working out."

"Yep, as a matter of fact, I am. I feel this whole process is off to a good start. Is there a crowd around, how about at Bill and Laverne's this afternoon?"

"George, you seem to draw a crowd anywhere you go these days. Bill was right. I had a good conversation with Monica. I'm not sure anyone thought that type of Link could be established. Mr. Eli even seemed surprised. By the way, he's here and would like a few words with you if that's okay?"

"Certainly!" he said.

In his rich baritone voice, Eli spoke, "George, things are indeed going well. I understand you intend to talk to Rev. Casey soon."

"Yes sir, my plans are to call him tomorrow and schedule a meeting as soon as possible. Any words of wisdom for me?" George asked.

"You're doing quite well," Eli continued, "Your ability to decide the best courses of action in these scenarios is really impressive. You seem to have an instinct for doing what's most effective. It's hard to tell how Rev. Casey is going to react. I know from his conversations with us, prayers as you might call them, reveal him to be a deeply religious person devoted to carrying forward the traditions of the Church, the Methodist Church in particular. I hope he'll come to understand that we don't feel the discovery is a threat to the Church but is, instead, an enhancement of its basic purpose; that is to teach people about God and to encourage them to live with each other in love and respect."

"I believe Richard, uh, Rev. Casey will listen with an open mind," George replied, "I've known him for many years. We've always been open with each other when it came to deeply rooted discussions. I feel my biggest problem is whether or not I can convince him to help us. As open as he may be, I fear the clergy upstream who he'll have to explain this to." In fact, George felt as if, in talking with Richard, his most important bridge to cross was yet before him. He couldn't see the bridge yet to know if he's crossing a raging river or a small babbling brook. Will the Church embrace this or will open battle ensue from what he had done and how he had opened this up to the world? The Link was real. The Church was real. If the Church failed to embrace this at this juncture and after all these centuries, would a significant split occur which would directly impact Home and all those who, like Eli, were responsible for its management?

"Very perceptive, George! No doubt, this may create some consternation to Rev. Casey as he pushes this information upstream. If we get a chance to work with those clergy through their conversations with us, perhaps we can lend some comfort and assistance to them over this as well," Eli said.

"I think it would be bad if they, not necessarily Richard, were to decide to start practicing territorialism and try to block this. It's occurred to me this sort of thing may have happened in the past whenever the process has surfaced," George added.

"Indeed, you're very perceptive. That's exactly what happened in at least two instances during the past two millenniums," Eli replied, "Your approach is going to make it difficult this time. To a certain degree, the population is much better educated than ever before. They're better able to decide for themselves what's significant and what's not. From that respect, the Church is not quite as powerful as it once was. That's a reason why your discovery is so important today. Don't forget to call me if you need me."

"Thanks, I will," George said even as he realized Eli was already gone.

Dana confirmed it, "He's gone, George. I bet you are tired as usual, after all, you aren't getting any younger. You continue to astound us here, by the way. I'm so proud of you. Katherine, your dad, all of us, are proud of you."

"I'll be tired when we break off. Right now, I still feel the euphoria of my time with our friends and the uplifting support that Eli always manages to instill in me. I'm glad we can talk even though you aren't here. I look forward to the day when I can join the clan there. Please tell everyone I think of you all often. This is George, signing off. Good night, Dana."

"Good night, George," as she watched him pull his weary body off the recliner and toward the bedroom. She wished she could be more helpful and wondered, with some concern, about the meaning in his comment about joining the clan at Home.

The call to Richard the next morning produced a meeting time of 2 o'clock for Tuesday. Monday was not exactly a boring day, however. About 4 o'clock, Monica called to say she had talked to another friend of hers and had passed along the information about the Link.

"I didn't think you'd mind. After all, you want us to get the word out, right?" she said.

"Yeah and what you did is okay. How'd it go and what can you tell me about your friend?" George asked in return.

"She's about ten years younger than Marvin and I. A couple of years ago, she lost her son and husband in a truck accident. They'd been somewhere in north Georgia on a hunting trip and ran off a winding mountain trail into a gorge," she related.

"I believe I remember Dana saying something about that. It was a real tragedy."

"Not only that but a year later she lost her mom to Alzheimer's. Her dad had passed away about five years earlier. She's all alone and hasn't really recovered. She's been the subject of a Church focus group for some time now. I even gave her a copy of your letter," Monica said.

"Have you heard from her since then?"

"Yeah I have," she said, "She's talked to her husband and her son. She's deliriously happy. I thought you'd want to know."

"I appreciate you calling me." About an hour later, Laverne called with a similar story about a widowed friend of hers. The process has begun. George needed to give the kids a call to see if anything was happening on their front.

"Hello,"

"Is this Michelle? This is George," he said.

"Hi Dad," she said. "Have you been doing all right?"

"Yeah, things are going great. Have you guys been okay?"

"Everything's fine with us. Actually, they're better than fine. Stewart's been linking up with Dana on a regular basis. You might be interested in knowing that I've told two of my friends about the Link. These are friends who each had lost a father. The information I got back from them is they were able to Link up and were able to get their moms linked up as well. This all seems so strange and wonderful. I gave them a version of the letter you gave us," she explained.

"Thanks! Looks like we're starting to spread the word. I told my friends this last weekend and they've started doing the same thing. Tomorrow, I'm going to bring Rev. Casey into the loop and get a sense about how the Church is going to react," George said.

"Good luck there," she added. Our conversation drifted to other things her family was been involved in.

Calls to the other kids yielded similar results. At least one person from each family had passed the information along to someone they knew. There was probably no way to stop the process now. Their friends would see other friends who would see their friends. It looked like a pyramid scheme, except in this case, there was no financial downside and everyone would come out winners, well almost everyone. Someone was going to learn about it who would not have anyone to link to. They might try it anyway. No doubt, there would be some disappointments.

Tuesday, 2 o'clock rolled around and found George in the Church parking lot. He was a little nervous. Not because of Richard but because of what he knew Richard would feel he would have to do with the information George was about to give him.

The Church secretary, Elaine, announced George's presence. Richard came out of his office with his hands extended and a big smile on his face. They really hadn't had a chance to talk since the funeral except in passing on Sunday. He was guessing Richard wanted to talk to him as well.

"George, I'm really glad you came in. I've wanted to call you and catch up on things. Have you been doing all right? Come on in and let's talk. Elaine, please hold my calls," Richard said to his secretary as he closed the doors to a typical pastor's office with moldy smells that only emanated from large quantities of books and papers. Richard's office was not neat but then when did any pastor keep a neat office. They needed the clutter to add to the mystique about how messages are developed for Sunday delivery. Richard delivered good messages so he was entitled to a cluttered office.

"I've been doing pretty well. Actually, I think I could describe it as great. Though, I've had a few rough periods since the funeral. You know that I loved Dana very much," George started right in.

George didn't know it but his Home entourage was with him. Eli was close by and wanted to observe Richard's reaction to the news he was about to get.

"You loved her very much, and she felt the same for you. A lot of people envied your relationship," he replied.

"Can I ask you a personal question?" George asked.

"Yes, sure! What would you like to know?" was his comeback.

"When you lost your parents, did you feel a deep sense of loss?"

Strange question, Richard thought, but he would see where George was going with this, "Yes, I was devastated for awhile. My Father was not only a dad to me but he was my mentor as I went through school preparing for the ministry. My mom was always there for me. Why do you ask?"

"I'd like to tell you a story about Stewart, my grandson who as you know belongs to Jason and Michelle," George began, "He's a very special little boy almost seven now, very bright and very sensitive to things about human nature. Before Dana passed away, he asked me if I missed Katherine and if I ever wanted to just talk to her. It was the strangest conversation. Richard, do you ever miss your mom and dad enough to want to talk to them?"

Boy, this was going off into a strange direction, Richard thought. "Yeah, particularly my dad. Often times when I'm getting a message ready to deliver on Sunday, I wish I could ask him about some of the finer points on Scripture. He was always three steps ahead of me in his knowledge about the Bible," he replied.

"I told you Stewart has a sensitive heart about human nature. I'm about to tell you he also has a sensitive Soul about the spiritual world. He's talked to Dana since her accident, several times. I know this for a fact," George said as he looked Richard straight in the eye from the edge of his chair. Eli was looking closely as well as he stood behind George.

Richard became visibly shaken at these statements. He sat upright in his chair and edged closer to his desk as he watched George. "What do you mean about Stewart talking to Dana and how, how is it you know that for a fact?" he stammered.

"Richard, dear Richard," George began, "I'm going to tell you a story you aren't going to believe. You're going to think I'm nuts, crazy, whatever. But in the end, I'm going to give you a simple way to prove me right or prove me wrong. Are you willing to listen to the wildest tale you've ever heard?"

Still on the edge of his chair and unmoving with his eyes pinned to George, he said simply, "Yes!"

George started off telling Richard about Stewart's first questions to him and then he went through the process with Katherine, Dana and Stewart. Richard sat motionless, mouth slightly open and eyes wide. George finished up by telling him about the importance of close relationships and the Link between two Souls. Then George told him how to try the process. "I simply ask that you try this," was his last statement and request.

Richard didn't interrupt with a single question. He suddenly looked tired as if he were trying to absorb all this while carrying some enormous weight on his shoulders. He was probably wondering how to tell his Bishop or even if he should tell the Bishop.

"I told you that you wouldn't believe it." George hesitated for a moment and added, "Richard you can speak now if you like."

Another moment of silence before he spoke, "This is the reason you asked me about Church history, isn't it?"

"Exactly! And you know what? I have some information for you about the incident which occurred in the 1950's when you're ready for it. You are not ready yet, believe me. Any other questions for now? I'll tell you this, I've told my family and friends. They've tried the Link. It's worked for them. You can ask them. They've already started passing the word to their friends. I have a lot of information to tell you but I need you to do one thing," George requested.

"What's that?"

"I need you to try the process.....then call me afterwards."

"George, I don't know," he hesitated.

"Look Richard, I know you pray on a regular basis. Before you try this, offer up a prayer and see if you get any feeling of direction for this. It might make you feel better. One other request; my guess is that sooner or later you'll call your Bishop. I ask that you try the process first." Eli had that faint look of respect as he was now watching George, Dana observed as she watched the whole affair.

"George, I'll try it....but tonight after I get home, if that's okay... and I'll wait to call Bishop Wright until some time later," he finally managed to get out feeling as if he's reeling from continued blows, only these were verbal blows from one of his best friends, "Meanwhile, you've given me some serious things to think about. Let me ask you what would happen if I call Bill or Laverne about this?"

"I strongly encourage you to do that. They'll tell you the same thing. As crazy as this sounds, it'll be one of the most significant things you'll ever do. I have a letter here for you. It explains some things about the process and it gives you a list of things to do to make it happen," George said as Richard wearily raised his arm to accept the letter. Richard knows Bill and Laverne better than his kids or Monica and Marvin. At one time Bill and Laverne attended church here. "If you want to call me after you try this, I wish you would."

By now Richard regained some of his composure, "Yes, I'll call you afterwards...regardless of the outcome," he added. "I don't think I've ever had a conversation quite like this. Do you have any more revelations for me, George?" He asked as he smiled at last. At that, all the others in the room smiled as well.

"No, but I'm glad you didn't throw me out on my ear. You've always been a good friend, Richard, and a good listener. I really appreciate it. I'll be listening for your call," as George got up to leave, returning Richard's smile with a warm one of his own.

Richard came around the desk to clasp George's hand with both of his. This was something of a trademark handshake for him.

It took George about an hour to get back home after Richard and he finished their little meeting. An almost empty refrigerator forced him to detour to the grocery store. He believed the meeting went okay. Richard seemed settled down when they finished. It was hard to tell if he was curious enough to try or if he had already dismissed it out of hand.

George wanted to check in but he had to put the groceries away first. This time though, he was going to try a different tact as he settled into the recliner, "Eli, are you here?" he wanted Eli's feedback in case he had been observing the session with Richard.

Sure enough, "Yes, George, I'm here. You want some feedback, right?" George had forgotten that he has capabilities beyond what Dana and Katherine possess.

"Yes sir, if you don't mind."

"Well, the feeling here is your meeting went well. Rev. Casey has already made contact with us through prayer," Eli said.

"Is there any way you can tell me what went on?" George asked.

"Ordinarily, we wouldn't reveal the contents or prayers or responses if there are any. In this case, however, I feel you have a right and a need to know. He was very concerned about the conversation he had with you and asked for some sign as to the direction he should take. The gist of our response, and you have to understand that our responses ordinarily are not as direct as my conversation with you, was that he should maintain an open mind. We were careful not to suggest he should not carry forward with his commitment to you. Anything more direct than that would be bordering on a violation of the freewill rules. Someday, I'll explain all that to you. By the way, I liked the way you involved Stewart," he explained.

"Stewart, you know Stewart?"

"In a manner of speaking, yes I do. He's a fine young man. He will do you and his Father proud one day."

Just then a suspicion crossed George's mind. "Let me ask you a question, if I might. You didn't have anything to do with the questions he asked me which got me started on this path, would you?"

After the briefest of pauses, Eli replied smiling to himself as he looked at George, "I think I have to give you a yes answer on that."

"Was there some ulterior motive in that?"

"I think that you already know the answer," Eli said, "In any event, we have been looking a long time for the right combination of personalities of two close people through whom we might initiate some suggestions through one person that might trigger the other person into a course of action leading exactly where we are now. We've tried many times. But it's only worked between you and Stewart. You see, George, the powers that be here have wanted this Link to work. We've had false starts. Your start looks to have all the trappings of success. We've wanted this a long time and you seem to be making it happen. Word is slowly beginning to spread as you predicted. We always thought the method you choose was the best way. You don't know this but about thirty people have now tried the Link successfully. The number will grow every day. I don't think the process can be stopped now."

"We'll keep trying, Sir," George said.

"George, I think the hard part of your work is behind you. We'll know tonight if Rev. Casey calls you. We really appreciate your work. Unless you have other comments or questions, I will leave you to attend to our new and increasing Link activity," Eli said as he left the conversation.

Eli was gone. All George had to do now was wait. Eli was correct about one thing. He was not sure what he would do if this works out with Richard. He's pretty much exhausted his list of close friends. All of a sudden, the phone rang. My goodness, he thought, "Richard is already done with this?"

"Hello," he answered.

"Is this Mr. George Mason who has a son named Jason?" the caller asked.

"Yes it is. To whom am I speaking?" George answered.

"My name is Marlene Sanders. Jason is a friend of my husband. He didn't think you'd mind if I called."

"That's all right. What can I do for you?" George asked.

"Jason gave us a copy of your letter. I just wanted to let you know I was able to talk to my father and sister both of whom died over a year ago. I wanted you to know how wonderful it is you discovered this and decided to share it," Marlene said.

"You know, I believe the discovery is a gift from God that needs to be shared. It would be great if you could let any of your friends know who might be able to use this."

'Thank you. I want to email this to some friends of mine," Marlene said.

"Oh my gosh! I forgot about email," George thought. This letter is going on the Internet. He could not stop it. He hoped those who get it use it responsibly. "Marlene, do you think your friends have loved ones they want to talk to?"

"Some of them do, I know," she said. "I really appreciate what you've done, thanks and goodbye."

With that, she was gone. No time to give her some valuable points to use. She wouldn't use them anyway, probably. There was no telling where this was going now. "Forgive me, Eli, forgive me God, I hope I haven't messed all this up. There's no telling how the internet crowd and websites will treat this," George told himself.

An hour later, the phone rang again. This time it was Richard. "George, George," he started with an obvious air of excitement in his voice, "It worked. I talked to my father and mom."

"Well, hello Richard. I know you had doubts but I didn't have any. I knew as long as you gave it a good try, you'd get results," George responded.

"My Father said you're like a celebrity there, at Home, I think they call it. Listen, I won't take up a lot of your time. I want to know if you can come by the office again, maybe tomorrow or, if you like, I could come to your house."

"I can come to your office. There's probably a lot I can tell you, that is unless you call your Father back and talk to him all night. Have you thought about calling the Bishop?" he asked Richard.

"Yes, I want to call him. Maybe you can help me do that, if you don't mind. And yeah, I believe I might call Dad back. There's so much to catch up on and learn. My gosh, think about it, there's loads and loads of stuff to learn," he answered.

"I think I need to tell you something, Richard. I had a phone call about an hour ago from one of Jason's friends. She's going to send the letter by email to some friends of hers. My guess is a wide spread distribution of this may not be far behind. Have you thought about this enough to decide if this is going to be a good thing or a bad thing for the Church?" George asked him. There, his main concern was out on the table. This would either be a mountain or a molehill.

Richard thought a long moment before responding, "My initial thoughts are it will be a good thing in the long run. There'll be some concerns, however, by some older members but maybe more so by the Bishops and other church leaders. We can talk about this tomorrow."

"Richard, I've thought about this. I believe it will be in everyone's best interest, after this settles down, for the people and the Church. I believe this has a high chance of positively impacting people's behaviors toward each other because it will offer them better assurances about the existence of Heaven. I'm concerned about adverse publicity before the settling down process is done, however. I'll see you tomorrow. Is 9 o'clock okay?"

"Yes!"

"Okay, good night," with that George hung up the phone.

George walked into the church promptly at nine. Elaine looked up with more than a little concern on her face and said, "He's expecting you. Go on in Mr. Mason. Can I get you some coffee or water or a soft drink?"

"Coffee, black and thanks, Elaine!"

George tapped once on the door and eased himself in. Richard looked in pretty bad shape in spite of the fresh shirt and tie he was wearing. He guessed that Richard got very little sleep last night. George bet he called his dad back.

"Good morning, George. I called my dad back. We must've talked for five or six hours. I bet I look like I have a hangover. I certainly feel like it. Did I say good morning?" Richard blurted out as his knuckles showed white where he was gripping the edge of his desk.

George laughed. Elaine handed him a steaming cup of hot coffee as she looked at Richard, "I think I need to get him a cup or two as well," she said.

George laughed again, "I think you're right."

To Richard, he said, "Good morning, sir. You look really chipper this morning," he added still chuckling.

"Yeah, and I got some of the ladies from the Auxiliary coming by later. I hope I look better by then," he stated. "You didn't tell me this was going to be so addictive."

"I'm sorry Richard. I really only wanted to tell you enough for you to try the process. I had a pretty good idea how you'd react but I couldn't tell you," George replied as he took a seat in front of Richard.

"I guess you're right. There is so much to learn. I also want to compare the generalities of Home to what is taught in the Bible. On the surface, many of the promises of Christ seem to pretty much parallel what I learned from Dad last night. It's amazing to me that I can't recall anything about this being in the Bible," he said.

"You know, Richard, I've thought about that a lot. Seems to me there're a lot of examples of conversations between the Prophets and God or his messengers scattered through the Old Testament. I'm certainly not a Bible scholar but in a lot of the Old Testament books, there were always conversations being recounted. Even in the New Testament, didn't Christ often speak of talking to his Father? It's just that perhaps there are no examples of people talking to their loved ones who had passed on."

"Well, you have a point there. My dad seemed to think this new, how shall I say it, re-discovery that you've made has a lot of people excited there, at Home. I'm learning a whole new language from him. The Elders, even the Elders, who he said we call Angels, are talking about this. Did you know that?" he asked.

"Yes! Would you believe it if I told you they have assigned an Elder to monitor what we are doing with all this? My guess is he's monitoring us as we talk. I bet your dad is too. As to you learning a new language, did you get the lecture on your continuing responsibilities with your earthly duties?" George asked him. Eli was indeed monitoring them as was Richard's dad along with George's dad and a whole host of others.

"Yes, and speaking of that, I need to call Bishop Wright. I'd like you to help me if you don't mind. Since his office is here in Atlanta, I may see if he can meet with us... maybe today. Is that all right?"

"Yeah, go ahead and call him," George responded.

George stepped out of Richard's office to allow him a private conversation with Bishop Wright. Five minutes later he came out and announced, "We have an appointment at 1:30 this afternoon. Elaine, please call the Ladies Auxiliary and see if we can reschedule for another day."

Richard and George spent the rest of the morning and lunch talking over the discovery and its meanings. By now, Richard was firmly on the belief side that it would be a good discovery for mankind but had concerns about Church leaders who could have selfish interests in preserving their positions of authority and ranking if the Church suddenly found attendance lagging due to this. Even so, he was unable to come up with a way the discovery could be covered up at this point. By 1:30, they were in downtown Atlanta outside the Bishop's office. George had never been this far into the Church hierarchy before. Bishop Wright welcomed them like long lost friends. Could be that he hadn't seen Richard for a while, but, for sure, he had never met George. It didn't seem to matter, George was now a friend as well.

"Richard, what brings you and George downtown on what you characterize as important Church business?" he asked as he looked at Richard and then at me. His glance at George seemed to last a little longer than normal.

"Bishop Wright, my friend here has made what appears to be an important discovery; one that I had not known about except through Church history studies; one that may have far reaching consequences for mankind and the Church alike. I, personally, have tested his discovery and can attest to its authenticity," Richard explained.

"And what's the nature of this discovery?" Bishop Wright inquired as he looked first at Richard and then George again.

Bishop Wright had occupied his office for an even dozen years. Prior to that, he was minister at the largest Methodist Church in Savannah. He appeared overweight by some fifty pounds on his six foot frame. His hair was balding and definitely gray over black. He had light gray eyes inset in a chiseled face. He had known Richard for an even longer time than his twelve years in Atlanta. He even knew Richard's dad quite well from earlier days when they were both young ministers in South Carolina. He was curious about Richard's call and now was doubly curious with George here and the talk of an important 'discovery'.

"George has discovered a Link that exists between people who love and trust each other; a Link that survives the death of one of the people involved; a Link that can be activated by the person who has not yet passed on; a Link that will allow the two people to communicate with each other. He has introduced this knowledge to his children and to his friends who are beginning to use the Link and to disseminate the information to their friends. One of his children's friends apparently has sent it out in emails to her friends. Here's a copy of the letter George developed as a way of introduction and instruction," Richard explained further as he passed the letter across the desk.

Bishop Wright took the letter and looked it over. He then opened his center desk drawer and withdrew another letter, looked at it, then at Richard's letter again and passed both of them to Richard. Richard looked at them and passed them to George.

The bodies of both documents were virtually identical. Obviously, the letters originated with George. The letter Bishop Wright produced from his desk, however, was headed up as an email message. Sometime earlier today, it had been faxed to the Bishop. The title of the email was simply 'Mason's Link'. A severe chill went up George's spine. Eli smiled.

"A pastor from a Church in Norcross faxed me this email this morning," Bishop Wright said. "The pastor told me the person who sent him the email had added it to his internet Blog this morning."

"Well it seems we're a little late with the news," Richard said.

"No, as a matter of fact, this letter and the phone call from the other pastor came to me after your call. There was no way I could have connected them until you showed me George's letter. Also, the meaning of the letter is now clearer once you told me," Bishop Wright replied.

Turning his attention to me, he asked, "George, how long have you known about this link?"

"About three months now."

"How did you discover it?" he asked. Eli was watching Bishop Wright closely.

George related the story of Stewart's initial questions and his thought processes as he pondered the idea which Stewart planted. He was not about to say to Bishop Wright and Richard anything about his direct conversations with Eli.

"Why did you decide to go public with this?" he asked.

"I really thought of not saying anything to anyone, except Dana, about any of this for a time. I felt I would subject myself and her to all sorts of ridicule if we went public with any of this. Also, I had a concern about how this would impact the Church. But then, after she had her accident and I lost her, I started rethinking all of this. It occurred to me that the behaviors of people might change for the better if the Link were introduced. It also occurred to me that perhaps negative behavior between people might diminish," George explained.

"I agree with George," Richard interjected. "In my own experience with the Link, I can tell you those people who can use the Link will consider it for what it is, a gift from Heaven, from God. They'll appreciate it immensely. It's possible that not everyone can use the Link but for those that can and do, it'll be a good thing. It'll encourage them to behave better toward others. It may even encourage some people to modify their behavior if they were headed down the wrong track."

George explained further, "To me, this is indeed a gift from God. It's probably existed for all time and has never been explored or understood. To me it seems with a few simple explanations and instructions, it'll be useful in our lives and should be able to coexist along with other teachings from the Bible."

Bishop Wright looked at George for a long moment before responding, "I think I agree with you, George. Obviously, I haven't tried it. I think I would like to experience this as well. What do you expect in bringing this to me?"

Richard responded, "It seems that while this is potentially a good, if not a great, discovery for man, it also occurred to me, and I believe to George, that those of us in the Church have some re-evaluations to undertake about how we use this discovery in the work of the Church as we try to carry out the mission given us by God and Christ. I would hate to think about the Church, at this point, trying to do anything to suppress this. Maybe I should have more faith in our Church leaders but if attendance is somehow negatively impacted, it's hard for me to predict how they'll react."

Bishop Wright said, "I believe I agree with you particularly if attendance drops. Church attendance in most denominations has steadily declined over the past ten years. If this causes the decline to accelerate, how will church leaders react? Right now, that is hard to predict. I also believe this may spread widely and quickly particularly since you've told me from personal experience about its success. The emails and the internet will enhance its dissemination much quicker than we could do it ourselves. We must prepare for this. As you might know, all Churches and religions will be in the same boat with this discovery. George, I'm going to go further into our Church hierarchy with this. It's possible that you, as the discoverer, could be useful in the next level of discussions if Richard is right about how the higher Church leaders will react. Would you be agreeable to that?"

"Yes sir, I would. Whatever you feel I could do to be useful, just ask."

"Mason's Link; I guess it now has a name," Bishop Wright said.

Richard and George just looked at each other. Eli grinned.

George decided he needed to give the Bishop a word of encouragement, "Bishop Wright, unless you feel you have to call today, I would respectfully suggest you take this home and think about it. I also suggest you try the Link yourself with a loved one who's passed on." George knew from looking at the Bishop that he was at least as old as he and probably has at least one parent at Home. Unfortunately, George had forgotten to ask Richard anything about the Bishop's personal life.

The Bishop surprised George by saying as he looked up from his hands clasped together in front of him with misty eyes, "Thank you, George. I was sitting here thinking about my Son, Jacob, whom I lost in Operation Desert Storm. His mother and I were devastated by the loss. Two years ago, I lost my wife of forty five years to a stroke. Yes, your Link is already tugging at my heart strings to give it a try."

They bade Bishop Wright goodbye. George expected to hear from him as he made calls to his superiors. Richard said he would stay in touch with George if anyone from Church came across the emails and wanted some explanation he couldn't provide. Otherwise the trip back to the Church was uneventful.

George was unbelievably tired and wanted to get home without delay. Before he called Dana, he wanted to check in with Eli to get his take on the day.

"Eli, are you here?" he asked as he settled into his recliner.

Almost immediately Eli answered, "Yes, George I'm here. You really have this thing going strong. By my last count a short while ago, there have been 3,564 Links by people outside your circle of family and friends. Things are really getting busy here."

George was pleased as he responded, "I heard today, perhaps you did too, that the message is now out in e-space in both emails and the web. I envisioned an environment where this would spread without anyone having to pay for it but the web was unexpected. Almost everything there is public domain stuff. Anyone with a computer will have access to this. I expect it may grow exponentially for a while."

"We are well pleased with the results. It's much, much better than we expected. It would also appear the Link now has a name, Mason's Link. That's all right with us. I can tell you the Bishop has already been talking with both his Son and his Wife. I cannot see the Church hierarchies will be a problem with the possible exception of the Roman Catholic Church and some of the Middle Eastern religions. We can talk about those later. You look tired. Perhaps you should retire early. I know you want to talk to Dana," Eli said.

"Thanks, Sir! I apologize for the name. Someone on the internet tagged it or so it seems. I'm glad my first name isn't listed. I'm going to advise my family and friends to keep my whole name out of this if they can. I really don't want the publicity or attention that may come from all this," George exclaimed.

"We know. Your humility speaks well of you. Good night, George."

"Good night, Sir," and he was gone. George wondered if it was night there or not. Probably not!

Before he called Dana, he took some time to send his own emails to the kids and his friends about the name issue. Hopefully, with the anonymity of the internet, his full name would not become associated with the Link.

Chapter 18

"Dana, are you here?" George asked from the comfort of his bed. He was dead tired but not too tired to call Dana. "I hope she isn't talking to one of the kids or Stewart," George thought.

After a moment, she answered, "Yes, dear George, I'm here. I was on with Jackie and begged off to talk to you. I'd been linked with her about an hour."

"Thanks, you've been okay, I assume," Now that was a dumb question. Everyone was always okay there.

"Yes, I've been fine. This whole place is abuzz about all the links which are now occurring. Anyone here who still has close ones there is hoping for a call. It's amazing with all we can do here and with all our capabilities, no one can force anyone on earth to make calls to them," she said as she watched him from the comfort of her side of the bed she used to share with him.

"My guess is there'll be a lot more calls coming. If you haven't heard, the news is now on the web. The introduction of my letter to the internet means it will likely spread to all parts of the world. I wanted to spread the word and this is one way to do it, I suppose. Sure makes my job casier. This means that I can retire sooner," George added.

"Ha! You are already retired," she quipped, "What're you going to do when you retire this time?"

"Come Home," I said.

"That's not very funny. We've had this discussion before,"

"No, I don't mean I would initiate anything. I'm getting tired too much. I give out too soon. I need time to rest and recuperate. I need a place to get away from all this for a while. You have a place there and there are places here. I'll look around. Don't worry about me," he said. "Is it okay if we say good night? I'm ready for bed."

"Sure, George! Good night! Please take care of yourself," Dana said tenderly and with an element of worry in her voice as she sat there looking down into his tired face. She could see the results of the strain he's been under. "George," she said to herself, "You may be joining us sooner than later although I can't say that to you." She leaned over and kissed him as had become her new custom.

"Good night!" and he signed off.

George turned on the 11 o'clock news just in time to hear the newscaster say, "Here is a strange story. It seems the internet and email servers are getting more and more requests to display the letter on Mason's Link. You can view the letter by going to our station website. What's all the excitement about it? Well, it seems there are instructions for contacting a loved one who has died. Most people who tried the instructions report success at making contact. Is that not strange? No one knows where the letter originated. At least it's not a computer virus. For more information, go to our website."

"Well," George thought, "There you have it. Today it's an Atlanta news story. Will it be national news tomorrow?" he turned off the TV and turned out the lights.

The morning dawned to gray skies. A promise of rain was in the air with a tropical depression that swept in from the Gulf overnight. He turned on the TV only to pick up the national morning show from New York. No mention of the tropical depression but Mason's Link was being discussed by the news team on ABC. Yep, national coverage overnight; the miracle of the Internet was not to be denied.

At least they didn't have his name yet.

About 10 o'clock, the phone rang. George noticed from Caller ID that it was an Atlanta number but not one he was familiar with. Cautiously, he said, "Hello," he didn't want to find myself on the phone with some reporter.

"Hello! Is this Mr. Mason who lives on Stonewell?" came the small shy voice.

The voice sounded like a young girl. "Yes, it is. To whom do I have the pleasure of speaking," he found it difficult to quickly dismiss the voice of a child even if he didn't know her.

She began, "Sir, I don't think you know me. My father and I live one street over from you. My Mother said she knows your wife. I believe she said her name was Dana."

"Yes, that was her name. And what is your name if you don't mind me asking?"

"My name is Deana. My mother used to visit your wife at the local art gallery. She was talking to her about giving me art lessons a couple of years ago," she said.

"So you are an artist. What kind of art do you do?" George asked.

"Well, I really never got started. You see, my Mother passed away shortly after that. She had cancer," Deana said.

A lump began to form in his throat as he heard those words. "Deana, how old are you?"

"I'm ten years old and in the 4th grade."

"Deana, I'm so sorry to hear about your mom. It sounds like you were very close to her."

"I still am. That's the reason I'm calling. A friend sent me an email about this letter called Mason's Link. I was calling to thank you for the letter," she said.

"Deana, I'm confused. How did you know to call me if you just got the letter? Is my name on the letter?" he asked now slightly alarmed at the direction this was going.

"No, only your last name in the title. My mom told me," she added.

"Deana, do you mean to tell me that you've talked to your mom based on instructions in the letter?"

"Yes sir! I wanted to call you to thank you very, very much. Mom is in Heaven, you know. She says she has talked to your wife who is there with her. She says everyone there knows who you are. I can rest now. I used to have nightmares about Mom. Not any more thanks to you," she said.

"I am so glad you've talked to your mom. I'm sure she watches over you every day."

"Yes sir, she says she does. I'm sorry to have bothered you," she said.

"That's all right. You seem to be a very bright young lady. What do you want to do when you grow up?" he asked.

"I want to be either an artist or a TV newsperson. I'm already a reporter for my class at school," she added. "I'm going to write a story about you and my mom for my school newspaper. You are famous, Mr. Mason. Goodbye, Mr. Mason."

There it was, his worst nightmare coming at 10 o'clock in the morning from a sweet ten year old girl. There was no way he was going to tell her not to write her story; a story that appeared to have given her a new lease on life. He would just face the consequences. After all, who read those little school newspapers anyway?

Well, George stayed anonymous for exactly another week. At 10 o'clock in the morning seven days later, his phone rang. It was the Atlanta Constitution calling. "Here goes," he thought.

It wasn't long before George changed his phone to an unlisted number. After the initial newspaper interview and the initial television interview that came two days later, he began to decline all offers for interviews. The street in front of his house was now full of slow moving vehicles looking for the Mason nut. That's not the right word. Actually, all of the press has been surprisingly kind and supportive of the Link. Most people wanted to express their thanks for what had been discovered. Some callers, however, were frustrated at being unable to complete a Link. Of course their complaints always registered higher in the media than the good news.

Where possible and where he had one-on-one situations, George was glad to talk to them and to accommodate them. He turned down all offers to write books, give autographs for pay or anything else that would generate income. He made it clear at every opportunity that Mason's Link was not for sale. It was free for the using, a gift from God.

George began to spend more time with his children, overnight stays, sometime for days at a time. He had less time for golf with Marvin and Bill. He still spent time with them on the weekends whenever one of them had a party or cookout. They had to be careful. Word had spread that he was one of their friends. They always had a couple of extra people at their parties, people who were their friends, people who wanted to meet George.

They always had fun and spent time talking about their Links and Home and what it was like. By now, a great deal of general knowledge about Home existed among Earth residents. An understanding about how society functioned at Home was slowly building.

Entire TV programs were starting to be aired where people described their Links and what they had learned about Home. Websites were being devoted to Home.

The impact on Churches of all faiths and locations was perhaps the most dramatic. George never heard from Bishop Wright. The imaginary mountain in George's mind turned out to be smaller than a molehill. The Church had enthusiastically embraced the Link. Church attendance was soaring. Services and Masses were filled. Extra services were being added. Richard told George one day that he was working him to an early grave. Church programs were being built around Link experiences. This was happening all over the world. Even the Roman Catholic Church had come around and had recognized the Link. All non-Christian faiths had also responded favorably.

Not surprising, most crimes were on the decline. Crime rates for most violent crimes were falling, all except white collar crime and internet fraud. There was an uptake of internet fraud based around the Link, of all things. Scams tagged to Link related schemes were also on the upswing. Never mind, those committing fraud based on the Link would, no doubt, face some severe scrutiny whenever they reach their Reconciliation.

Late August in Atlanta could be excruciatingly hot. This year was turning out to be no different. Jason told George to come whenever he wanted. He had a nice in-ground pool which was used regularly by the four of them. George knew they had completed their summer vacations and were in the throes of getting Stewart ready for the second grade. George thought maybe he could wrangle an invitation to spend several days before school started.

His call was answered by Michelle, "Hello!"

"Hi, Michelle, this is George. I didn't call at a bad time did I?" It was 9 o'clock in the morning.

"Dad, the timing is great. I just got in from the market and the kids have hit the pool," she replied. Both of them knew how to swim and knew how to look out for each other. Still, he knows Mom is also keeping an eye on them through the patio doors.

"Everyone okay at your house?" he asked.

"Everyone is fine. Are you okay? Are you still getting hounded by people and reporters?"

"Since I've changed my number and since the city police increased their patrols of the neighborhood, things are considerably quieter," George responded. "Michelle, I was wondering if it would be okay with you and Jason if I come over and spend a couple of days before Stewart gets back in school."

"I think that's a wonderful idea. Unless you are busy today, pack some clothes and come on over. Bring any dirty clothes you have and I'll throw'em in with ours. We thought we might take the kids to see that new Walt Disney movie at the cinema tonight and grab a pizza before we go. I bet you'll love to see it with us. The kids will absolutely go nuts when I tell them. How about it?"

"Sounds perfect, Michelle. Thanks for the clothes offer but I'm all caught up on laundry. Is there anything I need to pick up at the store? I could go by the meat market and pick up some steaks for tomorrow," he said.

"That's an idea. We could have a swim-party-cookout thing. It'll be fun," she responded.

"Okay, I'll see you later. And thanks a lot, Michelle."

Michelle called Jason to let him know the plans and to make double sure he expected to get off when he said this morning. "George needs to get out of that house," she told him.

George had the car packed in short order. After all, he wasn't going to be gone but a couple of days. He was already tired as he pulled out of the driveway for the forty five minute drive across town, an hour since he was stopping to buy steaks. They lived in Marietta on the northwest side of Atlanta. "Maybe I can grab a short nap sometime before the movie," he said to himself. "Who am I kidding; I want to be with the kids; that's why I'm going."

He didn't have to knock on the door when he pulled into their circle drive. It was a five year old two story with three bedrooms plus game room up and the master suite down. By any standards, it was a great home. He imagined with today's real estate market, they could sell it for a nice profit, not that they had any idea of doing it.

Stewart and Nicole came running out to meet him. They still had their swimming outfits on, which means they were going back into the pool and they undoubtedly wanted him to go with them.

Stewart started, "Grandad, Grandad, I'm sure glad you came."

Nicole added, "Yeah, Grandad, you wanna go swimming with us?"

How could you turn down an offer like that? Nicole didn't talk much so when she did, you had to listen and respond, "Yeah, should I put my swimming suit on or just go like this?"

"Grandad," she said with an element of glee in her voice, "You can't go like that. Mom would fuss," giggling as she responded.

She had the cutest dimples and a smile that warmed everyone exposed to it. Her hair was as blond as Stewart's.

After saying hello to Michelle and putting the steaks in the fridge, George took his one bag upstairs to the extra bedroom where he always stayed. Seemed like the stairs were steeper for some reason. He was huffing and puffing when he reached the upstairs landing.

In short order, George was out the door and into the pool. They played around for the next two hours before Michelle rang the bell signifying it was time to get out and get ready to go to the movie. Stewart told him several times he was still talking to Grannie. George told him that was great. Maybe she was watching them having a good time right now. She was, along with Katherine and a whole host of others.

Boy was he tired when he got back to the room. He thought, "If I lay down for just ten minutes, I can rejuvenate myself; better get ready for the movie first, though." His head hit the pillow and the next thing, he felt Stewart tugging at his sleeve. He opened his eyes to a big smile. Looking at his watch, he saw he was out for 45 minutes. Still, he felt good and was ready to go again. Dana and Katherine watched him with a definite concern.

The pizza was good. They went to a Greek Pizzeria where George had a pizza supreme loaded with all sorts of meats. He couldn't eat half of it even though it was only a single serving size. Some sort of stomach ailment kept him from eating his usual portions. The movie, Cars, was great. They all enjoyed it, even Nicole watched it to the end. Usually she gets restless. Maybe she's maturing some at the age of five.

It was about 9 o'clock when they got back to the house. George was tired once again. "Where is all my stamina?" he asked himself. He had a little bit of pain in his left arm which he attributed to the shrubbery trimming yesterday. He announced his intentions to turn in early. Tonight he was too tired to even call Home.

As he was about to turn out the lights, Nicole and Stewart wandered in. They just had their baths and were about to be put to bed as well. Nicole gave him a big hug and scooted out. Stewart sat down beside him for a moment. They talked about Grannie a little and how Stewart was going to call her tonight to tell her Grandad was spending the night with them.

"I think that'll be great. Tell her I miss her," George said.

"Don't worry, Grandad," he said in all earnest, "I believe she'll come to see you soon."

George looked at him for a moment before responding, "What do you mean by that? Do you know something I don't know?"

Then Stewart looked up at him for a long moment, "I don't know what I mean; it just popped in my mouth. Anyway, I hope you sleep well, Grandad. We can play some games tomorrow, right?"

"You got it, my man," he said as he hugged him. It bothered him when stuff 'just poped into Stewart's mouth' like that. He remembered what happened the last time that occurred. His arm was still stinging a little, so he got up and took an Advil.

He was asleep before the room darkened as he turned out the light. He didn't remember even turning it out. "Hey," he thought," Maybe it's still on. I should wake up and see," then he forgot about it.

George did wake up, only it was 3 in the morning. The light was off, but he could see the clock radio by his bed. He found himself trying to breath, but he was mainly gasping for air. His chest was hurting. His left arm was hurting. He seemed to be having some sort of heart problem but he couldn't get up and he didn't have enough breath to call out. He struggled to move but only managed to pull himself to the edge of the bed.

The last thing George remembered was what Stewart said as he hit the floor. Then he blacked out.

He was only out for a moment or so because the next thing he remembered was standing in the bedroom. He didn't remember standing up. The light was on, or was it? Just then the bedroom door burst open and Jason rushed in, flipping on the wall switch as he entered, "Dad, Dad, are you all right?"

"Yes, I'm all right, Jason. I didn't mean to scare you. I hope I didn't wake up the whole house."

Michelle came running in about that time. Jason acted as if he didn't hear George. He was kneeling on the floor. George walked around the bed to see what he was doing. It looked like he was about to give mouth to mouth resuscitation to someone. Who? George looked down and realized that person looked like him.

"My God, that is me. That's me lying there. Why am I lying there? Why am I standing here," he was saying but no one appeared to be listening.

From behind, George heard a now familiar baritone voice, "George, you see yourself lying there and standing here because you have just passed through."

George turned to see a tall person of African descent, "Eli, is that you? It sounds like you."

"Yes, George," he said, "I'm Eli. Pleased to meet you in person at last," as he extended large soft hands.

Eli was tall. He looked to be about six feet six inches and slender with graying hair, no extra weight on him. He was dressed in a light tan suit with a white turtleneck sweater under his jacket. George looked down and realized he didn't have his extra weight any longer. He was somehow dressed in street clothes and not his pajamas. Why was Eli here and not the other two? Wait, they're here as well. "Will I ever learn more about Eli; the Elder assigned to me by whom?" George thought.

After shaking his hand, George turned back to see Jason working feverishly. Somehow, he already knew he wasn't going to have any success. He was here. He had passed through. His physical body is lying on the floor where he landed some minutes ago. He guessed the thud must have brought them running. Now he felt so bad that they were going through this. Why couldn't this have happened when he was home all alone and he would've bothered no one?

Eli said, "George, let me assure you, Jason and your other three children would not have wanted you to have been home alone when this happened. Can you believe you brought yourself here for a purpose you were unaware of? I can. Even Stewart seemed to know. He's such a great person. He was right. Dana will to come see you soon."

George stood looking at Eli for a moment. Standing beyond him were a man and a woman. They stepped forward when they saw he'd noticed them.

The man extended his hand, "Mr. Mason, my name is John. I'm honored to meet you, sir."

The woman did the same, "George, my name is Helen and I'm also honored to meet you."

After shaking their hands, George said, "Your names sound familiar. Were you with Katherine and Dana when they passed through?"

"Yes," John replied, "And we were also with your mom and dad and most of your other relatives. You know they're going to be so glad to see you."

"I'll be glad to see them as well," he looked back at Jason and Michelle who were now holding each other and comforting each other as they cried.

Just then, Stewart came wandering in. He had a look of confusion on his little face. He looked at his mom and dad. Then he looked at his Grandad lying on the floor. He suddenly had a most amazing look as if he understood perfectly what was going on. He looked around the room as if he were looking for something or someone else. Just then, George barely heard him mouth the words as he kneeled to caress his Grandad's cheek for the last time, "I told you, Grandad, that Grannie would come see you soon." Then he hugged his mom and dad and began crying along with them.

"They'll be all right?" George asked to no one in particular now caught up in the sadness as he saw his family grieving. He knew how they felt from that time thirty-five years ago in a darkened hospital room.

Eli answered, "Yes, George, you know they'll be all right."

George did know. He also realized Eli had taken him gently by the arm and they began to move. He was not sure if he was walking or what but he was moving directly toward the outside wall. Now they were moving through the air; George, Eli, John and Helen.

The next thing he knew, they were walking on a winding path through a lightly wooded area next to a brook. They crossed over the brook on a small bridge and continued on through a meadow, then more woods.

"We're heading toward the arrival station, aren't we?" George asked.

"Yes, George. You know the routine. Thanks to you, more and more people will be arriving who'll also know the routine," Eli responded.

"Eli, will I be seeing you as I go through Orientation and Reconciliation?" he asked.

"I'll be around for some of the planning process when we discuss your activity options and I'll see you during your Reconciliation program."

About the only thing George was nervous about was the Reconciliation program. No one had really told him much about it. Apparently, that was an area where discussion was not allowed. He decided to ask, "What is it about the reconciliation process that has prevented me from learning about it?"

Eli looked at John and nodded. John answered, "The decision was made long ago that if the Link process was ever uncovered, which you did, it wouldn't be in the best interest of new arrivals or earthly residents to know the details about the Reconciliation process."

Eli then picked up on the explanation, "Because of your special situation, I'll tell you now, George. The Reconciliation program is all about giving you the chance to talk about all the situations you were in while on Earth where your interactions with other people didn't end on an amicable basis. These were situations where either you or someone else caused unhappy or unresolved endings regardless of whether or not you knew yourself. For any particular situation, the process involves meeting the other person, if they're here, or reviewing the situation visually to allow you to see what happened from a third party perspective; to allow you to talk about the situation and reconcile with the other person in order to correct the unresolved issues. It's all about resolving differences between people.

"All people have these situations as they progress through life. Some situations are major, most are minor. You'd be surprised at the situations which people were involved in and never knew they were the cause of someone else being hurt. The Reconciliation program will give you a chance to review these, explain your side of the event and, hopefully, resolve the issues with the other persons. An important part of the process is to allow someone else who caused some unresolved issue with you a chance to set their record straight. You may have a few of those to work through as well."

"Thanks for the explanation. I thought it was something like that," George said, "You mentioned my special situation. What is that? Also, you mentioned major situations, what are those?"

Eli responded again, "George, if you'll notice, I've been the one doing most of the talking as we move along. Ordinarily, an Elder wouldn't greet you when you pass through. Ordinarily, it would be someone like Helen and John. You, however, have become a Person of Special Interest here. I think it's interesting that you have yet to understand the magnitude of what you've discovered, first and second, how you managed the discovery. Seemingly, at every turn as you were dealing with it, your decisions and actions about the discovery gave rise here to the feeling that you possess extraordinary talent and perceptive skills, just as what you revealed in your last statement about the Reconciliation. From what little you heard, you developed a correct sense about its purpose. Based on what we have seen about you, I can tell you there are some unusual things in store for you. I hope you'll find them interesting and appealing.

"As to major situations, think of an incident when someone on earth dies directly at the hand of another or indirectly as a result of decisions made by another. The other person, whenever he or she arrives here, will be faced with that situation and offered a chance to explain and to face the victim or victims. Those are the most grave of situations. Unless it involved some kind of self defense or the people were facing each other such as soldiers on a battlefield, the resolution can be quite detrimental. You'll be told more about this later."

"Thanks! Looks like we're approaching the arrival station? I remember its description from Katherine and Dana. Also, I see an entrance that looks like the front of my house."

"We'll be taking our leave of you now," Eli said. "I'll see you later."

Helen added, "They are expecting you inside. Just go right in. This will be your temporary home until you re-settle later."

George thanked them and shook hands all around. "I'll be looking forward to talking with you some more, Eli," he said before turning toward the door.

Chapter 19

George didn't have to open the door. As he walked up, the door opened and Dana stood there looking just like the bride he married all those years ago, "Sweetheart," was all she said as she came running out.

They must have stood there a full minute holding onto each other before they started inside holding hands as they entered. Immediately, he saw Katherine just as he remembered her. Mom and Dad were there. They all laughed, giggled and hugged and hugged some more. It was a grand sight for his old eyes and a lift to his sagging spirits.

George looked around the room and thought that this looked exactly like he left the house yesterday. "Yes," Dana said, "This is home. I see you've made a few changes since I left. That's okay. You can do it again here. Welcome Home, Sweetheart."

"I'm glad to be here. I'm glad to see all of you. This is just like I dreamed it would be. My favorite people in the entire world. Wait, I can't say that. I just left a bunch of favorite people and... I'm not in that world anymore. I'm here... at Home, wherever that is."

He looked at Dana, "Stewart was right; he said you would see me soon,"

Katherine said, "Stewart is gonna be special, like you. Wait and see."

"I think so, too," Jefferson added.

There was another person in the room who hadn't spoken yet. Margaret stepped forward, "Hello, George! My name is Margaret."

"I thought you might be. Things seem to go in patterns around here," George said. He did a double take on Margaret. "You know, you look vaguely familiar to me."

Katherine said, "I said the same thing when I first arrived," as she looked at her.

"I know this isn't important but I seem to remember seeing your picture somewhere," George added as he was pondering. "Seems like it was a portrait with a man, your husband perhaps. Washington! Did you ever live in Washington; at the White House?"

"Yes," said Margaret as she appeared to be blushing.

"You were First Lady to, to…. Zachary Taylor. Is that right?"

"My goodness, Mr. Mason, you have a way with names and pictures," Margaret said.

"No, not really. I was something of a history nut. When I was a little boy, I visited the White House several times and I seem to remember your portrait there. Katherine and I also visited shortly before she became pregnant the first time. It's an honor to meet you, Mrs. Margaret Taylor," George replied.

"Mr. Mason, the honor's all mine. Let me say that you'll find yourself quite well known here at Home. You're quite the celebrity," she added. "You may know that one of my activities is an Orientation Coordinator. I went from the White House to the Great House at this arrival station. It'll be my pleasure to escort you around to all the different functions you'll be involved in during this program and the Reconciliation program. I wanted to be here to meet you.

I'm going to leave you alone for a short time while you catch up on things with your family. First though, I need to register you into our system so you can't get lost like some people I know," as she grinned and looked at Dana. Dana blushed and grinned back.

She walked over to George's living room wall and seemed to touch something, a switch or button or something. A small panel folded out from the wall. Funny, that didn't seem to be there in Atlanta. "George, if you will step over here, I need you to put your hand on this panel for a moment. It won't hurt a bit, I promise. In fact, I can promise you'll have no more pains, ever."

He walked over and placed his right hand on the panel. He felt a slight but pleasant tingling sensation.

"Now," she said, "We'll know exactly where you are at all times; just in case you decide to wander off like Dana. I'm sure she's told you the story."

"Yes, I told him," Dana said pretending indignity.

Margaret said, "George, I'll be back later to chat with you and start the Orientation," To Katherine she said, "Please let me know when you're back with him." With that, she was gone, vanished before his eyes, dematerialized into a mist, then nothing. "I have some new things to get used to," he thought.

Katherine said, "George, all that you'll experience in the next couple of days will be new even though you've heard from all of us about how things work here. Some of us will be with you all of the time except for when you're with Margaret."

"Eli said he may come by from time to time," George said rather casually.

They all looked at each other, then back at him. Dana asked, "George, did you say Eli?"

"Yes, didn't you see him as you opened the door to greet me? He and Helen and John were at Jason's to escort me to the door here," he said.

They looked at each other again. Dana said, "When I opened the door, all I saw were Helen and John. If Eli was there, either he had already left or I couldn't see him. What did he say?"

"I think he was just there to help Helen and John escort me. He did say he'd be seeing me off and on as I go through Orientation and Reconciliation. He told me some things about Reconciliation, mainly because I asked him," George replied.

"He told you that?" Jefferson said. "I didn't think they were supposed to say anything about that before you went through it. You must be a shoo in to pass. Something is going on with you, George. Any idea what it is?"

"The only thing he said was I'm a 'Person of Special Interest'. What do you think that means?" he asked.

Katherine said, "Coming from an Elder that could mean about anything. I think mainly it means they have something in mind for you that no one else I know of has been exposed to. Well, George, you continue to surprise us all. I have no idea what it's about, not a clue."

"Me either!" his dad chimed in.

"I do have a suggestion, however," Katherine continued, "Why don't we all go to our place to relax a bit. One of us will bring you back. Also, we'll monitor what's going on with the kids and see where they're gathering in Atlanta and we may drop in on them. I imagine they're devastated. Bless all of them; they've had a pretty rough year with both you and Dana passing through. Your friends, too, I expect."

"Okay!" they all said more or less in unison.

George looked at Dana then at Katherine. They looked young and relaxed. Does this mean they're doing well as roommates? He wondered if they're having any problems or second thoughts about their arrangement. He wondered how he would fit into their living arrangements. Have they thought of that?

Dana said, "All right, George, take my hand." He did and she mumbled, "My place, go there."

Before he could blink his eyes, he was in another place. Slowly, others arrived seemingly out of thin air. "Maybe there was no air here," he wondered to himself, "I don't remember breathing." He tried to exhale and nothing came out. How about that?

They were all standing in a large open room with six walls. Off to one side George could see a lake with mountains beyond. Another side opened into what appeared to be an open courtyard. He could see a swimming pool. Another wall opened into a huge kitchen. Two of the other walls opened into like foyers. This particular room was appointed with comfortable looking sofas, chairs, tables all atop massive Persian rugs. One wall contained a huge screen obviously for viewing something. One wall was blank. The ceiling was vaulted with a massive chandelier hanging directly over the center of the room which happened to be over open flooring covered with one of the rugs. If this was where Dana and Katherine lived, it looked like they spent a great deal of time here.

"Welcome to our home," Katherine said. "Dana will give you a tour while we rustle up something to nibble on while we visit."

"Come on George. Let's start with the pool area." They moved through the opening in the wall where the door just slid into the adjoining wall; how about that, an automatic door in a home. The outside temperature seemed to be the same as inside.

"The only reason we have doors at all is to keep the birds and butterflies from flying through the house," she said.

There was an outdoor cookout area here for anyone wanting to grill about anything. It looked virtually unused. "It needed a man around to use it, me for example," he thought.

"You can see we have some plants screening off the side of the yard which is exposed to the park. We left the lake side open for the view of the lake and the Prayer Mountains," she continued.

The pool seemed to be Olympic size. The lake, a short distance off, must have been a couple hundred acres at least. George could see houses on the other shore and up on the foothills of the mountains. The mountains were snow peaked and looked in the 10,000 to 12,000 foot range. The mountain range ran from one horizon to the other, although he could see passes in them about ten to fifteen miles apart. You could see ski runs scattered across the surface on this side. It was beautiful.

We walked around the row of plants into the edge of the park. There, inside a six car garage, sat four vehicles. One was a BMW two seater roadster. He knew who that belonged to. There were two SUVs and something that looked like an off road vehicle.

"These belong to you and Katherine?" he asked.

"Yeah, we don't use them much since it's so easy to get around by the Home travel method as you'll come to know it," she answered. "The roads here are somewhat confusing. They're made strictly for the occasional driver who just wants to go for a drive, not for the driver who must use them to get somewhere. Home is so big; I haven't even seen a map with all the road systems on it. But if you get lost, all you have to do is return home using the Home travel method."

The park was beautiful. There was the golf course his dad mentioned. George would be glad when his dad and he could play. There were several areas for children to play although there weren't many out. There were extensive walking and biking trails through the park and around the lake. He could even see some horses in the distance. He guessed they had their set of trails as well. Other than the absence of children, the park was fairly well populated. He could see other houses around the perimeter.

Dana and he walked around to the lake and re-entered the house from that side. From there, she led him to the kitchen. Every gadget imaginable was sitting around on counters. There were lots of counters and cabinet space. Most of it looked brand new as it if had never been used. "We have all this stuff but neither of us has cooked much since I arrived. We don't really have to eat so we rarely do," Dana said.

Right now though, Katherine and George's parents were busy hustling up some food. Dana and George watched for a brief time. "Come," she said, "Let me show you my suite." They moved back to the great room and into one of the foyers. She opened a door at the end and they moved into another section of the house consisting of several rooms off a smaller version of the great room.

"These are the rooms where I spend most of my time when I'm here," she said, "I have a studio for my art work." They walked into a massive room every bit as big as the main great room. Various pieces of paintings were scattered around on easels mostly in unfinished states. The ceiling was made of some sort of translucent material that allowed the outside light full access to all corners of the room.

As they walked back to her central room, she pointed out the painting she'd obtained from Monet when she first arrived. George remembered the story of the unscheduled trip. There were a number of other finished paintings on the wall. Some he recognized as her work.

Next, she led him into a couple of rooms resembling a bedroom suite. There was a bed that looked unused. He stood there staring for a couple of minutes. Dana stopped, turned and looked back at him then at the bed. "Don't even think about it," she said. "It doesn't happen here."

He looked up at her, smiled, "Yeah, I know but I still have the memories," and went on to the powder room. There was a shower but no toilet facilities. Guess you didn't need one here if you had no physical functions to attend to.

Then he turned to see a huge walk-in closet with row upon row of clothes and shoes. Her penchant for shopping hadn't let up.

"Katherine's rooms are similar to these," Dana said as we re-entered her central room, "She can give you the tour of her rooms later if you like. Katherine and I have become pretty good friends. Since we generally acknowledge that you were our best friend when we lived with you on Earth, we're hoping you'd like to live here with us. Katherine and I agreed to ask you. What do you think?"

"What did you have in mind?"

"In the great room, do you remember the blank wall?" she asked.

"Yes!"

"We thought of building another suite of rooms out from that wall to your specifications. We want to take you to the Design Section where they can help you with the layout and design. It might not take long and would be ready well before you finish your programs with Margaret. How does that sound?" she asked.

"Sounds like a plan I like. When can we go to the designer?"

"We could stop in after we end up here and give them some preliminary ideas. They'll let us know in a couple of days when they'll have a version we can review," she said.

George nodded then smiled as he turned directly at her, "Tell me about you and Katherine. I remember a moment back in Atlanta when you were pretty upset to learn I'd been talking to her. As much as I'd like to be with you, I'd hate to do something to cause friction between the two of us or between the three of us or the two of you."

"Tell me this, George," as she looked George square in the eyes as she could do sometimes, "I believe you love me. I'd like to hear you say that. But what do you feel for Katherine?"

"If you're asking do I love Katherine, I think I'd have to be honest with you and say yes. It's been so many years since I've thought about that. We had a relationship unique to the two of us. Some of those feelings still reside deep inside my Soul. Otherwise we wouldn't have been able to Link up. Are they romantic in nature? I can't say they are, at least not the same way I feel for you. My feelings for you are unique to the two of us and run deep as they did for Katherine; but my feelings for you are still more romantic. Hey, I know there's no sex here. It doesn't mean when I look at you, those memories and feelings don't come to the surface pretty readily. Do I love you? Passionately, even though some aspects of that may be without teeth, if you get my drift. I don't know if any of this makes any sense or not," as he tried to explain himself.

He looked at her for a long moment. She looked back. "I've missed you so much," he said slowly as he walked up to her. He held her tight, then, for another long moment.

"I've missed you too, George, even though I've watched you about every day. You never realized it, but each time we talked, I never left you without kissing or caressing your cheek. I'm really glad we're going to be together. I understand all of what you said particularly the way you feel about Katherine. She and I have talked a great deal about all this. Whatever differences we had are past us. We feel you are all that matters to the both of us. We would like you here and we would like you to not worry about our relationships. We may have bumps ahead of us from time to time, but most of the time, we expect to enjoy being together and having fun with each other. We want this to work, but do you think we'll ever tire of each other and all this."

"I can't see how, after all, not only is this Home for me, you and all of us; but it's Heaven, a place where everything is supposed to be perfect."

About that time, Katherine wandered in, "Am I interrupting anything?" she asked.

George turned and looked over at her. "Katherine, we've just been talking about your and Dana's invitation for me to live here. Ordinarily a three way relationship can be inherently dangerous. I've given her my thoughts, she gave me hers. Do you think this will work? I think the place you and Dana have here is great. I'd like to be a part of it," as he strode over to her, "I want to be a part of your life again and I want to be a part of Dana's life again. Can you see a way to make this happen without problems?"

She looked at Dana and then at him for a long moment and slowly broke into a huge grin as she walked into his arms, "This is the way to make it happen. You are here with us and that's where you belong," as she held him tight. Dana stood off to the side, hands clasped under her chin with tears streaming down her face.

Her tears seemed to match his and Katherine's as he pulled back from their embrace enough to look her in the face. He leaned down to kiss one of her tears. Strangely, it had a salty taste. "I'm Home at last," was all he could manage at the moment.

The gathering at Katherine's and Dana's probably lasted four or five hours. There was one clock in the place and it kept Earth time. Unless you kept up with activities by Earth time here, there was no other way to judge the passing of time. Usually, the clock was denominated in 24 hour per day segments and showed the date and day of the week, all in Earth time. He had been here less than 24 hours and had yet to witness darkness. He had not been sleepy or tired. He seemed to have abundant energy even though they didn't eat or drink a whole lot. They didn't fill plates or sit down at a table; instead, they ate as they might if they were sampling food. They were after the taste, not volumes of food to sustain their bodies. It was weird but pleasant.

On the way back to the arrival station, the three of them dropped into the Design Section's offices. This was a huge structure. George learned there are multiple offices like this scattered across the Home world all to accommodate the desires and wishes of residents. The building must have been fifty stories high with the base of the building easily covering a city block. They arrived into a massive lobby and approached a person sitting behind a counter. The counter was the length of a football field with perhaps a hundred people talking to arrivals like the three of them.

The arriving process for the people was interesting. There seemed to be a special section of the lobby where people arrived. 'Arrived' was not an adequate word to describe what George was witnessing. People would materialize from nothing to a faint misty cloud to a person. They would immediately vacate the arrival area as if to make room for the next person. Such was what he, Katherine and Dana did.

After they related their reason to be there to the counter person, Katherine obtained a card similar to a business card. They held hands while Katherine issued the travel words, "Go there!" That's all she said. Apparently the card provided the name and location of the person or persons they would be seeing.

Next, George realized they were in a small lobby, presumably, somewhere inside the building. She walked over to the receptionist and said, "My name is Katherine and we're here to see Howard."

The receptionist said, "Yes, I believe he's expecting you. Go down the hallway behind you. He'll be in the second office on the right."

When they walked into his office, he was coming around a huge desk on which sat five flat panel screens, "Hello, Katherine, it's good to see you again."

Howard was a pleasant looking man and looked to be in his early forties standing about five and a half feet. George was learning that looks don't mean anything relative to a person's real age. A person might look forty but could have been at Home 500 years. What a place. He was wearing khaki slacks with a pullover short sleeve shirt that had St. Andrews Golf The Old Course emblazoned on it. George wondered if he'd played there recently.

"You know Dana," as she conducted introductions, "And this is George."

"Mr. Mason, I know who you are. Let me say it's a real honor to meet you, sir. I've heard all about you and Mason's Link," as Howard extended his hand. Looks like George hadn't escaped the attention he was battling back in Atlanta. Howard shook all their hands and led them to a u-shaped conference table. He sat down in the inner portion of the table. Behind him was a huge view screen; maybe 40 inches square with a picture shown in high definition showing Katherine's and Dana's, and his place.

"George recently arrived from earth, and we want to talk about expanding our place to accommodate him. He will be living with us," Katherine explained and grinned as she smiled at George.

"What do you have in mind?" Howard asked.

Dana spoke up, "We have the sixth wall in the great room," As she spoke the view changed to the interior of the great room with the focus on the remaining blank wall, "We thought we could add a suite of rooms similar to what Katherine and I have but tailored to what George wants." Again, the screen changed to show a foyer and the other rooms from an overhead view which he was now familiar with.

"Okay, George, have you given any thought to what you want?" Howard asked.

"Not much, really! This is all pretty sudden. I guess I'd like the central room to be something like a media center with a large screen or two for watching TV, movies, things like that. How about a pool table and wet bar? Some nice leather couches and chairs. Back on earth, I had this favorite recliner I loved," as George said this, a corner of the view screen came up with a picture of his old recliner. "Yes, just like that. I guess I need a bedroom with closets and a shower and a small kitchen area. Off of the garage, I would like a workshop with some woodworking tools and mechanics tools for working on things mechanical. I'd like a lathe, drill press and a small hand brake press. How am I doing?" George asked.

As he was talking, things were appearing on the screen. Amazingly, the views they were watching were the same as George was picturing in his mind.

"I think you're doing well. Do we see all the things you mentioned?" Howard asked referring to the view screen.

"Everything seems to be fine. What if I need to make some changes or refinements?"

"I should have all these pretty much nailed down in a couple of days. Why don't the three of you drop back around to see the draft version? We can make changes then before we finalize and issue the production request," he said.

"I think you did well," Katherine said. "What say we leave Howard to his tasks and get you back to the arrival station? Margaret may be ready to start your programs." They all got up to leave. They took turns shaking Howard's hand again. Katherine issued the travel instruction and, next, they were standing in George's den at the arrival station. There was his favorite recliner across the room. Margaret arrived shortly after they did.

Chapter 20

Dana said, "Katherine and I are going back to our place. You're in good hands here. If you need either of us, just call us. You won't have to go through the routine you followed in Atlanta, just call our names."

"Okay!" George said. He hugged and kissed them both in turn.

Katherine said, "Welcome Home, dear George. We'll see you later; maybe tomorrow. We'll go to Atlanta to check on the family as they prepare for your funeral." With that she issued the travel instruction and was gone. Dana did the same. "Will I ever get used to this?" he thought.

He turned his attention to Margaret. She was looking through a folder she was carrying. "By chance, that isn't a schedule of sorts is it?" he asked.

"Sort of is a correct way to describe it," she responded, "There is considerable flexibility built into the things you'll be doing as we go along depending on the progress you make and the aptitudes you display. First, we're going to send you to an area where the Reconciliation program is performed. Second we'll put you in a class where you'll be paired up with another new arrival in a group setting. There you'll learn the art of navigating around Home. It's pretty simple, as you'll see, but it can be tricky as Dana found out. By the way, her getting lost was primarily due to the fact that I didn't register her before she and Katherine went off to check on you. Don't worry, she was never in any danger but had someone not directed her to an aid station, she could have wandered around for a while. Eli will be here in a moment or two to escort you to Reconciliation Hall."

This made him nervous. "I finally have to face my shortcomings whatever they are," he thought.

Sure enough, a couple of minutes later, Eli appeared smiling and as dapper as ever. "Good morning, George," he said in his rich baritone voice, "I'm going to take you to Reconciliation Hall and introduce you to the group you'll be working with as you move through this part of the Orientation program. Are you ready?"

George couldn't tell if it was morning or not. Maybe that's something of a universal greeting here for the beginning of something new. "Yes, sir, as ready as I'll ever be," he replied but still nervous.

He took George by the arm and they were gone, a marvelous way to travel.

They arrived outside another huge building. George couldn't see the top, it was so tall. It reminded him of standing at the base of the Sears Tower in Chicago on a cloudy day and looking up.

As they began walking to the entrance, Eli started explaining a few things, "Ordinarily, a Coordinator like Margaret would have escorted you here. I'm going to be with you most of the time you spend here so I thought I would perform that task."

"That's fine by me. I appreciate the time you are giving me."

"You can see this is a pretty large building. There are a lot of new arrivals, like you, going through the program at any one time. When we arrive at our appointed review room, you'll meet a panel of three Elders who'll conduct your review. Do you remember the conversation we had just after you passed through where I answered your questions about how this process works?"

"Yes, I do."

"Fine! One of the Reviewing Elders will go over more of the details before the session begins. We may see other Elders and new arrivals as we make our way to our room. I caution you not to speak with any of them. You will note that within this building, unlike any other facility at Home, the attitudes of people are serious because of the situations which are reviewed here some of which can carry the direst of consequences. This is similar to courtroom settings on Earth."

"Can I ask you what 'the direst of consequences' means?"

Eli responded, "I know your situations which will be reviewed. You'll have to wait until the Reviewing Elders go over them but I can tell you that none of yours should be assessed the harshest penalty. The harshest penalty is one where the Soul of the person being reviewed is forfeited. It's a true death sentence which is carried out rather quickly. The Soul is forfeited as if it never existed. All of the memories are destroyed and the person and Soul ceases to exist."

"So there is no appeal process?"

"No, not the way you're used to thinking about appeals. Don't let this alarm you but the process that's used is one where a person's Soul is opened like a book. The events surrounding a particular situation are absolute. Unlike a courtroom situation on earth, there is no need to presume that a person is guilty or not. The facts about the situation are revealed as they actually occurred. A person's mindset is shown as it actually was at that moment. There is no way a mindset can be disguised. The review shows it for what it really was. The person has no ability to deny what's in his own mind about the situation. The only thing left to do is ascertain why. The person will be given a rather limited chance to explain why they undertook certain actions versus alternate actions. You see, we have the ability to get inside a person's mind unlike an earthly courtroom situation where most times a case has to be developed from evidentiary matter. That's probably as much as I need to say until your situations are reviewed," Eli explained.

Katherine and Dana couldn't believe their eyes. Here they were, standing in the middle of George's family room in Atlanta watching a party going on. George's body was still at the funeral home waiting on the funeral service tomorrow and his family and friends were having an old fashioned good time at his house, eating his food, drinking what little booze he had left and generally having fun.

Marvin cooked some burgers on the grill. Bill and Laverne brought in extra drinks and sodas. Jackie and Michelle made some side dishes earlier today. The visitation at the funeral home was scheduled early to make way for this gathering. Mike and Stacie were here with their children.

Katherine said, "Know what I think? I think they're celebrating the fact that George is with us. They're glad for him. Almost all of them will be able to call him sometime later. They know he's Home; with us, I mean."

Dana agreed, "Yes. I've had a couple of calls already. Stewart was the first to call. He seems to be able to do it so easily. I wonder if it's his youth or that he just has some innate ability the rest of us don't have. Jason called as did Mike. We'll have to tell George when we see him next. Any idea when that'll be?"

"Probably won't be for another week. I understand he's about to begin his Reconciliation program," Katherine said.

Eli led George into an elevator in Reconciliation Hall and punched in a floor number on a keypad. The elevator began to move although there was very little sensation of upward motion. A few seconds later, the door opened at the 131st floor to a wide hallway that seemed to go a city block in each direction. The flooring was soft but wasn't carpeted; instead it gave the appearance of a wood grain material dark brown in color. The walls were a light shade of green and gave a good reflection from the ceiling light source. There weren't any visible light fixtures; rather, the entire ceiling glowed and emitted a bright light. Double doorways led off each side every hundred feet or so along the corridor.

After they had passed two sets of doors, they came to a set on the right. Just before Eli pushed through them, George noticed a name plate attached to the wall on the right side that said simply 'George Mason – Atlanta'. "Looks like I'm expected," he thought to himself.

As they entered the room, George noticed a set of three tables with chairs on the left center side of the room. On each table sat a flat panel screen probably 24 inches or so in size. An abbreviated keyboard was in front of the screen, abbreviated to the point of having no alphanumeric letters, just symbols. The tables were turned slightly so that each was focused directly on another table set to the right center side of the room. Another flat panel screen was visible on that table but without the keyboard. There were two chairs at the center table.

The room itself was about fifty feet square. On the floor, there was carpeting, plush and deep and light tan in color. The ceiling was about twelve feet off the floor and was providing light similar to the hallway except not quite so bright. On the left end of the room were three doors. The door on the left was light blue, the center one was bright red and the one on the right was emerald green. The wall opposite the main entry door contained three large windows looking out over a city which extended as far as the eye could see. The sky was bright blue and filled with sunlight. There were no clouds in sight. Against the wall on the right side of the room sat several chairs behind small tables on which also sat the same flat panel screens as were on the other tables. Eli had mentioned the possibility that some other Elders might be present to monitor the review. Directly in front of George on the other side of the Reviewers' tables and the center table was another table with two chairs and flat panel screens. There were no decorations, pictures, clocks or anything on the walls.

The doors closed behind them soundlessly and faded into the wall so they could not be seen. George guessed they were locked to prevent anyone else from entering or leaving. "Looks like I'm here for the duration," he thought. When the doors finished closing, the light blue door opened and three people entered dressed in robes similar to what one might see judges or ministers wearing on earth followed by five other people.

The three robed people made their way directly to Eli and George. Each extended a hand. The first one said, "Good day, Eli," and turning to George, "Good day, George, my name is Jacob. This is Elder Sarah and Elder Elias. Let me say what a pleasure it is to meet you at last." The other two echoed the same sentiment.

"I'm pleased to meet you as well," was all George could think to say. He guessed these two men and one woman held his fate in their hands. He hoped they would feel the same whenever they were finished here.

The three of them looked to be about fifty years old. George's learned, however, that looks can be deceiving whenever you look to see how old a person appears. "I need to stop worrying about that," he thought. These are Elders. They could be as old as Home itself for all he knew. Jacob and Elias looked to be of East Mediterranean descent with dark hair and olive skin with dark eyes. Sarah looked to have a Northern European background with light skin, blue eyes and blonde hair.

Eli led George to the table in the right center of the room. The robed Elders took seats at the three tables to his front. The other five found their way to the chairs behind George. The sun outside was still shining. He wondered how long it would remain that way.

Elder Jacob was the first to speak, "For the record," he said to no one in particular, "This is session one with George Mason, recently arrived from Atlanta, Georgia in the USA. Attending as Reviewers are Elders Sarah, Elias and I, Jacob. Accompanying Mr. Mason is Elder Eli. There are five visiting Elders at this time. They are free to come and go as they please."

To George he said, "If it's all right with you, we would like to address you as George. You are free to address us as Sarah, Elias," as he motioned to them, "and me as Jacob," as he motioned to himself. You should feel free to ask us questions at any time about anything that we'll be doing here.

"Given that you are a Person of Special Interest, which I hope Eli will explain to you, I believe Eli has already explained some of what goes on in our reviews here. The main purpose of our program is to review with you some of the transgressions or offenses which occurred between you and other humans while you lived on Earth. There are two types of transgressions. Type one is an occurrence against you caused by someone else. Type two is an occurrence against someone else caused by you.

"Just so you will know, over the course of a normal person's lifetime on Earth, there could have been hundreds or perhaps thousands of transgressions. Most events are minor and most are forgotten by both parties. We, in our Review, deal with the most serious offenses both against you and those caused by you. We deal with the ones which still reside unresolved inside a person's mind as incidents they have not had closure on.

"The fact that they occurred is not in question. We replay them directly from the Soul's memory bank. Sometimes we learn the Soul may have recorded a version of the incident without all the facts. These are the easiest to correct. In most other incidents, we are interested in understanding what happened and why. The procedure is that we will replay the incident with you from your perspective. We then bring in the other party, if they have passed through, and replay the incident from their perspective. If the other party has not yet passed through, we may put the incident in abeyance until they arrive and bring you back to review it at that time. We are mainly interested in having both parties eventually review the replayed incident together and give you a chance to reconcile the incident with the other party. George, do you understand all that I have explained to you?"

"Yes sir, I believe I do."

"Fine, let me explain one other thing to you. Normally, as we conduct Reviews, we do not have extra visitors. Today, however, we have with us five other Elders who have an interest either in you directly or perhaps one of the transgression incidents we will be reviewing. If these gentlemen make you nervous, we can ask them to leave," Jacob said.

George had forgotten about them. They had made no noise of any type. He turned to look at them and they all nodded silently and smiled briefly. They looked okay to him. "I don't mind their being here," he responded as he settled back to look at Jacob, Sarah and Elias. The sun was still shining outside.

Jacob began, "We have reviewed your memory bank and have cataloged ten incidents for review. There were a total of 398 but the others were deemed immaterial or trivial or have already been resolved. These ten have been ranked in order of severity with the most severe at the top. We want to go through them in that order if it's all right."

As if he had a choice, "Yes, that's fine with me." George wondered what the first and worst one was.

"Before we put the incident into play, let me give you some background to set the stage. The year was 1957 on a Saturday afternoon in August when you were 18 years old. You were driving your Father's Buick Roadmaster north on State Hwy 32 in Maryland with Bert Young as a passenger headed toward Columbia. The two of you were going to meet a couple of girls to see a movie and visit the local drive-in afterwards. Does any of this strike a familiar chord with you?" Jacob asked George.

"I remember the car and Bert certainly but the Saturday afternoon time frame may have been any one of several afternoons where we made that drive," George responded.

Jacob said, "We are going to put this review into motion first as seen through your eyes and then from a higher birds eye perspective to get a better view of others involved in this sequence."

All of a sudden, the windows changed from a clear view of the outside to a dark color that allowed no light entry. The overhead lights dimmed about 75 percent. The flat panel screens came alive with a two dimensional view of the scenery as seen from George's eyes. The area immediately behind the Reviewers turned into a three dimensional scene that allowed all people in the room to view the scene as if they were driving the auto; except George was driving the car. He now remembers perfectly.

He and Bert had the windows down and the radio turned up really loud. They were listening to a relatively new artist from Memphis named Elvis. He could really sing, and even though all the girls were crazy about him, there were some of guys who liked his music as well. They could do without the contortions he displayed on television, however.

George heard Bert say, "George, have you played golf with your dad this week?"

Bert was his best friend in high school. They'd both just graduated in June and were waiting on September to head off to college. Bert was bound for Penn State where he hoped to catch a slot on their freshman basketball team. He was about six feet four with a pretty good jump shot.

"Yeah, we played on Thursday afternoon. He got off work early. He waxed me good as usual. We played on that public course in Annapolis you and I played a month or so ago," George responded.

"I remember," Bert said as he took a swig on the Coke he had in his hand. Just at that moment, George blew through an intersection causing Bert to spill the drink on himself and his dad's car seat. George looked down trying to wipe off the excess liquid before it soaked in. "Oops, sorry about that," Bert said.

"Yeah, my dad will have my hide if that puts a stain on the seat or carpet," George said as they rode on. Slowly, the scene faded away. The view screens also went black.

George was confused. He remembered the incident but he sure didn't see anything that led him to think anything was amiss even after 49 years.

Jacob spoke up again, "Now, we'll see the scene played out from a bird's eye view. This time you'll see the activity with sound but without any conversations."

Sure enough, the scene replayed on the view screens and in the three dimensional setting. There Bert and George were cruising along highway 32 in the Roadmaster. As they approached the intersection of highway 29, George realized he was not slowing down to stop. Both roads were only two lanes with vehicles on highway 29 having the right of way. He took a deep breath and pushed his feet to the floor of the review room as he tried to make himself stop the car which plowed straight through the intersection. "My goodness," he exclaimed out loud, "I sure ran that stop sign."

As soon as George said that, he saw another car barreling southwest toward D.C. on highway 29 at what was obviously excessive speed. Unlike him however, the car swerved trying to avoid hitting his dad's Roadmaster. The other driver missed him and swerved to his left. He crossed the oncoming lane of traffic. Fortunately, no one was coming. His car continued on, running off the road down an embankment into a small park. George watched in horror as the car slammed into a lady walking along a park path by a small pond. The lady was knocked twenty or so feet to one side while the car continued into the shallow pond. Luckily for the driver, he appeared to be all right. Unlucky for the lady, she lay on the ground unmoving. The scene froze at that moment.

George sat there staring at the scene. The rest of the people in the room were looking at him. For the longest moment, he couldn't move or speak. Finally, he said, "My gosh, I caused that accident. I caused that accident," he repeated. "How, how did that guy and that lady make out in this? I never heard anything as Bert and I sped off to Columbia. I didn't stop. I should've stopped."

Elias spoke up for the first time, "The gentleman driving the other car was Tommy Quinn, at the time, a 33 year old carpenter and a father of three with a wife of fifteen years. He was coming home from work and was going well over the posted speed limit when he saw your car shoot through the intersection. He tried to miss you only to go barreling into the park. He was charged with vehicular homicide and spent five years in prison."

Sarah then spoke, "The lady was Emma Holcomb. She died in the accident. She was 48 years old and was out for a stroll in the park. She and her husband of 30 years lived about two blocks from the park. She walked there almost every day. She had two grown children and one grandson."

Jacob said, "Mr. Quinn tried to describe the car you were driving but was unable to furnish much more than the color and make. He had no chance to get the tag number. There was a John Doe warrant issued for you, the driver of the Roadmaster."

"I should have stopped. I never even heard anything about it on the news. I guess Dad didn't make any connection either since we lived near Annapolis." George's family lived a couple of counties away from the accident scene. "All these years and I never knew. What a mess I made of the lives of those people. What now?" George asked as he looked at Jacob.

"George, what do you suppose would've happened if you had gone back?" Sarah asked.

"I dunno! Maybe I could've done something," he said.

"Yes, and maybe your life would have turned out a lot different if you had. Have you thought of that?" Elias asked. "You could have gone to jail rather than Georgia Tech. You might not have met Katherine or Dana. You might not have ever seen the birth of your children. What about all that?"

George looked at Elias, then Jacob, then Sarah, then Eli, "Yes, all of that's possible, even probable. But, it still is what I should've done." His life would indeed have turned out different. If he had gone back, there would have been a radically different life for him even as hard as it might have been. It should have been that way. "How will I ever atone for this," he thought to himself.

Jacob said, "George, I want to bring Mr. Quinn and Mrs. Holcomb in now if you don't mind. They have been watching from an outer room."

George nodded as he turned to look at Jacob, "Yes sir, that's fine. I'd like to meet them."

The door opened. Mrs. Holcomb entered first followed by Mr. Quinn. She appeared as she was dressed in the scene just viewed, a short slightly overweight middle aged lady with grayish brown hair and hazel eyes. Mr. Quinn, also dressed as he was that day, was slender with a beard, sideburns, and blue eyes about six feet tall. George stood up unsure about what to do. He decided to walk over. "Mrs. Holcomb, Mr. Quinn," he said as he approached them, "I'm so very sorry about what I caused. I know that day changed everything for you and your families. It should have changed mine as well. I will do whatever I can to make amends here." George stood there looking at them for a long moment before anything happened.

Slowly, Emma Holcomb closed the gap to George. She reached up with both hands and hugged him lightly at first, then fiercely as if he were a long lost relative. Then Tommy Quinn approached and hugged them both. They all cried. "Why are we crying? I thought that wasn't possible here," George thought.

Jacob, Sarah, Elias and Eli all looked at each other then at the five men at the back and finally at the scene being played out across the room. They had not seen anything like this in a long time. Finally Jacob said, "We can continue if we all take our seats, please" as he acted to regain control of the review.

Emma and Tommy took their seats. George returned to his and looked at Jacob, "I'm sorry, sir. That was something I felt I needed to do."

Jacob, unsure, replied trying to ignore the scene just past and George's comments, "You asked 'what now'. What do you think? Your action resulted in three children left without a father and their mother without a husband for five years. You left a husband without a loving wife and a grandson without a grandmother. The ultimate penalty is forfeiture of your Soul. Do you think this is appropriate in this case?"

George looked at him. He looked at Emma and Tommy. He looked at Eli. He looked down at the table for a long moment, "Yes," he said. Then he looked back at Jacob, "Yes sir! That would be the appropriate way for me to pay for what I caused them."

Jacob continued to look at George for another long moment and said without turning his head, "Emma, do you have anything to say. You lost the most in that moment."

George looked over at Emma. She continued to have tears streaming down her cheeks. "I've often wondered," she said as she looked at Jacob, "If I'd ever get a chance to meet the driver of that car although I never saw it until I arrived here all those years ago in my first reconciliation setting. I have met him; I believe he's a good person who truly wishes something else had happened that day. I hope he has a long and fruitful life here at Home. I would like to be his friend," as she shifted her gaze to George.

"How about you, Tommy?" Jacob asked still looking at George.

Tommy looked at George, "I had five long years without my family. I lost five more after that trying to get back on my feet. I survived. My family survived. We all grew older and wiser and closer. But I was also a contributor that day because of the high speed I was driving. Mr. Mason is right. It should not have happened to any of us. However, now that he knows all the facts, he will have a long time to think about all this. Most actions have reactions and consequences. He's now aware of what we've known for 49 years. He's not likely to forget this in the next 49 years. I agree with Emma; he is a good man and I would also like to be his friend."

George looked at Tommy first, then at Emma. He thought, "All those years ago, I caused this tragedy to these two and their families, a tragedy that affected all of them for years. Yet here, they have shown forgiveness and hopefully their Souls now have closure. As for me......"

"How do you feel now, George?" Jacob asked.

Again, George looked at Jacob a long moment, then he looked again at Emma and Tommy, "I appreciate the comments from both of you and your willingness to move on with your lives. I'm glad you have closure. If I were in either of your shoes, I might have the same feelings. But I'm sorry, though. I cannot grant myself the same degree of forgiveness. I caused you and your families' horrible grief all those years ago without shouldering any of the responsibility or the consequences. I feel I must continue to assess myself the same penalty. I know I'm giving up my dreams of living many years with my family in this great place which God has so generously provided for his deserving people. I no longer feel I am deserving of his reward. Please do with me as you will," as he turned back to Jacob.

"George," Jacob said, "Are you willing to sacrifice your Soul for these two individuals and their families; to abandon your hopes and dreams for you and your own family forever?" Jacob couldn't believe he was asking these questions to a seemingly willing individual; questions that hadn't been asked for centuries of any prospective resident. George Mason was indeed a rare individual; one to be respected down to his last conscious moment and thereafter in all our memories.

"Yes sir," George replied trying to sit as straight as possible and to maintain his composure in the face of these dire questions and consequences.

Jacob sat there trying desperately not to look stunned at George's response. Eli, Sarah and Elias had the same emotions as did the five Elders across the back. Jacob looked at the five for the longest moment and nodded slightly before addressing George, "Very well, then," Jacob began in the most level voice he could command, "We will take the next step. George, please stand. Eli, please accompany George to the area immediately behind me and stand him in white circle facing the Red Door. George, I want you to stand in the circle and not move out of it regardless of what you see happening. Do you understand?"

"Yes sir," George managed to say as he stood. This is it, George thought, "My life is about to end. Never again will I see the smiling faces of Dana or Katherine, or Mom or Dad. Never again will I see my children or my grandchildren. My dream for our future will go unrealized for me. They will survive, however. They will remember me. They will remember that I loved each and every one. Never again will I have those pointed questions posed to me by Stewart. Hopefully, he will carry on in my stead. If I could, I would appoint him to pick up the banner I have carried so proudly for my family. I'm ready."

With that, Eli and George arose and walked around the three tables between the table where Emma and Jimmy were seated toward a white circle inlaid into the floor. "Eli," George said in barely a whisper as they made the short walk, "I want to thank you for all you've done for me over the past months. I would have loved for our friendship to have carried further than today," as he extended his hand to Eli.

Eli took the extended hand but could offer no words in return except, "It's been my pleasure to know you, George," as he struggled to get them out and maintain his demeanor.

The circle was about four feet in diameter. Once he was in the circle and stood facing the door, his feet seemed to plant themselves. He had no sensation, however, that he might fall.

Jacob asked, "George, do you affirm your choice to forfeit your soul based on this review with Mrs. Holcomb and Mr. Quinn.? If you do, please say yes."

"Yes," George replied as clearly as he could say it in an unwavering voice. Eli was standing off to George's left about ten feet; his face a mask with no emotion showing but his insides were screaming with compassion for this man standing before him now in the white circle facing his last conscious thoughts for all time.

"Let the process begin," Jacob said.

The room slowly became completely dark. The only thing that George could see was the Red door before him. Even the white circle vanished beneath his feet. There was no sound from anyone else in the room. George could not see his hand before his face except as he passed it between him and the door. The door opened slowly. Darkness was on the other side; complete and utter darkness. When the door was fully open, George had the sensation of moving through it. The door closed behind him. In twisting to see it, nothing was visible. He was bathed in total darkness. He had a sense of total void as if he were in outer space except there were no stars to see. He had no sense of standing nor could he sense movement in his arms or fingers. His immediate thought was being suspended in a black hole as if this is what it might have been like before the Big Bang. Slowly, images began flashing before his eyes; images from his earliest childhood moving into his teenage years and then into early adulthood onto middle age and finally to the moment of his heart attack in Jason's home. The images stopped at that moment. George suddenly realized he could not recall any of his earlier memories from before that time nor could he recall any memories from his brief stay at Home. George was at the point of his death on Earth and seemed to be stuck there. All of a sudden, even that memory was gone. Now he was at the point of his death at Home. Strangely, he suddenly felt himself falling. So this is what true death feels like as he lost consciousness, then nothing…..nothing..….nothing.

After some moments, Jacob said, "Please raise the lights."

Emma and Jimmy sat there motionless and stunned at what they had just witnessed. Emma began to cry uncontrollably.

Jimmy began to shake and his sobs came in great convulsions. Even Eli had trouble maintaining his composure.

One of the Elders from the back of the room rose and came forward with slow deliberateness and stopped outside the edge of the white circle. He knelt and reached his hand into the circle to touch the forehead of the individual lying prone on the floor and simply said, "Awaken." At that, he stood and slowly returned to his seat against the far wall with his head bowed.

By now, Jacob, Sarah and Elias were standing around the circle. Jacob and Elias reached down to touch the prone figure. Each of them shook the figure gently as if trying to awaken him.

Slowly consciousness returned. Where was he? All he remembers is the nothingness that settled over him inside the Red door. George opened his eyes and found himself peering at Eli standing across the room. Looking up he saw Jacob and Elias with Sarah. He felt himself being raised slowly and carefully off the floor by Jacob and Elias. They helped him gently back to his chair at the center table. Eli joined him. George looked at him and Eli was smiling. He looked at the three Elders; they were smiling. George looked around at the five Elders; they were smiling. Emma and Jimmy had regained their composure and were looking in amazement at what they'd just witnessed. The three Elders returned to their seats.

Jacob looked at George and asked, "Can you hear me? Can you remember the first birthday party you had in your backyard in Annapolis when you were three years old?"

George looked at Jacob, then at Eli and back to Jacob, "Yes sir, I can hear you. Yes sir, I remember that party. Would you like me to tell you about it?"

With that, the room erupted in applause. Everyone was smiling and clapping. George didn't understand it.

Jacob posed another question, "Do you remember entering the Red door?"

"Yes sir!"

"Do you remember images from your memory flashing before you and ending at the point of your death in your son's home? Then, do you remember the darkness and the nothingness that followed?" Jacob asked.

"Yes sir, to both questions," he said not yet comprehending all that'd just happened.

"George, do you know what just happened to you?" Jacob asked.

"No sir!" came his confused answer.

"George, you were granted the results of your decision. You forfeited your Soul. Your Soul died. You passed into the void of non-existence. Now you know what that feels like. You made your decision and suffered the consequences and now we will make ours," he said.

Jacob made it clearer, "George Mason, you will not forfeit your Soul over this incident. All primary parties involved are Reconciled. This incident is closed. We'll take a short recess while we prepare for the next incident." Jacob, himself, was still trying to recover from what just happened and regain control over his own senses. In all the reviews he had been in over the centuries, he never carried one to this extreme.

With that, Tommy and Emma rose to go, still visibly shaken over what they'd witnessed. George walked with them towards the door, "When this is over," he said to them, "Do you think it'll be possible for me to visit with you some more? Maybe I can have you out to where I'll be living."

They looked at each other and then back at him, "I'll never forget what I witnessed here today. I'll tell others what I saw and what you sacrificed. I think it will be wonderful to be your friend," Emma said, "Do you mind if my husband comes along?"

"Yes, I was going to ask you to bring him and your children if they would like to come. Mr. Quinn, is there anyone you would like to bring?" George asked.

"My wife and maybe my children as well," he said.

They shook hands and left but not before George got another huge hug from them; one that he didn't quite understand. Meanwhile, the five Elders who were sitting on the wall behind him also filed out. They wouldn't be back as it turned out.

"George," Eli said as he came up beside him watching the others leave, "I've never witnessed what just happened to you; in 1500 years, I have never seen someone lose their Soul and have it returned as if nothing happened. This is a very, very rare event. You sacrificed yourself for those two residents. Indeed, you are a Person of Special Interest. I'm impressed. You couldn't ask for that to go any better. The other five Elders who were here won't be back but we'll see them later. I'll try to explain all this after we're done.

"Eli," George responded, "I didn't think I had another choice. I guess the rarity of this is lost on me. That was really strange. If I really died and my Soul ceased to exist, how is it now that we are standing here talking? I guess I can now fully relate to the Reconciliation process."

Eli said, "You are here because of the help of another very special person. I'll explain that to you later as well."

Jacob, Sarah and Elias had been talking together while the roomed emptied. As soon as the door closed, Jacob said, "Can we continue?"

The next most severe incident involved a guy, Luke, whom George knew in school when Luke was twelve and George was nine. George was the victim and Luke was the school bully. He had grown out of his bullying ways by the time he was a junior in high school and had gone on to become an outstanding teacher and high school principal. One day when they were both young however, Luke and some of his friends caught George in the boys' rest room during recess. His friends watched as Luke shoved George around and eventually pushed his head down a toilet. They all laughed. Except George, who was thoroughly wet, humiliated and crying.

Today, Luke apologized profusely. Strange that George had never forgotten the incident but after seeing him and learning about his outstanding career in education, the incident seemed insignificant all those years ago. They reconciled the incident between them and vowed to be friends from here on.

Luke passed through about five years ago. George guessed from what he remembered about him was he had already faced others like George and would likely be doing this for some years as others pass through who he pushed around those many years ago.

During the break following, George asked Eli about Luke's status since he probably hadn't cleared all his incidents that need to be reconciled.

"He's a resident with a provisional status. Anytime someone passes through and cannot reconcile all their incidents because the victims haven't passed through earns a Provisional Resident status. He is subject to recall here at Reconciliation Hall to clear them up. He obtains his Unconditional Resident status only after the last incident is reconciled. These particular occurrences are relatively major in nature. Until they are all cleared up, some of their privileges are restricted. For example, they may not be able to travel to earth and they may not be able to summon or be summoned by anyone else who has passed through. Also, we've recently learned they cannot be Linked as you were doing before you passed through," Eli explained.

"So if they don't have communication privileges, they could be at Home but no one who knew them would know it. It's not as if they had to forfeit their Soul, right?" George asked.

"That's right," Eli responded.

"Thinking out loud then, that might be the case with Dana's father," George said as he looked at Eli closely.

Eli grinned and only said, "Indeed, you are very perceptive."

Of the remaining eight incidents to be reviewed, three were those where George was the victim and five were where others were victims from something he did. Almost all involved pranks and cruel jokes where the victims sustained lasting unpleasant memories. Six of them were cleared by reviews and face-to-face meetings with the other people.

They were down to the last two. They'd been going straight through without a significant break by the three Reviewers, Eli or George.

At that point, Jacob announced, "George, the last two can't be resolved yet because the other parties haven't passed through and they're the victims. We have reviewed them and have deemed them to be minor in nature. We're therefore granting you Unrestricted Residency with the stipulation that at some time in the future, you will return here to complete the resolution of these last two incidents. Do you understand this stipulation?"

"Yes sir!"

"Congratulations, Mr. George Mason, you're now an Unrestricted Resident," Jacob responded, "Let me add a personal comment if you don't mind."

"Yes sir?"

"I feel you'll become a valuable addition here at Home. Your accomplishments on Earth are widely known here. Mason's Link! Not many people have had such a significant achievement which is so important to all mankind. Also, with the fulfillment of your request on the first incident, you are now among a short list of only five residents who have ever had that process imposed and then reversed. It was a first for all of us here to have participated in and witnessed such an event. The three of us have considered it a high honor to have served you. I know your service to others is just beginning here at Home. I feel very confident that you'll be very successful. Welcome Home!" Jacob concluded as he and the others walked over to extend their hands and sincere smiles. "You may now exit through the green door to your future for the rest of eternity."

With that, they were gone. They walked back through the blue door rather than just disappearing which was the mode of departure George had noticed others use.

He turned to Eli who had already started for the green door, "Eli, you know I have a lot of questions. When can I start to ask them?" He noticed the white circle in front of the Red door wasn't there any longer.

"How about right now," Eli replied.

"Okay! If I didn't actually enter the Red door, what's behind it?"

"As I understand it, the process you went through is exactly what happens behind the Red door as its final step. Whenever we have a Subject who has failed the Review process and is about to forfeit his Soul, he's directed toward the red door and is escorted through by two Elders. Once on the other side, he is escorted to an area where the decommissioning is initiated; in other words, the black hole you witnessed. Before that, however, the incident which triggered the forfeiture decision is reviewed once again by five Elders who conduct the second review outside the presence of the Subject. If they detect any hesitancy in the testimony from the Subject as he is recounting his reasoning, they have the authority to reconvene the review. If nothing is found amiss, the decommissioning is completed and the process is over. The Subject ceases to exist, all memories are erased and the empty Soul is set for recycling. The entire process is managed and conducted by Elders. No residents are privy to any of this," Eli explained.

"Wait a minute; you said no residents are privy to this. Then why are you going into such detail with me?" George asked.

"In addition to the fact that you were a witness already, I'll explain the rest of it," Eli said.

Chapter 21

By now, they had moved through the green door. They entered a nice waiting area with a large screen TV or view screen. There was an area for food and drink. There was ample seating space consisting of comfortable chairs and lounges. There were reading materials. A closer look at the reading materials revealed a selection of newspapers from Earth and from Home. An even closer looked revealed a headline that simply read Mason's Link. George didn't pick it up.

Eli motioned to a couple of chairs and for them to sit down. "We've been going through the review now for a time period equivalent to five earth days without stopping. Do you feel tired, hungry, or thirsty?"

He thought a minute. Five days; he'd no idea they were in the Review for five straight days. After he recovered from that surprise, he realized that he wasn't tired or sleepy or hungry or thirsty, and he didn't have to go to the restroom. He felt he needed something in his hand however if they were going to have more discussions, "Can I get a Diet Coke?" He was surprised by his request. "Why would I need a diet drink here? Boy, I have a lot to get used to," he thought.

Eli mumbled something and handed him a Diet Coke on ice, "Is this all right?"

"Yes, thanks very much."

"Now the reason I told you all that, as part of the Orientation Program, you are evaluated to determine the responsibilities which will be assigned to you. The process normally takes some time during which someone talks to you about your interests, your background, education, occupation and so on. The idea is to find you something to do which you'll find interesting and fulfilling. This process may not apply to you. You've heard yourself described by me and Jacob and perhaps others as a Person of Special Interest haven't you?"

"Yes and I was going to ask what that meant."

"The arrival of a Person of Special Interest rarely occurs. Soon, you'll meet the One who gave you that designation. But as to what it means; it means if you're agreeable, we want to put you into a special training program where, at some point in the future, you'll become an Elder like me."

It's a good thing George was sitting down or else he would have collapsed. He almost spilled his drink.

"While you're in the Elder training program, you'll enjoy the life of an Unrestricted Resident. As such, we want you to work with me in the newly formed Department of Linking Services, the creation of which is almost solely due to your discovery and your efforts to spread the news about it," Eli continued. "I wasn't always an Elder. I've been an elder for over 1500 years. For 300 years before that, I was a resident like you. I still take on the appearance of a resident quite often."

"Appearance, what does that mean?"

"George, you have yet to learn all the new things that have been unleashed within your Soul simply by passing through. You'll learn there are lots of things you can do now that weren't possible on Earth in your old physical body. You're able to change certain aspects of your physical appearance. You can make yourself older or younger simply by willing it so. What you can't do is change your skin color or facial features except to look as you did as a young boy or as an old man. Whatever you looked like on Earth at any age, you can assume that appearance here.

"Elders, however, have a great deal more capabilities than regular residents. We can assume the look of almost anything except inanimate objects. We can look like anyone. For example, to you I look like a tall person of African descent with a baritone voice."

Slowly a metamorphosis began before George's eyes. Eli grew shorter. His skin assumed a fair complexion. His hair turned blond. His eyes became blue. "Eighteen hundred years ago, I passed through from a heavily wooded forest in a part of the world you know now as Finland. I was in a small hunting party when we were set upon by a larger rival group except they were a war party and not a hunting party. I, along with six of my friends perished in that brief, one sided fight. I left a wife and two small children all of whom soon perished as well because I wasn't there to protect them. They're all here with me now. I see them every chance I get. My name then and now as a resident is Eric."

He metamorphosed back to Eli. "Time requirements for Elders are different from residents who only have to devote about ten percent of their time to their responsibilities," he continued, "My time spent as an Elder is about fifty percent. The other thing is that aside from my wife and children, no one else here who I knew on Earth or who I meet now as a resident knows that I'm an Elder. It's very important to protect our identities. Now you know and I expect that you'll respect my other identity and keep it a secret.

"There'll be a lot of things you'll learn as an Elder which are not known by other residents. We'll let you know where the dividing lines are. About the only thing you'll be able to tell Katherine and Dana and your immediate children when they pass through is that you're an Elder as well as a resident. You won't be able to tell them anything about what you do or what you learn as an Elder. You won't even be able to tell them your Elder name. They won't be able to tell anyone else about your being an Elder. When you adopt your Elder appearance, they will not recognize you even though you may meet them face-to-face on the street."

George was still sitting there holding his drink mesmerized by what Eli was revealing. "Can I ask a question?" he asked.

"By all means."

"Maybe a couple of questions. First, how many Elders are there and how many were once residents?"

"In the beginning," Eli began, "When God created the universe and after mankind appeared on the scene, He also created about one hundred Elders. They were originally known as Angels. The name changed to Elders after the arrival of residents who perceived the Angels as having been here a long time and who appeared more elderly than they. This core group was given the responsibility of organizing the place we call Home and to ready it to accept residents. They also helped Him in the formation and placement of Souls into newly conceived infants. He eventually increased this number to around five hundred before Earth residents began to pass through in sufficient numbers to recruit from their ranks. After that, He recruited heavily from among new arrivals to meet the growing demands of new residents here. The number has now grown to about five hundred thousand. The recruitment efforts are not as focused as they once were. It seems that technology on earth when combined with the technology here puts fewer demands on the physical presence of Elders to get things done. I believe the recruiting ratio is now about one out of four hundred thousand new arrivals."

"I'm overwhelmed. Is this something that'll happen immediately?"

"No, as a matter of fact, you'll be in the training program without significant Elder responsibilities until all your transgressions are cleared. That may not be until the last person arrives here who you transgressed against. You'll have an Elder name and appearance immediately so you can undergo your training, but without a full range of Elder responsibilities. Is this something you want to think about?"

"I've been thinking as you were explaining. It's overwhelming for sure. It's an honor as well. I'm not quite sure why this is being offered to me," George added with a lot of trepidation.

All of a sudden, a door opened on the far end of the room. In walked four men. As George looked closer, he could tell they were present at his first incident review. There was a fifth and they all had left after the first review was finished. These four headed straight for Eli and him. They were all about the same height which was about five and a half feet and dressed in nice looking business suits. They were well groomed and looked eastern Mediterranean with dark hair and olive skins.

Then, before they were upon Eli and him, a metamorphosis occurred in all four. This was the third time George had witnessed such a thing within the past few minutes. They have to be Elders. Very quickly, their clothing changed to robes, multicolored robes. Their clean shaven faces changed to manicured beards and their hair became shoulder length.

Eli said, "George, let me introduce you to these gentlemen. You saw them a short time ago at your first incident review without the beards and robes. This is Andrew," as he brought George before the first man.

"Mr. Mason, I am honored to meet you at last. We've all heard so much about you over the past months," as he referenced earth time.

"Yes, sir, I'm pleased to meet you as well."

"And George," Eli continued, "This is Matthew."

"George, is it all right if I call you George, I am also honored to meet you," Matthew responded.

"Yes, sir, it's my pleasure and it's all right to call me George," he said as he shook his hand.

On to the next person; Eli introduced him as James.

"George, the gentleman who discovered Mason's Link; I've been eagerly waiting for a chance to shake your hand," James said with a wide smile as he grasped George's hand in both of his.

"I'm glad to meet you, James," George replied as he felt himself blushing. Wait, he thought, James... and Matthew... and Andrew. Where has he heard those names before?

Stepping along, Eli said, "And George, this is John."

John took his hand, "George, welcome Home. We hope you'll join our ranks as an Elder."

George took his hand but didn't immediately respond as he looked into John's eyes. Then he looked back at the other three. "Wait a minute, you are John," as he looked back. George released his hand and looked at the other three, "You are James, Matthew and Andrew. These were the names of four of Jesus' twelve disciples. This is just a coincidence, right?" as he glanced back at Eli.

"This is no coincidence, George. These gentlemen are Christ's disciples. Some of the others would have been here but they are busy on other assignments. You will meet them in due time," Eli said as he grinned.

Just then, the fifth Elder who had been at the review came into the room. He looked to be about five ten in height, same as George and dressed in a dark navy suit with white shirt and tie. Like the others, He was well groomed and with an olive complexion. He looked directly at George with royal blue eyes as He crossed the room. The others parted as He approached them. This time, Eli made no introduction; in fact, he said not a word.

George couldn't take his eyes off Him. As He approached, His suit metamorphosed into a white flowing robe. His hair, already dark, grew to slightly longer than shoulder length. On His face appeared a dark brown well trimmed beard. George was stunned as he quickly thought this could not be true. This couldn't be....

"George," He spoke in a gentle but firm voice, "I think we'll call you Joseph, after My earthly father. My name is Jesus," He said as He hugged George and kissed him on each cheek, "I have watched you from afar for a long while now and have heard volumes about your achievements and your inner struggles as you brought yourself to action in revealing the Link. Are you all right?" He stepped back and gazed at George while still holding his shoulders in each of His hands.

He probably saw George's mouth agape and felt his knees wobble but George brought himself under control as he replied, "Yes, Lord, I believe I'm okay. I am deeply honored that You would come to meet me. Will You tell me why?" George couldn't believe he was asking Him, the Lord Jesus, God Incarnate, any kind of question. "I should be on my knees before Him," he thought to himself.

"Yes," He replied, "I will tell you why and you don't have to kneel," as he read George's inner thoughts, "I wanted to meet you Myself and tell you face to face what you have done for us, for the Kingdom you now are in, which we call Home, and for Me, personally.

"Since I returned here to the Kingdom after My time on earth those two millenniums ago, I decided to modify the Souls we were giving humans to allow for a Link to be formed between two loving and caring people, the Link you discovered and aptly named. I thought the relationship between these people should not be lost just because one passes through to the Kingdom before the other.

"Joseph, the Link has existed dormant, undiscovered and misunderstood all these years until you found it. Please know and understand that Mason's Link and its dissemination is the most important achievement in Christendom since my Resurrection. Your service in bringing this forward will be etched forever in the hearts and minds of all mankind. They will make you a saint one day.

"From your first glimpse, I witnessed your amazement and confusion the first time you contacted Katherine. I witnessed your growth in understanding as you learned more. I saw your struggles as you came to grips with how to reveal its existence. I witnessed the decisions you made, all of them the right ones, as you moved to tell your children, friends and church leaders, knowing they in turn would reveal it to others. I saw your surprise as the new earth technology took hold of the information about Mason's Link and spread it further. I saw the humble manner in the way you refused to take credit or compensation for its existence. These are all qualities of a person I need. I could have let Eli tell you all this but I wanted to tell you in person.

"The results of your work have been phenomenal on Earth. Never have My churches and church leaders been so busy. Never has a single discovery had such an impact on behaviors. I and all of us here and those on earth who have yet to join us and those who will follow them, owe you a tremendous debt of gratitude. You have impacted millions of lives for the better. Your discovery will impact billions in the future. You are here at Home, with us, with Me and are now a permanent part of my Kingdom.

"A short time ago in your first incident review, I witnessed a personal sacrifice you made for two individuals and their families who had already forgiven you. A sacrifice you felt was necessary because you thought you had not given enough of yourself to make them whole. I am personally familiar with such sacrifices as you may know. That impressed me because almost no one else would offer up their Soul as you did.

"Joseph, you must say that you will join us as we make a place to use your talents and reward you for what you so humbly have done for all mankind and for Me."

George must have looked dumb struck as His words slowly soaked in. It seemed to take an eternity for him to respond, "Lord, everything You've said is most gracious and I thank You for the recognition. I need to point out a couple of things, if You don't mind."

"Please go ahead, Joseph."

George was also having trouble getting used to a new name. 'George' would have been just fine with him. "In my own thought processes," he began, "I've given credit to my grandson, Stewart, for triggering the questions about the Link which I explored before attempting it the first time. Whether it was him or some other external process that was using him, none of this would likely have transpired were it not for him.

"Also, I must say, when I was contemplating the Link and after I had successfully contacted Katherine, my motives were quite personal. It also took me some time to get beyond the fear that I might likely subject myself to ridicule if I told anyone, including my beloved Dana. It took me even longer to realize that the Link might actually have a positive influence on behaviors.

"I don't want to mislead anyone to think I started this for purely religious purposes. I've always considered myself to be only a middle-of-the-road Christian. Most things I've done during my life were considered from the standpoint of me first and not You first, Lord. I apologize for that but I have to be honest with You." George said in reply.

"Indeed, your grandson, Stewart, is a fine young man. He has great things ahead of him as you will see. As for yourself," replied Jesus, "Your honesty and forthrightness are qualities about you I highly admire. Would it surprise you to know that most people, including many who are called to be church leaders, all started out from a purely personal perspective? That is a human quality that's always existed. Your personal makeup is no different. All of these men here with us in this room started out that way." George looked around and everyone was nodding in agreement. "When I walked on Earth as a man and was going through the persecution and crucifixion, my own personal fears came to the surface.

"The fear of ridicule and derision and the possibility that someone would think you a little unusual would have driven most people in your position in a direction other than the one you chose. The fact that you stayed the course and plotted out the most effective way to achieve your objective and expected to receive nothing in return were what convinced us of your potential as an Elder. The fact that you insisted on giving Me the credit multiple times is what convinced Me about your character."

His words provided a very calming influence over George. "My answer then, Lord, is yes, I most humbly accept Your kind and generous invitation. I hope upon hope I don't disappoint You," George answered, "Let me also say of all the responsibilities and requirements on Your time, I appreciate You giving me the chance to meet You in person. This is something I never expected or even thought possible."

"Joseph, believe me when I say this is the most important thing I have to do at this time. Besides," he smiled, "I have multitasking abilities. One day, I'll show you how that works. Also, and this is important, if you ever feel you need to talk to Me, please just call My name and we will be together." With that, He gave George another hug, shook the hand of the other five Elders and turned to leave. By the time He was at the door, He was dressed again as one might expect in seeing some powerful business executive. "In an odd kind of way," George thought, "He could be considered a CEO; the CEO of the Kingdom of God."

Andrew shook George's hand and said, "I'll also take my leave. It will be a great pleasure to work along side you as an Elder, Joseph." The other three said basically the same as they all shook his and Eli's hand and turned to depart.

After they left, Eli turned to George and said, "How do you feel now that you've had a personal Audience with the Lord?"

"I'm overwhelmed beyond belief. It really did happen, didn't it? I mean I'm not just dreaming this am I? An Elder, huh! What are the odds of that happening?"

"As I said earlier," Eli replied, "I put the odds at about one in four hundred thousand. George, if you don't mind you will be George to me until we can get you into Elder training and we decide on your new alternate appearance. Let me just say that I've probably been in several hundred gatherings with the Lord over the past 1500 years, some small one-on-one settings, most were larger. I've never heard Him say to anyone what He said today about offering to show you how He multitasks. When He said that, I glanced at the other four Elders. They all looked at each other as I did them; with a look of surprise. I imagine it's hard to surprise any of them."

"Well, I'm sure I don't know what it means either," George retorted.

"There is one other fact you should know about the first incident review when you voluntarily surrendered your Soul. That act was only possible because Jesus was one of the five Elders attending as observer. They allowed you to forfeit your Soul only because Jesus was there to restore it. I know you don't remember it but the rest of us were witnesses. I thought you should know that."

"My gosh, Eli," George said, "How do I respond to that? Are you saying I was raised from the dead by Jesus?"

"Yes, I guess I am. Literally! Is that amazing or what? I've never witnessed that before in all my 1500 years. You are something, George."

"I....I...I'm just going to shut up because I don't know what to say."

"All right! George, there're two remaining steps before we turn you loose in Home society. Margaret will be here in a moment or two to escort you back to your home in the arrival station. You may find Katherine and Dana there by now. Margaret will begin your regular Orientation program where you'll learn to function as a resident. Then, after that's completed, I'll be back to take you to your first of many sessions of Elder training.

"Remember, the fact that you'll be an Elder must be kept from everyone except Katherine and Dana. You can tell your children as they arrive Home. Even Margaret need not know. You may also tell only Katherine and Dana about your Audience but they must not reveal it to anyone else.

"You'll hear again during Orientation that you'll be working with me at the Department of Linking Services. From there, you and I'll be able to carve out the training needed as an Elder without alerting other residents. George, I'm really looking forward to working with you and being your friend. I know you'll find your life here at Home to be rewarding and fulfilling. And, no one knows what the Lord really has in store for you."

"Thank you so much, Eli," George replied, "I am also looking forward to all of this. I hope you and I become close friends. There is so much new going on, so much unexpected, has there ever been a case of a new resident going off the deep end and being sent to the funny farm?"

Eli laughed; he had a really great laugh.

About that time Margaret came through the door. Eli looked up at her and then at George, "Has it occurred to you since we've been in Reconciliation Hall, George, that everyone has come and gone through doorways and not through the Home travel approach where you just materialize?"

"No, but you're right. Everyone I've seen has gone through a doorway."

"That's because of the sensitive nature of the things which go on in this building. To enter any area, everyone must be cleared in advance. Everyone you've met while here have been cleared to enter each door they've used. We wouldn't want people to unexpectedly enter and leave without prior approval," he said.

Margaret said, "Is this a good time for me?"

"You're just in time, Margaret," Eli said, then to George, "George, Margaret will get you back to your quarters now. Call me if you need me," as Eli shook his hand and left.

Chapter 22

Margaret turned to George, "We can go if you're ready, George. Congratulations on completing the Reconciliation program. You'll find the toughest part of arriving Home is now behind you."

"I'm ready," George said as he was contemplating all that had gone on here over the last four or five days particularly the last hour or so. She was right about toughness, but she had no idea about other surprises the Home office can pull.

They left by a doorway, went through another doorway and back into another hall leading to yet another bank of elevators. Apparently, the setup was that new arrivals going to Reconciliation would not meet new arrivals just completing Reconciliation. Once outside the building, Margaret issued the Home travel instructions, and they were off to his temporary residence. Sure enough, Katherine and Dana were awaiting his arrival.

They were smiling. "I guess that means they decided to let you stay," Dana said.

"It was close, but I squeaked by. Since I didn't see either of you there, I guess none of my major transgressions involved you. I was a little worried," George replied.

"Just how many transgressions were on your record?" Katherine asked laughing.

"A total of 398, of which ten were major,"

"Well that means that at least 380 of the others involved Dana and me," she said still laughing.

"Yeah, but about 370 of them favored me and were against the two of you," he retorted also laughing. By then, they were all cackling.

"Well, I can see you're all off to a great start in this three way relationship," Margaret said joining in the frivolity, "You have a good time. One of you can call me when George is ready for the rest of his Orientation." With that she mumbled something and dematerialized. "Will I ever get used to that?" he thought.

"We have some time before you move on," Katherine said as she looked at him, "What'll we do with it? I know we need to re-visit the Design Section about the additional space. Would you like to see our children?"

"Yes, I would."

It felt strange holding onto Dana's and Katherine's hands as they prepared for their travel back to Atlanta. There they were, looking all of thirty five and here he was looking all of sixty five. "I guess during Orientation," he thought, "they'll show me how to change my appearance. I think thirty-five is a good age."

Katherine and Dana seemed to be good friends after only a short time; what was it now, five months since Dana's arrival? Their mutual connection was their families and George but beyond that, they had also developed, by now, a deeper respect and kinship between themselves. Katherine had birthed two of his children and Dana the other two. Dana had raised all four. Katherine had watched the whole process. Then there was George, a husband to both of them at different times. Now, after his arrival, they have re-claimed him much like they would have one of their children who may have gotten lost. That was it; he felt like a child with each of them now as co-mothers. They were responsible for him, to make sure he didn't get lost. They have him for a while and have to bring him back here just like driving him to school.

How do they feel about him now? George had loved them both during their respective times together. How did he feel about them now? Then he realized he still loved them. They were his best friends on Earth; they were still his best friends at Home.

Was this possible here, to care for two people at once? Then came the second realization: his love for both of them was indeed possible. Not only was it possible but the very nature of the Home that God made for all of them was conducive to the concepts and realities of love and caring and trust and respect between all people. It just so happened these were his favorite two people among all who were here and next to the four children who had yet to join them. That makes a total of seven people who were inextricably linked as a Family albeit one still separated by the veil which existed between residents of Earth and residents of Home. One day, they would all be together; he felt this in his heart: this would come to be.

But this day, Katherine and Dana were taking him to see their four children. By now, four days after his body was buried near the burial plots of Katherine and Dana, they had all returned to their homes with their families. The funeral was history, but the memories his children possess were alive and burning within their hearts and Souls. They had all talked to Dana at various times. They all knew George was in Orientation. He hoped it wouldn't be long before they could call him. Maybe Stewart could reach him as well.

Their first stop was at Jason and Michelle's. The time was Sunday morning. They arrived in the foyer. Katherine said the recommended arrival spot was somewhere inside a front door. This gave the visitors a chance to see what was going on in the rest of the house without violating the privacy rules which were universally observed by Home visitors. If the privacy rules were not in jeopardy of being violated, then they could move anywhere inside the home they wanted to.

Stewart and Nicole were already dressed and in the family room looking at a cartoon movie. They were fussing over the remote control; something they did quite often. George heard Michelle's voice from the master bedroom as she tried to regain control over the situation, "Okay, guys, quit your fussing or both of you will spend the afternoon in your rooms with no TV privileges."

That seemed to work. Momma had spoken and her word was law. George moved to their bedroom and watched as she and Jason finished their preparations for church. It was strange. This scenario was one that he'd never seen before when he lived among them.

"It'll be strange today. We'll be at church for the first time in years when neither Dad nor Mom will be there," Jason said. They attended the same church where Dana and George had been members for decades. Jason had grown up there from the preschool programs through the youth programs. After he and Michelle started dating, they both attended and were married by George's friend, Richard, about ten years ago.

"Yes, it will. What're you going to do about the request from Rev. Casey you got yesterday?" Michelle asked. What request, George wondered.

"I'm not sure," Jason said, "I talked to Jackie late yesterday. She was going to call Stacie and Mike. It's all so soon after the funeral." George was listening closely and wanted so badly to ask questions. He looked at Katherine.

Katherine said, "Sorry, George, there's no way to prod them. Maybe they'll give us more information. Dana may have to wait for a call." he nodded in understanding.

"Besides," Jason said, "How can Dad's discovery create such a furor?"

"Well," Michelle added, "Mason's Link is certainly getting a lot of press and media attention these days. Your dad's association with the Link is now pretty common knowledge. I think the Church Council is concerned about your dad's house and property sitting there unoccupied. It does need watching and protecting seems to me."

"Yeah, but the Atlanta Church Council; why are they the ones who're concerned enough to ask us to allow them to put it under guard and provide security?" Jason asked.

"I think," Michelle continued, "the Council has come to realize Mason's Link has been at least partially responsible for the overflow crowds appearing in churches all across the country. It also occurs to me they may feel your dad's residence may some day be looked upon as some sort of shrine or something as more and more people begin to associate your dad, his home and the Link as something…well something spiritual. I mean, I'm even in awe of what he did and the fact that he shared it with us. I'll never forget that night as long as I live. It was a life changing event for me. I'm sure others will come to feel the same way and will want to see where it all started."

"Well, at least we've cleared it of most things of value. I know Bill has many of his other papers. He told me so at the party we had over there. I hope Dad didn't mind us doing that. Bill and Marvin thought it would be a good idea and we were all there anyway. It was a good way to say goodbye to Dad and the home we grew up in. We all know where Dad is and it's only a matter of time before we can talk with him again. You know, Michelle, I agree, with you; what he discovered was a life altering event for me as well. I bet most people who've used the Link would agree," Jason stated. "Hey, we better get started or we'll be sitting in the outer lobby again in folding chairs." With that, they gathered up Stewart and Nicole and made their way out the door.

Dana said it first after they had gone, "I guess we now know what's going on. Michelle was right. I've been following the earth media from Home, and Mason's Link has created waves all over the world. What they're all so amazed about is apparently it's made a huge impact among Christians and Non-Christians alike, in every country and on every continent. They are saying they've never seen or heard of anything which has made such a profound impact on people's lives. You did it, George."

George looked at her and smiled, "No Dana, I only discovered it. You both would be shocked at how I worried about how or even if I should tell you. I was a bundle of contradictions about what to do. And then after you passed through, I worried even more about what to do. Eventually, though, reason won out. I thought it might help others, but I had no idea an avalanche of this magnitude would ensue. It's still all so overwhelming to me." He couldn't even tell them about his Audience or the invitation to be an Elder which he realized only happened a short time ago and how that overwhelmed him as well.

Katherine, in looking at Dana but talking to George, said, "Don't worry, George, Dana and I will keep you in check. You're just George to us, the guy we both fell in love with. We'll make sure that you stay 'just George' to us."

Little did she know what was ahead for him. Wait, what was he thinking, he could tell them. Why not do it now? He could tell them here, in Jason's home on Earth, as well as anywhere else.

"I've got something to tell you," he started, "Might as well be here in Jason's living room as anywhere. Have a seat."

They both looked at him and each other but they sat down anyway. What ever could he tell us now; he could see the questions in their eyes.

"Remember when I first saw you in the arrival station and I said that Eli had accompanied me along with Helen and John?" They both nodded yes.

"Well, Eli was with me through the entire Reconciliation review. He stayed with me the whole time and left there with me. There were also five other Elders at the review observing the first incident," They looked astonished at hearing this, "Not only that, but in all the conversations we had, he and others kept saying that I was a Person of Special Interest." Katherine and Dana looked even more astonished.

"Did you know that Eli has been an Elder for 1500 years?" he asked them. They shook their head no and looked even more astonished if that was possible.

"What I'm about to tell you cannot be repeated to anyone else. You must promise me or else I can't tell."

Another moment of silence, then, "I promise," Katherine said. Dana said as much. George imagined their curiosity had peaked about now.

"When they said I was a Person of Special Interest, Eli said that meant they wanted me to become an Elder. Also, he wants me to work with him in the newly formed Department of Linking Services."

"An Elder, how can you become an Elder?" Katherine asked, "I thought they had all been around forever." Both of them were now riveted to Jason's chairs, eyes focused on him.

"I just learned that isn't so. Most Elders have been recruited from the resident population. There're a couple of hitches you should know about."

"What are they?" Dana asked, not moving except to ask her question.

"First, there will be some additional time requirements on me over and above what other residents have. I understand it's not much more, but it will be more. Second, I will adopt another name as an Elder. I can't tell you what it'll be. I'll also assume another appearance. I can't show that to you either. Apparently, there're some special abilities I'll inherit as an Elder. You'll always see me and know me as George. All the rest of my friends and relatives will do the same except they won't know about my alter role. As our children arrive Home, I'll be able to tell them but no one else," George paused to allow them to catch up with what he just said. They looked pretty stunned.

"But that's not all and not even the best part," as he continued, "I had an Audience."

"A what?" Dana asked, her mouth agape.

"An Audience," George replied, "An Audience with the Lord, Jesus." From their looks, they could have been pushed off a cliff without complaining in hearing this.

"Remember me saying there were five other Elders observing my review? Well, four of the five were named Andrew, Matthew, James and John. Do these names ring a bell?" he asked but continued without waiting for any reply, "They are names of four of Jesus' twelve disciples. The fifth Elder at the review was Jesus. All of them were in disguise. They came to Eli and me after the reviews were done in their original two millennia old robes and appearance. Jesus was dressed in white robes.

"He spoke to me for a long time explaining why He wanted me to be an Elder and thanking me for bringing the discovery of the Link into the open for everyone to use. He called the discovery and its dissemination the most important achievement in Christendom since His Resurrection. He says it will impact billions of people now and into the future," George said as he finally wound down, "That's it, that's what I wanted to tell you."

George didn't think he should scare them with the tale of forfeiting his Soul. Well why not? "Well, there is one more thing I will tell you. It involves the first incident in the Reconciliation review. I'll tell you because there were two residents who witnessed it. I did something terrible as a transgression for which I offered to forfeit my Soul," They gasped, "Instead, the two I transgressed against forgave me for the incident I caused. I didn't think that was sufficient so I offered up my Soul a second time," They gasped louder, "The reviewing Elder received permission to let me undergo the forfeiture without me knowing. It was strange. I witnessed all my memories being stripped out of my Soul and witnessed the black void of nothingness before they plunged me into it. I was dead, my Soul really died. I thought I was gone forever without a chance at ever seeing either of you or my family again," Katherine and Dana were crying now, "One of the five Elders was Jesus in disguise. He came forward and brought my Soul back to life. I wasn't even aware of it until Eli told me. I later learned that I was only one of five individuals who have ever undergone this death and restoration. There, now, I'm really finished telling you."

Silence permeated the room as they both sat there sobbing quietly, stunned, mute, staring and thinking. They both ran to him. He embraced them. Katherine was the first to speak, "You died and came back to life? You spoke to Jesus? I've been at Home for thirty five years and this is first time, blockbuster news for me. For all the time I've been here, I don't recall hearing of anyone ever going through that or saying they ever had a word even in passing with Jesus. I've seen Him maybe a dozen times always from afar. There were always huge crowds at his appearances."

"I've only been here a few months and I learn something new and breathtaking every day and I don't even have to breathe," Dana added, "This is by far the most stunning and significant new development to date. And I can't even tell anyone. When will you become an Elder? Should we start calling you Lazarus?"

"No, I'm not Lazarus; just George to you. There are a few minor unresolved transgressions of mine involving people who haven't passed through; could be years before the last one is settled. Meanwhile, I'll be in some sort of Elder training program as well as doing a regular resident's job. I still have to finish Orientation too. Are you two still going to let me live with you?"

Katherine and Dana looked at each other, "You're not going to be doing any sort of strange things are you?" Katherine asked.

"Nothing stranger than what I've always done."

"Promise?"

"Promise!"

"Well, I guess that'll be all right," Katherine said, "This is so different than anything I could've imagined. It's going to take some getting used to. It seems that strange things follow you on a regular basis. You are going to be quite dull when all this settles down."

"I thought I was always dull. My guess is that you'll never know any difference. I just won't be around as much as I might otherwise."

George just realized a downside to being an Elder. He would be doing things he couldn't share with them. He'd always been open with all he'd been involved in over the years. This would be different.

"Wait a minute," Dana said, "You said you can't tell us your name or allow us to know what you look like. That means that we won't know what you're doing either. Is that right?"

"I'm afraid so. Could be you might see me but you won't know it's me. Are you still all right with all this?" I asked.

Both of them nodded yes.

"I guess we can go check on the other kids," George said.

"Grab our hands," Dana said and they were off to Jackie's house. They weren't home. They caught up with them at church. Jackie's family was Baptist. They watched them awhile during their Sunday morning service. Jackie and Tom were the only ones in the service. The kids were in the church's child care center. They walked around to see them before they moved on.

The visit to the church was strange. They could see the congregation members. They could also see others, Home residents like them, not many but a few, who were there watching the service and perhaps relatives of their own. The others saw them, and they exchanged acknowledgements. One couple in particular looked at them. The wife was looking directly at George and mentioned something to her husband who looked more closely at him; then both waved at them again as if she recognized George. George would have to get used to a certain amount of that. It didn't go unnoticed by either Katherine or Dana.

Next they visited Stacie and Robert. Unlike Jackie or Jason, they were at home this Sunday morning in St Louis with little Lisa who was scampering around their family room while Stacie puttered around her kitchen. Robert was in the garage working on his lawnmower. Katherine, Dana and George watched awhile. No conversations were going on between them.

Next, they joined Mike and Elizabeth near their home in Cincinnati in a local park watching Todd play with a couple other children on a jungle gym set. The weather was delightful for early fall. The trees were starting to change but still retained their leaves. Some were bright yellow. Mike and Elizabeth were talking as they watched their little fellow. They were smiling and laughing and generally enjoying themselves. They were even holding hands.

What a family George had raised. Now that Dana and he were gone, they had all picked up their lives and were moving on. Little did they realize it but they were building their own families now. In fifteen years, they would be independent unto themselves, only occasionally calling or seeing each other. In thirty years, they would be overseeing their own family gatherings and chasing after their grandchildren. By then, they might start arriving at Home. The cycle would go on as God intended. They would adapt to events and conditions of the day. They would love and care for each other as they were taught. George smiled at the scene as did Dana and Katherine. They were ready to go back Home now.

Katherine looked around one last time then at Dana and George. "Let's stop into the Design Section to see if the preliminary sketches for George's complex are ready. Mike's family is happy and settled. They all are. We can leave them in peace and us with a peace of mind."

They clasped hands, Katherine mumbled the travel instructions and they were at the Design Center. What a system.

Howard was not there but they spoke with an associate of his who showed them the plans. George looked them over pretty quickly but thoroughly as he was prone to do being an experienced engineer. When asked by Dana when the changes would be done, they were promised a span of no more than two earth days. Again, what a system. George was going to like it at Home very much.

Next, they dropped by to see George's mom and his dad who had just finished his daily round of golf. Mom had just returned from a visit with a couple of her childhood friends. They were pleased to learn George was about to go into the Orientation phase. No mention was made of the second career path he was about to embark upon or the Audience just for him. They would never know those things about George.

The next stop was at Katherine and Dana's place and George's now as well, before they departed for the arrival station for George to continue Orientation. They wanted to unwind a little. George took to the grill and seared some steaks while Katherine and Dana decided to take a short swim. They looked pretty good in their thirty-fiveish bodies.

He desperately needed to learn how to make his body look a little better. Even though they didn't need the nourishment, the meal was nevertheless scrumptious. A little Merlot didn't hurt either.

Chapter 23

The trip back to George's temporary quarters at the arrival station was short as usual. It was so strange to be wandering around the replica of his old home in Atlanta. He remembered the conversation between Michelle and Jason about the house going under the care and protection of the Atlanta Church Council. What a strange thing to hear. He wondered how Richard was dealing with all this. As soon as he could, George would drop in to see how he was doing.

It wasn't long before Margaret arrived. George expected her. She was about to escort him to the main part of his Orientation.

"George, I hope your little R&R with Katherine and Dana was refreshing," she said.

"It was indeed. I saw all my family. They all appear to be doing well. Are we ready for me to continue?"

"I'm ready if you are," she said.

"Let's go then."

"First, here's an envelope. I need you to put this in your pocket. You'll need this during your first session," she said. He put it in his jacket pocket. "Take my hand and we'll get you started."

George took her hand, she mumbled something and they were gone. Next, they appeared in a hallway vaguely resembling a school with doors up and down the hall leading into rooms. She opened a door and as they entered, they faced a large group of maybe two hundred people. He remembered either Katherine or Dana describing this. A lot of the group were milling around looking dazed. George assumed these were new arrivals like him. Others among them were probably coordinators like Margaret. Pretty soon, they started to disappear as they made their way back to wherever they stay while 'class' is in.

The room was about 150 feet square. The walls were white and about fifteen feet high with floors covered in a soft but solid material light tan in color. In the center of the room an object was suspended about three feet from the ceiling resembling something akin to a projector except it was round.

After a bit, an elderly gentleman standing on a small raised platform beneath the suspended object spoke up so they could all hear. Those talking quieted down to allow him the floor, "My name is Steve Williams," his voice boomed out; "I welcome all of you Home. You'll find Home to be an extraordinary place, much better than you were taught back on Earth. Up until recently, there was no way anyone on Earth could have known exactly how great we have it here. That's expected to change now that the knowledge of Mason's Link is rapidly spreading across the world," he said as he gave George only the briefest of glances. George shivered a little.

"At any rate," he continued, "This is the first of several sets of instructions you will receive during the program we call Orientation. We'll teach you to navigate around our vast expanse we call Home. You might have known it as Heaven or some other term used to describe the place you go after you die. By the way, you didn't 'die' on Earth, you 'passed through', much like you would do in going through a veil.

"We'll teach you how to communicate and how to receive news and entertainment media. On Earth, you had computers, the Internet, TV, newspapers, magazines, and movie houses. You'll have all that here and more. You'll find our systems for acquiring and disseminating information much further advanced than you were accustomed on Earth.

"We'll teach you how to acquire things you want or need. From a physical standpoint, you'll find you need very little. You're here with me; yet you are not breathing. You'll find you don't have to eat to sustain yourself; you will not have to go to the bathroom to relieve yourself nor will you have to sleep if you don't want to. All of those things you did on earth were physical necessities so that your body could sustain itself and sustain your Soul.

"Your Soul is the part of you that passed through. None of the physical aspects of your previous existence passed through. Your memories came with you and you retained all your sensory skills such as sight, smell and hearing. When you were conceived those many years ago by your parents on Earth, God and his great staff of people, put a Soul into your embryo body. When your body died on Earth, it stayed behind but God has re-claimed your Soul. Your Soul is what sustains you here. You'll find your Soul has been unleashed at Home. You'll find your Soul can do many more things than it could do while housed in your physical body on Earth.

"The purpose of Orientation is to teach you about all the new things you can do. Seemingly, you may feel these new skills you have are magical. At first, you may have to think about how to do things. Soon, however, you'll begin taking them for granted and their use for you will become second nature. Are there any questions?"

The room was completely silent. "Very good then," he continued, "We'll proceed. Your coordinator should have given you an envelope before you arrived here. Do each of you have your envelope? If you do not, please raise your hand."

No hands were raised. There was a general shuffling in the room as people reached for their envelopes. George pulled his out and examined it for the first time. Margaret gave it to him just before they arrived, and he had not taken the time to look at it. It was not made of paper but felt like plastic. Who knows what it was? It did have his name on the front with a notation that it wasn't to be opened until instructed.

"If you have not done so," Steve said, "please open your envelope now."

George turned the flap and removed a one page document along with a card. The document was more or less a recitation of the opening speech Steve just made. The card had George's name on it along with the name 'Orientation Session' in embossed lettering followed by the numbers 2007-194893. There was also another name shown at the bottom, the name of Jonathan Adams. There was a large red 1 encircled in the upper right corner. The card was about the size of a business card.

"During all Orientation sessions," he continued, "You'll be paired with another individual. That individual's name is shown on the bottom of your card. The first lesson we're going to learn is the Travel Instruction. Simply said, this is the method you'll use to navigate around our Home world. We'll use it now to allow you to find and introduce yourself to your Orientation partner.

"The Travel Instruction works in several ways. The operative words are 'Go There'. The instruction works in a sequence. First you either read or visualize the place you want to go and then you say 'Go There'. Is that clear?" Without waiting for anyone to answer, he continued, "Don't worry, we haven't yet activated the part of your Soul that allows this to work.

"Does everyone see the object suspended over my head?" Everyone was looking from him to the object and back to him. "In just a moment, you'll see a brief flash from this device. This flash will let you know that your Travel Instruction program has been activated in your Soul. After that occurs and for those of you who have the red number one in the upper right corner of your card, I want you to look at the name of your partner shown on the bottom of your card and say 'Go There'. Ready?"

As soon as he said ready, the light flashed on the suspended object. The flash routine had been recently added to the Orientation program to prevent any premature travel before the training could be done. Before the flash, travel was theoretically possible immediately after a person passed through. Steve remembered an incident a short time ago when a new arrival inadvertently sent herself to a shopping center.

George had the number one on his card so he looked at the name of Jonathan Adams and said, "Go there."

In a flash, George was standing across the room facing a gentleman about his height who jumped as did George. George stood looking at him for a moment before asking, "Are you Jonathan Adams?"

He looked at George, then at his card and said, "Yes, you must be George Mason. At least that's what my card says."

"I am!" as George extended his hand, "Pleased to meet you. Where are you from?"

"I'm from Des Moines, Iowa and I'm 70 years old or at least I was when I passed away some days ago. How about you?"

"I'm from Atlanta. I think I've been here about a week."

"You know," Jonathan said, "Your name is familiar. I'm trying to remember where I've heard it before. From Atlanta, huh; you wouldn't be that guy they're talking about on TV that discovered Mason's Link, would you?"

"Yeah, I'm afraid I am."

"Well, it's a real honor to meet you then. You did a marvelous thing with that discovery. I used the Link to talk to my Mother and Father who'd passed away twenty years ago. I think it's great."

"Thank you," George said. An awkward moment of silence followed before he added, "I wonder what they'll have us doing next."

Just then, Mr. Williams shouted, "Okay, is there anyone who did not find and meet your partner?" Before anyone could answer again, he continued, "All right, for those who made their first trip, I want you to say 'previous location' followed by 'Go There'."

George did just that and found himself back across the room more or less where he started out.

Next Steve said, "Now for the partner who has the red number two on their card, I want you to say the name of the partner you just met followed by the words 'Go There'.

In just a moment, Jonathan was standing in front of George grinning, "I think this will be fun," he stated. George grinned back and nodded.

"Is everyone paired up once again?" Steve asked and then continued as before without hesitating, "This time we're going further afield. There's a park outside this building called Orientation Park. Each pair of you will make a trip to the park, obtain a soda pop from one of the vendors in the food service area and return to this room with the soda. But instead of going individually, you will go as a pair.

"To go as a pair, you must designate one of yourselves to give the Travel Instruction. The designee will say the name of the other partner, then 'the name of the park' and then 'Go There'. Stay there no longer than one hour; then it'll be the responsibility of the other partner to bring the pair of you back to this room by saying 'the room of 2007-194893' which is your class number. Don't worry, if you get lost, we'll find you. I'll see you in an hour."

"Jonathan, you wanna do the honors?"

"Sure! Let's see, George Mason, Orientation Park, go there!"

The next thing George knew, both of them were standing in Orientation Park. "This sure is fast, isn't it?" George commented without expecting an answer.

"Yeah!" Jonathan said. The park was probably a half mile square. Orientation Hall was the largest building on its border. Other buildings were no more than ten stories high and may have been offices or shopping facilities or whatever. The park was heavily populated with residents in addition to the sudden influx of new arrivals looking for soda pops.

George and Jonathan walked around awhile swapping family stories. Jonathan was here ahead of his wife of fifty years. She was back in Iowa in a nursing home stricken with Alzheimer's disease, and it was doubtful she had even missed Jonathan according to his story. The park was beautifully manicured. It reminded George of Disney World where so much time and resources are spent to keep the park clean, except here he didn't see any paper wrappers or drink cups to pick up. Looking back, the Orientation Center was huge, not unlike the building where the Reconciliation programs were conducted. In fact, looking off several miles distant stood the unmistakably tall Reconciliation Hall. Thinking back to when he was looking out the 131st floor of that building, they must be in part of the huge city he saw from that window.

Looking at his watch, George saw that forty-five minutes had passed since they arrived, "Jonathan, time is getting on, we should think about getting those sodas and going back. I'd hate for Mr. Williams to send someone looking for us."

"I agree," he said.

They only had to walk a short distance further before they saw a food vendor. George walked up to the vendor only to realize he didn't have any money to pay for the drinks. George saw on the shirt that the vendor's name was Herbert. He looked to be of Asian descent.

George looked at Jonathan then at Herbert and said, "Herbert, we were asked to get a couple of sodas to take back to our class but we don't have any way to pay for them. Can you suggest something?"

Herbert spoke in what sounded like an Indian accent while laughing, "Don't tell me, you're in your first Orientation session, yes?"

Jonathan and he nodded sheepishly, "Yep!" they replied together.

"Well here's another lesson for you; you don't need money here. It's yours for the asking. What'll you have? I've got a wide range of flavors."

"I'd like a Coke," George said not embarrassing himself by asking for a Diet Coke again.

"You got a Dr. Pepper?" Jonathan asked.

"Coming right up," Herbert said, while he began pouring the drinks over ice, "Here you go."

"Thanks, we appreciate it," George said as Herbert handed them the drinks complete with lids and straws. "It feels strange not paying for it."

"Your thanks will be payment sufficient."

They nodded appreciatively as they walked off. George guessed it was his turn to get them back to the classroom, which seemed an appropriate description although he doesn't remember seeing any chairs or desks. He started, "Jonathan Adams, the room for 2007-194893, go there!"

"Well, it's absolutely magic I don't care what anyone says. Here we are, in our designated place with five minutes to spare," George thought. Many other pairs had already returned. Some, not all, even had sodas and were sipping on them. Some had yet to arrive. He saw three more pairs materialize as they stood watching before the time allotment expired.

Mr. Williams stepped up on his platform. "I see we still have some groups out. We'll give 'em five more minutes," he said. Several more groups arrived meanwhile, but at the end of the time extension, about five pairs and some singles were still absent. Either they didn't have access to a watch or clock or they were lost or they misused the travel instruction. George remembers seeing several clocks in the park on pedestals.

"Okay, time's up. We'll fetch 'em back ourselves," he announced as he turned to someone against the far wall, "Maria, please bring 'em back."

"Yes sir, I'll go activate the recovery routine," they heard her reply except she spoke in Spanish but George heard her in English. She immediately left the room.

George looked at Jonathan who looked amazed. Steve said, "Did everyone hear Maria's response to my request? She spoke in Spanish and you heard her response in your head in English, right? You have automatic translation capability built into your Souls so you don't have to worry about language barriers. You speak in your native tongue and you will be heard by them in their native tongue. Maria heard my request in Spanish. The process reverses itself if you receive a reply."

Jonathan was still amazed. George told him, "I'd learned this from my wife before I arrived here. It's the first time for me to witness it, however."

About that time twelve people consisting of the five missing pairs and two singles all arrived simultaneously, all looking a bit bewildered. George heard one of them say, "I guess we got the instructions wrong, we were at some zoo on Earth in front of the ape exhibit."

They all laughed including Mr. Williams. "Good," he said, "The twelve of you and your other two partners get to stay for some extra training. The rest of you can return to your respective quarters. All you need do is say 'my quarters' then 'go there'. Be back here tomorrow at 9 o'clock sharp Earth time. Let's see if you can figure out how to get there and back. Hang onto the card you got earlier."

George looked at Jonathan and asked, "Think you'll have any trouble getting to your quarters?"

"No, I'll see you tomorrow."

"Okay!" George replied. He issued the travel instruction and was immediately back at his arrival station quarters. There was no one there. He still held the soda from the park as he walked over to his favorite recliner and sat down. He picked up the TV remote, turned on the TV and was astonished to see the Atlanta stations appear. What a place.

George sat for a while and suddenly thought about clothes. It occurred to him that he hadn't changed clothes since he'd been here. His closet was full of the clothes he had in Atlanta so he picked out a pair of khaki slacks and a blue pullover shirt. He added a light jacket to his ensemble just in case the temperature turned cool. Of course, he knew it wouldn't, but he figured an extra pocket or two wouldn't hurt.

Then he wondered where Katherine and Dana were. He also wondered if he could experiment a little with the Travel Instruction and find them. So with fresh looking clothes and a little knowledge, here he went. He pictured Dana in his mind and said, "Dana, go there."

George was surprised that it worked. He was even more surprised to learn he wasn't at their place. He arrived in some store. It resembled a store similar to Kirklands where home décor items were displayed in a wide variety of sizes shapes and colors, except this store was much larger than any Kirklands he'd ever been in. At first, he didn't see her. There were several other ladies around and he'd forgotten she'd adopted a thirty-fiveish look. She turned and saw him when some other lady gasped at the arrival of someone so close to her.

George received a wide grin along with a hug and kiss as she welcomed me. He guessed everyone thought he must be her father. Well, who cares what anyone else thought. He grinned and hugged in return. It was good to see her.

"My goodness," she said, "where did you come from?"

"They let us out of our Orientation session a short while ago and I wondered what you were up to. I should've known I'd find you shopping."

"Well, you know my passion. The possibilities are endless here. You want to wander around with me?" She asked as she stepped back to look at him. "When is the last time you went shopping for any new clothes? I remember that shirt as one we bought you about five years ago."

"I can't remember the last time I went shopping for clothes."

"Well, this is your lucky day. Come on, we're going shopping just for you."

Suddenly George remembered and forgot at the same time. He remembered he didn't have any money or plastic and forgot he couldn't use it here anyway. "Wait," he said, "I don't have a credit card."

"Well, it's good you don't have one. It wouldn't be of any use here anyway. I bet you forgot that as well."

George grinned, "Yeah, I did. So how does this work, and where do we go?"

"Okay, here we go," she said as she started the travel instruction, "George, men's clothing, go there."

All of a sudden, they were in some store where all he could see was men's clothing. It was bigger than any store he'd ever seen. Looking closer at the displays, he saw that each style only had one piece on display. Also, it had no size shown on an inside label.

"Now, I haven't shopped at Home for any men before, but my guess is the same process works here as for women's clothing," she said, "You see something you like, and we acquire it for you. The size is guaranteed to fit. So look around. Let's find you some things."

They shopped for at least a couple of hours. George had bags full of stuff before they had finished: everything from shirts, pants, shoes, belts, coats and caps. He even bought a new pair of golf shoes on the expectation that he'd get to play with his dad soon. After they were done, they returned to his quarters so he could put the stuff away.

No sooner had they arrived than Katherine showed up to say they had finished his complex at their place. So now it was known as Katherine, Dana and George's place. George said, "I think we'll call it the Bird's Nest after the three high flyers who'll be living there." They all laughed. "So how do we get all my stuff there? Can I go ahead and move in and go to Orientation from there?"

"Questions, questions, questions! Except for the things you just brought in, all your stuff is already there, even down to your favorite recliner. Yes, you can commute to Orientation from there now that you have your Travel Instruction procedure under your belt," Katherine said.

"Let's go then," George grabbed his new clothes and said, "Let me try it. Katherine and Dana, Bird's Nest, go there."

Next, there they were. It worked even with the new name. The place looked great as he wandered through his complex with the two of them. There it was, his favorite recliner. Now there was also one back at the arrival station. How many of them could there be anyway, didn't matter. He was really Home now. They had some wine and snacks as they showed him how to work his new entertainment system.

They talked for hours about the past, about their children and more importantly about the future. George gave them his vision of the future when all of them, children and grandchildren alike, would be together. They talked about him being an Elder. Since he knew nothing about it, he could speculate about what it might be like. Once the Elders tell him, then he'll be unable to tell these two, better to speculate now. They talked all the way up to the time for him to return to class at room 2007-194893.

George's confidence in traveling was high. He arrived on time at the appointed place. Yeah, he was starting to take this for granted. Jonathan made his way back as well. They were on a roll. The first assignment of the day was to take a half day trip to Central Park in New York back on Earth. There was nothing they could bring back since all of them were mere spectators there. They did have to count the ducks in the lake and report back with a headcount. This time, all pairings made their way back by the appointed time.

Other trips were made over the next several days over a broader portion of the Home world. Trips were made to sporting arenas and other recreational locations where they were allowed to spend longer periods of time.

Next up was something of a geography lesson for the Home world. After all, according to Mr. Williams, "We should understand something about Home if we expect to avail ourselves of all that's here for us." They received a fold out map of the Home world, a little cheesy but certainly helpful.

"The map being handed out is a high level representation of your new Home. It may look a lot like planet Earth but in fact, it's quite different," Steve explained. "You'll note most of the area is represented as land mass. Remember, Home was built to provide for the needs of residents. Few residents have need for large oceans. There are masses of water for those residents who love the sea and sailing, but they're about the size of the Earth-bound Great Lakes.

"The larger cities are shown, including Kingdom City where we are now. It's the largest city with a population of about 100 million inhabitants. All told, the current population of Home is about 4 billion Souls and is growing by about 50,000 per day. Unlike Earth's population which has births and deaths, Home's population is constantly increasing with few or no losses. Consequently, the requirement for additional land mass is ever increasing. From time to time, the land mass will undergo additions, whereas Earth's land mass is constant.

"Most residents travel within only a small segment of the Home world. Everything they need or want to do is generally available within a relatively short distance from their place of residence. However, for the more ambitious travelers, any place on the Home World is accessible by the Travel procedure if you know where you want to go. In the Communications orientation segment, you'll be shown a way to access other places, including cities, shopping facilities, recreation facilities and the like," Steve continued.

"The next segment we'll cover is called Acquisitions. In this segment," Mr. Williams explained, "We'll teach you how to acquire goods and services you need or you want. This will involve several trips to several shopping areas. We'll show you where you can do your shopping, the correct procedures to follow, and how to turn back or dispose of items you no longer want or need. Items and services available to you generally include most anything you found accessible on Earth. The only difference here is you will not be required to pay money or use credit to acquire things. So if you could not afford certain items on Earth, this will not be a problem here.

"Also, we'll show you, in general terms, other items or services only available. We require that you not share with Earth residents any technology which has yet to be discovered or developed on earth. We've always issued this warning but," he said as he looked at George, "the discovery of Mason's Link now demands that we stress this rule more clearly. We only ask that you acquire items you might use and not acquire things simply to have them lying around. Otherwise, you could find your living spaces quite cluttered with useless objects.

"In addition to many shopping areas, you'll also find shopping available interactively from your place of residence. If you used the Internet while on Earth, you'll find our systems have similarities with the Internet. We'll show you how to do this.

"The basic instruction to acquire an object or service is similar to travel," Steve continued, "When you see something you want, you need to fix a picture of it in your mind and if you know its name, say it along with the phrase 'Bring Here'. It's as simple as that. For example, say that I want a basketball. I have a picture of a basketball in my mind and I say 'basketball, bring here'." Within a moment or two, a basketball appeared in his hand. For this, Mr. Williams got an ovation from the class.

"We'll have you try this in a moment," he added, "But first, we have to activate the program in your Soul that makes this possible." As soon as he finished speaking, the suspended object over his head flashed, similarly to the process for travel.

"All right, I want everyone to visualize either a pen or a wrist watch, say its name followed by the acquisition phrase."

Since the girls had already given him a Rolex, George visualized a Montblanc Rollerball pen, spoke its name and said 'bring here'. In a moment, he had the pen in his hand. He actually needed a pen. This was a good one from his other life experience. He opened it, tested it on a slip of paper, and put it in his pocket. Mission accomplished. Nothing to it!

"I have to advise you to be careful what you ask for; because you're likely to get it. For example, if you want a refrigerator, you should ask for it at the place you intend to use it. If you ask for it in a store, you'll have to take possession of it there and you'll have to transport it to where you want to use it. You'll find that no stores here offer delivery services. Bottom line, plan your acquisitions. Know what you want and where you want it to be," Mr. Williams explained.

Over the next several days, Jonathan and George made several assigned trips to shopping centers to practice the acquisition routine and to learn a little about the shopping centers. As it turned out, the shopping centers were huge as one might expect them to be for a city servicing 100 million residents. Actually, the centers were available for anyone coming from anywhere.

There were at least two dozen major centers in Kingdom City alone. The main difference in these centers from the shopping centers on Earth was that only one store here displays, for example, men's clothing as opposed to multiple store brands selling men's clothing on Earth. That was the reason for the size of the store Dana and George visited. Everything men wear was in one place. To him, that made a lot of sense, but he wasn't sure others would agree.

"Another place you'll want to visit," Steve said, "Is the Design Section. Most of you are residing in the temporary quarters in the arrival center. You can select other quarters or places of residence if you like. The process is similar to the Acquisitions Procedure except there is a staff of designers who will help you select a design and suggest locations. When you have a chance after Orientation, you can designate the Design Center as a travel location and visit them to begin this process."

By now, another week had passed and they were ready for the next phase of the program which happened to be Communications. "In this segment, "Mr. Williams began,

"We'll go over the communication systems available to you as new residents. You'll find them to be quite comprehensive, and they will include communications from Home and Earth. Your main access to information, news and entertainment media will be by our systems which are similar to television and computers on earth, only the systems we have here are more technologically advanced. We call them 'view screens' or simply 'screens' for short. Once you have a permanent place of residence, you'll be able to acquire any number of model screens. There are also small portable handheld screen devices you can acquire.

"These screens are mainly voice activated. With your voice and with images generated in your mind, you can command the screens to display news content, sporting events, movies, and other programming from Home or Earth. These screens are accompanied by keyboards to make them completely interactive. Most types of Earth based computer programs are also available on these screens, all of which are accessible simply by voice command and keystrokes. Of course, any live event from Earth available for screen viewing at Home can also be accessed by you simply by traveling to Earth to attend the event live and in person. Ticket availability and seating will never be an issue.

"For training purposes, I'm going to display a short selection of hand-held screen devices around the walls of our training center here. Specifications will also be shown for those of you with the skills to read and understand them. I would like each of you to walk around the room and look at the various models. None of these are available yet on Earth but may become so since technology is advancing so rapidly there. When you've looked at all of them, make a selection and use the Acquisition Procedure to obtain one now which we can use for training. You have an hour to complete this."

Jonathan and George walked around together. Jonathan admitted his computer skills on Earth were sadly behind most of society. George understood computers and how they work pretty well so he volunteered to give Jonathan the benefit of his experience as they reviewed the various models. George suggested one of the simpler models for Jonathan, one that wouldn't require him to advance his computer skills much beyond where he is at present. The screen was almost all voice activated.

For himself, George chose the most advanced model, not because he understood it or all it could do, but because he felt he had the ability to learn its capabilities.

They both issued the Acquisition Procedure and in a short time, they were holding their new gadgets. The view screens were in the best high definition. The screens were about three inches square for Jonathan and about four inches square for George. They easily fit them into their pockets. They both found a quiet corner while they did some preliminary exploring of their new toys. George was excited about this. Jonathan didn't move too far from George, however, because of his need to ask George a constant stream of questions about how to do this or that.

Shortly, Mr. Williams began the formal training program. They all used their hand held devices to follow his instructions which, they learned, will work on any screen devices they run across. There was a simple sign on procedure where the screen would recognize each of them, meaning that they would be recognized by the central system which operated all of the screens wherever they are.

As it turned out, each screen was just that, a screen. Once they were signed on, all instructions between them and the screen were communicated back to a central system where all the program execution occurred. Everything was done at much higher speeds than George ever witnessed on Earth. He guessed the operation of the central system must be another of those massive operations which existed. He wondered if there were a number of the operating centers scattered about. He had to remember to ask his dad about that.

The better parts of two days were spent practicing the use of the screens and accessing the large number of the options available. They broke their session between two days, at which point George returned to his new residence. He had two huge screens in his living area which came with the complex because he'd ordered them. At first, he thought they were large televisions. Now, he knows they're just screens. He spent all night playing around with them, watching movies, sporting events and news programs from all over the Home world and Earth and accessing computer programs. Katherine and Dana would occasionally wander in, stay awhile, shake their heads and leave. They knew him well enough to know he was in his element with this system.

After another break following the completion of the Communications training, Steve was ready to move on. "Today will be a short session," he announced, "We're going over some rules. I hate to tell you this but just because this is Home, it doesn't mean you can escape the rules that govern all our conduct. There is a major difference in the rules here and the rules on Earth, however. The difference is that your Soul is conditioned never to violate them, unlike Earth where you had voluntary compliance and free will. This may sound rather harsh, but the rules here are held inviolate because to do otherwise could cause some rather serious disruptions to the way things operate at Home which would be to everyone's detriment.

"Here are the basic rules. They should require no explanation, but I'll answer questions if you have any.

"You will not injure or harm anyone.

"You will not lie, cheat or steal.

"You will not interfere with Earth activities.

"You will not reveal Home technology to Earth residents."

After he finished, no one raised a hand for questions. They apparently were simple enough and, thus, required no explanation. Afterwards, Mr. Williams dismissed the group for the day.

George was back home within an hour of when he left. A thought occurred to him since it appeared he had the day off. He searched out his dad.

"Hey Dad," George shouted as he found him milling around the yard outside his home nestled at the foothills of the Prayer Mountains, "You got any plans this morning?"

"Well, good morning to you too. I was about to head over to the club to see if I could pick up some players for a round of golf. Why do you ask?"

"Would you mind if I joined you? I have to tell you, though, I don't have any clubs yet," George answered back.

"Hey, that's no problem. We'll get you a set at the club. You can even store them there assuming we'll play together on some regular basis," Jefferson said.

"Let's do it then. I don't have to be back to Orientation until tomorrow and it's been so long since you and I were on the links together."

"Okay, they haven't taken you through the Appearance Modification program yet, have they?"

"No, I look like I'm as old as I was when I left Atlanta, sixty-seven. Why?" George wanted to know.

"Because, old man, this young man is going to kick your butt on the course," Jefferson said as he was grinning.

To look at his dad, he didn't look a day over 40. "Yep," he thought, "I'm in trouble." In the old days when his dad was the old man and he was the young whippersnapper, George could take him by ten strokes. Today, his Dad could well take all of'em back. "Let's see what you got," George said laughing.

The day turned out perfect for golf. The temperature seemed to be about 75. There was no appreciable wind. The sun was out the whole time; in fact it seemed to hover overhead the whole round. George wondered if the Home world was flat and the sun never sets. He hit'em as usual. His dad hit'em great and beat him by fifteen strokes. "Oh well, there'll be lots of other days and other rounds and other courses," George thought. "Just wait til I shave some years off this old frame." He enjoyed this day and the time with his dad.

The next day was the one George was waiting for. "Today," Mr. Williams said, "will be the day you discover the fountain of youth," he said, smiling as the suspended object over his head flashed.

"Today will also wind up your Orientation. After we finish, you should return to your place of residence and your Orientation Coordinator will contact you for the next event which is the job activity selection process. You'll undergo screening and interviewing to determine the best fit based on your preferences and abilities. Within a week, you'll be finished with all this and will take your place as permanent members of heavenly society.

"Now, I want all of you to acquire a small mirror."

They did as he requested. Looking into it, George could see an old man's face complete with sagging skin, wrinkles and an almost bald head. Strangely though, he didn't feel as old as he looked except for a few creaking bones.

"All right, now look back into your memory and visualize the person you were twenty-five years ago. Everyone have their image fixed? Now, say to yourself, 'this is me'."

"This is me," George said quietly to himself all the while watching the mirror. To his great surprise, changes in his face occurred as he watched. He felt a general tightening of muscles in his waist, across his back and in his legs. The sleeves in his shirt got a little tighter as the muscles grew to their old natural size. His wrinkles smoothed out as if he'd ironed them. His clothes were fitting tighter momentarily until they also changed to match his newly acquired physique. George also had a head of hair. What a place!

A short time later, Mr. Williams again took to the raised platform, "All of you look much better. Just so you know, you can take the aging process the other way. If you want to appear older than you were when you passed through, just visualize yourself at some advanced age and repeat the phrase. It works every time."

All of a sudden, the light flashed again. "Does anyone care to guess what that flash meant?" he asked. No one ventured an opinion.

"Let me relate an interesting story I've alluded to a couple of times," he began as he turned to look at George, "George, will you please come forward and join me here on the platform. I want everyone to get a good look at you."

George walked forward nervously and climbed aboard. "You see, folks, there is a phenomenon sweeping our mother Earth as I speak. It's become known as Mason's Link. If you haven't heard about it, this is a mechanism whereby someone on Earth can contact and talk to someone they care dearly about who has passed through. George's last name is Mason," as he put his arm around George's shoulder, "George Mason, the discoverer of Mason's Link. Some of you here may have known this fact about George, but I wanted to recognize him to give you a chance to meet him in person. You can tell your loved ones that you went through Orientation with the discoverer of Mason's Link. The light flashed because you are now eligible to receive calls from Earth."

The room erupted in a round of shouts and applause. As George made his way off the platform, everyone crowded around to shake his hand. It was all pretty embarrassing. He was glad when the furor subsided.

"All right, now does anyone have anything you'd like to say before we break this little group apart?" he asked as the room returned to normal.

All was quiet for a few moments. All of a sudden the room erupted into wild applause, laughter, whooping and generally a high state of expressed happiness. George wondered if they passed out diplomas.

As the session wound down, people began to leave. They just dematerialized before George's eyes. Several came by again to shake his hand. He spoke with Jonathan before he took his leave. They promised to stay in touch.

George had a feeling that his job activity program might go a little different than most others. As he arrived back at the Bird's Nest, he found Katherine and Dana waiting. Margaret was there as well as Eli.

Dana startled everyone with, "Oh my gosh, look at you. You look great and twenty-five years younger."

George blushed or something because everyone laughed.

Margaret came over to congratulate him, "Just wanted to let you know that Eli is going to explain your next phase. I understand you'll be working with him. I also wanted to tell you what a great pleasure it's been serving you and all the members of your family over the years. I hope to continue this role."

"Thank you, Margaret!" George said, "Do you think it'll be possible to meet your husband, Mr. President Zachary Taylor, some day?"

"So you haven't forgotten," she said beaming with a smile, "Absolutely! All you need do is call me and we'll have you and the ladies join us one day. He's told me he wants to meet you as well." With that she smiled, waved to Katherine and Dana and was off.

Eli was next, "George, why don't you take a couple of Earth days off and call me. I'll come get you and introduce you to the new activities you'll undertake," as he winked at George. "You've done quite well. You'll find we're still quite pleased with Mason's Link and all that's going on with it."

"Okay, I'll do that. Thanks for the support and all your help and information. I'm not sure that I ever told you how your pep talks kept me charged and upbeat when I was rolling out the Link. Those little discussions really helped me get through some tough emotional lows," George replied as he warmly shook Eli's hand.

Eli was taken aback as he replied, "George, you really are a special person. I am honored you feel that way. I'll catch up with you in a couple of days." He turned to smile at Katherine and Dana, then he was off.

"Okay, ladies," George said as he turned to Katherine and Dana who were grinning like Cheshire cats, "What'll we do first?"

Just then, George got a call….a call from Stewart, "Grandad, are you here?" came his little voice from across the veil. George smiled as he looked at Katherine and Dana.

He grabbed their hands and said," Yes, Stewart my man, I'm here," as The Three Musketeers materialized in Stewart's bedroom. This was going to be fun…………

Epilogue

George stood looking across the courtyard of the Bird's Nest. Before him lay the Olympic size swimming pool, the expanse of the two hundred acre lake adjacent to their residence, and the high snow covered passes and peaks of the Prayer Mountains in the background. A beehive of activity was going on before him as about seventy-five people milled about in various stages of conversation, yard sport activities, swimming and food preparation.

He couldn't believe that 250 years had gone by like winds through a sail since he passed through. Being an engineer, he tended to keep statistics. One of his favorites was to track his descendents. When he was on Earth, he tracked his ancestors. At Home, with genealogy as a hobby, he tracked descendants as closely as he did ancestors. This made his family tree look like an hour glass. Since his four children were born, his family has grown to some 1800 people. Of this number, 700 had already passed through while some 1100 still resided as Earth residents. This didn't include all the spouses that his descendents had through the years. These were just his direct descendents.

Another amazing statistic: Of the 700 descendents who had passed through, all of them had become residents and none had been dispatched to the void of non-existence. Just goes to show that the Masons were generally good parents who instilled good values in their children.

Katherine walked out of the kitchen with a load of goodies to deposit on the expanse of outdoor tables they had set up for food. George was busy cooking steaks and chops on several grills with smoke billowing up before him. Marvin was hovering around him like a mother hen dispensing a constant stream of advice. Dana was the bartender aided by his dad. Katherine had a small core of helpers in the kitchen doing various tasks readying the tables with food and materials before they lined everyone up to serve their own plates, smorgasbord style.

George's parents were here. Dana's parents were here. Her dad finally got himself out of hot water and was released some time ago to become an unrestricted resident. Katherine's parents were here. Monica and Marvin as well as Laverne and Bill were here. Richard was here. Jackie, Jason, Stacie and Mike were here along with their spouses, all of the Mason grandchildren, great grandchildren and all their spouses. Emma Holcomb and Tommy Quinn were here with their families.

There were hundreds of their descendents who could have been here but the crowd would have grown unwieldy plus the fact that the further down the chain, the less likely the crowd would be cozy and friendly. It would be a crowd of strangers for the most part.

George had a surprise about 200 years ago as Stewart was approaching his advanced age on Earth. His skill levels in achieving a Link with his family at Home were at a level above anything anyone else had exhibited. He could seemingly complete a Link in almost any circumstance. As a young adult, he also developed the unheard of ability to project his Soul out of his body enabling him to see and converse with any other Souls from Home who happened to be around him. He was unique and became another Person of Special Interest.

Even before he passed through, there were discussions of moving him into the Elder Training program as George had done. In fact, that's exactly what happened. To the family members, he will always be known as Stewart. To the Elders, he is known as Elder Zachariah. George calls him Zack for short whenever they are alone. Zack called George, 'Joe' for his Elder name Joseph. George had the privilege of being in the Audience he had with Jesus when he was introduced and recruited. George was in his Elder Joseph persona, but Stewart didn't recognize him until after the Audience was over when they were alone with Eli. He was ecstatic as was George.

Other special guests were in attendance as well. Since George lead a secret life as an Elder, some of his friends from that branch of his existence were here as well, incognito. Eric, of Finland, a.k.a. Eli, along with his wife, Joann, were mingling about and enjoying themselves. Eli and George had become close friends. Didn't matter if it was Eli or Eric, they did a lot of things together. As Eric, he along with his wife visited quite often. They had joined George's group of other close friends now including Laverne and Bill, Monica and Marvin and Richard. Eric had become the regular fourth member of their golf foursome. George's dad was the substitute if one of the others couldn't be available. They often played as a five some. They taught Eric how to play golf. He could almost beat George now.

There was another guest, a certain five foot ten clean shaven gentleman with piercing royal blue eyes, with a gentle but firm voice wearing khaki trousers with a white open collar pullover shirt who George affectionately called the Boss but otherwise known to the crowd here as Ben, as in Gentle Ben. He seemed to be thoroughly enjoying Himself as He made his way from group to group and person to person stopping along the way to engage in conversation. It amused George to think about how his family and friends would react if they knew who He really was, God. Of course Eric and Stewart knew who He was.

At this morning's golf outing, George had developed the pairings since this was his party. Besides himself, he put Bill, Marvin, his dad, Jason and Mike in charge of foursomes. For his own foursome, George had Eric, Stewart and Ben. A ruling was issued by George, prior to the first group teeing off, advising all players to play honestly and not do anything to artificially influence the flight of the golf balls. Ostensibly, the ruling was directed at all players but George, Eric and Stewart knew the rule was really directed at Ben. As the Boss, Ben could cause a wide range of things to happen. George, after 200 years, finally convinced the Boss to take up the game but knew His propensity to want to avoid mistakes.

At the first tee on a 400 yard par 4 hole, Ben hit His drive only some 150 yards down the fairway and off to the left beneath some trees. They all carefully watched the flight of the ball to make sure no special force had been used to influence its flight. Would Ben do that? Never! Ben was His usual self and smiled after his swing. To clear the overhanging limbs, however, for His second shot, He took out a one iron. On this swing, Ben only hit His ball 145 yards and He missed the fairway as His ball landed some 50 yards off to the right in the middle of a briar patch. They all cringed as He obviously wasn't happy with this shot.

Stewart whispered to George as they watched, "Just goes to show that even God can't hit a one iron."

They were all relatively satisfied because, again, Ben's ball seemed to fly without any special influence. However with the ball buried in the briar patch, He would have to take a drop and a penalty. But by the time they arrived down the fairway where the briar patch was, the ground was now covered with a nice patch of fairway grass with a clear shot to the green, hence, no penalty. The ball hadn't been moved, thus George's ruling hadn't been violated, but the course had been altered. Ben just grinned as He shrugged and said, "I decided the fairway needed widening at this point." The others just threw up their hands and laughed.

"The Boss sure seems to be enjoying Himself this year," Eric said as he and George watched him mingle with the other guests back at the party, "I understand He really looks forward to your gatherings."

"He should, especially after today's golf round. This is about the tenth Mason gathering He's attended," George said grinning with a smile of satisfaction over finally getting Him to take on a few leisure activities in addition to His job of running the universe.

They had been having these gatherings about every five years. Oh, it was not like they didn't see everyone more often. Truth is George's children and grandchildren had reunions of their respective family branches at various times scattered during the intervening four years. George, Katherine and Dana, now affectionately known as the Three Musketeers, went to at least four of these reunions every year.

This particular gathering would last about three days. There would be more golf, horseback riding and family discussions on various topics of the day. To accommodate such a crowd, they had a building constructed on the grounds similar to a hotel complete with rooms sufficient in number to accommodate all the attending families' needs.

It was interesting to see what everyone had been up to over the past five years. There were always some of the family who had changed job activities. Residents were allowed to change jobs if they became bored with what they had been doing. New jobs were discussed. Politics, clothing styles, and technology issues on Earth were discussed. Someone always had an interesting story to relate about one or more of their descendents still living there. They also asked that someone update the group on the names of the latest family arrivals.

As for himself, George was still working in the Dept. of Linking Services with Eli. He was the senior resident in the department and presided over the activities of about 75,000 residents who work there. In his other role as Elder Joseph, except for Katherine, Dana, his four children, his special guests and Stewart, no one else here knew about it. George had been out of Elder training now about 200 years. The activities he had been involved in had grown over the years to ever higher levels of responsibility too numerous to mention.

As far as this gathering of the Mason Family, this was what it was all about. George's vision had been fulfilled. To be surrounded by family and friends was the best that anyone can ever expect, whether it was on Earth or at Home. Here, the Mason Family gatherings were perfect. George's life was almost always perfect. Very rarely, but on occasion, disagreements arose among the Three Musketeers. Usually though, they were resolved in short order and life went on as nearly as perfectly as possible. It seemed like George had always had the good life; even on Earth when they were all subject to the trials and pains of a physical existence. There were no pains here and never would be, all thanks to a loving God who with His perfect foresight had made this heavenly world and other worlds for His own children all over the universe of which the Mason family were prominently counted as members and who had joined them today as Ben.

George traveled back home to Atlanta on occasion. Their old home on Stonewell had now become a major tourist attraction. Most of the surrounding neighborhood had given way to parking lots and souvenir shops for the tourists who come by the bus load to visit the home and walk the grounds of the man who discovered Mason's Link. The Atlanta

Church Council still presided over the facility which had been added to the national list of historic places, and it was now a national landmark. The lawns were kept as George did all those years ago. The inside rooms were maintained almost exactly as George left them the day he visited Jason's family before his heart attack. It was strange to visit because George could see almost as many visitors from Home touring the grounds as from mother Earth.

As to Mason's Link, it had apparently earned its place in world history as one of the more important discoveries of all time. Everyone now took its existence for granted. It was credited with the rebirth of Family values and highlighted the importance of family ties. It had gone a long way in galvanizing the world's population around Christianity. Churches were as full as ever but without the stifling controls the Church exercised during the Inquisition days of the Middle Ages. Entire curriculums had developed around the ways and means of Home. The percentages of entrants into Home society versus those that forfeited their Souls had risen to about ninety eight percent. Only the truly evil and the ignorant found themselves in the two percent category. George was thankful that all his Family members were present and accounted for either at Home or on Earth.

George finished up the grilling details, with Marvin's mother-hen-like approval, and was about to announce that dinner was ready. But first he needed to ask, "Okay, who will say the blessing over this food and this family?" As he uttered these words he glanced at the Boss who winked at him. He saw an arm rise from beyond where Ben was standing, an arm which was attached to the person also exhibiting Stewart's smiling face; the boy who had the first word and now, as a man, wanted the last word.

THE END

Mason's Link
Discussion Points

1. *Mason's Link* is a novel about a beautiful and benevolent Heaven. What Biblical verse formed the basis for the construction of the Heaven described in *Mason's Link?* What other scenarios might be developed to describe Heaven along with the activities of those who enter therein and what Bible support can be associated with these scenarios?

2. *Mason's Link* chronicled a particular outcome for Souls of unborn babies. What was that outcome and what could other possible outcomes be? What are some circumstances which would cause these Souls to be unborn? In the Reconciliation process described in *Mason's Link*, how might the fate of those responsible, for these unborn Souls, be handled?

3. How do you think those who foster and commit terrorism against innocent people in today's world would fare in the Heaven described by *Mason's Link*? Can you envision a scenario where they would be allowed to enter Heaven as residents?

4. In *Mason's Link*, the Soul of one individual was condemned. What was the punishment this Soul endured? Can you find any scriptural support in the Bible for this method of punishment? What other punishments, if any, are described in the Bible for condemned Souls?